Steampunk Revolution

D1314283

STEAMPUNK REVOLUTION

EDITED BY

ANN VANDERMEER

TACHYON — SAN FRANCISCO

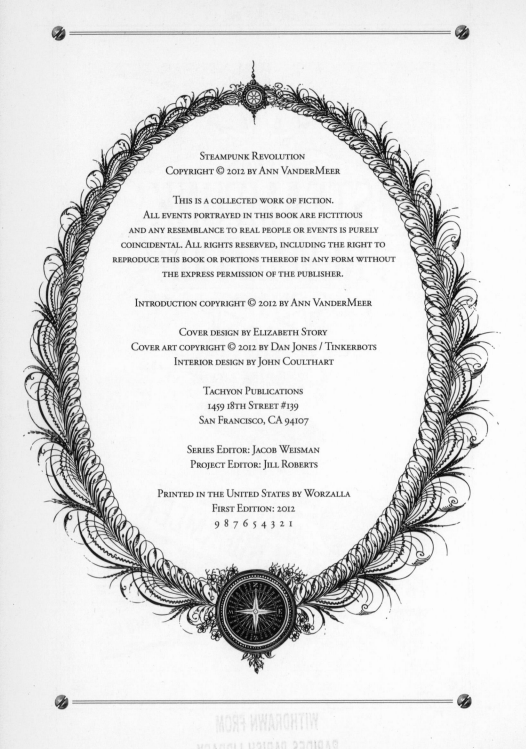

Introduction copyright © 2012 by Ann VanderMeer

Cover design by Elizabeth Story
Cover art copyright © 2012 by Dan Jones / Tinkerbots
Interior design by John Coulthart

Tachyon Publications
1459 18th Street #139
San Francisco, CA 94107

Series Editor: Jacob Weisman
Project Editor: Jill Roberts

Printed in the United States by Worzalla
First Edition: 2012
9 8 7 6 5 4 3 2 1

In memory of my grandmother Florence Merlin
who taught me how to be a rebel by how she lived her life

CONTENTS

Nonfiction

Introduction

Ann VanderMeer

"After all, what our world is and can be are more about human imagination than well…anything else. And isn't that a lot of what steampunk has to say? Imagine! Play! Create! Push past the artificial boundary of time to ask the real questions: What does it mean to be human? What are we going to do with all this technology? How can we create the future we want and need?"
—James H. Carrott (Cultural Historian, 2011)

WHEN JEFF VANDERMEER AND I published *Steampunk* (the first book in this series) in 2008, we approached the concept through the literature. At that time we had no idea that an entire subculture had grown up around this form of retro-futurism. We had done a lot of research around the fiction but only briefly delved into film, comics, and other creative endeavors. Then we found *Steampunk Magazine*, which gave us another view of this fast-growing subculture, attended a Steampunk convention, and soon had a better sense of it all. It's not surprising that we weren't more aware, given that it wasn't until the *New York Times* article in 2008, the month our anthology was published, that the Steampunk subculture became mainstream.

From there, however, steampunk seemed to go viral. We were even approached for an interview by the Weather Channel. I, being a weather geek, was thrilled for the opportunity but asked the interviewer, why us? Why would the Weather Channel be interested in Steampunk? He answered global warming, alternate energy sources, recycling, DIY thinking. This got me to take an even closer look at what was going on in this subculture.

When we agreed to do the second book in 2010, *Steampunk Reloaded*, we wanted to show how the fiction of this subgenre had grown and transformed. It had expanded beyond just science fiction featuring the Victorian era, and we were able to include many more alternative Steampunk backgrounds and approaches. Correspondingly, the subculture had also expanded and become more diverse and more international—in a very short period of time.

Which brings me to the volume you hold in your hands. So many people asked me to publish a third, but what could I do in a third volume that hadn't already been done in the first and second? The Weather Channel experience seemed to be the key: I was interested in looking at how Steampunk could change the world, could really make a difference. When I attended WorldCon in 2009 I had participated in a Steampunk panel, along with writer Lev Grossman and editor Liz Gorinsky. We also had a Victorian scholar on the panel, who spoke about all the ways that that time period was horrible. But Steampunk is an opportunity to force us to address those issues of the past, examine what went wrong, what we can do to put it right and make a better world. Just as traditional science fiction uses the future to discuss issues that concern us now, Steampunk fiction can use the past (or alternate pasts) to bring to light issues that we might otherwise have trouble discussing.

During the panel, someone asked if Steampunk would ever be a political force. Could there possibly be a Steampunk candidate in our future? I said yes and everyone laughed. Perhaps it is folly, but I still think the ideas that spring from a Steampunk point of view are valid for a political movement. How else can we make positive change without understanding our past? Let's not run away from our past, but examine it, take it apart, and put it back together again—the right way. (In a way, civilization depends on some kind of critical self-evaluation, given current global warming and human rights concerns.)

But it is also true that many of us don't know our own history, much less the histories of other parts of our shared planet, and this is another reason Steampunk is relevant. At the Steampunk Worlds Fair in 2011, Emma Goldman (aka Miriam Rosenberg Roček) organized a mock late-1800s Worker's Union Labor rally to illustrate to all what it was really like back in those days. Can you think of a better way to teach about a moment in history, to explain to a modern audience how things were then? She used creative ways to challenge the status quo and to think about change—and she used Steampunk to do this.

Revolution—how else can you effect a positive change? In the Steampunk context, it means to examine our relationship with technology, with each other, and with the world around us. And by doing that through the lens of Steampunk, it allows our imaginations to take off. Let's use *creative play* to look at creation, invention. For example, Bruce Sterling calls his story in this book salvagepunk, not Steampunk. Well, maybe so, but it seems to me that something like salvagepunk is one direction in which Steampunk is headed. Which raises other questions. Does a story have to have steam in it? Does it have to take place during the Victorian Era in an alternate UK or US? I say no, that's not punk. Clearly defined boundaries? Pah! Boring. If you want to start a revolution, you must challenge the current situation, and if that means Steampunk becomes something other than its origins indicate, or a part of Steampunk pushes beyond that…it's all to the good.

So here I present to you stories that largely challenge or comment on the status quo. Stories that provide a different perspective and help us to see the existing world in a new light as we read about an alternative past, or perhaps a possible yet impossible future. What would Friedrich Engels do if he really did liberate a factory and its workers? Would it be as he expected? What happens when a woman challenges the roles that she is forced into? Can people from different walks of life, different backgrounds get along and respect each other's abilities, intellects, and passions?

But these are not the only situations explored in these stories. How do we view transportation? What is our relationship between the modes of transportation and our social status in the world? Is transportation a political issue? Should it be? Cherie Priest's "Clockroach" shows us not only what we can create to solve a problem, but how these creations can be stifled by misunderstanding and fear. And just how closely related are man and machine? Lev Grossman tackles this in a more humorous way in "Sir Ranulph…" Do we build a better human with immortality? Just ask Ben Peek in "Possession." And what about Christopher Rowe's "Nowhere Fast," which provides us a look at a true revolutionary? Good fiction is all about the questions. For example, are we the master of our machines—and should we be? Samantha Henderson's story "Beside Calias" explores bravery and responsibility, broken relationships, and where one can find reserves of strength where one previously thought there was only weakness.

Such questions cut across race and gender. Some of these stories take a closer look at not just the larger society but the individuals as well. What happens when we cross boundaries and reach out to the *other?* What do we learn from such interactions? Is that a scary notion? In Paolo Chikiamco's story "On Wooden Wings," two young people from different cultures come to understand each other amidst the prejudices of their communities.

Beyond individuals and societies, there is also the idea of family. What is a family? Is the idea of a nuclear family the base, the goal, the foundation? And when did that notion take hold? It wasn't always that way, so let's tackle that as well. Malissa Kent's "The Heart Is the Matter" looks at how far a sister will go for another, while Catherynne M. Valente has a new take on motherhood in "Mother Is a Machine." And what is love, and how do our assumptions undercut love? Karin Tidbeck's "Beatrice" takes an unflinching look at this question.

All of these stories are Steampunk stories, by most definitions of the term, and yet did my description of them conjure up the term "Steampunk"? Probably not, which is part of my point. Steampunk allows us to address so many different kinds of situations and issues.

At its best, I think that Steampunk allows us to take some of these ideas, throw them out there and build a better mousetrap, flying machine, and, dare I say it, a better place to live, a better society. Let's strengthen our relationships by reaching out and truly knowing others. Let's stretch our hands across all those boundaries. Let's have a Steampunk Revolution.

FICTION

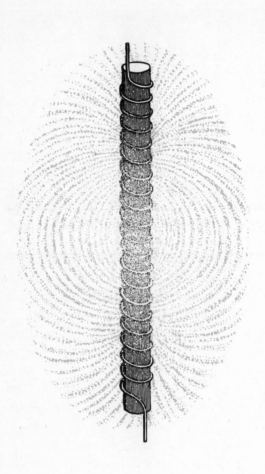

Harry and Marlowe and the Talisman of the Cult of Egil

Carrie Vaughn

HERE IT WAS, lying on a bed of stone, inert. Such an innocuous artifact, one that would go unnoticed on any machinist's workbench. A coil of copper wire wrapped around a steel cylinder just a few inches long, inset with an otherworldly crystal that seemed to glow faintly green with its own light, like a distant aurora. Truly otherworldly, as it happened.

Harry had searched for the object for more than a year, scouring ancient manuscripts, picking apart the threads of unlikely stories, tracking down reliable eyewitness accounts and separating them from fabrications, deciding which myths had a seed of fact within them and which were pure folly. Finally, she planned the expedition and arranged her disappearance from polite society for a month or more to embark on said expedition—leading to the moment that would make all the effort worthwhile. Or confirm that she had wasted her time utterly.

It would seem, she was pleased to note, that she hadn't.

The Aetherian craft that crashed in Surrey in 1869—her entire lifetime, twenty-five years ago now—was not the first such visitor to this world, some hypothesized. This artifact proved that they were right, that another Aetherian being had arrived a thousand years before and left this mechanism behind. A spare part to the Aetherians, but worshipped as a trinket of the gods in this obscure corner of Iceland ever since.

Some would say the Cult of Egil was not far wrong, to take the artifact as a holy talisman. Harry couldn't be bothered with the theology of the matter. She needed it for more mundane purposes. This was a piece of Aetherian technology that no one else in the world possessed. Britain had brought Aetherian wonders to the rest of humanity; by rights, it should have this as well, before anyone else. *If* she could convey it back home successfully.

Carefully, with gloved hands, she removed the object from its stone niche, where it had rested for centuries deep underground, inside the dormant volcano where the mysterious Icelandic cult that guarded it made its home. It hardly weighed anything. Surely the tingling she felt from it was her mind playing tricks. Merely the anticipation of finally having it in her possession. Nerves, that was all.

The artifact was hers. She set it safely inside the padded metal box she'd brought to transport it in, and slipped the box back inside her canvas rucksack, which she slung over her shoulder. Taking a moment to prepare for the next stage of the journey, she arranged herself and her tools. She wore a leather vest over a shirt, khaki trousers, and thick work boots. Along with her rucksack she wore a belt with several pouches, containing a rock hammer, lock picks, compass, hand lantern, and a holster with her pistol. Everything was in place. Now, to get out before they ever realized she'd been here.

The Cult of Egil's Temple of Sky Fire was located in an ancient lava tube, a twisting set of caves carved into the very earth by rivers of molten lava and searing gas. The air still smelled of sulfur, the reek of distant, burning stone. Heat rose up through the black rock, evidence that the fires that had once flowed through here still lingered beneath the crust. The tunnels had merged into a large cavern; oblique shafts had been dug to the surface to let in faint glimmers of arctic light. Polished squares of silver reflected the sunlight, directing the rays to strike a mural above the altar: a mosaic of bone and shell, in the shape of some inhuman god—an Aetherian pilot, Harry knew, with its plates of bone and curling tentacles.

The niche was one of dozens ringing the cavern and its altar, all containing carved stone figurines, polished jewels, elaborate gold ornaments. This niche didn't seem any larger than the others, or have any significance of placement. Surely no one would miss this artifact, which must have seemed incomprehensible to them.

Just then, the shouting of a crowd, like the roaring of a wave, echoed from the main tunnel of the cavern complex. *Well, then.* She'd lingered too long. A dozen tunnels led out of the cavern; the only one she'd identified for certain was the one she came in through. Her exit, if she wished to avoid the wrath of the angry cultists, would have to be via a different route. She turned to the tunnel that sloped upward out of the chamber—to the surface of the mountain and not its depths, she hoped—and ran.

She wasn't stealing, not really; she had so much more use for the object than these northern heathens possibly could. But clearly they would not understand her reasoning; a hundred voices raised in fury, shouting rolling curses in an ancient tongue, followed her. Harry didn't dare stop, but risked a glance over her shoulder.

These men, this horde—descendants of a lost tribe of Vikings trapped under the Icelandic volcano—had degenerated to a level of barbarity that would have shocked even their own bloodthirsty ancestors. The first of the cultists appeared in the cavern just in time to see which way she'd gone. A caricature of an ancient Scandinavian warrior, the hide-draped brute wore a crude helmet, and carried a chipped stone spear. His hair and beard shrouded his face in a filthy mask. His fellows swarmed behind him, antlike, one barbarian form almost indistinguishable from the next. Their blond and red heads of hair were unwashed, matted beyond rescue, but the cultists cared nothing for such civilized matters. Their only concern was the temple to their hideous alien god, and the artifacts they had made in worship of it, in imitation of the one they'd found that had fallen from the sky.

Of course Harry ran for her life—and for the artifact in her pouch, which had damned well better be worth it. Marlowe had better be waiting for her, as they'd planned, as he'd *promised*. She had no reason to expect he would fail her; he hadn't yet, not in all the years she'd known him. He wouldn't now.

She ran in darkness, for a time, when the tunnel curved away from the silver glow of the cavern. Hoping she didn't run smack into a wall, she had to fumble for the hand lantern in her belt pouch as she ran; she didn't dare slow down to fish for it properly. Her vision swam, searching out the way in front of her, following the wall by the sound of her breath echoing off it. Finally, her hand found the lantern, and she pressed the switch to activate its green Aetherian glow. By this light she could see only a few feet before her, but it was enough.

A hundred leather-clad footsteps pounded on the stone behind her.

Up ahead, a spot of sunlight shone—the tunnel entrance. Escape—or *rescue,* rather. The light ahead expanded, and the stink of sulfur in the basalt tunnel gave way to a touch of icy arctic air. When the tunnel opened, Harry skidded to a stop, balanced at the edge of a cliff that dropped away a thousand feet to a rocky, blasted landscape below.

Marlowe wasn't there.

The mountain had dozens of caves, places where the volcanic heat steamed forth. Marlowe would be keeping watch on them all, searching for her. She still had time. An hour before he gave her up as lost. Shoving her lantern back in its pouch, she reached into another one for a flare, struck the flint on the fuel, pointed it to the sky, and launched the charge. A fiery missile, sparking green, arced upward, trailing thick black smoke behind it. If that didn't work....

Before her was a long fall on hard rocks. Behind her, the cultists. She inched to the edge of the drop, keeping a hand on the tunnel wall for balance. If she had to, she'd jump. Slow her fall down the rocky slope as much as she could, and maybe Marlowe could pick up the pieces of her broken body. Or find and rescue the artifact, if there weren't enough pieces of *her* to collect. The flare's smoke hung in the air, a trail leading back to her—while it lasted.

She drew her Aetherian pistol from its holster, though it hardly mattered—the gun's charge would only last long enough to stop a handful of the cultists. The fiery glow of torches preceded their assault. She prepared to slide over the edge.

Suddenly, the flare's trail of smoke dissipated, scattered by a blast of wind that pressed Harry to the wall. Arm over her face, she chanced a look—and saw the airship drop down the side of the mountain, to the tunnel entrance. Its curved bladder and sleek gondola blocked the sun and threw a shadow over her.

Stone-filled bags fell from the gondola—ballast dropping, slowing the ship's descent. Marlowe had timed this very close indeed.

The Aetherian engine in the back of the airship whined, throwing off green-tinted sparks behind it. When the gondola came alongside the mouth of the tunnel, the door to the cabin was wide open, and there was Marlowe, just like he was supposed to be. The pilot was obscured, made larger and more terrifying by the greatcoat and leather-padded goggles masking his features. He held his rifle at the ready.

Harry clutched her satchel, her pistol in her right hand, and didn't look back, leaping from the cliff's edge to the airship cabin. Marlowe stepped in behind her, slammed shut the door, and lunged to the airship's controls. A Viking spear *thunked* against the gondola's side. Out the window, Harry saw the horde reach the edge of the cliff—in fact, two of the fellows fell over, pushed by their enthusiastic brethren rushing too fast behind. *Good riddance.*

The airship sank a few more feet, then stopped, and with another bag of ballast gone, rose up again. The guidance propeller spun faster, and the ship jumped forward, wind whipping across the bladder above them. The ship raced away from the tunnel, along the slope of the shattered volcano, and soon the cultists' berserker shouting faded against the sound of wind and rumbling engine.

They'd done it.

Marlowe turned another set of levers and the sound changed, drive motors coming online, whirring, moving the craft laterally. The mountain, its black crags and broken clefts, slid past, like a painting on a roller. In moments, the ship turned to the coast of Iceland, and open sky lay before them.

Settling her breathing, Harry took in lungfuls of cool clean air, letting its touch calm her. She slouched against the plush seat at the side of the cabin.

Marlowe turned in his pilot's chair to face her, pulling the goggles down to hang around his neck. In his early thirties, he was weathered in a way that spoke of experience rather than hardship, his brown hair unkempt and his cheeks covered with stubble because he simply didn't have time to bother rather than because he was sloppy. His clothing was simple, practical. His eyes shone, and his smile was playful. Butterflies fluttered in her stomach.

"If you'd misjudged the ballast you dropped by a *pound,* you'd have lost me," she said, scowling.

"But I didn't. You knew I wouldn't," he said.

"Bloody hell," she sighed.

The motor droned, sending vibration through the cabin. The rattling soothed her.

"You got it," he said, a declaration of fact rather than a question of her ability.

"Do you even have to ask?"

"I never doubted. May I see?"

Moving to the copilot's chair, she retrieved the box from her satchel and rested it on her lap. Marlowe leaned forward, watching as she revealed the artifact. She smiled—he clutched his hands together in an effort to keep from grabbing the thing from her. She presented the cylinder to him cupped in her hands, and admired his flat, astonished expression. He sighed a quiet breath and picked it up.

"I'm not sure I even know what it is," he said, holding it up to the cockpit window, turning it this way and that in the light. "Part of a generation coil, perhaps, or an amplification rod."

"But it's Aetherian. The stories were true."

"Yes," he murmured. "It most certainly is, and they were."

The possibilities presented by this new artifact clearly entranced Marlowe, but Harry was taken by a larger question: The Aetherians had visited Earth before. Perhaps often, even. There might even be artifacts—new pieces to the Aetherian puzzle—scattered all over the world. No one had even known to look for them.

"Where do you suppose they found it? The cultists?" she said.

"The stories say they found it frozen in ice that had drifted from the north."

"But there had to be another ship—another crash, even. Where is the rest of it?"

"It might be a tool left behind. Perhaps they didn't crash at all."

She stared out the window to a sun-bleached sky. "It rather begs the question, doesn't it? This proves they've traveled here more than once. What do we do if the Aetherians ever come back?"

Marlowe looked up from the coil, and she met his gaze. Neither of them had an answer. In the twilight shadow of the volcano, the crystal gave off a faint glow.

"All this time, and the power source is still active. Weak, but active," he said. He produced a jewelers' loupe from an inside vest pocket and tucked it over his eye. "Usual switching circuitry here—we saw this sort of thing in all the shipboard systems of the Surrey crash. Used to route power. I wonder... Harry, my toolkit is under the bench, if you wouldn't mind—"

"Are you sure this is wise? Shouldn't you wait until you're in your laboratory?"

"This will only take a moment."

A little digging in the bench cupboard revealed the kit, a slim aluminum case containing the tools for manipulation of finer mechanisms. He chose a wire probe from the collection. When he tapped it against the alien cylinder, his hands were steady as a surgeon's.

The device emitted a hissing noise—gas released under pressure.

"What was that?" Harry asked.

Marlow tapped the cylinder again, and the hissing stopped. Bringing the artifact close to his face, he sniffed.

"Smell that," he said, offering it to her.

She hated to get too close to the coil, but she didn't have to, to identify the reek. "It's sulphur."

"Some kind of gas exchange, I'd wager," Marlowe said. "God, I really need to take this apart...."

"We'll know more, once we're back in London."

"Oh. About that." He handed the device back to her. "We may have a bit of a problem getting home."

"Good of you to mention it," she said, smirking, wrapping the coil again and securing it safely in the box. "What kind of a problem?"

"The Germans have established a blockade."

She harrumphed. "We knew that was coming. We'll simply avoid the Channel and approach from the north."

"Ah, no. Not just the Channel." She raised a brow, and he continued. "They've blockaded the entire British Isles."

A bit of a problem, indeed.

The battle had been raging for a week—naturally, the Queen and the Empire could not let a blockade of the home country stand. Marlowe had spent the time, while Harry had been infiltrating the volcanic tunnels in Iceland, hiding the *Kestrel* in valleys and ravines, going aloft at intervals to intercept wireless transmissions to try to get some kind of news.

They were too far away yet to see signs of fighting. Knowing the respective strength of each of the forces, though, Harry was certain she and Marlowe wouldn't be able to avoid the battle for long. They weren't at all equipped for it—the *Kestrel* was a courier ship, built for speed and agility. She had no armor and little in the way of weapons. Perhaps they'd do better to find a safe port and wait out the blockade.

Except they had to get the coil to Prince George, and to Marlowe's laboratory. The artifact could change everything. She thought through a multitude of plans—land elsewhere, make their way home by some other route. Make for the Americas and rendezvous with a more capable warship. Or did they dare attempt to run the blockade? She knew what Marlowe would say.

"So, do we go above or below the fray?" she asked.

"Above. They've got surface ships on the water."

"Right, then."

She went to the safe in the back, a square of thick steel tucked over the driveshaft, put her satchel containing the artifact inside, locked it tight, and tied the key to a cord around her neck. Even if the ship didn't make it through, no one would be able to gain access to the box without destroying its contents. Not without her.

"What can I do to help?" she asked.

"Don't jostle the boat," he said. "Or if you'd like you can pour us some brandy." He glanced over his shoulder and quirked a grin.

"I'm your maid, then?" she said.

"I stashed the bottle in the cupboard under the seat there." He nodded to the bench by the hatch.

The bench seat was hinged, revealing the promised cupboard, packed tightly with boxes, slots, canvas bags, blankets and fur coats for high altitudes, provisions for an extended journey, and her own package of supplies. Good. In a slot that looked as if it had been specially made to enclose it, she found the bottle of brandy and a pair of glass tumblers.

She joined him at the front of the cabin. The dashboard had enough of a ledge for her to set the tumblers on it and pour. After, she tucked the bottle in a pouch on the wall to keep it from sliding or falling. Marlowe took the glass before she could hand it to him.

"Cheers," he said, and they clinked glasses.

The liquid went down smoothly and warmed her blood in an instant. Marlowe always kept the good stuff on hand.

Before them, through the thick glass at the front of the cabin, the ocean extended. This had become the simplest part of the journey. Marlowe's piloting would manage the ocean winds and unpredictable weather. She had no idea what awaited them once they reached home. Harry squinted, searching for the haze of gun smoke and fires.

Best to drink up while they could.

"How high are we going to have to get to avoid it, then?"

He frowned. "They've got rockets that reach higher than anything that flies. We'll do what we can, but it probably won't be high enough."

"Rockets? How?"

"They stole them, in the time-honored fashion," he said.

She slumped in the chair. Had the entire journey been wasted? "It's all been for nothing," she murmured.

"If that were true, I wouldn't have bothered coming for you." He gave her that smile again. And it was true. She imagined herself waiting at the cave entrance, the horde of cultists coming up behind her. Having to jump....

She drained the brandy and poured herself another glass.

"That bad?"

"I hate this," she said.

"Amen," he murmured.

The sun set, and the air grew cold. Below them, the ocean was the color of pewter and seemed still, frozen, like a painting. No moon shone.

Harry slept for an hour or so, then offered to watch over the ship while Marlowe slept. That he didn't hesitate to take the offer she took as a great compliment. He stretched out on the bench in the back of the cabin, rolled a blanket around him, and instantly fell asleep in the way only long-time soldiers could manage. He snored, softly, the noise like just another exhaust or gear on the airship. If she told him he snored, he wouldn't have believed her.

They'd reach Ireland by dawn. Then, Marlowe would ascend as high as the *Kestrel* was able. Breathable air would fail before the engines did, yet they had to climb high enough to avoid the blockade and not draw attention from scouts; they had to skirt that boundary without crossing it and blacking out.

She wouldn't have to touch the controls unless something went wrong—the winds changed, or they were attacked. She watched pressure gauges, altitude monitors, and compass readings. Their course remained steady; she had to add a little gas to the bladders to maintain altitude. Marlowe had left his goggles hanging on a hook above the window.

The cabin was dark except for a dim lamp near the control board, the faint glow of the engine in back, and a tea light for warmth near the cage where a pair of carrier pigeons slept. Too much light—a fire in the stove, for example—would make them a target. And it was only going to get colder, this high up, at night.

Once the sky darkened, the first signs of battle became visible. On the eastern horizon, tracers arced, distant shooting stars, orange, yellow, green. Fireballs rose up from unseen explosions and dissipated into raining sparks. At the moment, the scene was a remote tableau, an unreal moving picture. She could imagine the hint of pyrotechnics was a harmless show put on for her benefit. Except for all the thousands of people dying underneath it.

Dim lamplight turned the cabin ghostly, flat, unreal. She wrapped the blanket more tightly around her. For the moment, she could believe she drifted between worlds, and oddly enough the sensation came as a relief. In this suspended place, she could breathe easy, let down her guard, and pretend that all was well.

At dawn, Marlowe's snoring stopped, and soon after he shifted, the blanket rustling as he pushed it away, the cabin shivering with his movements. He pulled a pair of heavy fur coats from the storage cupboard and brought them to the front.

"How are we doing, then?" he asked.

"Steady as she goes, captain." She smiled at his crazily ruffled hair.

He gazed out the cabin's front window. The sky had grown hazy with the smoke of battle. A particularly large explosion bronzed his face for a moment, even at this distance. That would have been one of the larger airships going down, hit by a rocket maybe, all its gas and munitions igniting. Debris fell after the initial fireball, flaming bits of fabric and metal plunging to earth, like diving birds.

He said. "God, would you look at that. I wonder if that was one of ours or one of theirs?"

"We've no way of knowing, and nothing we could do to help even if we knew." She tried to sound offhand about it, but only managed bitter.

Marlowe put his hand on her arm, where it rested on the edge of the pilot's chair. Warm, comforting, an anchor. They both looked at it there. The impropriety of it seemed very distant, and she imagined everything she might do—touch his cheek, turn his face toward her, kiss him—and her brother and grandmother would be none the wiser.

He quickly pulled his hand away—but not before she could catch it, squeeze it, then let it go. Just a moment of contact, gloved hand to gloved hand. It would have to be enough. They had more important things to think about.

"We've got to get over this before the scouts see us," he said.

She moved out of the way so he could take over the pilot's seat. They bundled up in the coats. He pulled back a pair of levers, the engines buzzed, and the cabin tipped back, pressing them into their seats. The *Kestrel* climbed, and climbed.

The battle climbed with them. It wasn't just rockets reaching this height; airships climbed with them, exchanging broadsides. Harry was already panting for breath, using her whole chest to suck in too little air. She couldn't imagine fighting like this. But they were headed for the thick of it.

"I thought coming in from the north would avoid most of this mess," Marlowe said, the words punctuated with gulps for air.

"What must it be like on the Channel?"

He pointed. "See there, at two o'clock. Is it coming closer?"

The triple-motored airship wasn't just coming closer—it was set to intercept them. "We can't let them stop us, even if it's one of ours."

"Especially if it's one of ours," he said, giving half a grin.

"Do I dare hoist a signal flag?" she said.

"Give it a moment. Let's see if we can outrun 'em."

"Bloody hell."

Marlowe started throwing levers, and the motor's humming changed in pitch. The ship rose, and the horizon tilted as they changed course.

Their ship was small and fast, but their opponent was an interceptor, all lift and motor and guns, specifically designed to stop ships like this one.

"It's one of theirs," she said. "Look at the flag."

When the sun hit it directly, the red field with the black eagle painted on the bladder was clear. Marlowe would crash the ship rather than let them be boarded now. Though they'd most likely get blown from the sky before it came to that. They couldn't risk letting the Germans take possession of the coil.

"You said all we have is a pair of rifles?" she said.

"I would never lie to you about my weaponry, Harry," he said, eyebrow arched. And why exactly did she want to laugh at a time like this?

She grabbed Marlowe's goggles and put them on, adjusting the strap. Then she found the rifle and checked that its charge was full. "Where's the harness?"

"Hanging across from the door, there."

She found the gear and hooked the leather straps over her shoulders and around her chest, checking the buckles three times. The straps and hardware were all well-oiled and in excellent repair—but of course they were, this was Marlowe's ship, after all. One end of the line hooked to the front of the harness. The rest of it she hung coiled around her forearm while she opened to the door to cabin.

Wind tore at her. She hadn't buttoned the coat all the way, and the collar flapped around her neck, sending a freezing draft across her skin, but that didn't matter. The other end of the line hooked to the track ringing the outside of the cabin. Normally, the track and harness were used as a safety measure for mechanics making repairs. But she'd always thought it looked like fun.

She gripped the rifle, and jumped.

The line caught, and she swung out as the harness caught, dug into her shoulders and ribs, and arched her toward the cabin's side. Sticking her feet out, she landed and ran until the line came up against the first bracket. Leaning forward, she had a view across the nose of the *Kestrel*. Bracing, she held the rifle steady to her shoulder, aimed along the barrel, and waited for Marlowe to swing the ship around and give her a shot. She wished she'd thought of tying her hair back first; it whipped behind her, catching on the line.

Her best chance would be to rip a shot through the enemy ship's air bladders. Even if she didn't start an explosion that destroyed the airship, it would lose lift and maneuverability, giving Marlowe time to get them out of this. The *Kestrel*'s motor droned, increasing in pitch, and the craft lurched upward, the nose tipping down, as if the whole thing had been caught in an updraft. Harry shifted her feet to keep her balance.

There it was, the Kaiser's black eagle staring at her with contempt, or so it seemed. Cannons mounted on the base of the cabin swung around. They were still too far away for Harry to bother firing at them. But soon.

An explosive scream cut through the air, and in spite of herself Harry flinched back. When she looked, she saw the long trail of black smoke, but never saw what made it. The trail led to the enemy airship, which transformed into a fireball a moment later. The heat of it washed over her, and she ducked, clinging to her line, pulling herself close to the cabin for shelter. The *Kestrel* rocked with the shockwave, but Marlowe increased altitude yet again and got them above the worst of it. Breathing was very difficult now; blackness flashed at the edges of her vision. It was all wind and no air up here.

Below her, gas from the German ship ignited in blue flames that quickly faded to yellow and dispersed, munitions vanishing in bursts of orange fire; the ship disintegrated and fell, pieces trailing arcs of smoke and sparks. Bodies fell. Harry saw one man, still alive, limbs flailing as he tumbled through air. She imagined she could hear his screams, but of course could hear nothing over the roar of the wind.

There was only the one fortuitous rocket, sent to destroy their enemy. She might never learn if that had been by chance or design.

Marlowe waved at her through the front window, his expression showing concern. He was too sensible to actually yell at her to come back inside. Clutching both her safety line and the rifle, she didn't have a free hand to wave back. Carefully, she braced against the harness, freeing herself to signal back at him. He pressed his lips and nodded. He moved a lever. The nose tipped down, beginning a descent. She made herself stay still and focus on breathing, imagining she could tell that the air grew thicker. The goggles brought her eyesight to a narrow focus, and she sought to see beyond the edges of her vision.

The horizon was a distant smudge; the gray haze made it impossible to see where ground ended and sky began. She could imagine seeing the curve of the Earth from here. When she looked up, the sky became like night, shifting from pale blue to a deep indigo, then darker still, to the black of twilight. And beyond that, stars.

If man were ever to travel to the upper reaches, past the atmosphere and into Aetherian spaces, they had a serious problem to solve: They had to learn to bring their air with them. Or they had to learn to stop breathing. There was some debate about which alternative the Aetherians had used. Finding a solution for these reckless airship pilots venturing forth, as far as they could until they couldn't breathe at all, that was the key to all. If only....

Marlowe knocked on the window this time, and she brought herself back.

Sliding the line along its track, she walked along the cabin hull to the door and tried to pretend that her legs weren't shaking. Marlowe was waiting for her. Handing the rifle to him, she swung inside, unhooking herself from the track. When he shut the door, she finally breathed easy again.

"You all right?"

"I didn't even get a chance to fire," she said, pulling the goggles off, handing them back to him. Her legs were still trembling, and she lowered herself to the bench.

"Never mind that we'd never have gotten close enough before they blew us out of the air."

"Oh, yes, indeed. You'll have to find out who I ought to send a bottle of wine to for that rocket."

"A bottle of wine? Seems this would be worth at least your firstborn."

"I'm afraid my firstborn, should such a person ever exist, is already promised to my grandmother and brother."

"Ah. Of course."

She fumbled with the buckles, and Marlowe managed to pretend not to notice, but still helped, coiling the rope and pulling the harness off her shoulders once she'd finally managed to unfasten it. She sighed and rolled her shoulders—they were going to be very sore for a couple of days, and she'd probably have bruising around her ribs. Not anywhere that anyone would be likely to notice, so they didn't matter at all.

"I think I could use another finger of your brandy, Marlowe."

He was already reaching for the bottle.

They had managed to circumvent the worst of the blockade, and reached the shores of Scotland. There, they put up their flags and lit the cabin lights, to prevent any misunderstandings. In friendly territory now, Marlowe felt comfortable using the wireless. He posed as a standard military courier ship that had been damaged in fighting and was seeking the safety of a mooring in Liverpool. He used the coded phrase that would, in fact, get them permission to continue on to London.

Harry's preferred choice of communication was more primitive, but less prone to eavesdropping than the wireless. This would go straight where she wanted it, and there was little chance someone could intercept. She wrote a note on a strip of paper, using her and her brother's code, rolled it tightly, and put it in the tiny canister that she then fit to the leg of one of the pigeons. She held the cooing creature gently to her chest, smoothing its feathers and whispering comforts to it, before throwing it out the open portal window, into the bright sun. Its white wings flashed as the bird dipped around the ship, then seemed to vanish as it raced on.

Harry went back to the front of the cabin, where Marlowe sat.

She sighed. "I don't think I'm ready to be back just yet."

"I could turn us around, head toward the battle," he said.

"Do you really think that piece of metal will help us end the war?"

"Strange, isn't it? So much hope in that little thing. But I do think it's worth it."

Not strange at all. Little things had often changed the world. Whatever it was worth, this was better than sitting at Marlborough House, waiting for something to happen.

They reached the Thames and followed it to the mooring station outside Windsor.

"Well then," she sighed. "I suppose I ought to make myself presentable."

"I'm sorry I haven't got anything like a decent room for you—"

"Nonsense. We'll make do."

He blushed, pointedly turning away.

She retrieved her luggage from the bench. From it, she unfolded her proper lady's attire and all its attendant architecture. She ought to have a good wash before putting it on, but there was no chance of that. She would have to make do. She stripped the old rugged shirt and trousers she'd been in for the last week and donned the crisp linen shift, smoothing out the wrinkles as best she could. She'd had the corset made with fasteners in front for just such occasions as this. Her sisters would be scandalized, to see her dressing herself. In front of a soldier, even. She had her back to Marlowe; he could have been sneaking glances at her all this time. Of course, the worse scandal was that she rather hoped he was.

Then came the gown, which she'd managed to pack well enough to prevent the worst of the wrinkles. The fasteners in back, however, presented some difficulty. She could feel the hook and eye at the back of her neck, but no matter how she contorted herself, couldn't get them to catch.

She turned to the pilot's chair. "Marlowe—"

He sprang to his feet, as if he'd been watching. Waiting for her to ask.

At her back, he fumbled with the tiny hooks, the tips of his fingers brushing along the bare skin of her neck. Closing her eyes, she reveled in the warm flush his touch inspired. The breath of his sigh tickled her skin. If she took a step back, she would be leaning against him, and she was very tempted.

If only they could only stand like this for the rest of the hour. The rest of the war....

He moved away, but only after smoothing away a lock of her hair. Back at his seat, he clasped his hands together and gazed at her with a look of blank innocence.

They both practiced that look.

"Thank you," she said. He nodded.

She continued with buttons, hooks, earrings, necklace, arranging them all properly. Next she used the little tray of cosmetics with the tiny foldout mirror. After some powder, some color on her lips and cheeks, and a few pins in her hair, she'd be able to pass in the most respectable society without comment. She saw the gown, with its corset, ribbing, and petticoats, as armor.

"All right, I'm finished. How do I look?" She gave her skirt a last brush.

He said simply. "Your Highness. Princess Maud returns."

She ducked her gaze. She wasn't ready for Princess Maud to return.

"It's amazing how you do that," he continued, when she didn't speak. "You're a chameleon."

"I think you are the only one who sees my true form."

His smile flashed, and fled. "Sometimes I'm not sure I've seen it yet."

Marlowe steered them to an upper landing platform at the air port. He followed the signals of the tower controller, sending back his reply with the lantern at the window.

"I'll get the line," she said, intending to throw out the mooring lines to the deckhands.

"You'd better not," he said, nodding at her current dress. "Why don't you gather your things?"

She unlocked the safe and retrieved the prize, which she put in the valise that had hidden her gown, burying it in her dirty clothes. She tucked her pistol in a pocket in the side, and remembered to keep that side of the bag closest to her. Not that she expected to encounter any trouble here; rather, it was habit.

Marlowe and the deckhands got the ship anchored perfectly well without her, of course. But she felt useless, standing there, stiff as a statue in this clothing.

Out the window, she could see the street leading toward the village and castle, and the carriage drawn by a pair of large bay horses parked there. The carriage door would have her brother's crest painted on it. The royal crest belonging to the Crown Prince. He'd gotten her message, then, and made it as easy as possible to bring the box straight to him.

Anchored and still against the tugging of the bladder above it, the ship felt like a rock instead of a bird. As soon as the door to the cabin opened, she'd have to leave. She and Marlowe stood together, regarding one another. She never knew what to say in these moments, when their missions ended. Whatever she said felt awkward and artificial, and as soon as he was gone she'd think of everything she should have said.

"You'll come to the Royal Academy? To be on hand when they examine the artifact?" she asked.

"I hope to. But I suspect the general will send me and the *Kestrel* to Plymouth, to assist in the defense."

That hadn't been part of the original plan. The war had crept far too close to home shores; she preferred to forget.

"But I will see you again, soon?"

"As soon as possible, I should think," he said.

They shook hands, as if they were familiar colleagues and not...she couldn't decide exactly *what* they were. There was no civilized name for it. As she made her way down the steps from the platform to the street and Prince George's carriage, she could feel Marlowe watching her, and was glad of it.

Addison Howell and the Clockroach

Cherie Priest

AN EYEWITNESS ACCOUNT BY PETRA OBERG (1902–1996), RESIDENT OF
HUMPTULIPS

ADDISON HOWELL DIDN'T so much arrive in the town of Humptulips as
appear there sometime around 1875. He had money, which set him apart from
everybody else—because everybody else was working for the logging company,
and mostly they didn't have a pot to piss in, as my Daddy put it.

At first, Mr. Howell didn't make much of a stir. He built himself a house,
way outside of town, a big three-story place set back in the hills—and you
couldn't see it until you were right on top of it, what with all the trees. He had
a wife with him at one point, but she died up there. Folks said he'd murdered
her with an axe, but there was never any proof of that and we didn't have any
law at the time nohow, not a sheriff or anything, much less a jail, what with
less than three hundred souls. We had a mayor, though—a fellow named Herp
Jones—and I think if Herp could've rounded up enough warm bodies, he
would've seen to a lynch mob. But everyone he might've asked was either working or drinking, so I guess that didn't happen.

The town gave Mrs. Howell a Christian burial in a little plot back behind
the only church we had, and her guilty-as-sin husband paid a pretty penny to
have a crypt built up around her. It was a real big deal, because nobody else in
town had ever gotten a crypt, and only about half the folks who ever died even

got a tombstone. That rankled a bit, even though he gave a tithe in honor of our St. Hubert, protector of woodsmen. But then Mr. Howell went back to his house in the trees, and for the most part, nobody hardly ever saw him again.

But a few years later, as I heard it, after he'd been out of people's minds, laying low so to speak, Addison Howell was out and about doing whatever it is a wicked man does on a Sunday, and he came across a homesteader's camp just off the old logging road. There was a wagon with a broken axle, and two dead men lying beside a campfire. It looked like they'd been tore up by wolves, or maybe mountain lions, or some such creature. But inside the wagon he heard a little girl crying. He looked inside and she screamed, and she bit him—because like attracts like, I suppose, and the girl had a bad streak in her too. That's why he took her home with him.

She was maybe eight or nine when he brought her inside, and legend has it she was mute. Or maybe she didn't feel like talking, I couldn't say. But we all thought the girl was too scairt to speak after wild animals all ate her family, and thought it a scandal that he took her in rather than bringing her into town. No matter what a bad seed she might've been, Mr. Howell was worse for having lived longer.

Anyway, he raised her as his own, and they lived together in the house in the hills, and nobody ever visited them because everybody knew they were doing evil things up there. If they weren't up to mischief, they would've just moved to town like civilized people.

But people started telling stories about hearing strange noises out there at night, like someone was whacking on metal with a hammer, or sawing through steel. Word got around that he was building a machine that looked like a big bug, or a lobster, or something. It had a big stack on top and it was steam powered, or coal powered, or anyway it was supposed to move around when he was sitting inside it. The stack was strange, they said, because it curved back into the machine. That made a lot of the folks down at the tavern laugh. I don't know who was fool-headed enough to get close enough to listen, but somebody did, and somebody talked.

Of course, I worried about the girl, and later on, the mayor and some friends of his, all of them with guns and itchy trigger fingers, went up to that house and demanded to know what was going on up there. For all they knew he was summoning Satan, or beating up that girl, or raising whatever kind of hell I just don't know.

Addison Howell told them they were welcome to look around, so they did. They didn't find anything, and they were mad about it. They asked the girl what was going on, but she wouldn't say nothing and they thought maybe she was scared of Howell, and that's why she wasn't being helpful. But she was a teenager by then, or old enough that she could live there with a dirty old man if she felt like it, and people'd look askance, but no one would take her away.

Not long after that, Addison Howell went into town to do some business—he was over at the logging foreman's place, and nobody has any idea why, or what they were talking about. They got into some kind of fight—the foreman's wife overheard it and she came out and saw them struggling, so she took her husband's shotgun and she blew the back of Addison Howell's head clean off, and he died right then and there.

The foreman went and got Herp Jones, and between 'em, they figured it was good riddance. They decided they should just leave him in the crypt with his wife, since there was a slot for him and everything, and that's what they did. They wrapped up his body and carried it off.

When they got to the crypt, they found that one of the doors was hanging open—and that was odd, but they didn't make nothing of it. They thought maybe there'd been an earthquake, a little one that wasn't much noticed, and the place had gone a little crooked. It happens all the time. But inside the thing, they found the floor all tore up. There used to be marble tiles down there, and now they were gone. Nothing but dirt was left.

I expect they wondered if someone hadn't gotten inside and stolen them. Marble might've been worth something.

They didn't worry about it much, though. They just dumped old Addison Howell into his slot, scooted the lid over him, and shut the place up behind them. Then they remembered the girl who lived at Howell's place—nobody knew her name, on account of she'd never said it—and they headed up there to let her know what had happened.

I think privately they thought maybe now she'd come into town and pick a husband, somebody normal and good for her. There weren't enough women to go around as it was, and she was pretty enough to get a lot of interest.

When they told her the news she started screaming. They dragged her into town to try and calm her down, but she wasn't having any of it. Around that time there was a doctor passing through, or maybe Humptulips had gotten one of its own. Regardless, this doctor gave her something to make her sleep, trying to settle her. They left her in the back room of the general store, passed out on a cot.

And that night, the town woke up to a terrible commotion coming from the cemetery behind Saint Hubert's. Everybody jumped out of bed, and people grabbed their guns and their logging axes, and they went running down to the church to see what was happening—and the whole place was just in ruins. The church was on fire, and the cemetery looked like someone had set off a bunch of dynamite all over it. The Howell crypt was just a bunch of rubble, and there was a big old crater where it used to be.

And by the light of the burning church, the mayor and the logging foreman and about a dozen other people all swear by the saints and Jesus too...they saw a big machine with that ridiculous tall black stack curving back into itself... crawling away—and sitting inside it was the demon Addison Howell, driving the thing straight back to hell. Some said he was laughing, some said he was crying. We were so glad he was leaving, no one followed him, and it would have been difficult to track him anyway because no smoke belched from the black stack.

That's how it happened, and it's God's honest truth. As for the girl, when they went back to tend to her in the general store, she had fled. That's how we knew she had no innocence in her, either. We went looking, but we never found her. Most everyone thought she'd finally gone to join her family, and in the same way: devoured by beasts in the forest. If she had ever come back, we would have treated her like a ghost.

A Brief Perspective from Historian Julia Frimpendump, University of Washington Professor

My research began with the church, as perhaps the most accurate repository of information. Though Saint Hubert's was in fact subjected to a fire in 1889, it did not burn in its entirety and most of its records were preserved. I found a record of burial for a woman named "Rose M. Howell" on October 2, 1878, lending credence that the story of Addison Howell may hold a grain of truth; but there is no record for Mr. Howell's death, nor any subsequent burial.

After consulting with an archeo-industrialist in Cincinnati, I have concluded that the peculiar device known locally as "the clockroach" was very likely intended for use in the logging industry. Its forward claws suggest a machine capable of carrying tremendous weight, and the multiple legs imply that it could have traversed difficult terrain while successfully bearing a load.

Based on this information, one could speculate a kinder story for the tragic Addison Howell. It's reasonable to guess that he might have been a lonely man who, driven west, adopted an orphaned girl, and in his spare time he devoted himself once again to the very thing that had been his downfall back east: tinkering…eventually coming up with this peculiar engine, which might have revolutionized the industry—perhaps even the history of the internal combustion engine—had it been adopted and mass-produced. His conversation-turned-argument with the logging foreman may have been some patent dispute, or an altercation over the invention's worth—there's no way to know.

The casual record-keeping and insular nature of a tiny homesteader's town has left us little with which to speculate.

However, the remains of a marble crypt can be found in Saint Hubert's churchyard. The church's present minister, Father Frowd, says that it collapsed during an earthquake well before his time—and to the best of his knowledge, it was salvaged for materials.

As for the wagon with the murdered occupants and the sole surviving child, evidence suggests that a family by the name of Sanders left Olympia, Washington, intending to homestead near Humptulips in 1881. This family consisted of a widower, Jacob, and his brother, Daniel, and his brother's daughter, Emily. The small family never reached Humptulips, and no record of their demise or reappearance has ever been found.

In one tantalizing clue located (once again) via Saint Hubert's, a spinster named "Emily Howell" reportedly passed away in 1931, at the estimated age of sixty. Her age was merely estimated because she never gave it, and she passed away without family members or identification. She was found dead alone in the large home she kept outside the city limits—her cause of death unknown.

But she is buried behind the church, and her tombstone reads simply, "Emily Howell, d. 1931. She never forgave us, and never forgot him."

"Pioneer Myths and Lore in Peninsular Victoriana": An Exhibit at the Stackpole Museum of Prototypical Industry (Port Angeles, Washington)

The Olympic Peninsula has long been home to a number of Native American tribes, including the Hoh, the Makah, and the Quileute; but it was not until the second half of the nineteenth century that it became settled by white homesteaders. Primarily these homesteaders were farmers and loggers, lured by the Homestead Act of 1862 and the promise of a temperate climate.

Though much can be said about the Native traditions and myths, this exhibit focuses on the rural homesteaders and their inevitable bedtime or campfire stories—some of which were regarded with a seriousness that borders on the charmingly naïve or dangerously optimistic, as evidenced by the items on display. Highlights of the collection include the "Clockroach" (1953.99) created by Addison Sobiesky Howell (America, born 1828 in Chicago, IL, died 1899 in Humptulips, WA). The "Clockroach," built in 1878(?) was a one-man, quasi-lobster-shaped vehicle allegedly designed and driven by the aloof, peculiar craftsman whom the townsfolk of Humptulips came to believe was a minion of the devil himself. Howell's early past is mostly unknown to historians, but it is believed that he worked as a designer and consultant at a factory that produced train parts, before a falling out with the owner of the company led to his trek from Chicago to Washington State.

The "Clockroach" was discovered by loggers in 1903 abandoned by the side of a remote road in the forests of Washington State, overgrown by moss but otherwise marvelously intact. A private collector bought the "Clockroach" and upon his death in 1953, the museum acquired the piece at auction.

The "Clockroach" measures 40 feet long by 15 feet wide and is composed primarily of steel, cast iron, rubber tubing, and glass. The nature of the machine's mechanical operation has been the subject of some debate, as it does not conform to the known properties of the internal combustion engine. Indeed, experts have concluded that the "Clockroach" could not have run on gasoline or, as some have postulated, a wood-fed furnace. Speculation that Addison had stumbled upon a safe hybrid steam-powered energy alternative in creating his curiosity has yet to be substantiated by evidence. What it did run on, or whether it ever really worked at all, remains a mystery.

The museum understands the fascination that the "Clockroach" holds for "children of all ages," but due to liability issues, we can no longer allow anyone to climb the machine. Please remain behind the safety rope at all times. Remember that for energy conservation reasons, we now close at 3 p.m.

On Wooden Wings

Paolo Chikiamco

"No place like home, right Clarita?"

Had she lived in any other city, Clarita Leschot Esteybar might have suspected that Nur was being facetious. Even people who had lived in Jolo all their lives still marveled at its brass minarets, its narrow-gauge wagonways, the retractable sheets over its smaller streets and alleys. The city of Jolo had been a center of trade and commerce even before it was integrated into the Qudarat Sultanate, but in the century since the Spaniards had been repulsed from Zamboanga, the nature of its goods had changed. Junks from China and prahus from Celebes now sought the Fleet of Wisdom's artifices and scholarly treatises more than the pearls and precious shells that used to be Jolo's stock in trade. Clarita took great pride in being a part of the Fleet, the strength of the Sultanate. She just hoped that she'd be able to remain a part of it after today.

"Look at them all." Clarita looked at the crowd which had gathered in the square before the Kutta Bato. Even if they still called it a "stone fort," the old citadel had been much improved over the years, its high walls bristling with the pneumatic and powder-based canons, the very latest of the War Makers' designs.

Nur patted Clarita on the back. "Don't be nervous. It's the same as every other time we've been here."

The most distinctive contribution of the Fleet to Jolo had nothing to do with its defense—the square was dominated by the Elephant Tower, a five-story re-creation of Al-Jazari's famed Elephant Clock. Sultan Qudarat himself had commissioned it to commemorate the union of Maguindanao and Sulu. It was by this Tower that a platform had been set up for students engaging in their Promotion Trials. Competition for patrons was fierce among the Çelebi, and many ambitious students chose to hold off their Trials until they had an audience saturated with the elite of the Sultanate; short of the capital of Maguindanao itself, Jolo was a prime hunting ground.

Another cheer went up from the crowd. From their position behind the platform, the girls could see an older student propel himself up a ramp and into the air. He flipped once, twice, then landed on his feet, smoke trailing from the rockets strapped to the sledlike conveyance on which he perched.

"Parlor tricks," Nur said, sniffing as if in the presence of something rank. "His ambition flies only as high as he does."

"At least his project works," Clarita said, unable to keep the bitterness from her voice. Even beneath its sheltering tarpaulin, her Auto-bird looked misshapen, hard angles pushing out the fabric without rhyme or symmetry. That they'd managed to put its pieces back in a semblance of working order was a miracle in itself, but Clarita knew that the chances that it would be flight ready were almost zero.

Nevertheless.

"I'll do it."

Nur's normally stoic face creased in concern. "We've run no tests on—"

"I'm sick of tests," Clarita snapped. She massaged her temples and took a deep breath. "If the weather stays fair, the wings will hold—and if they don't, well, that's why we added in the Homo Valens."

Nur set her jaw, but then inclined her head in the barest nod. "Then I shall inform the Çelebi that you've made your decision," she said, but before Nur could step onto the platform, Çelebi Husin addressed the spectators.

"While student Udtong prepares for his final demonstration, we have a very young candidate who has signified her intent to undergo a Trial today, one who hails from this very city!"

Clarita looked at Nur, but her friend seemed equally surprised. "We'll figure it out later," Nur said, before turning to wave a few nearby alipin toward the Auto-bird. "Get this up on the platform, quickly!"

But Clarita had more immediate concerns. She stepped up onto the platform, and was immediately greeted by a spontaneous round of applause

Paolo Chikiamco

from the crowd. Clarita ignored the noise, and Çelebi Husin's unnecessary introduction, her eyes scything through the crowd until they met a pair of hazel eyes identical to her own. Her father gave her a grave nod, acknowledging her without communicating an ounce of belief in her endeavor. He already seemed resigned to having to enforce their bargain, "for her own good."

Then, to Clarita's surprise, her father looked up and away from her. The rest of the crowd followed suit, and it was only then that she realized that Çelebi Husin was still speaking.

"—yes, at the very highest point of your fair city, we find the brave young man who has volunteered to pilot student Esteybar's machine in its first ever flight!"

It was as if the Çelebi's words had stretched out time: it took an hour for her vision to travel from her father to the top of the Elephant Tower, a year for her to recognize the face of the boy strapped to a machine that she had not created, a century to whisper his name in horror.

"Domingo…"

And then he began to fall.

Eight months earlier:

When Clarita was young, she'd been fascinated by Scheherazade. Now, all of fifteen years of age, Clarita liked to think that she and the Queen were very much alike. After all, Clarita had read the books of literature, philosophy, and, well… mechanics, in her case. She knew gears by heart, had studied da Vinci's note-books, and was acquainted with the works of Albertus Magnus. She was—or at least liked to think of herself as—intelligent, knowledgeable, and refined.

Definitely refined. After all, this was the only reason that she was knocking, for the fifth time, on Domingo Malong's door, instead of breaking it down with Nur's Guericke-pump catapult.

"I know you're in there, kafir!" Sometime during the five minutes she'd been standing outside the door to Domingo's room, her polite knocking had turned into a vigorous battering. "I can keep this up all day!"

"Go away!" answered a deeper voice from behind the door, in heavily accented Arabic.

Clarita gave the door a final kick, then stepped back. "Fine. I'm coming back with a Çelebi." While standing in place she began to stomp her feet, gradually decreasing the force of her steps to mimic the sound of receding footsteps. With her right hand, she took a brass ruler from her sidebag and stopped moving. She waited crouched before the door. *One...two...*

The door opened just a crack, and a suspicious eye peered out at the corridor. Before the door could slam shut Clarita lunged forward and wedged the ruler in the gap.

"Ha!" Clarita shouted, using the ruler as a lever to pry open the door. Defeated, the boy stepped back and crossed his arms, glaring at Clarita as she entered his room.

Clarita tapped the tip of the ruler against her forehead, flushed with pleasure at her success. "You've got a lot to learn before you can best me."

"My apologies," Domingo said, his jaw jutting out like the bow of a galleon. "I forget how good you Spaniards are at invading the homes of others."

And that was the reason that Clarita and Domingo could never be friends. It wasn't the fact that Clarita was the best student in the Fleet, or that the Çelebi had turned her into Domingo's personal overseer and tutor. No, it was the simple fact that Domingo was a Filipino, and Clarita was "Spanish"—never mind that she had never seen Spain, or that her father was French, or that her mother came from a Muslim minority that was more persecuted in Spain than Domingo's people were in Luzon. It was obvious to Clarita that as far as Domingo was concerned, she was The Enemy. Considering that many of her fantasies involved using the Tagalog as a test subject for one of Nur's more unstable inventions, maybe he was right.

Clarita let her eyes roam around Domingo's room. It was the first time she'd ever been inside, and, except for canvas sacks piled in the corner, the small space looked surprisingly clean.

"You've been here three months now, and you still haven't unpacked?"

"I don't see how that's any of your business." Domingo took a step back as she moved forward, eyes flicking away, then back at her.

"And I don't see how my question is a call for rudeness," she snapped.

"Rudeness?" Domingo laughed. "You're a Spaniard. That's a wrong which calls for a wrong. Why are you even here? I don't have falsafa scheduled today."

"Would it even matter to you if you did?" She pointed a finger at the younger boy. "You haven't met with any of the Çelebi for a week—and I know that Çelebi Jalal was supposed to see you yesterday, so don't even try to lie."

Clarita heard some of her anger creeping into her voice. She couldn't help it. Here he was, with access to a level of instruction that was the envy of the world, and he seemed dead set on squandering it. Why the Çelebi had granted Domingo admission was a mystery to Clarita, but less so than the fact that they seemed so invested in his academic advancement. *If I missed two falsafa in a row*, Clarita though bitterly, *they'd have me on a ship to Jolo within the day, best student or no.* The thought of having to leave the Fleet and face her father under such a circumstance, even imagined, stoked the fires of her anger even higher.

"And if I'm not interested in making graceless, clanking machines, what is it to you?" Domingo waved a hand at her; dismissive, imperious. "Get out of my room, *moro.* You have no right to be here."

Clarita's eyes narrowed. "Funny, I was thinking the same thing. Since you hate it here so much, I think you should just leave." With a burst of speed, she brushed past him. "In fact, why don't I help you pack?"

"Don't touch those!" Domingo caught Clarita's arm, but even as he pulled her back, Clarita kicked out at one of the bags. As soon as her toes hit the canvas, a cloud of sawdust and wood chips erupted from the bag.

Clarita coughed, and took a step back, waving the dust away from her face. Domingo moved quickly to pick up the bag, but by then she had already glimpsed the rest of its contents.

"Is that…what you've been doing in here, all this time?"

Domingo lurched away, holding the bag she'd kicked, but Clarita merely reached down and picked up another. She thrust her hand inside, and pulled out a wooden figure, about half a cubit in length.

"It isn't…it isn't what you think it is," Domingo said, his voice tremulous, but Clarita was too entranced by the carving to pay him any mind. It was only half finished, but it was clearly meant to be a middle-aged woman. Clarita marveled at the level of detail that had been painstakingly etched in the wood, from the embroidery along the sleeves of the woman's blouse, to the fine lines at the corners of her eyes, lines that somehow conveyed the certainty that they had been stamped by suffering, rather than time.

Clarita looked back up at Domingo, who seemed ready to make a break for the door. "Did *you* make this?"

The boy licked his lips, then seemed to recover some semblance of the belligerence with which he usually addressed her. "Yes. And again, I don't know why that's any of your—"

"It's beautiful."

"—your, uhm…" He stopped. "Wait, you're not angry?"

"Angry? Why would I be...Allah give patience to my soul," Clarita threw up her hands. "Did you think I'd take this as blasphemy? Is that what they teach you Christians?"

"I wasn't sure," he said, his voice cautious. "I don't know a lot about you people."

"That's because you've gone out of your way to keep from getting to know us, kafir. As long as you're not planning on praying to this thing, we'll have no problems."

Clarita watched as the anxiety leaked from the boy, leaving him with an almost comical look of relief. "Thank God. If I had to tell Father I'd been expelled..."

Clarita felt a twinge of sympathy. Who would have thought she'd have something in common with the Christian boy? She looked at the figure again. *And who'd have thought he'd actually be good at something.* As she let her fingers follow the contours of the shaped wood, felt the weight of it in her hand, an idea sparked in the recesses of her mind. She handed the carving of the woman back to Domingo, then placed a friendly hand on his shoulder.

"Listen, promise me that you'll be at falsafa tomorrow so that the Çelebi will get off both our backs," she said, "and in return, I'll give you a reason to keep going."

When Clarita pushed open the door to the workshop, Domingo's nose wrinkled immediately. "What is that *smell?*"

"Some concoction the alchemists came up with to keep us from burning down the ship," Clarita sniffed. It had been some time since she'd last noticed the pungent aroma. "You'll get used to it. Watch your head."

Clarita ducked beneath a series of pipes that seemed to have been positioned intentionally for maximum mischief. A muffled thunk later, Domingo emerged on the other side, rubbing his forehead and wearing a sour expression—but that changed as soon as he got his first good look at the workshop.

When the first Çelebi had allied themselves with Sultan Qudarat over a hundred years ago, the Fleet had consisted of nothing but two ragged vessels, barely able to stay afloat. Now, the Fleet numbered nine self-propelling Khaliya Safin—and numerous smaller craft for defense and trade—each of which was dedicated to one of the major branches of learning. The Jazari was home to machinists like Clarita who studied the mechanical arts, and while she had grown used to the place over the last two years, she still remembered how it had felt like when she first found herself amidst the hissing, clanging, smoldering chaos of the student workshop.

The Jazari was one of the most populated ships, and at any given time there could be a dozen students and twenty different projects jostling for space within the high-ceilinged room. As a result, the students learned to build around each other, their inventions and experimental apparatus entwined like tree limbs in a rainforest of hard brass and shorn wood, piles of books and loose pages serving as the underbrush.

"Watch out!" came the call of a familiar voice, and Clarita pulled Domingo to the ground just as a large object hurtled past them, to shatter against the wall in a spray of water and ceramic.

Clarita straightened her kombong. "Water pressure still giving you problems?" she asked the lanky girl who had just popped out from behind a particularly sturdy worktable.

"I think I'm putting too many contortions in the pipe." Like Clarita, she too wore a kombong around her head, and tight, black sawal pants beneath a loose, long-sleeved blouse with embroidered geometric designs. The taller girl, however, had a blade sheathed at her hip, an auto-kris which Clarita had once seen cut through an inch of iron. "Is this your Tagalog? He looks a bit fragile."

Clarita made a face. "Domingo Malong, meet Nur bint Jamal Hassim al Maguindanao."

"Just Nur," Nur said as she offered her hand to Domingo. The boy took it, though his eyes were a bit wild.

"Was that some kind of weapon?" Domingo asked.

The taller girl snorted. "If I built a weapon that couldn't pierce a reinforced hull, I'd slit my throat."

"Nur's from the Rammah," said Clarita, referring to the home ship of the War Makers, "but she's working on a project for Çelebi Samira, on the side. Penance for almost sinking the Jazari a few months back."

"It wouldn't have sunk," said Nur, in a long-suffering tone of voice. "Maybe it would have listed a little, but no one was in any real danger."

"So then what—"

"It's an odorless privy," Nur said, then at Domingo's blank look: "You Tagalogs would call it an arinola."

Clarita laughed at Domingo's expression. "Çelebi Samira is a woman of acute sensibilities…and little patience. We'd best let Nur get back to work."

"Good to meet you Tagalog," Nur said. "Nice of you to help Clarita with her research."

"Research?" Domingo asked, casting a suspicious look toward Clarita as she led him further into the maze of metal struts and stained cabinets. "What research?"

Clarita cursed under her breath. "Later. I promised to show you something first."

She stopped in front of her own modest worktable, most of it occupied by her latest project, hidden from view by a specially treated tarpaulin. Clarita ducked down beneath the table, and after a few minutes of rummaging, she emerged with a dusty wooden box, about twice the size of a loaf of bread. She opened the box and smiled at Domingo's sharp intake of breath as he saw the wooden figures inside. Clarita set the box on the table, then began to remove them one by one, a lute player, a knight, and a princess, each one exquisitely detailed and small enough to fit in her hand.

"Did you—?"

Clarita shook her head. "My father used to work with a man named Jacques de Vaucanson. When Father left Europe, de Vaucanson gave them to him as a parting gift."

Domingo was barely listening. His eyes traced over every line of the figures as if to carve them indelibly into his memory. And she hadn't even delivered the coup de grâce yet.

She gently inserted a small key into the back of the princess and twisted. Immediately the figure began to bow, stopping when it reached mid-waist, then straightening again, repeating the somewhat rickety motion while Clarita keyed the other figures into action, the knight lifting and lowering its sword, the musician moving the lute back and forth.

"I thought you might find these more impressive than a cord pulley or a pump engine," Clarita said, her tone smug, but she could see from the rapture in his eyes that she'd already won. There was something about his expression of absolute stupefaction that gave her a warm feeling.

"See? Not every machine needs to be graceless and noisy." She clapped him on the shoulder. "Just think of these beauties every time Çelebi Jalal is rambling on about valves and sprockets—it may not seem like it, but you can use mechanics to build art, if you're good enough."

Domingo tore his eyes away from the clockwork pieces, his face oddly conflicted. "I'm not here to learn about art," he said, but his next words betrayed him. "Could I borrow them?"

Clarita smiled. *Got you.* "I don't know, kafir, these are priceless family heirlooms we're talking about…I'd be foolish to just loan them out for nothing."

Domingo gave her a sour look. "You're as subtle as a flying arinola. I suppose this is where that research comes in?"

Clarita's smile grew wider. With a flourish, she pulled the tarpaulin off her table, to reveal a pair of folded mechanical wings, attached to a complicated apparatus of wood and brass, cogs and levers, roughly in the shape of a throne that had been cut off at the armrests, dangling from an iron stand by leather straps.

"This," Clarita said with pride, "is the Auto-bird, my prototype human-operated, heavier-than-air flying harness."

"What does it do?" Domingo asked in a dry tone, then grinned as Clarita sputtered in indignation. "Look, it's impressive, but if you're having trouble getting it off the ground, I can't help. I'm no machinist."

"No," Clarita grinned. "But you have another skill I'd like to borrow."

"Move your head a little bit to the left."

Clarita let out a breath. "You've been working on my nose for more than a week."

In response, Domingo set down his chisel, this one with a v-shaped head (she was beginning to wonder how many he owned), and stared at her with supreme patience. Clarita sighed, then turned her face to the left. Behind him, the door stood open, a compromise for the sake of her modesty as Domingo refused to carve anywhere else. As she heard the methodical sound of metal biting into wood, she tried to distract herself by letting her eyes wander around Domingo's room. It was poor entertainment, considering that she'd long since memorized even the grain patterns of the floorboards.

It had been a simple enough plan: have Domingo craft a wooden model of her so that she could safely test her flight harness. The Auto-bird was her masterpiece, something that would guarantee her the rank of Çelebi if demonstrated at a Promotion Trial. The masters of the Fleet held a special weakness for those who could master the winds and seize the legacy of their spiritual founder, Ahmet Çelebi. Clarita believed that she'd created a mechanical harness capable of wing-assisted flight, but she wasn't crazy enough to attempt a test flight herself. The only way she was going to get any useful results would be if she could approximate how the harness would react with her strapped into it, and that meant creating an accurate model, or, in this case, finding someone to create it for her.

A sound plan. She just hadn't expected that it would take *months*.

It wasn't that Clarita didn't appreciate the effort that Domingo was putting into the project. After all—except for that hellish week where she had to pose with her arms suspended, resting on an imaginary brace—she just stood still (or sat) while Domingo hammered, chiseled, and cut. But the Auto-bird was almost ready for a field test and Clarita was getting impatient. The next docking at Jolo was less than half a year away.

Clarita stood up, and Domingo made a small, exasperated noise. "Clarita…"

"Dom, listen, I don't need something that can take my place in falsafa. I can't afford to waste too much time on—"

"Waste?" Domingo asked, in an injured tone. He laid down his chisel and picked up a hammer.

"I didn't mean that," Clarita said, picking her words carefully. While Domingo had, surprisingly, turned out to be good company, she'd learned the hard way that he was vindictive and easily offended. "The model is fine, it's good enough—"

"Good *enough?*"

The hammer hit the wood with unusual force, and Clarita jumped back, unnerved by how loud the harsh cracking sound was in the small space.

"What does that even mean? You're going to be hundreds of feet in the air!" Domingo was glaring at her as if he found the thought of her leaving the ground to be personally insulting. "What if something goes wrong? What if you turn the wrong way or pull the wrong lever because, because when you did your test I got your hip wrong, or your elbow, or, or your nose?"

Clarita was ready to answer his rising anger with her own, but there was something in his voice, in the strain on his face, that gave the girl pause. She smiled.

"Domingo Malong…are you *worried* about me? Little moro me?"

To her great delight, Domingo actually blushed, looking quickly down and busying himself with carving a notch between the fingers of the model. "Don't be ridiculous. I just…I think it's crazy what you're doing. You're taking a huge risk, and for what?"

Clarita sat back down, and for a few minutes there were no sounds other than those Domingo's tools made as they steadily chipped away at the wood.

"I made a promise." The words were out before she realized that she had decided to confide in him. "A deal...with my father. If I'm promoted to Çelebi by my next homecoming, then I get to stay on the Fleet for good."

"That sounds like an easy enough deadline to avoid."

Clarita barked out a harsh laugh. "I come from Jolo. The Fleet docks there at least twice a year. At the worst case, I've only got six months."

For a long moment, Domingo was quiet. "A Çelebi at fifteen, huh?"

Clarita felt heat rush to her face. Most students studied for more than a decade before they passed their Promotion Trials, the demonstrations of learning and ingenuity required before one was allowed to teach at the Fleet. Without another word, she rose once more to her feet and headed toward the doorway. Domingo intercepted her, his hand encircling her wrist.

"You're the smartest student I've met here. If anyone can do it, you can." His eyes were earnest and searching, and Clarita felt like one of the Vaucanson figures which had so captured his imagination. "And whatever I can do to help, I will."

Maybe Clarita's surprise showed on her face, or maybe the boy hadn't really meant to be so direct, but Domingo let go of her wrist abruptly and turned away. "I'll...see you tomorrow."

Clarita stepped out into the hallway, then turned and smiled at the back of Domingo's head. The boy had begun to clean the chips and wood shavings from the floor, and was studiously avoiding any glances in her direction.

"See you tomorrow," she said.

"What do you mean you're not testing it today?"

"I think the statement speaks for itself, Nur," Clarita said, before her eyes were drawn to a circular saw, its handle inscribed with jewel-like beads. "Oooh! How much?"

The Fleet had docked at the coastal town of Baras that morning for one of its periodic mail and resupply runs. A docked Fleet meant a free day for the students. Clarita, like most of her peers, had decided to spend the free day browsing the wares at the portside tiangue, just beyond the town walls. While most of the vendors still displayed their wares on nothing more advanced than old carpets, the various clockwork mechanisms on sale—not to mention the new watchtower, twice as tall as the old bantayan—were a testament to the impact of commerce with the Fleet. Students were always welcome at the tiangue, and that was where Nur found her.

"For a pretty young girl like you, only two Lujine," said the old woman. Clarita gagged.

"There are towns in the Visayas where I could buy *you* for that much!"

"Well, you're not in the hinterlands, girl." The vendor bit down hard on her betel chew and spat; a black smear appeared on the grass. "You're in the Qudarat Sultanate, and if you're not willing to pay for quality, then back to the ship with you!"

Before Clarita could muster a retort, Nur dragged her away. "Clarita, you've got bigger problems than a mouthy vendor."

Clarita shook off the taller girl's grip. "Nur, I told you, the Auto-bird is done, but Dom says the model isn't ready yet—so no, I won't be conducting a field test today. How many times are you going to ask me the same question?"

"Let me try another one then," Nur said. "When did you stop taking your deal with your father seriously?"

Clarita went still. "Nur...you of all people should know better"

"No, *you* should know better," Nur said. She held up a hand to forestall Clarita's objections. "It's just the facts. You used to spend all your free time tinkering with that machine, double checking your calculations, stealing supplies...now, you're a permanent resident of the Tagalog's room."

"His name is Domingo," Clarita said, scowling at her friend, but Nur simply raised an eyebrow. Domingo's name wasn't the real issue here, and Clarita knew it.

It was true that she's been spending a lot of time with Domingo in the past few... Had it really been months since she'd asked for Domingo's help? The days seemed a blur.

"I know what I'm doing." Clarita wished Domingo were here—he'd be able to tell Nur just how committed Clarita still was to her goal. But the Çelebi had been keeping Domingo's family updated as to his progress, and an aunt in Baras had insisted on having him visit while the Fleet was here. "We've still got two months before I meet my father, so there's plenty of—"

She stopped when she saw the look on Nur's face.

"No wonder you've been taking your sweet time." Nur gripped Clarita by the shoulders. "There was a Spanish raid on Dapitan a few weeks ago. If you'd

⚙ ◎ ✥ ✦ ✺ ⊰ **Paolo Chikiamco** ⊱

been spending more time in the common areas you'd have heard. The Çelebi changed our route—we'll be docking at Jolo in ten days."

Clarita's body went rigid. She heard Nur continue to speak, but her friend's voice seemed like it came from far away. Clarita was already running the calculations in her mind, doling out the little time she suddenly had left amidst all the things that she now remembered had yet to be done, the little details that needed to be taken care of, the tests…

"Come on," she said, grabbing Nur's arm and pulling the taller girl along behind her. "No time to lose!"

They made it to the Da Vinci—the Khaliya Safin where most of the kafir resided—in less than an hour. Domingo had fallen out of the habit of locking his door ever since Clarita's modeling sessions began. Nur pushed the door open, then let out a low whistle, coming to a stop just as she stepped over the threshold.

"You didn't tell me he was *this* good."

Clarita couldn't remember the last time she had looked, really looked at the wooden figure. It had almost become part of the scenery, just another piece of a room that had become so familiar. Now, in the mid-afternoon light slanting through the sole window, the wooden figure took on an almost luminous quality, every chiseled line and smoothened contour thrown into stark relief. Clarita had asked Domingo to re-create her in wood, and he'd done so with exacting accuracy.

"It looks finished to me," Nur said, leaning in to take a closer look at the horsehair wig they'd glued into place on the wooden head. Her eyes flicked down to the carving's chest before slanting toward Clarita. "My, my, he really did play close attention, didn't he?"

"I don't know what you mean," Clarita said, but avoided looking at her friend as she took a firm hold of one of the carving's legs. "A little help here?"

By the time that Clarita and Nur had retrieved their equipment from the workshop and returned to Baras, the sun had begun to set, its colors muted behind a gathering of dark clouds, forming a heavy line across the horizon. Fortunately, it didn't take them long to find the perfect location for the flight test.

"Perhaps next time…you'd consider using small scale models for your tests," Nur said, breathing heavily, the tall girl still not fully recovered from the ordeal of carrying the wooden carving to the top of the abandoned bantayan. Clarita ignored her implied complaint, intent on making sure that the carving was fastened tight.

"All set," Clarita said, taking a step back to survey her work. The carving, dressed in tight clothes similar to what Clarita would wear on her own flight, was tied to a simple winged harness—no sense in risking the actual Auto-bird. This streamlined iteration, its flapping motion powered by basic clockwork— would be enough to discover whether her wing design could provide enough lift to keep a body with her weight and dimensions aloft.

Nur had a hand on her head to keep her kombong from being caught by the wind. "The weather's deteriorating, Clarita. Are you certain you want to do this today?"

"You're the one who told me to take this seriously," Clarita snapped. She shook her head. "The Fleet leaves tomorrow. I'm out of time." With two quick key twists, she set into motion the clockwork mechanism in the wings. "On three: one, two—"

With the girls standing on either side of the carving, they pushed it off the roof of the bantayan. It began to drop almost immediately, the whirr and click-clack of the mechanical frame almost drowned out by the wind, which howled as if to reject the trespass to its domain. But after a two-foot freefall (which Clarita's stomach mimicked) the wooden frame shuddered, and its wings began to move in a steady rhythm. In the span of a few seconds, the downward spiral tapered off, and the mechanical frame and its human-shaped cargo began to rise.

"It works!" Clarita laughed, digging her fingers into Nur's arm, heedless of the wind ripping her kombong from her head. "I told you Nur! I told you it—"

That was when she heard the screech of protesting machinery. In the almost darkness, Clarita had only a moment to stare in horror at the two wings of the frame—tangled perversely in the cloth of her kombong—before there was a fractured crack, and frame and carving both hurtled to the ground.

There was absolute silence at the top of the bantayan as Clarita and Nur gazed down at the wreckage, a good fifty feet below them. Perhaps it was the distance that allowed Clarita to view the disaster with a strange detachment, her mind already working on foreign object counter-measures even as she saw a wooden replica of her head break off and roll across the packed earth.

"Another strap might work," Clarita mumbled to herself, "up and under the chin and around the neck…"

"Clarita…"

"…can use that frictionless substance, maybe trade a few workshop hours to…"

"Clarita!"

Nur was pointing urgently down to the ground. A figure knelt at the foot of the bantayan, cradling the detached head. A moment later it stood, let the head drop to the ground, and looked straight up at Clarita. Distance was no protection from the fury that seemed to emanate from Domingo in waves.

Clarita and Nur rushed down the bantayan, but by the time they reached the wreckage, Domingo was almost out of sight, running straight for the docked ships of the Fleet. The girls reached the dock in time to see Domingo reach a ship and duck below decks—but it wasn't the Da Vinci.

"What could he want in Jazari?"

Clarita didn't answer, but desperation lent her flagging leg muscles new strength, and soon she left Nur behind. Clarita was afraid that she knew exactly what he wanted. Down the stairs and through the almost empty halls she ran, but as she neared the workshop she could hear Domingo's inarticulate screams, and the sounds of splintering wood.

Clarita entered the workshop, then let out a strangled cry when she saw what he had done.

Pieces of the Auto-bird littered the floor of the workroom, some still spinning in place from the force with which Domingo had slammed the machine against the reinforced hull of the ship. Pieces of the wings, broken at the joints, hung from fume pipes and notched gears, torn canvas fluttering disconsolately... And in the center of it all stood Domingo, tears streaking his cheeks as he wrenched one last lever from its socket.

Nur surged past Clarita, crashing against Domingo and bending him backwards over a table. Her auto-kris was at his neck before he could react, but Domingo ignored the blade, his eyes locked on Clarita's.

"Nur..." Clarita whispered.

"You spineless bastard! Do you know what you've done?" Nur thumbed the exposed cog and the kris began to hum, its blade vibrating as if in anticipation. "In ten days, we dock at Jolo!"

Domingo blinked. "Ten...days?" he asked, but Nur ignored him.

"Her father is going to withdraw his support," she hissed. "The best of us, sent home—and for what? A pig-eating, no-good Christian?"

"Nur," Clarita said, and pulled her away. "Enough."

Nur stared at her in shock. "Are you telling me that he walks away from this?"

"A wrong for a wrong," Clarita whispered. She gazed into Domingo's eyes and did not flinch. "We're even."

Domingo picked himself up from the table. He averted his gaze, ever so slightly. Was that remorse that she saw flicker across his face before he turned away?

Too late now.

Now:

It took less than two seconds for Domingo's wings to deploy and his trajectory to level out. The stretched canvas flapped down-and-up in a rapid motion, faster than Clarita's original design—and it *was* Clarita's design, or at least appeared to be at this distance.

"He replicated the Auto-bird," Nur said, a grudging admiration coloring her tone. She came to a stop beside Clarita and clucked her tongue. "In ten days too…looks like your Tagalog can work quickly when he wants to. I'm having trouble even believing this is possible."

But Clarita was watching Domingo's flight path with growing concern. "It isn't," she whispered, then whirled on Nur. "Get me strapped in, quickly!"

"What—"

"He's going to fall!" she shouted, just as the first gasps drifted up from the crowd. Clarita resisted the urge to look up, as Nur helped Clarita buckle herself into the repaired Auto-bird. "The wings don't have enough twist or fold to their movement, just up-and-down up-and—"

"The fool replicated the form, not the science." Nur cursed as she tightened the chin strap which secured Clarita's kombong to her head. "But we're not high enough for take-off and we don't have time to—"

"Excuse me!" Clarita shouted, as she lumbered toward the older student, Udtong, but he was transfixed by the spectacle in the sky. Without further preamble she aligned his sled with the ramp, then stepped atop it.

"Hey!" Udtong protested, as the sound of her heavy feet brought him back to earth. "What are you—"

"Ignite the rockets!"

"You're out of your mind!" Udtong said, but then Nur pushed him to the ground, taking the fire strikers from him. Nur twisted the keys on the Auto-bird's flanks, then handed Clarita her auto-kris, before stooping down to light both sets of rockets.

>i Paolo Chikiamco k

"Good lu—"

The roar of the gunpowder igniting beneath Clarita's feet drowned out the rest of Nur's words. Clarita swayed, struggling to keep her balance as the sled thundered forward, then up the prepared incline. At the height of the upward arc, the sled fell away from beneath her and Clarita was standing on nothing but air, working the levers desperately as she prayed: *Let it be enough, let it be enough...!*

She let out a shout of victory when her wings deployed, but that turned into a scream when the first gust of wind threatened to break apart her improvised repairs. But she was airborne, if unsteadily so, and she quickly scanned the skies for Domingo. He was almost directly above her, wrestling with his controls, the movements of his wings jerky and desperate. Clarita climbed up in little bursts, her hobbled Auto-bird sputtering and stalling every ten seconds, but soon she was close enough to reach out to him.

"Grab hold!" she said, one hand reaching toward Domingo while her other clutched the auto-kris. He was panicking, his eyes wide and his teeth chattering, and the hand which closed around hers was ice cold. Clarita began to slice the straps which bound Domingo to his machine. They were at least five stories up in the air. She managed to cut all but one tether before she heard an ominous screech. She looked up in time to see the wings of her Auto-bird entangled with his before her jury-rigged stitching came undone, both of her wings tearing themselves away as she and Domingo plummeted to the ground.

"Pull the cord pull the cord!" Clarita screamed, as she stabbed desperately at the last remaining tether with one hand, the other wrapped around Domingo's waist. The leather gave out just as Domingo grabbed the bit of rope streaming out from over her left shoulder, and pulled it with all his might.

Domingo's harness fell away from them as the Homo Valens unfurled behind them, catching the air in its bulging canvas as it arrested their fall, the harness straps digging painfully into Clarita's body. But the ground was still rushing toward them at an alarming rate, and the last thing Clarita felt before the shock of impact was Domingo moving beneath her and enfolding her body in his.

When Clarita came to, she found herself buried beneath the billowing cloth of the Homo Valens. She'd lost the auto-kris at some point after she hit the earth, so she laboriously unfastened each buckle and crawled out from beneath the suffocating canvas, her right side throbbing as if it had been flayed.

"Domingo?" she called out, her voice a rasp. She cleared her throat. "Domingo!"

"Here," came a small voice, followed by a moan. Domingo was a few feet away from her. For a horrifying second, it seemed as if he lay in a pool of blood, but then she realized it was fruit pulp—he lay against the remains of an overturned produce cart. But his cough was liquid, and Clarita rushed to his side.

"I guess I didn't quite get the wings right, huh?"

She stared at him. *"That's* what you have to say to me?" It was as if a dam had broken within her, and the words spilled out. "You destroy a year's worth of work, then, instead of apologizing, you decide in your wisdom that what you *really* need to do is make a flying machine on your own, tell everyone it's mine, and throw yourself off a tower?"

"I—"

"Did it not even occur to you that I'd try to repair the Auto-bird? Did you think I'd just give up?" Clarita shook her head. "When I think about how much progress we would have made if we'd just combined efforts… Argh!"

"I—"

Clarita forced herself to her feet, ignoring the pain in her side, and jabbed her finger at the boy. "Domingo Malong, from now on, you work with me, understood?"

Domingo stared at her, incredulous. Then he began to laugh.

"What about your father?" he asked, after she had helped him to his feet. "If you don't pass the Trial…"

"Domingo," she said, in a patient tone, "I just demonstrated a heavier than air flying machine in front of the richest men in the Sultanate. I don't think I need to depend on my father for funding anymore."

"Oh. That makes sense." Domingo licked his lips. "I'm sorry, 'rita."

"I know." She beamed at him. "But it's good to hear it."

The Elephant Tower tolled the passing of the half-hour from high above the city. Clarita closed her eyes, and let her triumph seep down into her bones. For the first time in her life, the future that lay before her was subject to no grand design. She opened her eyes then, and locked them on to the boy that stood beside her.

Well…none but her own, anyway.

Still smiling, Clarita linked arms with Domingo and the pair began the painful journey back to the square.

Sir Ranulph Wykeham-Rackham, GBE, a.k.a. Roboticus the All-Knowing

Lev Grossman

Sir Ranulph Wykeham-Rackham was born in 1877. As heir to the legendary Wykeham-Rackham wainscoting fortune he was assured a life of leisure and privilege, if not any particular utility. But no one suspected that his life would still be going on 130 years later, after a fashion.

A brilliant student, he went up to Oxford at the age of 16 and was sent down again almost immediately for drunkenness, card-playing and lewdness. Given the popularity of these pastimes among the undergraduate body one can only imagine the energy and initiative with which young Ranulph pursued them.

Although he had no artistic talent himself, Wykeham-Rackham preferred the company of artists, who appreciated his caustic wit, his exquisite wardrobe and his significant annual allowance. He moved to London and rapidly descended into dissipation in the company of the members of the Aesthetes, chief among them Oscar Wilde. Wykeham-Rackham was a regular presence in the gallery during Wilde's trial for gross indecency, and after Wilde's release from prison it is strongly suspected that wainscoting money bankrolled the elaborate ruse surrounding Wilde's supposed death, and his actual relocation to a comfortable island in the remote West Indies where such advanced Victorian ideas as "gross indecency" did not exist.

The real Wilde died in 1914, leaving Wykeham-Rackham alone and feeling, at 37, that his era was already passing away. Pater and Swinburne and

Burne-Jones and the other aesthetes were long gone. The outbreak of World War I further deepened his pessimism about the future of modern civilization. Rich, bored and extravagantly melancholy, he enlisted in the 28TH Battalion of the London Regiment, popularly known as the "Artists Rifles," because, as he said, he "liked the uniform, and hated life." One can only imagine his surprise when the Artists Rifles were retained as an active fighting force and sent on a tour of the war's most viciously contested battlefields, including Ypres, the Somme and Passchendaele. All told the Artists Rifles would sustain more personnel killed in World War I than any other British battalion.

But Wykeham-Rackham survived, and not only survived but flourished. He discovered within himself either an inner wellspring of bravery or a stylish indifference to his own fate—the line between them is a fine one—and over the course of three years of trench combat he was awarded a raft of medals, including the Military Cross for gallantry in the face of the enemy at Bapaume.

His luck ran out in 1918, during the infamous 100-days assault on Germany's Hindenburg Line. Wykeham-Rackham was attempting to negotiate a barbed-wire barrier when a sharpshooter's bullet clipped a white phosphorus grenade that he carried on his belt. White phosphorus, then the cutting edge of anti-personnel weaponry, offered one of the grimmest deaths available to a soldier in the Great War. In short order the chemical had burned away much of Wykeham-Rackham's lower body, from the hips down. As he writhed in agony, the German sharpshooter, evidently not satisfied with his work, fired twice more, removing the bridge of Wykeham-Rackham's nose, his left cheekbone and half his lower jaw.

But not, strangely, ending his life. The former dandy's soul clung tenaciously to his ruined body, even as it was trundled from aid station to field hospital to Paris and then across the channel to London. There he became the focus of one of the strangest collaborations to which the 20TH century would bear witness.

At that time the allied fields of prosthetics and cosmesis were being marched rapidly out of their infancy and into a painful adolescence in order to cope with the shocking wounds being inflicted on the human body by the new mechanized weaponry of World War I. Soldiers were returning from the battlefield with disfigurements of a severity undreamt of by earlier generations. When word of Wykeham-Rackham's grievous injury reached his family, from whom he had long been estranged, rather than attend his bedside personally they opted to send a great deal of money. It was just as well.

In short order Wykeham-Rackham's feet, legs and hips had been rebuilt, in skeletal form, out of a new martensitic alloy known as stainless steel which had just been invented in nearby Sheffield. They were provided with rudimentary muscular power by a hydraulic network fashioned out of gutta-percha tubing. The whole contraption was then fused to the base of Wykeham-Rackham's spine.

It was a groundbreaking achievement, of course, but not without precedent. The field of robotics did not yet exist—the word "robot" would not be coined till 1920—but the history of prosthetic automata went back at least as far back as the 16ᵀᴴ century and the legendary German mercenary Götz von Berlichingen, who lost his right arm in a freak accident when a stray cannonball caused it to be cut off with his own sword. The spring-loaded mechanical iron arm he had built as a replacement could grip a lance and write with a quill. (Wykeham-Rackham was fond of quoting from Goethe's *Goetz von Berlichingen*, based on von Berlichingen's life, in which the playwright coined a useful phrase: *"Leck mich am Arsch,"* or loosely, "kiss my ass.")

To replace Wykeham-Rackham's shattered face, a wholly different approach was required. When he was sufficiently recovered from his first operation, Wykeham-Rackham was removed to Sidcup, a suburb of London, home to a special hospital dedicated to the care of those with grotesque facial injuries. It was an eerie place. Mirrors were forbidden. Throughout the town were placed special benches, painted blue, where it was understood that the townspeople should expect that anyone sitting there would present a gravely disturbing appearance.

Wykeham-Rackham's old artist friends, those who were left, rallied around him. Facial reconstruction at that time was accomplished by means of masks. A plaster cast was made of the wounded man's face, a process which brought the patient to within seconds of suffocation. The cast was then used to make a mask made of paper-thin galvanized copper. Prominent painters competed with one another to produce the most lifelike reproduction of Wykeham-Rackham's vanished features, which were then reproduced in enamel that was bonded to the copper.

In all, 12 such masks were produced, suitable for various occasions and displaying a range of facial expressions. On seeing them for the first time, Wykeham-Rackham held one up, like Hamlet holding up Yorick's skull, and quoted from his old friend Wilde: "Man is least himself when he talks in his own person. Give him a mask, and he will tell you the truth."

Following the end of the war, Wykeham-Rackham enjoyed a second heyday. His fantastical appearance made him the toast of the European avantgarde. A pioneer of kinetic sculpture, Marcel Duchamp was enraptured by Wykeham-Rackham, who agreed to be exhibited alongside Duchamp's other "readymades"; he even allowed Duchamp to sign his steel calf with his distinctive "R. Mutt." Man Ray photographed him. Cocteau filmed him. Stravinsky wrote a ballet based on his life, choreographed by Nijinsky.

Picasso created a special mask for him, a Cubist nightmare that he never wore. (Wykeham-Rackham remarked that Picasso seemed to have missed the point, as the mask was more grotesque than what lay beneath it, not less.) Prosthetics became increasingly fashionable, and not a few deaths and grievous injuries among the fashionable set were explained as attempts to reproduce Wykeham-Rackham's distinctive "look."

Meanwhile he was continuously undergoing mechanical upgrades and improvements as the available technology progressed. He regularly entertained whole salons of inventors and engineers who vied to try out their innovations on him. Nikolai Tesla submitted an elaborate, wildly visionary set of schematics for powering his movements electrically. They were, characteristically for Tesla, the subject of a defamation campaign by Edison, then a blizzard of lawsuits by others who claimed credit for them, and then, finally and decisively, lost in a fire.

But as time wore on Wykeham-Rackham became increasingly aware that while his metal parts were largely unscathed by the passage of time, his human parts were not. At a scandalous 50TH birthday party thrown for him by the infamous Bright Young Things of London, Evelyn Waugh among them, Wykeham-Rackham was heard to remark that he was both picture and Dorian Gray in one man.

It was not long afterwards, in 1932, that Wykeham-Rackham opted to have the remainder of his face removed. He was tired, he said, of having his mask touched up to look older, to match his surviving features. Why not become all mask, and look however he wished? It is not known with any certainty who performed this "voluntary disfigurement" operation, but it is strongly suspected that Lambshead's steady if not overly fastidious hand held the scalpel, judging by the fact that Wykeham-Rackham took a *sub rosa* trip to Madagascar at around this time.

Meanwhile stormclouds of international tension were once again massing.

For a brief period Wykeham-Rackham's lower limbs were declared a state secret, and he was required to wear specially designed pantaloons to conceal them. There were numerous attempts by Soviet emissaries to lure Wykeham-Rackham to Moscow—Stalin was said to have been obsessed with the idea of acquiring a literal "man of steel" to lead the glorious proletariat revolution.

No one was wholly surprised when Wykeham-Rackham re-enlisted following Germany's invasion of Poland in 1939. He had grown increasingly disenchanted with 20TH-century urban life, with its buzzing electric lights, blaring radios and roaring automobiles, even though he himself existed as its living, walking avatar. (He had reluctantly submitted to the electrification of his nether regions in the mid-1920s, after a series of messy, embarrassing hydraulic failures at public functions.) He mourned the elegance of his vanished late-Victorian world.

He was also lonely. His romantic life had stalled, in part because he lacked anything in the way of genitals. (It is rumored, although not confirmed, that attempts to add sexual functionality to Wykeham-Rackham's steel groin had to be abandoned after a catastrophic injury to a test partner.) At one time he had hoped that the same procedure that made him what he was would be performed on others, who would share his strange predicament. But all attempts to repeat the experiment failed. It has been argued, most notably in Dominic Fibrous' definitive *Wykeham-Rackham: Awesome or Hokum?*, that this is because Wykeham-Rackham's condition was "medically impossible" and "made utterly no sense at all."

His one, platonic, romance seems to have been with a young mathematician and computer scientist named Alan Turing. Their dalliance led to the latter's formulation of his famous Wykeham-Rackham Test, which raised the question of whether it would be possible to devise a robot so lifelike that it would be impossible to tell it apart from a human being while making love to it.

Now in his 60s, Wykeham-Rackham was far too old for active service, but the physical stamina resulting from his unusual physical make-up, and his value to the troops as a source of morale, made him indispensable. For public relations purposes he joined the invasion of Normandy on D-Day, and the famous photograph of him striding from the surf onto Omaha Beach, his steel pelvis dripping seafoam, a bullet pinging off his enamel face, remains one of the iconic images of the Second World War. The American GIs cheered him on and called him "Tin Man."

But Wykeham-Rackham's excessive bravery was again his downfall. Emboldened by this taste of his former glory, he refused the offer of transport back to England and stayed with the Allied forces pressing forward through the Norman hedgerows. A close-range encounter with the infamous German *Flammenwerfer* seared his arms and torso almost to the bone. Once again he made the perilous journey back across the Channel to the hospitals of London. This time it was necessary to replace almost his entire upper body, leaving only his head and major organs in place.

Astoundingly, he lived on.

Indeed, some began to speculate that out of the crucible of the world wars, humanity's first immortal being had emerged. Wykeham-Rackham showed no obvious signs of aging, apart from his mane of white hair, which he took to dyeing to match its original lustrous black.

But inside, his soul was wasting away. A dark time began for Wykeham-Rackham. Owing to the precipitous decline in sales of wainscoting and wainscoting accessories since the Victorian period, his family fortune had dwindled almost to nothing. He was able to survive only on his military pension, and whatever he received making promotional appearances for the British Armed Forces. Twice he was caught stealing lubricants for his joints and convicted of petty larceny. He became silent and morose. He sold off eleven of his masks, and the Picasso, leaving only the one entitled "Melancholia." It was, he said, the only one he needed.

Wykeham-Rackham's last moment in the spotlight came in the 1960s, when he became one of the oddities and grotesques taken up by Andy Warhol and the Factory scene in New York. He appeared in several of Warhol's movies, to the lasting detriment of his dignity, and was of course the subject of Warhol's seminal silkscreen *Wykeham-Rackham Triptych*. It was at Warhol's suggestion that Wykeham-Rackham commissioned the final surgery that turned him into an entirely synthetic being: the replacement of his skull with a steel casing, and his brain with a large lightbulb.

Conventional wisdom would argue that this was the end of Wykeham-Rackham's existence as a sentient being, but in truth it was difficult to tell. As the 1960s wound down he had spoken and moved less and less. One Warhol hanger-on remarked, in a display of sub-Wildean wit, that after the operation his conversation was "more brilliant than ever."

But Warhol cast Wykeham-Rackham off as lightly as he took him up, and he passed the 1970s and 1980s in obscurity. It's difficult to track his movements during this lost period, but curatorial notes found in Lambshead's basement suggest that some of Warhol's junkie friends eventually sold him to a traveling carnival, where he was put to use as a fortune-telling machine.

Even there he was exiled to a gloomy corner of the midway. The proprietors despaired of ever making money off him, because, they said, no matter how they fiddled with his settings, he only ever predicted the imminent and painful demise of whoever consulted him.

His glorious past had been entirely forgotten but for a single trace. On the sign above his booth was painted, in swirly circus calligraphy, a quotation from Oscar Wilde:

"A mask tells us more than a face."

CHAMP DE
MARS

PALAIS DE
L'ÉLECTRICITÉ

PALAIS
PAR M^R
E. HÉNARD
ARCHITECTE

The Heart Is the Matter

Malissa Kent

This is a fact: The muscles of the hand and arm cramp and spasm while becoming acclimated to a regular repetitive motion, especially one that must be repeated sixty to eighty times a minute. More if there is any cause for excitement.

At the Hôpital du Salut, the strangest sights are not the men and women with metal instead of flesh, not the children with gas flames in place of eyes, not the veterans who race down the hallway to see if they're spry enough on the wheels that replace their legs to join the police corps. The strangest sights are the docteurs and nurses, all of whom are completely flesh.

The children stop and point at me, too. I'm a straddler; I don't belong in the world of the Hôpital anymore than I do in the world outside. I'm not fully flesh, but my metal workings are carefully kept hidden under the long lace at the ends of my sleeves. Only five others in the world know of my metal plates: my parents, my sister, Docteur Suvi, and his nurse. The nurse stays in the room from the moment I step behind the screen to undo my blouse to the moment the docteur escorts me back out into the world. It's childish, certainly, but she provides a security that not even my parents can give me. My sister Eva could, if she chose. But she doesn't.

Today my fingers are numb with cold, even after warming them in front of the fire in the waiting room, so it's hard to undo each of the tiny buttons that line my spine, then to pull the tight sleeve off my left arm, the hand ever pumping, then to shake the sleeve off my right arm. It feels whorish to leave my blouse dangling from the waist of my skirt so I pull it off completely, meeting the docteur in only my corset and combination above my long skirt. He's never embarrassed; all he cares about is the metal.

"Looking good despite the rain," he mutters as he forces his fingers into my palm in the few seconds that my fingers relax. He removes his chef d'oeuvre from my grip carefully, squeezing the metal heart for the few moments it takes to slip it into the huge steam-powered pump where he tests the endurance of each new heart. My hand hovers above my captive heart, unable to stop clenching and unclenching. I have to stay within inches of the hot metal and steam; my metal vessels won't let me stray any further from my heart. "We could try putting it back between your ribs and your bicep," the docteur says, examining my heart for wear. The nurse takes quick notes from the desk, never looking at her paper. "Then you'd have both hands again."

"No." It was bad enough having a metal plate instead of the ribs that shattered under the force required to pump my heart. I could live one-handed.

He shrugs. "How is your arm?" he asks, checking the flexible metal tubes just under the skin of my left hand. They enter on the underside of my wrist, connecting to the large blood vessels there. At the time of the operation, the docteur told my parents, Eva, and I that the metal might get corroded. That I would die if it did.

"Fine." I swallow. "Docteur, did you see that Monsieur Edison is coming for the Exposition? I've been following his experiments with electricity.... I think he may be interested in creating an electric heart."

Dr. Suvi snorts. "First you refuse to be shown as my crowning achievement, and now you speak of electric hearts? You're a silly girl, mademoiselle." He steps away, wiping his hands on his white coat as if he's been sullied by hearing my question. "I'll see you in a week."

And with that I'm back behind the screen. I'm better at buttoning up than I am unbuttoning. Before I step out to rejoin the docteur and his nurse, I shake my sleeves so that the long lace covers both hands equally.

This is a fact: An adult human heart has the same mass as two clenched fists. A child's heart has the same mass as one clenched fist. It took years of innovation for Dr. Suvi to develop a metal heart that fit in one hand.

If Eva had gone to the hospital, our parents would have sent Marie to accompany her. I go on my own. I prefer it this way; Marie is not a stifling governess, but I've seen enough of her in my nineteen years. She was hired to take care of Eva, and me by extension once I was born six years later.

Rather than taking the stairs up to the zeppelin station like most people of gentle birth, I walk to the corner to hail the horse-driven omnibus. I tell Eva that I prefer being on the ground, but in reality I'd rather be in the air. I get too excited by heights for my hand to keep up with my brain's need for oxygen. The city view from our family's flat is the most beautiful thing I know, and the excitement of seeing all of Paris spread below me like a toy begging to be played with is too much. Since the operation, I faint every time I take a zeppelin, causing sensations. I'd rather not have well-dressed bourgeois ladies poke at my metal heart with their silk fans while their husbands debate over who will have to carry me off. I know they do this; I woke in the middle of the debate once. They probably all thought I was dead, despite the spasms in my left hand that kept my blood moving. My hand resembles a heart more than a hand now; it wouldn't stop clenching and unclenching if I told it to, even when I sleep. It took months of practice and conditioning before the operation, but nothing can stop it now. Just like a true heart, it never tires.

The omnibus is full of half-metals and the working class, grimy from a day in the cafeterias, laundry halls, whorehouses, and construction sites of Paris. The construction sites are everywhere, and the only one complete is Mr. Eiffel's tower. Everyone else hurries to be ready for the Exposition Universelle, just two months away now. Eva just ordered a whole new set of gowns; she ordered the first set made a year ago, so naturally they're out of style now. I'm working on pumping even faster so that I can handle more excitement—like meeting Monsieur Edison. I won't mention it again to the docteur, but nothing he says will stop me from speaking to the wizard himself.

I'm so wrapped up in my dreams of electric hearts that I don't think twice about jumping off at my stop; only once I'm on the ground do I realize that I hadn't meant to return until this evening. By then it's too late to turn back— the omnibus is clattering away, and I know that Marie will be hanging off our balcony as she does every time she hears an omnibus while I'm out. It annoys Eva to no end, as she's informed me on numerous occasions. Even my parents have scolded Marie for her silliness.

I turn toward our building and give Marie a resigned wave. I can see the relief that I've returned unharmed on her face even from here. Then she disappears back into the flat to come open the back door for me. I move forward, dragging my feet, and plunge my good hand into the velvet purse dangling off my belt to feel the stiff paper of the invitation that Eva had given me that morning. An invitation to one of her exclusive salons. It was only the latest of many, but this time it was different—she'd invited planners for the Exposition. Planners who might know Monsieur Edison. I had decided to stay far from the temptation of returning and being forced into a society that prefers not to see me.

The alley between buildings is clean except for the occasional mound of dog dirt. From here I can peer into courtyards around thick hedges and iron gates—courtyards that are invisible from the street, where the buildings appear blocky and impenetrable.

"Mon dieu, you and your omnibuses! Ça va?" Marie repeats the question over and over, brushing imaginary dust from my shoulders while shepherding me through our small courtyard. Once we reach the wide, short stairs, she turns on me.

"It's already started—we must make you presentable quickly."

"No, Marie. I'm not going."

"Bah! It's about time you entered society. There are ten members of her literary salon; the rest are scientists."

My stomach clenches. Eva spends time in the company of literary geniuses, complaining bitterly about it afterward; now that I have a weak heart, the only excitement I'm allowed is my weekly visit to the Hôpital.

"But Mother and Father...."

Marie pats my arm. "Don't worry yourself; they gave Eva their approval. Venez!" She pulls me up the stairs. My parents have taken the day to stroll around the Bois de Vincennes, giving Eva the run of the apartment and the servants. If my introduction to society goes poorly, there will be no one to save me.

This is a fact: The human heart weighs an average of ten ounces. My heart weighs three pounds, nearly five times that of its flesh counterpart.

"Now, this must go," Marie says, picking at the sleeve of my blouse. It is made of the same free-flowing brown fabric as my skirt so as to look like a dress covered with tiny white and red flowers. It is the height of Artistic fashion, according to

Eva's magazines and my fellow omnibus riders. None of the bourgeois women at Eva's salon would be caught dead wearing anything similar, with only a loosely laced corset and no bustle.

"Here—your mother had this made up, but she hasn't worn it yet." Marie swirls a dark blue dress made of some heavy fabric I can't even name out of a large box.

"Marie, I couldn't...." I trail off under the force of her glare, reaching for my buttons. She helps me out of my simple dress and buckles me into a cagelike bustle before I even have time to protest. The ridiculous thing has cream-colored linen ruffles along the bottom, and I bite my lip to keep from laughing at my own silhouette.

Marie sighs and shakes her head. "We need to tighten the corset a little, non? Your bust must balance your bustle."

"I can do without the bustle."

"And where would all the skirt's fabric go then?" Marie shakes her head in amazement at my suggestion. She tightens my corset efficiently, making me cough with the sudden constriction of my lungs, then wrestles the blue gown over my head. My mother is taller than me and has longer arms, so even though there is no lace at the edges of the sleeves, my mechanical heart is easily hidden. Mother and I both favor a high neck; in the end, the dress is close enough to something I would have picked myself to make me feel comfortable.

Marie pulls my hair out of its braid and into a tight chignon, allowing a few strands to frame my face. Then she pins the extra meters of fabric in the skirt's back up to the bustle, arranging it to look like an oversized bow on my backside and exposing the ruffles on the bustle. I barely recognize myself.

"Beautiful," Marie pronounces as she powders my face. She shoves the invitation into my hand and opens the door. She gives me a quick, rare smile, then pushes me into the hallway and shuts the door behind me.

I steel myself, shivering with anticipation. There's still time to turn back. I knock on the door to the study, and our butler opens it. He takes the invitation before I can scurry away, then bows me into the room.

A phonograph is playing under the chatter of voices, and skirts swirl over bustles as two couples waltz. The drapes are thrown open to the view of Mr. Eiffel's tower, and a group of three men and a woman are looking out at it. I scan the room for Eva and spot her being escorted to the dance floor by a sandy-haired man in a dark suit and top hat. She is stunning in a red gown with a low décolleté that shows off the top half of her scar. I finger my identical scar, hidden under the high neck of Mother's dress, as I edge around the dancers. How long can I avoid Eva and her introduction?

I go to the one place in our apartment where I feel powerful: the window with its awe-inspiring view. The group standing there is silent as I join them.

"Such a beautiful view," I say to fill the silence, my hand clenching as quickly as my muscles allow. I wish Marie hadn't pulled my corset so tight. Or maybe it's just nerves that make my head so light.

Two of the men turn to me. "Is that so?" the first asks. His accent makes me think of sunshine and lavender.

Heat rushes to my cheeks. "Of course! Seeing the city spread out before you like a pomegranate...."

The second man snorts. "What, with that monstrosity looming over everything? Eiffel ought to be sent to America, if they like his work so much."

"It's as if he wants to remind the world how many metal men there are in Paris," the first adds. "An abomination!"

"It's a work of genius," I say. This grabs the attention of the other two, as well, and they all stare at me. "You must not have read Monsieur Eiffel's interviews regarding the mathematics and the wind resistance of the structure. Nothing in the world can be compared to it. And if it reminds foreigners at the Exposition of French metal men, then it will also remind them of our medical sciences, which make the metal men possible in the first place. Imagine how many lives would have been lost in the war of 1870 if Docteur Suvi had not understood how to fuse metal and flesh!"

"Bravo, mademoiselle," the third man says, clapping his gloved hands. His green eyes are alight with humor—and, I think, admiration. "How do you know so much about Mr. Eiffel's tower?"

"I find the design intriguing and daring, and I appreciate his homage to the metal men. I have visited the Hôpital du Salut many times, and I have seen the miracles performed there firsthand. I know that the technology of Dr. Suvi and his colleagues can do much good in the world." My hand slows slightly as I calm down, and I hide it behind my back so that my little group of listeners doesn't notice its compulsive clenching.

"You see, Raoul and Henri? This tower cannot be all bad if such a pretty demoiselle defends it so! What is your name?"

 → Malissa Kent ←

"Coraline," I reply before realizing that I can't tell him the truth. "Devillers," I add, substituting my mother's maiden name for my own last name.

"Enchanté, Mademoiselle Devillers. I'm Jean d'Ivernay, and your sour-faced adversaries are Raoul Davi and Henri Meurier. And this charming lady is my sister, Sophie."

"Enchanté," I reply in turn, giving them each a slight curtsy for lack of anything better. Raoul is the one with the accent that makes me think of lavender, and I hope to drive the conversation toward his native region and away from the dangerous waters it's currently floundering in.

"Your attitude seems unique, Mademoiselle Devillers," Raoul says, dashing my hopes. "I have heard our hostess speak highly of Dr. Suvi as well, but her opinions of the tower are more…shall we say, normalized."

"Are people no longer allowed differing opinions, Raoul?" Jean asks lightly. He seems like a kind man, and I wonder how he knows the two other boors.

"I read the papers, too," Henri breaks in. "*International* papers. Papers that claim that Paris has become a metal-loving hotbed, and that Dr. Suvi's 'technology' is in fact nothing more than the black magic that Napoleon Bonaparte brought out of Egypt."

"Nonsense," I snap before I can help it. "Look at our hostess! She would not be here without Dr. Suvi's technology. Can you imagine Eva being under the sway of such magic?"

"Claims about Bonaparte's Egyptian magic have always existed," Raoul replies, waving a hand. "What does that matter? It's the rumors about Paris loving metal that concern me. It's bad enough that these half-humans are protected as if they were fully human! Can you imagine some foreigner approaching you and asking, 'Are all Frenchmen metal? Is your wife?'" He shudders. "The day when any man or woman is permitted to marry a metal is the day the Third Republic must end."

This is a fact: The ancient Egyptians weighed the heart against the feather of truth to determine if the dead soul could gain admittance to paradise. If the heart was heavier, the soul was devoured by Ammit, a demon part hippopotamus, part lion, part crocodile.

Before the surgery, I could go into a flying rage and throw a tantrum that neighbors an arrondissement away would hear. My tantrums always surprised my parents; Eva's failing heart never allowed for such explosive displays of emotion. Sometimes I wonder if they realized that the operation would calm me down to Eva's level.

Hearing Raoul's obscenely ignorant comments, I wish I could still fly into a rage. But I can do nothing more than snarl a tart response and stalk off, my hand pumping as quickly as possible.

I stop near the phonograph, struggling to take deep breaths to calm my pulse. The damn corset makes deep breathing nearly impossible, and the bustle is starting to weigh heavily on my back. Sweat beads my forehead under the powder.

"I feel as though I must apologize for Raoul," Jean's voice comes at my elbow, making me jump and my pulse go up even more. This is even worse than the zeppelin!

"He's from Provence, you know, so he's not completely comfortable in the salons of Paris, or with Parisiennes," Jean continued.

"Yes; I heard his accent."

"I hope you do not judge us for being part of that." He waves his hand in the general direction of Raoul and Henri. Then he pauses, looking me up and down slowly. "Mademoiselle Malsante told us that her salon would have a surprise; could it be you? I've never seen you at a salon before, though you seem to know her quite well."

I swallow hard. "Do I?"

His lips twitched. "You called her by her first name."

"We were…childhood friends." It isn't a complete lie. We were friends as children. When all I wanted was to help my older sister. When she was grateful beyond words, and promised me over and over that she'd do anything for me once she had my heart. Anything at all.

"I see. Was she much different then? I've always wondered…did living with another person's heart change her?"

"Not as much as it changed the donor, surely."

"Undoubtedly, since the donor is dead."

"No, she isn't." I don't stop to think until after the words are out of my mouth. I should run out of the room now, before I say anything more. But something in Jean's kind eyes won't let me. If the strange electricity between a man and a woman could be harnessed, ours would power my heart for the rest of my life.

He raises one eyebrow. "No? But surely the donor can't use Evaline's heart?"

I note that he's started calling my sister by her given name, too, and wonder for the first time why he's so interested. Is he one of her suitors? "No; her heart was too small to sustain anyone. Her donor has a metal heart. So I've heard," I add, realizing that it's already too late. He must know who I am by now.

His face lights up and he rocks back on his heels. "I had no idea metallurgy had advanced so far! Such an accomplishment should be mentioned in the Exposition; it will change the world's opinion of metallurgy. I shall mention it to my colleagues at the Exposition Universelle."

"Oh, please don't!" I cry in a panic. Dr. Suvi tried to convince me it would be an honor to be paraded around the Exposition like an object, but I refuse to debase myself—or any other metal man or metal woman—in such a way. "If Eva or her donor should ever find out I've said anything, why...." I back away from him, right into the phonograph. Its three-legged stool wobbles and falls, and I crash down next to it as the music dies.

This is a fact: Aristotle and the Roman physician Galen were wrong. The seat of emotion is not in the heart.

Even before Jean can recover enough to disentangle me from the phonograph, I hear Eva shriek, "What is *this?*" Her face is flushed beneath her powder, and her scar blends into the redness of her upper chest as she pushes to the front of the crowd. "Oh, Cora!" She smiles, though it trembles, and puts a hand over her heart. "Are you all right?"

In the years leading up to the operation, Eva and I used to play guessing games about how we'd change once I had a metal heart and she had mine. I was convinced that she'd understand me completely once my heart was safely inside her. I feared that I'd lose who I was. As the operation drew nearer—Dr. Suvi refused to perform it before my heart was fully developed and its pulse had stabilized with adulthood—Eva's main concern was that my heart would change her feelings for certain men.

My heart did nothing but stabilize her pulse and gave her full range of normal activities that had been denied her for twenty-four years. That was enough for her—for all of us. Dr. Suvi had cautioned our parents with tales of rejected donor organs when it first became apparent that Eva's heart would only get worse as she aged. She was eighteen then, and I twelve. We tested our servants. Our entire extended family. Ourselves. I was the best match. I love my sister, and wanted to do anything to help her. With my parents' francs, Dr. Suvi developed the metal heart, promising them that they'd keep both their daughters.

Jean helps me up. Eva sweeps toward me and takes my right hand. Jean's hand is still on my left arm.

"Mesdemoiselles and messieurs, allow me to introduce my surprise in her first entrance into société: my sister and donor, Coraline Malsante."

There's a quiet murmuring, a polite smattering of applause. I'm not sure what I expected, but certainly not this feigned interest. Then Raoul elbows his way forward.

"Donor?" Raoul spits the word. "But how does she live?"

Jean laughs quietly next to me. "You will eat your words, Raoul. The demoiselle has a metal heart."

I try to flinch away as the salon gives a collective gasp, but neither Jean nor Eva lets me go.

"Coraline," Jean murmurs. I look at him, my pleading eyes boring into his bright green ones. I'm suddenly short of breath. If he asked me to show him what was in my hand, I would. If he asked me to stop pumping, I would try. All for those eyes.

His hand moving down my arm sends electric tingles throughout my body. Is this how Eva feels when she sneaks off with her latest beau? His fingers find mine and lift my hand up, pulling away the sleeve and exposing the spasms of my hand for all to see. "It's all right," he says, his voice deep and oddly seductive.

I can only nod. His hand caresses mine, then pries my fingers apart. So gently. "Incroyable," he whispers. My fingers clench and unclench around metal, clench and unclench around metal and flesh, clench and unclench around flesh, and I cry out as he pulls my heart out of my palm. The salon erupts into shouts as people push and shove toward me, jostling to see the girl with the metal heart. Their words spin around my light head like confetti.

Just when I'm about to faint, my vision black, Jean crams my heart back into my hand. I gasp and pump frantically, the edges of my vision slowly clearing. Eva is staring at Jean, her face pale. She must have forced him to return my heart.

"Cora, please," Jean says. "You simply *must* be part of the Exposition. I can introduce you to everyone—Eva has already agreed."

"Jean could get you a meeting with your dear Monsieur Edison," Eva adds. She winks at me.

I try again to pull away. "I already told Dr. Suvi—I will not be put on display for people such as *him.*" I point to Raoul.

"This is about science, not about people," Jean says. "You, of all people, should understand that. You helped revolutionize science."

"Only so that I could help my sister. Not for the sake of science. For the sake of my sister." I look at Eva.

"I didn't ask for your heart," she whispers.

"You didn't have to. I'm your sister. What else could I have done?"

"It was willingly given," Jean says, speaking over me. My hand unclenches in shock, and he catches my heart as it tumbles away. "We'll keep it safe for you, Coraline," he tells me. "I'm sure Monsieur Edison will come to see you in the exposition hall."

The greatest man of science, come to view me as a curiosity? Men like Raoul, spitting at me because my metal parts are unobtrusive enough that they don't know to harangue me? Men like Jean, holding my heart in their hands but not realizing they have to pump it?

I collapse; neither Eva nor Jean expects it. Jean doesn't move fast enough. A fountain of red bursts from my wrist and I close my eyes.

This is a fact: The one completely automatic organ is the heart. The brain can tell the lungs to stop breathing, the bladder to stop peeing, the stomach to stop grumbling. But any conscious effort to stop the heart is in vain. The heart is the closest thing to a machine of perpetual motion known to man.

I hear voices around me, sense lights and shadows. My throat swallows when liquid is pushed into it. But I don't open my eyes.

I try hard to not recognize the voices. To imagine my visitors as less than human, less than animals, even. Mere dust that is beneath my attention. I know that if I pay attention to the voices, to the words they utter, I will know my fate. As long as I smell the tang of metal on the air, as long as I hear the squeaks of new parts getting tested for the first time, I know that I am safe. The Hôpital du Salut has no part in the Exposition.

I try hard not to think, not to wonder. Not to dream. But it's impossible not to; I seem to sleep all the time. I dream of rivers of red blood. After the first few times waking from this dream, I began to find it soothing. And every time my fist clenches around my metal heart, I remind myself to forget and forgive. Forget and forgive.

I dream that lights are flashing, that people are screaming a foreign name over and over. My left hand is clenching, but there is no metal. Just flesh. My nails bite into my palms, drawing blood. My left arm is warm, probably from Dr. Suvi's steam-powered heart pump. I sway, but do not fall, supported at the waist by a wide, padded circle. I feel like a doll propped up for display. The shouts are getting louder, but they're strangely muffled.

For the first time since the disastrous salon, I open my eyes.

The dream was not a dream.

I'm standing in a glass box, my hips supported by the padded circle, only some of my weight on my feet. Something presses into the center of my spine to keep my back above my waist, and my corset keeps my spine straight. My heart is not in my hand, nor anywhere in the box. I can hardly see beyond my four transparent walls; there are lights trained on my box from all directions. But I follow the flexible metal of my veins and arteries from my left wrist to a small window in the box.

My heart is outside the box, cradled in the steam-powered pump. I examine all the walls, craning around as much as my supports allow, but I see no door. Eva wouldn't have allowed that. Surely not. And our parents would have protested…Marie…and Dr. Suvi. Dr. Suvi would have told them it was for my benefit, surely. And they would trust him, once more, with my life. My head is light, and I wonder what the crowd would do if I fainted.

A strident voice, one I know well, rouses me. A dual current of hope and fear surges through my mind, and I search for his face with my weakened eyes, which I realize have been closed for months. For I am in the Exposition Universelle.

Representing science. Not sisterly love or human compassion. Just science.

That voice again, and this time I can make out his words through my display box: "Monsieur Edison, if you would kindly step this way."

Edison. The name that pulled me from my stupor in the first place, the name that had been shouted on the lips of so many. I wish I could faint on command like some ladies seem able to do. Anything to keep these tears from falling. Edison really is here. He really will see me. And that voice of sunshine and lavender will make my introduction.

I want to wail, to thrash against my constraints and demand to see Eva, our parents, even Dr. Suvi. Even Jean, who must be somewhere nearby. But I do none of these things, for my savior is standing in front of me. I cannot allow myself to miss a single word he utters.

Raoul stops in front of my box, and I notice that there's a velvet rope in front of it, keeping the masses from getting too close. He sees that I'm awake and turns away from me, to the frowning man next to him.

"Monsieur Edison, allow me to present Mademoiselle Coraline Malsante." He shouts for Edison's benefit, but Edison shouts even louder when he cuts him off in fluent French.

"I told you, boy, take me to Eiffel's tower. I must speak to him about sending telegraphs from the top."

Raoul's smile falters, then spreads wider. I'm willing him to say anything, anything to make Edison look at me. Just one glance, I'm sure that's all the great inventor will need to decide to help.

"Monsieur Eiffel and his tower will not be leaving anytime soon," another voice says. Jean pushes through the crowd to appear on Edison's other side. "And this young lady is a marvel not to be missed."

"That's right," Raoul says now that he has Edison's attention once more. "You see that metal heart there, in the machine? That has replaced her real heart." He goes on, explains my entire story at a shout. The reporters grouped behind them scribble furiously in their notebooks, gawking at me. I'm not here for them.

Edison seems interested in my story now, his eyes following Raoul's hand as he points at my heart, at my metal veins. I will Edison to meet my gaze, but he focuses instead on the box that surrounds me. His hair is messy, as if he forgot to comb it before leaving his bed, and his pale face is surprisingly clean-shaven. His expression is melancholy, and I dare to hope he's moved by my imprisonment. There are stains on his vest, though his suit jacket covers most of them. His eyes drift from the top of my glass cage to the placard at my feet; from the band holding me by the hips to the steam-powered machine that contains my heart.

Something flashes across his face, and his eyes light up. I lean forward, amazed despite my predicament that I just witnessed a flash of inspiration on the face of a genius. He realized how to make my heart electric. Or the inhumanity of keeping me on display. Either way, he'll make a fuss and Raoul and Jean will have no choice but to let me out.

"These lights," Edison says. "Are they DC?"

Raoul blinks. "Monsieur?"

"What does it matter?" I cry. I want him to see me, not to think about electricity! I struggle to reach the glass with my right hand, but it's too far away. "Look at my heart! Look! S'il vous plaît, monsieur, help me!"

Edison points at the lights. "Those are electric lights, non? Direct current, I hope?"

Raoul opens and closes his mouth, and the crowd starts to move behind him as reporters push one another in an attempt to hear the bumbling Exposition official's answer. Jean takes one of Edison's arms and says something in his ear, gesturing at Raoul with the other. They're going to move on.

"Monsieur Edison!" I scream. The glass muffles my voice. Edison can hardly hear Raoul or Jean, even when they shout practically in his ear. I have no hope of making my voice loud enough to be heard.

Mother Is a Machine

Catherynne M. Valente

THEY GNASH FROM the door, the slavering parent-golems, offering wire hangers and arsenic cakes with grimy grins, teeth slid their heads, grunting their nicotine-paean in 4/4 time.

They lurch and leer, sewing their fingertips to my mouth—

Hush, child, hush.

There are windows in their bellies, and in them I can see homunculi vomiting earthly delights onto the titanium floor. In them I can see the quantum zygote, the almost-me, the tiny machine might have been daughters echoing in and out of each other with quiet, regular clicks.

Clockwork girl, shine and smile, polish the apples of your cheeks, we've company tonight.

Mother is a machine. Father is a factory. He stamps out hundreds of tiny fathers a day from his bronze-age femur, two by two by two. Her tin breasts are bolted to a steel-drum chest; his hydraulic arms pump up and down on my rot-soft stomach, cut biscuit-daughters from my liver, from my kidneys: little pig-tailed pancreatic automata that scowl and weep and scowl and weep. And on nights when the moon is fat and yeasty as unbaked bread, Mother opens her ribs and tells me, tells me, with her mouth flapping open like a swinging door, to crawl inside, baby girl, crawl crawl crawl. Her wheedle-voice hisses, steam-sighing, from a copper jaw, hinged with a platinum pin.

See, saw, Margaery Daw, sold her bed and lay upon straw!

She beckons into herself with eight-jointed hands. I am afraid to be inside Mother, whose window looks in but never out;

I am afraid to be inside Mother, whose ribs are made from beaten spoons and the spittle of Spanish silversmiths;

I am afraid to be inside Mother, whose doors slam hungry and grim. Her kettle-cry reverberates and conjugates the nursery-verb into she and I, she and I:

Oh! One misty, moisty morning, when cloudy was the weather! There I met an old man, clothed all in leather!

Father bangs on the womb-dead-door and she eats his electroplated thumb-knuckles with slurping candy-smiles—I touch the back of her breasts and try to hear a code tapped out, a code mapped out on her steely lungs.

Cilia, cilia, all this delicate lace! Mother is a machine, and I am empty space.

I am wire, ash, and never a beanstalk floating out of my throat, sliding up to the Father-press, sliding up to the warehouse window. Mother pats her belly, full and warm. Mother slaps her chest-door shut and dances her banshee-shuffle, crouched and laughing:

The cat's in the cupboard and she can't see!

Here they come and here they are, the parent-golems with their eyes in their hair, and when I am let out, when I am let out of the steel-drum torso, the metal tans my skin gill-gray.

Ask me, Father, ask me which biscuit-girl I will have for breakfast, which of my selves I shall eat while you chortle above my pretty sea-snail scalp and sew my skin to a stucco wall—which shall I have, the I that dresses for Christmas in syringes and horse hoof-glue, the I that slavers just like you?

Ask me, Mother, ask me if I thirst to breathe the fluid of your cylinder-self, ask me if I leap to be closed in, folded in, tucked into you?

Now I lay me down to sleep inside your engine-bones. And should I die before I wake, the clocks will eat their own.

Ask me when you hem my hips, ask me when you thread my nose, ask me when you solder pilgrim's palm to pilgrim's palm, ask me when you hide me in your silver bowels if I would not rather have my own hands to eat?

I see the moon, the moon sees me, bright as only the moon can be!

Father is a factory. Mother is a machine. Father presses out my skin like a book—fifth edition, Coptic binding; out of his mouth drops copy, copy, copy. Mother pulls me back in until there is only one of her, and I am under the larynx, stitching the old electric umbilicus together with glabrous teeth.

Stitch it up, and stitch it down, then I'll give you half a crown!

Push it in, Father, all this metal! Make it mine, my pure mercury, pour it cool and trickling into my marrow and I will wake up strong and shining, I will wake up new. Into your belly, Mother, in I go, and if there is enough wire and lead, I can make a merrily clanging creature, I can build a child like you.

Mother is copper, Father is tin. But I am bone, but I am skin.

THREE DAYS BEFORE Eliana Stein found the girl made from bronze, the stocky Botanist noted the passing of her twelfth year living in the Aremika Shaft, though she did not celebrate it. That was the kind of woman she was: pragmatic because she lived alone, modest because her vanity did not extend to her celebrating her own successes, and fatalistic, because surviving the passage of time, she believed, was an act of submission, not rebellion.

The Shaft (so shortened by all who lived in it) was best described by what it was not: an immense absence of soil. On the yearly journeys Eliana made outside the Shaft and into the low, sprawling, ash-stained Aremika City that circled the Shaft, she told those few who asked that she could not describe the huge emptiness of the Shaft. Rather, she could only explain by its horrific absence. The Shaft, she said, was a deep, burnt scar and was like the woman who had lost an arm: you did not describe the missing limb to friends, but instead noted its loss, and the way in which that loss cast a shadow over the remaining parts of the individual, and rendered them out of harmony with the whole. That is what Eliana felt when she stood in the dark, endless, windy hole that dove through the Earth. The pressure of the disfigurement was always present in the hole: it was the walls, the ground, and the wide emptiness before her. She could feel it constantly, and knew if any part of the Shaft broke, that it would collapse and smother her. There would be nothing that she could do in that eventuality. Even the shifting collection of faint, glowing dots that were scattered farther up along the Shaft—the dots that signaled other Botanists who, like herself, wore the luminous clothing of the trade so not to be lost or forgotten by the Botanist Counters outside—even they were nothing against the deep wound that was the Shaft.

For her part, Eliana felt it more than others Botanists did, because she had gone deeper than any other had. It had not been asked of her to do this, but she had chosen the depth through some yet fully self-explained reason. Still, without knowing the reason, she performed her job of monitoring the soil and helping it heal and grow in density and strength with the pellets that she planted. At her depth, the soil around her alternated between dark, brittle burns and thick, healing brown of varying types; but if she could have gone down farther, where there was less life and the soil was hard and brittle like tightly packed blocks of cinder, she would have. The Department of Botany had told her it was simply not safe to go beyond her depth, however, and that they could not lower the unit for her to live in or hook up a cable for her to leave, not until the soil farther up was stronger.

On the day that Eliana found the girl made from bronze, thick black ash had fallen into the Shaft during the night. Smoke rose from the factories outside Aremika City daily, and it was perpetually in the sky and ground, but the ash was only thick enough to bother her when all these elements combined. When they did, the ash fell so prodigiously that when Eliana awoke, she found the pathway around her slim, bronze unit coated in black, and the pale fungi that grew across the walls and that served as the only natural light was dim beneath it.

It was the ash, however, that led her to the girl.

When Eliana stepped from the unit, she did so holding a thickheaded broom. A brass track ran around the Shaft's circumference like a tarnished halo. Her unit was mounted on it, and from inside, a gear system allowed her to move manually along the track. However, at the moment, she walked, and swept the paths as she did. If she didn't clean straight away, the ash would contaminate the soil and leave a horrid stink, especially because it took her a day to walk the circumference of the Shaft. She had no complaints, however, and dutifully followed the path that ran to a bronze plate that anchored a thick, taunt cable into the ground. The cable led up into the dark, joining hundreds of others that disappeared in thin lines up to the surface and the hint of a scabbed red sky that sat at the start of the Shaft. Through the cables, a Botanist received mail and food and, in a swaying, narrow bar that served as a chair, was raised out of the Shaft. Eliana had no mail, left the Shaft only once a year, and was not due a food drop for another two weeks, so it was only by her attention to the detail of sweeping that she found the girl, who had fallen next to the cable. The truth of it was, if the ash fall had not been so heavy, the girl might not have been found alive at all.

But she was.

The girl made from bronze, the Returned, because she was not a real girl, this artificial girl had a loud, irregular moan in her chest: a broken machine whine that announced itself in a grinding of gears. It was loud and troublesome to the woman who held her, and every now and then, it stopped, as if in death.

When Eliana, holding the heavy, broken figure, first experienced the pause, she did indeed think of it as death, so long and final did the lack of life seem. She stepped to the uneven edge of her path in the Shaft, ready to release the body. To dump the refuse. But with a ragged howl that gargled and coughed life back in a spasm through the girl's body, her heart returned to its stuttering, moaning journey. Still holding her, Eliana watched as the girl's eyes flickered open, met the Botanist's, and then drifted shut.

She was pretty, Eliana thought as she turned, and continued down the rough path, even now. It was a created beauty, however, for Eliana doubted that she had been born with such a cute face, and such smooth, white skin and large, dark eyes. The girl's short black hair did not feel right against her skin, either: it was too dry, too hard to be real hair, even if it was tangled and dirty, and a patch on the back of her head had been torn away to reveal the bronze skull underneath. There were cuts down her pale face and neck and her clothing was torn, though neither cuts nor clothes showed sign of blood. Not all the Returned bled, however, and in this case, Eliana was pleased. The girl had lost her legs in the fall: they had splintered and broken upon landing, leaving a sharp, twisting mess of jagged bronze and internal silver and bronze wiring dangled out of her open thighs. Eliana had left a single, preserved foot back at the cable. There was no way to reattach it, and the girl weighed so much already that there was no point in bringing it. In addition to the loss of her legs, the girl had also lost her left hand. It had been torn off from just above the wrist, perhaps as she had grabbed at something, perhaps the cable that ran down to Eliana's level, the cable that the girl frantically reached for as she fell, as the desperation forced her to struggle to touch it, to grab it, but where the speed of her decent—

Well, who knew?

A cold fluid from the girl was staining the Botanist's hands, but Eliana ignored it. Worse had touched her hands in her life, but still, she hoped it was not urine. There was no smell to the girl, but Returned ate, drank, and pissed and shat, simulating the life that they had been born into, once, so it would only be a matter of time before the internal parts of her body began to fail if they were as broken as the external parts.

Ahead of her, the slim, pale lit, shadowed outline of her unit drew closer. Eliana thanked the God That Could Not See Her that she knew the narrow tracks of the Shaft's circumference so well that she need not look down, that she did not need her gaze to direct every step. Though she did wish, squat and strong as she was, that she had not aged so much in the Shaft, that she still had the strength of the thirty-year-old woman who had descended so long ago and who could have carried the girl without the strain she felt.

In the end, Eliana was forced to set her down to gain her strength before continuing. She sat, for a few minutes, on the path, in the pale glow of her uniform and a brighter cluster of fungi. She was used to seeing things in that eerie glow, but even so, the girl did not look healthy, or functional, or whatever other term you might use for a made person. Did a Returned die like her? Did they go pale and cold? Well, perhaps not cold. The Returned were always cold to touch. With a grunt, Eliana resumed her sure walk with the girl. If she had not been so close to the tarnished, bronze door of her unit when the strain began to tell again, she would have had to rest a second time. Instead, her muscles burning, the Botanist shouldered her way into the narrow unit and, thankful for once that she did not keep her bed upstairs, placed the girl down on the dark blue sheets.

In the bright, yellow light inside the unit, Eliana could see that the girl was made not just from bronze but brass as well. The darker and lighter coloring that shone through the tattered remains of skin around her arms and legs suggested imperfection and sickness that had existed long before her fall. The girl's clothes, which were made from red and brown, likewise hinted at blood and defecation. As if listening to her morbid thoughts, the sick machine moan of the girl's heart grew louder, as if threatening to burst from its casing, struggling, pushing…and then silent, silent, *silent,* before with a spasm and a cough, it started again.

Though her arms still ached from carrying the girl, Eliana descended to the bottom level of her unit. It was, like all single Botanist units, made from three narrow floors, linked by a set of rungs down the middle. The center floor was where she slept: there were tall, narrow closets and a comfortable chair that she sat and read in. The top floor held a small kitchen and the single, narrow table that she ate at. The knives and forks and cooking utensils were suspended from the ceiling and dangled like pit of spikes reversed. When strong winds buffeted the unit, they swayed dangerously and occasionally fell—she had been hit more than once, though thankfully she sheathed all the blades. There was an opening up there that she could push open to release smoke and odors from cooking. On the bottom floor was the workbench where she kept her samples, notes, and where she could manufacture pellets. There was also a tiny shower and toilet, the drains of which opened out into the Shaft in what she considered a small contradiction to her work of healing. In the opposite corner was a large cage that ran from floor to floor and that held a single, medium-size crow, all black and smooth, and that watched her with cold glass eyes.

Under those eyes, she sat at her workstation and pulled free a piece of paper. In a thick, bold script, she wrote to the Department of Botany and explained what had happened. In her opinion, Eliana stated, she did not believe the Returned had much time left. She did not ask how the girl had come to be at the Shaft, or how she fell, though she might have, because it was difficult to do either without help; but she did not ask, because she was afraid of upsetting someone, which would result in aid not being sent. In her own mind, Eliana had decided that a Botanist had let her through, and the resulting theories of murder and mystery flowered in her mind. Who knew if they were true, however.

Once she had finished the letter, she placed the note in a small brass case and walked over to the cage. The crow slipped out and perched on her arm with cold claws. It waited patiently as she attached the case to its leg. Once that was done, she climbed up a floor, and released it into the dark of the Shaft.

When Eliana could no longer see the crow, she turned and regarded the girl who lay on her bed, slowly staining her sheets. A smell had begun to emerge: an oil machine mix of urine and shit and something as equally unpleasant. The girl's body was still moaning, though it reminded her of growling, now, as if were fighting for life while the rest of it lay dying.

When the girl made from bronze awoke that night, she did not scream.

Eliana had expected her to. She spent the evening in her narrow kitchen, expecting the cry at any moment. Returned or not, the Botanist believed that the sight of shattered limbs and torn skin would be reason enough for horror. At the very least, she had expected tears. But the girl gave neither. Instead, she pushed herself into a sitting position and waited, quietly, until Eliana descended from the kitchen. Having placed her flowing, luminous Botanist uniform in the closet, she now wore a blue shirt and a pair of comfortable, faded black pants. Her tattoos, words and patterns made from red and black ink, twisted along her thick left arm, and around the exposed left-hand side of her neck and foot. It was not until that foot, with its slightly crooked toes, and the nail missing from the smallest, touched the cool bronze floor of the unit, that the girl spoke:

"I appear to be broken."

Her voice was faint, but purposefully so, rendering it a pampered girl's voice, the quality of which instantly annoyed the other woman. "Yes," Eliana replied, curt where she had not planned to be. "You fell."

"This—this is the—"

"Shaft, yes."

The girl spoke slowly, each word a chore, the stuttering moan in her chest causing her to pause after every short sentence. "Yes, I fell."

"You remember falling?"

"Yes."

"Landing?"

"No."

Eliana approached the bed. The noxious odor grew, and she struggled to keep it from showing on her face. Folding her thick arms in front of her, Eliana gazed down at the girl, but the latter did not return her gaze. Finally, she said, "I have sent a bird to my department, telling them of you—"

"What? *No!*"

It was her turn to be cut off now, her turn to pause. Her thick eyebrows rose in her only hint of surprise. Before her, the girl, the fragile, lost girl who had fallen, and who had sat before Eliana in a confused haze, disappeared. Evaporated like water beneath the hot red sun. In response, the pity that Eliana had meant to be feeling, but that she could not, for reasons she had not been given time to explore, was no longer required, and her dislike, her hostility, which she had been ashamed of, had sudden reason for purchase inside her.

The girl spat out, "Why did you do that?"

"Who are you?"

"Why?"

"You're dying."

"Ha!"

"You are."

"Of course I am!"

Eliana had no reply, had not expected that.

The girl made from bronze gave a coughing splutter of a laugh. It was caught between self-pity, self-hate, and desperation, and it ended raggedly as the struggling moan in her chest choked it off. Finally, pushing her single good hand through the tattered remains of her hair, she said, "I won't be thanking you for this."

"I think," Eliana said slowly, out of her depth, trying to find a way to understand the situation. "I think you best explain to me what is going on here."

"As if I would explain anything to someone marked like you are!"

The tattoos. Of course, it was the tattoos that spoke of Eliana's religion, of where she had been born. The clean skin of the Returned did as much for her as the tattoos did for Eliana. The intricate words and designs that ran across the Botanist's body recorded the forty-two years she had been alive. Parents, siblings, her growth into adulthood, her failed jobs and relationships: the words of each ran beneath her clothes and spent most of the time on the left-hand side of her body, before crossing at her shoulders and neck and descending down her right side. Once a year she left the Shaft for those markings. Once a year a Mortician's needle and ink set down her life so that when she died, God would be able to read her body, her life, and judge her, for Life, for Heaven, for Damnation, for Obliteration.

"There is no God in the Shaft," Eliana said, finally. "Have you not heard that?"

The girl laughed, again, but this time it was forced, angry, and each broken movement she made in the laughter stripped the appearance of youth from her. Finally, when she could force no more out, the woman, the woman who was much, much older than Eliana, and who smelt of decay, lowered her head. With her very real eyes staring at the woman who looked her senior, she said, "I need a drink. Do you have one?"

She did.

It was cheap wine that Eliana bought down for the Returned. The bottle was green, the label plain and simple, and she had used a quarter of it some weeks back in a meal that had not been improved by its inclusion. It was not an act of friendship, nor was it an act of trust, but it was a signal that the Botanist was, at the very least, understanding of the situation. No woman was at her best while dying. When the Returned took the bottle with her one good hand, she did so quickly, snatching it, ripping it from Eliana's strong, blunt fingers, before taking a long drink—and that helped too with her decision.

"How old are you?" Eliana asked, watching. She held a second, unopened, good bottle of wine in her hand, and did not bother to hide it.

The Returned swallowed, then said, "This is like vinegar."

"You didn't answer my question," Eliana repeated.

"No, I did not." Her good hand placed the bottle between the shattered stumps of her legs. Loose silver wiring was reflected dully against it. "My name is Rachel, by the way."

"I didn't ask that."

"No." Her dark eyes met Eliana's. "You're too busy trying to figure out *what* I am, rather than who."

The Botanist unscrewed the cap off her wine bottle, said nothing.

"I'm 128," the Returned said, a hint of defiance in her tone. "Happy?"

"Yes."

Eliana didn't say it, but the Returned's—*Rachel's*—words had affected her. She had turned, given the back to her after she had replied, but the Botanist knew that she had been treating the woman as a thing. She thought that she had left that kind of prejudice behind when she had entered the Shaft, but Rachel's words suggested that she had not.

Grabbing her orange chair that had a colorful array of patches over it, she swung it around and dragged it near the bed. Once it was close enough, but not so close that the stink of the girl assaulted her overly, she sank into it, propped her feet up on the edge of the bed, and took a long drink in front of the other woman.

"I bet yours tastes better," Rachel said.

"Let that be a lesson." Shame had not made her more sympathetic. "Politeness has its rewards."

At that, the Returned laughed: a short burst, different from the earlier laughter, natural this time. A faint, unwilling smile creased Eliana's face in response.

"This is going well, don't you think?" Rachel asked. Her broken arm lifted, paused. She grunted and her good hand picked up the bottle. "When I was standing on the edge of the Shaft, Joseph—do you know Joseph?"

"Callagary?"

"Yes."

A tall, thin, white, clean-skinned man on the Department of Botany's Board of Directors. He had a stylish bronze eyepiece that recorded everything. "I know him," Eliana said, and not kindly.

"Yes, that was my response, too." Rachel lifted the bottle, drunk. Around the stumps of her legs and the torn pants of her genitals, the stain was refreshed in both wetness and odor. "I've known worse, mind. Much worse. He showed me the Shaft when I asked, at least. Was more than happy too. I was his student for a little while. It turned him on, I think. He told me the Shaft had been made by lava—that the center of the Earth had ruptured, leaving the heat nowhere to go. So it burst out. It scarred the world, he said. Such a dramatic boy. I still remember that little drop in his voice. Scarred the world, he said quietly."

"That's the theory," she said.

"Believe it?"

"No one has seen the center."

"No." She fell silent. Then, "No, he said that. He said that some had journeyed down. He said that they had never returned."

"And you?" Eliana pulled her legs off the bed, leaned forward.

"What?"

"What was your plan? Were you running from Joseph?"

Rachel let out a breath, half a laugh, half a grunt, and rubbed her chest as if it were in pain. Perhaps it was. "Joseph was just a man for the night."

She frowned. "You're a prostitute?"

"Yes." The Returned lifted the bottle, regarded her with the defiance she had shown earlier. "I'm a prostitute. A dirty *whore*. Are you morally outraged now?"

"I've known whores."

The other woman started at her.

"Just not Returned whores," Eliana finished. "I've never heard of it before."

"You live in a giant hole in the ground." Rachel took a long drink and the dark stain across the bedsheet increased. The wine was going right through her—her thirst, her need, would never be sated by it. Seemingly unaware, she added, "In this case, however, I do admit: there aren't many of us. It's expensive. Being Returned is expensive. You have a body partly carved and partly found. It has to look real. That's not cheap, so to buy us is not cheap. No."

Eliana did not know how to respond. She was not, and had never had been, a woman who could connect with others quickly. She responded to situations better and was able to meet a moment with the appropriate emotional response without difficulty. But sitting in front of Rachel, watching the wine stain her bed, trying to hide her growing revulsion at the smell that was growing stronger, and aware that the woman's voice was not really focused on her, Eliana was being asked not to react to the moment, but to the person; and here, she did not know what to say. Fortunately, she did not need to.

"I have over a hundred years of being fucked," Rachel said. Her good hand tightened around the neck of the bottle and a faint cracking followed. "In eight days, I will have been a Return for a hundred years. Another month, and I'll have been working for a hundred seven years. Working! Do you know what that means? Do you have any idea? How many men and women have fucked me? How many have looked at me as if I was nothing—as if I was an object!

"My boss looks at me just like that. She organizes who sees me. She keeps me in drugs. She makes sure I get what I need to live. She's surely a lot better than some of the pimps I've seen, but she doesn't see me. She doesn't talk to me. She talks about me. She talks around me." She stopped, gave a faint *ha*, then fell silent.

"I don't—"

"She's my eleventh boss," Rachel said, not even noticing that she interrupted the other woman. "My eleventh *pimp*. I hate that old term. But she's my number eleven. I have watched ten others get old. I have watched clients get old. I've watched them all go gray and small. It doesn't matter how rich, how intelligent, how whatever they were. They each faded, they—"

"I had worked for two years before I was Returned." The woman switched topics without pause, her mind erratic. "I wanted money. I had plans—*plans*. The world—this world—I wanted to see it. With the money I had left I could buy a house. I wouldn't owe anything to anyone. But there was a problem. I got sick. I had a hole in my heart. A *hole*. Surgeons told me I wouldn't live past twenty-eight unless I got it fixed. And you can earn a lot of money on your back, but it's not enough to get a new heart. No. You need help for that.

"The man who paid for my Return ran *the Brothel of Exotics*. That's what he called it. He was a Returned himself: Baron De'Mediala. His real name was Gregory. I—I didn't want to die. Twenty-eight is too young to die. He sat me down in his office. It was filled with statues of birds: flamingos, cockatoos, seagulls, and dozens of other birds, colored yellow and green and pink—every color but black and red. If there was a hint of black or red in it, it wasn't there. I later learned that he had a strange obsession with bright colors. Bright colors meant life. He had even dyed his hair a shocking lemon.

"He said to me, 'The price, it is great.' He had that way of talking. A theatrical way. I heard a rumor that he had once been a stage magician. I told him that no price was too high, that I would pay it. Even if it meant a hundred years on my back, I would pay. He told me that I would probably never be free from the debt. He said, he said, 'M'dear, m'dear, each year a repair must be done, a part of you fixed. Each year you will have to fix your appearance. Each year your living tissue will require ointments. Each year the wires in you will need to be cleaned. Each year your look and fashion will need updating.' Each year, he said. But it didn't matter—I told him it didn't matter. I was so afraid. I didn't see endless service as a problem. I thought, 'What's so different about that to the life I currently live?'

"I learned. The Baron—that's what I called him, *the Baron*—he knew. He had Returned himself. He knew the cost. He kept himself free with our servitude and—and—" Rachel's voice trailed off for a moment. Eliana, having not moved once during her speech, shifted her bottle, but did not drink. Opposite her, the Returned lifted the bottle, took a short, sharp drink, then said, "He was killed for bodysnatching. They caught him one night standing in an open grave. That's what I heard. There were eight of them and they burnt the skin from him. When he didn't die, they removed his organs. You only need the heart—" she tapped her chest, rubbed the spot where the moan gurgled "—that mechanical heart to live. I don't know how long it took them to get to that. I know you can live without everything else. I once had lungs. A liver. I had all my organs, and they worked—but now? Now, now I have supplements. I can't afford real livers, real replacements. I have fakes. I have simulations for sensations. I simulate. I—

"The Baron was right. There's no end to your debt. The debt—it is to a Surgeon, or a Hospital, but it's not just for one job. Not just for the Return. It's for every day of living you do after it. Every day is debt. My debt would be passed from boss to boss, and I would work to pay it off, and I would work to make sure that I was kept alive.

"It wasn't such a bad life in the start. There is an attraction to be exotic. A power. *Ha.* A power. I've wanted to stop so many times. One boss even let me. She was a terribly obese woman, caught in her own addictions. I think she understood it. I had been working for fifty-six years, by then. I—there are no jobs that will pay a Returned what she needs. I was free for two weeks before I went back to her. When I got back, I decided I would train myself. I enrolled in a college, but I never finished any course. I kept telling myself I would. I kept telling myself I could. I said it for forty years. I said it in four different cities. I said it with five different bosses. Eventually, I just—I had to just admit that I couldn't change. I hated that.

"It was simple, really. I told Joseph I wanted to see the Shaft—I used my best girl's voice." The last of the bottle was tipped into her throat. She did it roughly, angrily, and wiped her mouth with the back of her good hand after. When she spoke, there was only self-loathing in her voice, "It's hard to kill yourself when you've already died once. A girl I—a girl I was *friends* with did it. Not so long ago. A month. We'd—we had known each other for sixty years. The night before, we got drunk and talked about how you would do it. You couldn't cut veins, we said. You couldn't poison yourself. You couldn't drown. You couldn't suffocate. There was only the heart and the head. It was like a nursery rhyme. Do you know what she did?"

There was a pause, but not long enough for Eliana to answer.

"She paid a man to cave her head in with a hammer. A hammer! *A hammer!* I—I saw her the day after. She had had the man chain her to a chair. He had left her in the basement—and—and—

"I figured the Shaft would be a good choice. That was my idea. The Shaft. All you had to do was to jump. I could never sit there and let a man cave my head in. That waiting, that—no. *No.* All I had to do was push Joseph back—let him get me in close, first, tell him I wanted to stand on the edge, tell him it excited me. That was all. Then I could just push him back. Then I could just jump. Then—then—I would free, then."

Rachel stopped, her good hand releasing its hold on the bottle.

In the silence that followed, it occurred to Eliana that it was now her turn to speak, that she should say something. She should offer sympathy. Understanding. At the very least she should acknowledge the other woman. But she couldn't. The silence between the two stretched until it was taut and Rachel's eyes closed slowly and her head sank and Eliana looked down at the smooth floor and tried to find words…and had almost succeeded when a faint scratching at the door interrupted her.

It was the crow: its sharp, glass beak was pecking against the door.

When Eliana opened the door, it flapped through to the cushioned armchair silently and sat, shaking flakes of ash out of its black feathers. They fell over the fabric, over the floor, the residue of its journey outside the Shaft and beneath the red sun. Once it had done that, it waited, patiently, for the Botanist to open the brass casing on its leg.

Across from it, Rachel gazed at the crow in what Eliana considered a sudden lucidity that was inspired by apprehension and fear. There was no resignation in her gaze, however; no sense that she had accepted her fate, or even knew it, though it was impossible that she could have imagined that the tiny scrawl on the tiny note on the crow's leg brought her any news that she would want to hear. The Department of Botany would send a man or woman to repair her. At the very least they would stabilize her before she was taken out of the Shaft.

Surely, she could not hope.

Surely.

"I don't want to hear," Rachel said. "If they are coming for me, don't tell me."

Eliana picked up her bottle of wine from next to the couch, ignored the crow, and passed it to her.

"Don't waste it," the other said, quietly. Her gaze never left the bird. "It just goes right through me."

"Take it, anyway."

Silence.

"Go on."

"I want to—"

"They're coming."

"—You haven't—"

"They were always coming." She thrust the bottle a little. "Take it."

"Okay." Rachel's voice was quiet with submission. Instinctively, her broken arm reached up—she must have been left-handed—but a moment later, her good one found the bottle. The first one, made from cheap glass, lay on the bed, the neck splintered in a web of cracks. When she took the bottle, Rachel's eyes, the eyes she had never been born with, but which had been born to someone else, those dark, dark eyes held Eliana's with a terrible fragility. "Please read the note to me."

Eliana approached the crow. It scratched gently at her hand and she rubbed its cold, bronze head through its feathers. The crow had been in the Shaft as long as she had—had, in fact, come down when the unit was lowered and put into place. It had been her only companion for the years, but she had never named it; nor did she know if it were male or female. The crow was, as Rachel had said of herself, an object, a thing. It responded to Eliana's touch only because it had been taught to do so when it was alive. At least, that is what she told herself, though she was unable to fully believe it.

"What does it say?" Rachel said, her voice still quiet, still soft.

"It is from Callagary," she began, then stopped. She had her back to the other woman and, conscious of it, she could not continue. She turned. "Joseph. He wrote this. He said that there was an accident on the top. That they had feared the worse. A Surgeon is on his way down as he writes."

"A Surgeon?"

"Yes." Silence. The crow's cold claws pulled at the fabric of the chair. Awkwardly, Eliana added, "I'm sorry."

Still, Rachel did not reply.

"I—"

"How do you live here?"

"What?" Rachel had spoken hard and quick, as if she were accusing her, and it caught Eliana off guard. "What are—"

"It's awful, down here." Her voice softened and took on, once again, the tone that a woman might use when she talked to herself, and did not require an answer. In her hand, the bottle lay still, drunk only by Eliana; but the stain, still growing in size and accompanied by an ever-growing sharp odor, had finally began to drop faint traces of discolored red wine on the bronze floor. "There's no fresh air. It's so dark. Your light—it's not like the light up there. It's harder. Brittle. Everything feels like it is burning. How can you stand it?"

"No one watches down here." Eliana hesitated. Rachel's eyes were not focused on her: they wandered about the narrow unit, as if everything were new, and slippery, and she could not grasp it. Her good hand no longer gripped the bottle, but rested on it. Quite clearly, the strength, strangely for a body made, and without muscle, was gone. *She's dying. She might not be alive by the time the Surgeon arrives.* Quietly, Eliana said, "On the surface, all we worry about is life. Who comes back. Who has what rights. Who is dominant. We fight, because we think God is watching. Or God isn't watching. The world is dying around us and we fight and we try to make people live a certain way, never understanding that it doesn't matter. That the world we live on is—"

Rachel's eyes focused, suddenly, on her, and Eliana's voice faltered, the last word unspoken on her lips.

"Don't let them take me," the dying woman said.

A single luminescent dot was descending toward her.

Eliana shifted. In her straining arms, Rachel was heavy, and the stuttering, gurgling moan of her chest was the only sign that she was still alive. She spoke softly, now, a continual murmur as if she were speaking to a mother, or an older sister, and her cold, hard head was pressed in to Eliana's neck and shoulder, as if she were a child. Because of this, the Botanist did not tell her of the figure who rode the thin bar down her cable, and who, in an hour or so, would be upon her unit. She wondered if he—it would be a he, she decided, on instinct—she wondered if he could see her, standing barefoot in her faded black and blue, her hard, bare feet walking off the dirt trail and to the edge of the path. The pale glow of the fungus around her did light the area, if poorly, and yellow light did fall out of the unit's doorway. It was possible that he could see her, if he were looking.

It didn't matter. It simply didn't. A stone stabbed into the sole of her foot, and she grunted from the pain, but kept walking. The moan in Rachel's chest began to grow louder. It rattled as if she were empty. As if all she was could be described by a heart that had been made from bronze. Perhaps, even, that was true, as the sharp, putrid smell that had been about her in the unit when Eliana picked her up had all but disappeared in the Shaft. Perhaps all that was left of her was a struggling, dying heart.

The Shaft was before her. Its emptiness yawned wide and full, and she could see the track that ran its circumference like a giant, fallen halo; a broken halo, for she could not see the wall on the opposite side. It was as if, on her ledge, she stood at the very edge of a burnt, broken world, and that there was just nothing, an absolute nothingness before her.

"It's okay."

Rachel's whisper barely rose over the sound of her heart. If her cold lips had not been so close to Eliana's ear, the dark wind of the Shaft would have stolen it, the now grinding growl of her heart smothered it. When Eliana met her gaze, she found Rachel's eyes open, partly lucid, partly aware, but not fully. She was not gone, but she was going.

"It's okay," Rachel repeated. "It's okay—God is not watching, not down here."

"No. He never is."

And she let go.

Beatrice

Karin Tidbeck

FRANZ HILLER, A physician, fell in love with an airship. He was visiting a fair in Berlin to see the wonders of the modern age that were on display: automobiles, propeller planes, mechanical servants, difference engines and other things that would accompany man into the future.

The airship was moored in the middle of the aviation exhibit. According to the small sign by the cordon, her name was Beatrice.

> *In contrast to the large commercial airships, Beatrice is built for a maximum of two passengers. An excellent choice for those who live far from public airship masts or do not wish to be crowded in with strangers. Manufacturing will start soon. Order yours today, from Lefleur et Fils!*

Franz had had no previous interest in airships. He had never seen one up close, let alone travelled in one. Neither had he had any interest in love. At thirty, he was still a bachelor; his prospects were good, but he had been profoundly disinterested in any potential wives his parents had presented to him. His mother was becoming more and more insistent, and sooner or later Franz would have to make up his mind. But then he found himself here, in Berlin, facing this airship: Beatrice, her name tolling like a bell.

Franz couldn't stop looking at her. Her body was a voluptuous oblong, matte skin wrapped tightly over a gently rounded skeleton. The little gondola was made of dark wood *(finest mahogany!)* and embellished with brass details *(every part hand-wrought!),* the thick glass windows rounded at the edges. Inside, the plush seat was embroidered with French lilies, facing an immaculately polished console. Beatrice was perfect. She bobbed in a slow up-down motion, like a sleeping whale. But she was very much awake. Franz could feel her attention turn to him and remain there, the heat of her sightless gaze.

He came back the next day, and the next, just to look at Beatrice and feel her gaze upon him. They could never touch; he once tried to step inside the cordon but was brusquely reprimanded by the guards. Franz could sense the same want from her that filled himself, a longing to be touched.

He sought out the representative of Lefleur et Fils, Lefleur the younger in fact, a thin man with oil-stained fingers who looked uncomfortable in his suit. Franz offered to buy Beatrice outright; he would write a check on the spot, or pay in cash if needed. Out of the question, was Lefleur the younger's reply. That airship there was a prototype. Not at any price? Not at any price. How could they start manufacture without the prototype? Of course, monsieur Hiller was welcome to order an airship, just not this one.

Franz didn't dare explain why he wanted the prototype so badly. He accepted the catalogue offered to him, and returned home. He thought of Beatrice, caressing her picture in the catalogue. Her smooth skin, her little gondola. How he wanted to climb into her little gondola.

After two weeks, the fair closed. Beatrice was taken home to Lefleur et Fils' factory in Paris. Franz fantasised about travelling to the factory, breaking into it at night and stealing her; or pleading his case to the owners, who were so touched by his story that they let go of her. Franz did none of this. Instead, he moved out of his parents' home, much to their consternation, and left for Berlin where he found new employment and rented a warehouse on Stahlwerkstrasse. Then he placed an order.

Two months later, a transport arrived at the warehouse on Stahlwerkstrasse. Four burly men who didn't speak a word of German unloaded four enormous boxes, and proceeded to unpack the various parts of a small airship. When they left, an exact copy of Beatrice was moored in the warehouse.

The realization dawned on Franz as he stood alone in the warehouse, studying his airship. This new Beatrice was disinterested. She hovered quietly in the space without a trace of warmth. Franz walked along her length. He stroked her skin with a hand. It was cool. He traced the smooth, polished mahogany of her gondola with his fingers, breathing in the aroma of fresh wood and varnish. Then he opened the little door and gingerly seated himself inside, where a musky undertone mingled with the smells of copper and fresh rubber. He imagined that it was Beatrice. He summoned the sensation of warm cushions receiving him, how she dipped under his weight. But this Beatrice, Beatrice II, had a seat with firm stuffing that didn't give.

"We'll manage," said Franz to the console. "We'll manage. You can be my Beatrice. We'll get used to each other."

Anna Goldberg, a printer's assistant, fell in love with a steam engine. She was the youngest and ugliest daughter in a well-to-do family in Hamburg; her father owned one of the largest printing works in the country. Since Anna showed intellectual talent, she was allowed schooling and worked for her father as his secretary. In that way she would at least earn her keep. Anna was happy with her employment, but not because she loved the art of printing or the art of being a secretary. It was the printing presses. When other girls her age mooned over boys, she had a violent crush on a Koenig & Bauer. However, it wouldn't do to start a romance openly in front of her father. She saved every pfennig of her income, so that when the day came she could afford to follow her love. At twenty-eight, she was still waiting for the right opportunity.

It finally came the day she met Hercules at the Berlin fair. He was a semi-portable steam engine: a round-bellied oven coupled to an upright, broad-shouldered engine. He exuded a heavy aroma of hot iron with a tart overtone of coal smoke that made her thighs tingle. And he was for sale. Although Anna came to the fair every day for a week to get to know him properly, she had really made up her mind on the first day. She could just about afford him. Anna announced to her parents that she intended to visit a friend and her husband in Berlin, and possibly find a suitor there. Her parents made no resistance, and Anna didn't tell them her stay would be indefinite. She rented a warehouse on Stahlwerkstrasse, and moved her possessions there.

Arriving at the warehouse with Hercules, Anna was greeted by a confused gentleman and a miniature airship who already occupied the space. The gentleman introduced himself as Dr. Hiller, and wouldn't meet her gaze, but showed her a document. They seemed to have identical leases for the warehouse on Stahlwerkstrasse. Anna and Franz visited the landlord's office, where a small seborrhoeic woman regretted the mix-up. Sadly, it was too late to save the situation as all warehouses were now occupied. She was, however, convinced that Dr. Hiller and Fräulein Goldberg could solve the situation between them. As long as the rent was paid every month, it wasn't very important how. They would even get a discount for their troubles. With that, she thanked them for their visit and asked them to leave.

"I can't have people burning things in the warehouse," said Franz once they exited onto the street. "The airship is very flammable."

"What does Dr. Hiller do with it?" said Anna.

"I don't think that is of Fräulein Goldberg's concern," said Franz. "What is Fräulein Goldberg going to power with her steam engine?"

Anna stared at him with a blush that started at her neck and crept up her cheeks. "His name is Hercules," she said quietly.

Franz stopped and looked at her. "Oh," he said after a moment, and his eyes softened. "I apologise. I think we share the same fate."

Returning to the warehouse, Franz led Anna to the airship moored in the far end of the room. "This is Beatrice," he said, and laid a possessive hand on Beatrice's gondola.

Anna greeted Beatrice with a nod. "My congratulations," she told Franz. "She is very beautiful."

They agreed on sharing the warehouse, with a partition in the middle. Anna brought a simple wood stove. After she pointed out that he, too, would need to cook for himself, Franz allowed her to install it in an alcove in the middle of the far wall of the warehouse, as far away from Beatrice as possible. The alcove became a shared kitchen and sitting room. It even took on a cosy air.

Anna was constantly at work shovelling coal into Hercules' gaping maw and topping up water for the steam. At night, she would get up every other hour to feed him. Franz, who left for the clinic each morning, imagined she would do the same in the daytime as well, as she was often busy shovelling coal no matter what time of day he came home. Other than that, she mostly seemed to be busy reading technical manuals and papers. She had brought an entire bookcase full of them.

Beatrice remained cold and distant, no matter how Franz tried to warm their relationship. He was meticulous in his care for her. He read newspapers to her daily; he made love to her with great care. Nothing seemed to get her attention. Should he have tried harder to win the first Beatrice? Should he have pursued her more? Why hadn't he? And the question that plagued him the most—had Beatrice loved him as violently as he loved her? One night, he told Anna the whole story over a shared supper.

"I'll never find out," he said. "Did she really love me? Would I have loved her at all, once I got to know her? Perhaps it was just a dream. She might be nothing like I thought she was."

Anna shook her head, smoothing the pages of the journal she was reading. "I learned something from falling in love with that Koenig & Bauer. Infatuation is worth nothing. It has nothing to do with the real world." She nodded at the steam engine looming in the corner by her bed. "Me and Hercules, we have an understanding. We take care of each other. It's a better kind of love, I think."

"This Beatrice might come to love me, don't you think?" Franz said.

"She might," said Anna. "And you have her right here. That's more than you can say about the other."

Anna's relationship to Hercules did seem much happier in comparison, especially when her belly started to swell. The pregnancy was uncomplicated, even though Anna sometimes complained of strange sensations in her stomach. When Franz laid an ear to her belly, he could hear clicking and whirring sounds in there.

"What will you do when it's time?" he asked.

"I can't go to the hospital," said Anna. "They'll take the child from me. You'll have to help me."

Franz couldn't say no. He stole what he might need from the clinic, a little at a time: suture, tongs, morphine, iodine solution. He had only delivered babies twice, and never on his own, but he didn't tell Anna this.

Even when she had contractions, Anna kept feeding Hercules. She wouldn't let Franz do it. She didn't stop until she went into labour. The delivery was a quick process. The child was small but healthy, its pistons well integrated in the flesh. But once the placenta had emerged, the bleeding wouldn't stop. Anna bled out in the warehouse, the child on her belly.

"Put me in Hercules," were her last faint words. "I want to be inside him."

Franz did as she asked. First he gently washed the child, wrapped it in clean linen and put it in a basket next to Anna's bed. Then he turned to Anna where she lay on the bed. He wiped the blood off her body with a wet cloth, and folded a clean sheet around her. He lifted her off the bed with some difficulty and carried her over to where Hercules waited. She fit in the oven perfectly.

"That's the last you'll get," he told Hercules. "I'm not going to feed you."

The steam engine seemed to glare at Franz from its corner. The oven hatch glowed with the heat from Anna's body. Franz turned his back on it and picked the baby up, cradling it in his arms. It opened its mouth and cried with a whistling noise. Franz walked over to his side of the warehouse, holding the baby up in front of his airship.

"We're foster parents now, Beatrice," he said.

For the first time he could sense a reaction from her. It felt like approval, but it wasn't directed at him.

The child was a girl. Franz named her Josephine. He tried to feed her cow's milk at first, but she spit it out, hissing. She steadily lost weight, her pistons squealing and rasping, until Franz in desperation dissolved some coal in water, dipped the end of a rag in it and stuck it in her mouth. When Josephine immediately sucked the rag dry, Franz understood what kind of care his foster daughter needed. He took the box of maintenance tools Anna had kept for Hercules, and greased Josephine's pistons carefully with good oil. He fed her a steady diet of coal-water, gradually increasing the coal until it was a thick paste. When she had enough teeth, he gave her small bits of coal to gnaw on. The girl didn't need diapers, as she didn't produce any waste; she seemed to spend whatever she ate as body heat. If he fed her too much, she became unbearably hot to the touch, her pistons burning his hands. These peculiarities aside, she behaved much like a normal baby.

Franz wrote a letter of resignation to the clinic. He sold Hercules to a factory, and Anna's furniture to an auction house. The money would be enough for rent and food for a long time to come, if he spent it wisely. He would at least be able to take care of his airship and his foster daughter. Whenever he had to leave their home, he put the baby in Beatrice's gondola. When he came back, the baby was always in a good humour, comfortably cradled in the otherwise hard seat, cooing and playing with dials or tubes that had somehow come loose from the console. When Josephine was old enough not to need constant feeding, he found work at another clinic. Josephine seemed content to spend her days in the gondola. Beatrice radiated affection whenever the girl was near.

The catastrophe came when Josephine was four years old. The little girl didn't have vocal cords, but a set of minuscule pipes arrayed in her larynx. She whistled and tweeted until her fourth birthday, when she suddenly started modulating the noise into speech. It was early morning. They had just finished breakfast. Josephine was sitting on the table, Franz lubricating the pistons in her arms. Josephine opened her mouth and said in a high, fluting voice:

"Father, her name isn't Beatrice."

"Is that so," said Franz, dripping oil on her finger joints.

"She says so every time you call her Beatrice. That's not my name, she says."

Franz blinked. "Do you understand everything she says?"

"Her name isn't Beatrice," Josephine repeated. "It's something else. And she wants to say some things to you."

Josephine sat with her legs dangling from the gondola, warbling the airship's thoughts without seeming to grasp their meaning. Franz was informed of the following: The airship's name wasn't Beatrice. It was something entirely different. She had lived as a slave under her husband, and he had raped her while pretending her to be someone else. She hated him.

"That can't be right," said Franz. "We worked on this marriage together. She was the one who wouldn't make an effort."

"She says, I had no choice," said Josephine. "She says, you're holding me captive."

Franz felt his throat constrict. "I certainly am not," he said. "I've worked so hard." He shoved his hands in his pockets to stop them from trembling. "I've worked so hard," he repeated.

"She wants to fly," said Josephine.

Franz opened the great double doors to the warehouse, and slowly towed Beatrice outside. He knew what was going to happen. That Josephine was going to climb up into the gondola while he was busy sorting out the tethers. That Beatrice II would tear free of her moorings and swiftly rise up into the sky, drifting east. That she would be gone in a matter of minutes, leaving him alone on the ground.

He sorted out the tethers. Meanwhile, Josephine climbed up in the gondola. Beatrice II suddenly pulled at the moorings, which snapped, and she ascended without a sound. Franz stood outside the warehouse, watching the sky, until night fell.

1. The Transformation Problem

In glancing over my correspondence with Herr Marx, especially the letters written during the period in which he struggled to complete his opus, *Capital*, even whilst I was remanded to the Victoria Mill of Ermen and Engels in Weaste to simultaneously betray the class I was born into and the class to which I'd dedicated my life, I was struck again by the sheer audacity of my plan. I've moved beyond political organizing or even investigations of natural philosophy and have used my family's money and the labour of my workers—even now, after a lifetime of railing against the bourgeoisie, their peculiar logic limns my language—to encode my old friend's thoughts in a way I hope will prove fruitful for the struggles to come.

I am a fox, ever hunted by agents of the state, but also by political rivals and even the occasional enthusiastic student intellectual *manqué*. For two weeks, I have been making a very public display of destroying my friend's voluminous correspondence. The girls come in each day and carry letters and covers both in their aprons to the roof of the mill to burn them in a soot-stained metal drum. It's a bit of a spectacle, especially as the girls wear cowls to avoid smoke inhalation and have rather pronounced limps as they walk the bulk of letters along the roof, but we are ever attracted to spectacle, are we not? The strings of electrical lights in the petit-bourgeois districts that twinkle all night, the iridescent skins of the dirigibles that litter the skies over The City like peculiar flying fish leaping from the ocean—they even appear overhead here in Manchester, much to the shock, and more recently, glee of the street urchins who shout and yawp whenever one passes under the clouds, and the only slightly more composed women on their way to squalid Deansgate market. A fortnight ago I took in a theatrical production, a local production of Mr Peake's *Presumption: or the Fate of Frankenstein*, already a hoary old play given new life and revived, ironically enough, by recent innovations in electrified machine-works. How bright the lights, how stunning the arc of actual lightning, tamed and obedient, how thunderous the ovations and the crumbling of the glacial cliffs! All the bombast of German opera in a space no larger than a middle-class parlour. And yet, throughout the entire evening, the great and hulking monster never spoke. *Contra* Madame Shelley's engaging novel, the "new Adam" never learns of philosophy, and the total of her excellent speeches of critique against the social institutions of her, and our, day are expurgated. Instead, the monster is ever an infant, given only to explosions of rage. Yet the audience, which contained a fair number of working-men who had managed to save or secure 5d. for "penny-stinker" seating, were enthralled. The play's Christian morality, alien to the original novel, was spelled out as if on a slate for the audience, and the monster was rendered as nothing more than an artefact of unholy vice. But lights blazed, and living snow from coils of refrigeration fell from the ceiling, and spectacle won the day.

My burning of Marx's letters is just such a spectacle—the true correspondence is secreted among a number of the safe houses I have acquired in Manchester and London. The girls on the roof-top are burning unmarked leaves, schoolboy doggerel, sketches, and whatever else I have laying about. The police have infiltrated Victoria Mill, but all their agents are men, as the work of espionage is considered too vile for the gentler sex. So the men watch the girls come from my office with letters by the bushel and burn them, then report every lick of flame and wafting cinder to their superiors.

My brief digression regarding the *Frankenstein* play is apposite, not only as it has to do with spectacle but with my current operation at Victoria Mill. Surely, Reader, you are familiar with Mr Babbage's remarkable Difference Engine, perfected in 1822—a year prior to the first production of Mr Peake's theatrical adaptation of *Frankenstein*—given the remarkable changes to the political economy that took place in the years after its introduction. How did we put it, back in the heady 1840s? *Subjection of Nature's forces to man, machinery, application of chemistry to industry and agriculture, steam-navigation, railways, electric telegraphs, clearing of whole continents for cultivation, canalisation of rivers, whole populations conjured out of the ground—what earlier century had even a presentiment that such productive forces slumbered in the lap of social labour?* That was just the beginning. Ever more I was reminded not of my old work with Marx, but of Samuel Butler's prose fancy *Erewhon—the time will come when the machines will hold the real supremacy over the world and its inhabitants is what no person of a truly philosophic mind can for a moment question.*

With the rise of the Difference Engine and the subsequent rationalization of market calculations, the bourgeoisie's revolutionary aspect continued unabated. Steam-navigation took to the air; railways gave way to horseless carriages; electric telegraphs to instantaneous wireless aethereal communications; the development of applied volcanisation to radically increase the amount of arable land, and to tame the great prize of Africa, the creation of automata for all but the basest of labour…ah, if only Marx were still here. That, I say to myself each morning upon rising. *If only Marx were still here!* The stockholders demand to know why I have not automated my factory, as though the clanking stove-pipe limbs of the steam-workers aren't just more dead labor! As though *Arbeitskraft*—labour-power—is not the source of all value! *If only Marx were still here!* And he'd say, to me, *Freddie, perhaps we were wrong.* Then he'd laugh and say, *I'm just having some fun with you.*

But we were not wrong. The internal contradictions of capitalism have not peacefully resolved themselves; the proletariat still may become the new revolutionary class, even as steam-worker builds steam-worker under the guidance of the of Difference Engine No. 53. The politico-economic chasm between bourgeoisie and proletarian has grown ever wider, despite the best efforts of the Fabian Society and other gradualists to improve the position of the working-class vis-à-vis their esteemed—and *en-steamed*, if you would forgive the pun—rulers. The Difference Engine is a device of formal logic, limited by the size of its gear-work and the tensile strength of the metals used in its construction. What I propose is a device of *dialectical logic*, a repurposing of the looms, a recording of unity of conflicts and opposites drawn on the finest of threads to pull innumerable switches, based on a linguistic programme derived from the correspondence of my comrade-in-arms.

I am negating the negation, transforming my factory into a massive Dialectical Engine that replicates not the arithmetical operations of an abacus but the cogitations of a human brain. I am rebuilding Karl Marx on the factory floor, repurposing the looms of the factory to create punch-cloths of over one thousand columns, and I will speak to my friend again.

2. THE LITTLE MATCH GIRLS

Under the arclights of Fairfield Road I saw them, on my last trip to The City. The evening's amusement had been invigorating if empty, a fine meal had been consumed immediately thereafter, and a digestif imbibed. I'd dismissed my London driver for the evening, for a cross-town constitutional. I'd catch the late airship, I thought. Match girls, leaving their shift in groups, though I could hardly tell them from steam-workers at first, given their awkward gaits and the gleam of metal under the lights, so like the monster in the play, caught my eye.

Steam-workers still have trouble with the finest work—the construction of Difference Engine gears is skilled labour performed by a well-remunerated aristocracy of working-men. High-quality cotton garments and bedclothes too are the remit of proletarians of the *flesh*, thus Victoria Mill. But there are commodities whose production still requires living labour not because of the precision needed to create the item, but due to the danger of the job. The production of white phosphorous matches is one of these. The matchsticks are too slim for steam-worker claws, which are limited to a trio of pincers on the All-Purpose Models, and to less refined appendages—sledges, sharp blades—on Special-Purpose Models. Furthermore, the aluminium outer skin, or shell, of the steam-worker tends to heat up to the point of combusting certain compounds, or even plain foolscap. So Bryant and May Factory in Bow, London, retained young girls, ages fourteen and up, to perform the work.

The stories in *The Link* and other reformist periodicals are well-known. Twelve-hour days for wages of 4s. a week, though it's a lucky girl who isn't fined for tardiness, who doesn't suffer deductions for having dirty feet, for dropping matches from her frame, for allowing the machines to falter rather than sacrifice her fingers to it. The girls eat their bread and butter—most can afford more only rarely, and then it's marmalade—on the line, leading to ingestion of white phosphorous. And there were the many cases of "phossy jaw"—swollen gums, foul breath, and some physicians even claimed that the jawbones of the afflicted would glow, like a candle shaded by a leaf of onion skin paper. I saw the gleaming of these girls' jaws as I passed and swore to myself. They were too young for phossy jaw; it takes years for the deposition of phosphorous to build. But as they passed me by, I saw the truth.

Their jaws had all been removed, a typical intervention for the disease, and they'd been replaced with prostheses. All the girls, most of whom were likely plain before their transformations, were now half-man half-machine, monstrosities! I couldn't help but accost them.

"Girls! Pardon me!" There were four of them; the tallest was perhaps fully mature, and the rest were mere children. They stopped, obedient. I realized that their metallic jaws that gleamed so brightly under the new electrical streetlamps might not be functional and I was flushed with concern. Had I humiliated them?

The youngest-seeming opened her mouth and said in a voice that had a greater similarity to the product of a phonographic cylinder than a human throat, "Buy Bryant and May matchsticks, Sir."

"Oh no, I don't need any matchsticks. I simply—"

"Buy Bryant and May matchsticks, Sir," she said again. Two of the others—the middle girls—lifted their hands and presented boxes of matchsticks for my perusal. One of those girls had two silvery digits where a thumb and forefinger had presumably once been. They were cleverly designed to articulate on the knuckles, and through some mechanism occulted to me did move in a lifelike way.

"Are any of you girls capable of independent speech?" The trio looked to the tallest girl, who nodded solemnly and said, "I." She struggled with the word, as though it were unfamiliar. "My Bryant and May mandible," she continued, "I was given it by…Bryant and May…long ago."

"So, with some struggle, you are able to compel speech of your own?"

"Buy…but Bryant and May match…made it hard," the girl said. Her eyes gleamed nearly as brightly as her metallic jaw.

The smallest of the four started suddenly, then turned her head, looking past her compatriots. "Buy!" she said hurriedly, almost rudely. She grabbed the oldest girl's hand and tried to pull her away from our conversation. I followed her eyes and saw the telltale plume of a police wagon rounding the corner. Lacking any choice, I ran with the girls to the end of the street and then turned a corner.

For a long moment, we were at a loss. Girls such as these are the refuse of society—often the sole support of their families, and existing in horrific poverty, they nonetheless hold to all the feminine rules of comportment. Even a troupe of them, if spotted in the public company of an older man in his evening suit, would simply be ruined women—sacked from their positions for moral turpitude, barred from renting in any situation save for those reserved for women engaged in prostitution; ever surrounded by criminals and other lumpen elements. The bourgeois sees in his wife a mere instrument of production, but in every female of the labouring classes he sees his wife. What monsters Misters Bryant and May must have at home! I dared not follow the girls for fear of terrifying them, nor could I even attempt to persuade them to accompany me to my safe-house. I let them leave, and proceeded to follow them as best I could. The girls ran crookedly, their legs bowed in some manner obscured by the work aprons, so they were easy enough to tail. They stopped at a small cellar two blocks from the Bryant and May works, and carefully stepped into the darkness, the tallest one closing the slanted doors behind her. With naught else to do, I made a note of the address and back at my London lodgings I arranged for a livery to take me back there at half past five o'clock in the morning, when the girls would arise again to begin their working day.

I brought with me some sweets, and wore a threadbare fustian suit. My driver, Wilkins, and I did not have long to wait, for at twenty-two minutes after the hour of five, the cellar door swung open and a tiny head popped out. The smallest of the girls! But she immediately ducked back down into the cellar. I took a step forward and the largest girl partially emerged, though she was careful to keep her remarkable prosthetic jaw obscured from possible passing trade. The gutters on the edge of the pavement were filled with refuse and dank water, but the girl did not so much as wrinkle her nose, for she had long since grown accustomed to life in the working-class quarters.

"Hello," I said. I squatted down, then offered the butterscotch sweets with one hand and removed my hat with the other. "Do you remember me?"

"Buy Brya…" she began. Then, with visible effort, she stopped herself and said. "Yes." Behind her the smallest girl appeared again and completed the slogan. "Buy Bryant and May matchsticks, Sir."

"I would very much like to speak with you."

"We must…work," the older said. "Bryant and May matchsticks, Sir!" said the other. "Before the sun rises," the older one said. "Buy Bryant and May—" I cast the younger girl a dirty look, I'm shamed to say, and she ducked her head back down into the cellar.

"Yes, well, I understand completely. There is no greater friend the working-man has than I, I assure. Look, a treat!" I proffered the sweets again. If a brass jaw with greater familial resemblance to a bear-trap than a human mandible could quiver, this girl's did right then.

"Come in," she said finally.

The cellar was very similar to the many I had seen in Manchester during my exploration of the living conditions of the English proletariat. The floor was dirt and the furnishings limited to bails of hay covered in rough cloth. A dank and filthy smell from the refuse, garbage, and excrements that choked the gutter right outside the cellar entrance, hung in the air. A small, squat, and wax-splattered table in the middle of the room held a soot-stained lantern. The girls wore the same smocks they had the evening before, and there was no sign of water for their toilet. Presumably, what grooming needs they had they attempted to meet at the factory itself, which was known to have a pump for personal use. Most cellar dwellings of this sort have a small cache of food in one corner—a sack of potatoes, butter wrapped in paper, and very occasionally a crust of bread. In this dwelling, there was something else entirely—a peculiar crank-driven contraption from which several pipes extruded.

The big girl walked toward it and with her phonographic voice told me, "We can't have sweets no more." Then she attached the pipes, which ended in toothy clips similar to the pincers of steam-workers, to either side of her mechanical mandible and began to crank the machine. A great buzzing rose up from the device and a flickering illumination filled the room. I could finally see the other girls in their corners, standing and staring at me. The large girl's hair stood on end from the static electricity she was generating, bringing to mind Miss Shelley's famed novel. I was fascinated and repulsed at once, though I wondered how such a generator could work if what it powered, the girl, itself powered the generator via the crank. Was it collecting a static charge from the air, as the skins of the newest airships did?

"Is this…generator your sustenance now?" I asked. She stopped cranking and the room dimmed again. "Buy…" she started, then recovered, "no more food. Better that way. Too much phossy in the food anyhow; it was poisonin' us."

In a moment, I realized my manners. Truly, I'd been half-expecting at least an offer of tea, it had been so long since I'd organized workers. "I'm terrible sorry, I've been so rude. What are you all called, girls?"

"No names now, better that way."

"You no longer eat!" I said. "And no longer have names. Incredible! The bosses did this to you?"

"No, Sir," the tall girl said. "The Fabians."

The smallest girl, the one who had never said anything save the Bryant and May slogan, finally spoke. "This is re-form, they said. This is us, in our re-form."

3. What Is To Be Done?

I struck a deal with the girls immediately, not in my role as agitator and organizer, but in my function as a manager for the family concern. Our driver took us to his home and woke his wife, who was sent to the shops for changes of clothes, soap, and other essentials for the girls. We kept the quartet in the carriage for most of the morning whilst Wilkins attempted to explain to his wife what she should see when we brought the girls into her home. She was a strong woman, no-nonsense, certainly no Angel of the House but effective nevertheless. The first thing she told the girls was, "There's to be no fretting and fussing. Do not speak, simply use gestures to communicate if you need to. Now, line up for a scrubbing. I presume your…equipment will not rust under some hot water and soap."

In the sitting room, Wilkins leaned over and whispered to me. "It's the saliva, you see. My Lizzie's a smart one. If the girls' mouths are still full of spit, it can't be that their jaws can rust. Clever, innit?" He lit his pipe with a white phosphorous match and then told me that one of the girls had sold him a Bryant and May matchbox whilst I booked passage for five on the next dirigible to Manchester. "They'd kept offerin', and it made 'em happy when I bought one," he said. "I'll add 5d. to the invoice, if you don't mind."

I had little to do but to agree and eat the butterscotch I had so foolishly bought for the girls. Presently the girls marched into the sitting room, looking like Moors in robes and headwraps. "You'll get odd looks," the driver's wife explained, "but not so odd as the looks you might have otherwise received."

The woman was right. We were stared at by the passengers and conductors of the airship both, though I had changed into a proper suit and even made a show of explaining the wonders of bourgeois England to the girls from our window seat. "Look girls, there's St. Paul's, where all the good people worship the triune God," I said. Then as we passed over the countryside I made note of the agricultural steam-workers that looked more like the vehicles they were than the men their urbanized brethren pretended to be. "These are our crops, which feed this great nation and strengthen the limbs of the Empire!" I explained. "That is why the warlords of your distant lands were so easily brought to heel. God was on our side, as was the minds of our greatest men, the sinew of our bravest soldiers and the power classical elements themselves—water, air, fire, and ore—*steam!*" I had spent enough time observing the bourgeoisie to generate sufficient hot air for the entire dirigible.

Back in Manchester, I had some trusted comrades prepare living quarters for the girls, and to arrange for the delivery of a generator sufficient for their needs. Then I began to make inquires into the Socialistic and Communistic communities, which I admit that I had been ignoring whilst I worked on the theoretical basis for the Dialectical Engine. Just as Marx used to say, commenting on the French "Marxists" of the late '70s: "All I know is that I am not a Marxist." The steam-workers broke what proletarian solidarity there was in the United Kingdom, and British airships eliminated most resistance in France, Germany, and beyond. What we are left with, here on the far left, are several literary young men, windy Labour MPs concerned almost entirely with airship mooring towers and placement of the same in their home districts, and…the Fabians.

The Fabians are gradualists, believers in parliamentary reforms and moral suasion. Not revolution, but evolution, not class struggle but class collaboration. They call themselves socialists, and many of them are as well-meaning as a yipping pup, but ultimately they wish to save capitalism from the hammers of the working-class. But if they were truly responsible somehow for the state of these girls, they would have moved beyond reformism into complete capitulation to the bourgeoisie. *But we must never capitulate, never collaborate!*

The irony does not escape me. I run a factory on behalf of my bourgeois family. I live fairly well, and indeed, am only the revolutionary I am because of the profits extracted from the workers on the floor below. Now I risk all, their livelihoods and mine, to complete the Dialectical Engine. The looms have been reconfigured; we haven't sent out any cotton in weeks. The work floor looks as though a small volcano had been drawn forth from beneath the crust—the machinists work fifteen hours a day, and smile at me when I come downstairs and roll up my sleeves to help them. They call me Freddie, but I know they despise me. And not even for my status as a bourgeois—they hate me for my continued allegiance to the working-class. There's a word they use when they think I cannot hear them. "Slummer." A man who lives in, or even simply visits, the working-men districts to experience some sort of prurient thrill of rebellion and *faux* class allegiance.

But that is it! That's what I must do. The little match girls must strike! Put their prostheses on display for the public via flying pickets. Challenge the bourgeoisie on their own moral terms—are these the daughters of Albion? Girls who are ever-starving, who can never be loved, forced to skulk in the shadows, living Frankenstein's monsters? The dailies will eat it up, the working-class will be roused, first by economic and moral issues, but then soon by their own collective interest as a class. Behind me, the whir and chatter of loom shuttles kicked up. The Dialectical Engine was being fed the medium on which the raw knowledge of my friend's old letters and missives were to be etched. *Steam,* was all I could think. *What can you not do?*

4. The Spark

I was an old hand at organizing workers, though girls who consumed electricity rather than bread were a bit beyond my remit. It took several days to teach the girls to speak with their jaws beyond the Bryant and May slogan, and several more to convince them of the task. "Why should we go back?" one asked. Her name was once Sally, as she was finally able to tell me, and she was the second-smallest. "They won't have us."

"To free your fellows," I had said. "To express workers' power and, ultimately, take back the profits for yourselves!"

"But then we'd be the bosses," the oldest girl said. "Cruel and mean."

"Yes, well no. It depends on all of the workers of a nation rising up to eliminate the employing class," I explained. "We must go back—"

"I don't want to ever go back!" said the very smallest. "That place was horrid!"

The tedious debate raged long into the night. They were sure that the foreman would clout their heads in for even appearing near the factory gates, but I had arranged for some newspapermen and even electro-photographers sympathetic to Christian socialism, if not Communism, to meet us as we handed out leaflets to the passing trade and swing shift.

We were met at the gate by a retinue of three burly looking men in fustian suits. One of them fondled a sap in his hand and tipped his hat. The journalists hung back, believers to the end in the objectivity of the disinterested observer, especially when they might get hurt for being rather too interested.

"Leaflets, eh?" the man with the sap asked. "You know this lot can't read, yeah?"

"And this street's been cleared," one of the others said. "You can toss that rubbish in the bin, then."

"Yes, that's how your employers like them, isn't it? Illiterate, desperate, without value to their families as members of the female of the species?" I asked. "And the ordinary working men, cowed by the muscle of a handful of hooligans."

"Buy Bryant and May matchsticks, Sir!" the second-tallest girl said, brightly as she could. The thuggish guards saw her mandible and backed away. Excited, she clacked away at them, and the others joined in.

"How do you like that?" I said to both the guards and the press. "Innocent girls, more machine than living being. We all know what factory labour does to children, or thought we did. But now, behold the new monsters the age of steam and electricity hath wrought. We shall lead an exodus through the streets, and you can put that in your sheets!" The thugs let us by, then slammed the gates behind us, leaving us on the factory grounds and them outside. Clearly, one or more of the police agents who monitor my activities had caught wind of our plans, but I was confident that victory would be ours. Once we roused the other match girls, we'd engage in a *sit-down* strike, if necessary. The girls could not be starved out like ordinary workers, and I had more than enough confederates in London to ring the factory and sneak food and tea for me through the bars if necessary. But I was not prepared for what awaited us.

The girls were gone, but the factory's labours continued apace. Steam-workers attended the machines, carried frames of matches down the steps to the loading dock, and clanked about with the precision of clockwork. Along a catwalk, a man waved to us, a handkerchief in his hand. "Hallo!" he said.

"That's not the foreman," Sally told me. "It's the dentist!" She did not appear at all relieved that the factory's dentist rather than its foreman, who had been described to me as rather like an ourang-outan, was approaching us. I noticed that a pair of steam-workers left their posts and followed him as he walked up to us.

"Mister Friedrich Engels! Is that you?" he asked me. I admitted that I was, but that further I was sure he had been forewarned of my coming. He ignored my rhetorical jab and pumped my hand like an American cowboy of some fashion. "Wonderful, wonderful," he said. He smiled at the girls, and I noticed that his teeth were no better than anyone else's. "I'm Doctor Flint. Bryant and May hired me to deal with worker pains that come from exposure to white phosphorus. We're leading the fight for healthy workers here; I'm sure you'll agree that we're quite progressive. Let me show you what we've accomplished here at Bryant and May."

"Where are the girls?" the tallest of my party asked, her phonographic voice shrill and quick, as if the needle had been drawn over the wax too quickly.

"Liberated!" the dentist said. He pointed to me. "They owe it all to you, you know. I reckon it was your book that started me on my path into politics. Dirtier work than dentistry." He saw my bemused look and carried on eagerly. "Remember what you wrote about the large factories of Birmingham—*the use of steam-power admit of the employment of a great multitude of women and children.* Too true, too true!"

"Indeed, sir," I started, but he interrupted me.

"But of course we can't put steam back in the kettle, can we?" He rapped a knuckle on the pot-belly torso of one of the ever-placid steam-workers behind him. "But then I read your philosophical treatise. I was especially interested in your contention that quantitative change can become qualitative. So, I thought to myself, Self, if steam-power is the trouble when it comes to the subjugation of child labour, cannot more steam-power spell the liberation of child labour?"

"No, not by itself. The class strugg—"

"But no, Engels, you're wrong!" he said. "At first I sought to repair the girls, using steam-power. Have you seen the phoss up close? Through carious teeth, and the poor girls know little of hygiene so they have plenty of caries, the vapours of white phosphorous make gains into the jawbone itself, leading to putrefaction. Stinking hunks of bone work right through the cheek, even after extractions of the carious teeth."

"Yes, we are all familiar with phossy jaw," I said. "Seems to me that the minimalist programme would be legislative—bar white phosphorous. Even whatever sort of Liberal or Fabian you are can agree with that."

"Ah, but I can't!" he said. "You enjoy your pipe? I can smell it on you."

"That's from Wilkins, my driver."

"Well then observe your Mr Wilkins. It's human nature to desire a strike-anywhere match. We simply cannot eliminate white phosphorous from the marketplace. People demand it. What we can do, however, is use steam to remove the human element from the equation of production."

"I understood that this sort of work is too detailed for steam-workers."

"It was," the dentist said. "But then our practice on the girls led to certain innovations." As if on cue, the steam-workers held up their forelimbs and displayed to me a set of ten fingers with the dexterity of any primates. "So now I have eliminated child labour—without any sort of agitation or rabble-rousing I might add—from this factory and others like it, in less than a fortnight. Indeed, the girls were made redundant this past Tuesday."

"And what do you plan to do for them," I said. "A good Fabian like you knows that these girls will now—"

"Will now what? Starve? You know they won't, not as long as there are lampposts in London. They all contain receptacles. Mature and breed, further filling the working-men's districts with the unemployable, uneducable? No, they won't. Find themselves abused and exploited in manners venereal? No, not possible, even if there was a man so drunk as to overlook their new prosthetic mandibles. Indeed, we had hoped to move the girls into the sales area, which is why their voiceboxes are rather…focused, but as it happens few people wish to buy matches from young girls. Something about it feels immoral, I suppose. So they are free to never work again. Herr Engels, their problems are solved."

For a long moment, we both stood our ground, a bit unsure as to what we should do next, either as socialist agitators or as gentlemen. We were both keenly aware that our conversation was the first of its type in all history. The contradictions of capitalism, resolved? The poor would always be with us, but also immortal and incapable of reproduction. Finally the dentist looked at his watch—he wore one with rotating shutters of numerals on his wrist, as is the fashion among wealthy morons—and declared that he had an appointment to make. "The steam-workers will show you out," he said, and in a moment their fingers were on my arms, and they dragged me to the entrance of the factory as if I were made of straw. The girls followed, confused and, if the way their metallic jaws were set was telling, they were actually relieved. The press pestered us with questions on the way out, but I sulked past them without remark. Let them put Doctor Flint above the fold tomorrow morning, for all the good it will do them. Soon enough there'd be steam-workers capable of recording conversations and events with perfect audio-visual fidelity, and with a dial to be twisted for different settings of the editing of newsreels: Tory, Liberal, or Fabian. Indeed, one would never have to twist the dial at all.

We returned to Wilkins and our autocarriage, defeated and atomised. Flint spoke true; as we drove through the streets of the East End, I did espy several former match girls standing on corners or in gutters, directionless and likely cast out from whatever home they may have once had.

"We have to..." but I knew that I couldn't.

Wilkins said, "The autocarriage is overburdened already. Those girlies weigh more than they appear to, eh? You can't go 'round collecting every stray."

No—charity is a salve at best, a bourgeois affectation at worst. But even those concerns were secondary. As the autocarriage moved sluggishly toward the airship field, I brooded on the question of value. If value comes from labour, and capital is but dead labour, what are steam-workers? So long as they needed to be created by human hands, clearly steam-workers were just another capital good, albeit a complex one. But now, given the dexterity of the latest generation of steam-workers, they would clearly be put to work building their own descendents, and those that issue forth from that subsequent generation would also be improved, without a single quantum of labour-power expended. The bourgeoisie might have problems of their own; with no incomes at all, the working-class could not even afford the basic necessities of life. Steam-workers don't buy bread or cloth, nor do they drop farthings into the alms box at church on Sunday. How would bourgeois society survive without workers who also must be driven to consume the very products they made?

The petit-bourgeoisie, I realized, the landed gentry, perhaps they could be catered to exclusively, and the empire would continue to expand and open new markets down to the tips of the Americas and through to the end of the Orient— foreign money and resources would be enough for capital, for the time being. But what of the proletariat? If the bourgeoisie no longer need the labour of the workers, and with the immense power in their hands, wouldn't they simply rid themselves of the toiling classes the way the lord of a manor might rid a stable of vermin? They could kill us all from the air—firebombing the slums and industrial districts. Send whole troupes of steam-workers to tear men apart till the cobblestones ran red with the blood of the proletariat. Gears would be greased, all right.

We didn't dare take an airship home to Manchester. The mooring station was sure to be mobbed with writers from the tabloids and Tory sheets. So we settled in for the long and silent drive up north.

I had no appetite for supper, which wasn't unusual after an hour in an airship, but tonight was worse for the steel ball of dread in my stomach. I stared at my pudding for a long time. I wished I could offer it to the girls, but they were beyond treats. On a whim, I went back to the factory to check in on the Dialectical Engine, which had been processing all day and evening. A skeleton crew had clocked out when the hour struck nine, and I was alone with my creation. No, with the creation of the labour of my workers. No, *the* workers. If only I could make myself obsolete, as the steam-workers threatened the proletariat.

The factory floor, from the vantage point of my small office atop the catwalk, was a sight to behold. A mass of cloth, like huge overlapping sails, obscured the looms, filling the scaffolding that had been built up six storeys to hold and "read" the long punched sheets. A human brain in replica, with more power than any Difference Engine, fuelled by steam for the creation not of figures, but dialectics. Quantitative change had become qualitative, or would as soon as the steam engines in the basement were ignited. I lacked the ability to do it myself, or I would have just then, allowing me to talk to my old friend, or as close a facsimile as I could build with my fortune and knowledge. All the machinery came to its apex in my office, where a set of styluses waited in position over sheets of foolscap. I would prepare a question, and the machine would produce an answer that would be translated, I hoped, into comprehensible declarative sentences upon the sheets. A letter from Marx, from beyond the grave! Men have no souls to capture, but the mind, yes. The mind is but the emergent properties of the brain, and I rebuilt Marx's brain, though I hoped not simply to see all his theories melt into air.

With a start, I realized that down on the floor I saw a spark. The factory was dark and coated with the shadows of the punched sheets, so the momentary red streak fifty feet below was obvious to me. Then I smelled it, the smoke of a pipe. Only a fool would light up in the midst of so much yardage of inflammable cotton, which was perplexing, because Wilkins was no fool.

"Wilkins!" I shouted. "Extinguish that pipe immediately! You'll burn down the factory and kill us both! These textiles are highly combustible."

"Sow-ry," floated up from the void. But then another spark flitted in the darkness, and a second and a third. Wilkins held a fistful of matches high, and I could make out the contours of his face. "Quite a mechanism you've got all set up here, Mister Engels. Are these to be sails for the masts of your yacht?"

"No sir, they won't be for anything if you don't extinguish those matches!"

"Extinguish, eh? Well, you got a good look, and so did I, so I think I will." And he blew out the matches. All was dark again. What happened next was quick. I heard the heavy thudding—no, a heavy *ringing* of boots along the catwalk and in a moment a steam-worker was upon me. I wrestled with it for a moment, but I was no match for its pistons, and it threw me over the parapet. My breath left my body as I fell—as if my soul had decided to abandon me and leap right for heaven. But I didn't fall far. I landed on a taut sheet of fine cotton, then rolled off of it and fell less than a yard onto another. I threw out my arms and legs as I took the third layer of sheet, and then scuttled across it to the edge of the scaffold on which I rested. Sitting, I grasped the edge with my hands and lowered myself as much as I dare, then let go. Wilkins was there, having tracked my movements from the fluttering of the sheets and my undignified oopses and oofs. He lit another match and showed me his eyes.

"Pretty fit for an older gentlemen, Mister Engels. But take a gander at the tin of Scotch broth up there." He lifted the match. The steam-worker's metallic skin glinted in what light there was. It stood atop the parapet of the catwalk and with a leap flung itself into the air, plummeting the six storeys down and landing in a crouch like a circus acrobat. Remarkable, but I was so thankful that it did not simply throw itself through the coded sheets I had spent so long trying to manufacture, ruining the Dialectical Engine before it could even be engaged. Then I understood.

"Wilkins!" I cried. "You're a police agent!"

Wilkins shrugged, and swung onto his right shoulder a heavy sledge. "'Fraid so. But can you blame me, sir? I've seen the writing on the wall—or the automaton on the assembly line," he said, nodding past me and toward the steam-worker, who had taken the flank opposite my treacherous driver. "I know what's coming. Won't nobody be needing me to drive 'em around with these wind-up toys doing all the work, and there won't be no other jobs to be had but rat and fink. So I took a little fee from the police, to keep an eye on you and your..." He was at a loss for words for a moment. "Machinations. Yes, that's it. And anyhow, they'll pay me triple to put all this to the torch, so I will, then retire to Cheshire with old Lizzie and have a nice garden."

"And it?" I asked, glancing at the automaton on my left.

"Go figure," Wilkins said. "My employers wanted one of their own on the job, in case you somehow bamboozled me with your radical cant into switching sides a second time."

"They don't trust you," I said.

"Aye, but they pay me, half in advance." And he blew out the match, putting us in darkness again. Without the benefit of sight, my other senses flared to life. I could smell Wilkins stepping forward, hear the tiny grunt as he hefted the sledge. I could nearly taste the brass and aluminium of the steam-worker on my tongue, and I certainly felt its oppressive weight approaching me.

I wish I could say I was brave and through a clever manoeuvre defeated both my foes simultaneously. But a Communist revolutionary must always endeavour to be honest to the working-class—Reader, I fell into a swoon. Through nothing more than a stroke of luck, as my legs gave way beneath me, Wilkins's sledgehammer flew over my head and hit the steam-worker square on the faceplate. It flew free in a shower of sparks. Facing an attack, the steam-worker staved in Wilkins's sternum with a single blow, then turned back to me, only to suddenly shudder and collapse atop me. I regained full consciousness for a moment, thanks to the putrid smell of dead flesh and fresh blood. I could see little, but when I reached to touch the exposed face of the steam-worker, I understood. I felt not gears and wirework, but slick sinew and a trace of human bone. Then the floor began to shake. An arclight in the corner flickered to life, illuminating a part of the factory floor. I was pinned under the automaton, but then the tallest of the girls—and I'm ashamed to say I never learned what she was called—with a preternatural strength of her own took up one of the machine's limbs and dragged him off of me.

I didn't even catch my breath before exclaiming, "Aha, of course! The new steam-workers aren't automata, they're men! Men imprisoned in suits of metal to enslave them utterly to the bourgeoisie!" I coughed and sputtered. "You! Such as you, you see," I told the girl, who stared at me dumbly. Or perhaps I was the dumb one, and she simply looked upon me as a pitiable old idiot who was the very last to figure out what she considered obvious. "Replace the body of a man with a machine, encase the human brain within a cage, and dead labour lives again! That's how the steam-workers are able to use their limbs and appendages with a facility otherwise reserved for humans. All the advantages of the proletariat, but the steam-workers neither need to consume nor reproduce!" Sally was at my side now, with my pudding, which she had rescued from my supper table. She was a clever girl, Sally. "The others started all the engines they could find," she said, and only then I realized that I had been shouting in order to hear myself. All around me, the Dialectical Engine was in full operation.

5. All That Is Solid Melts Into Air

In my office, the styluses scribbled for hours. I spent a night and a day feeding it foolscap. The Dialectical Engine did not work as I'd hoped it would—it took no input from me, answered none of the questions I had prepared, but instead wrote out a single long monograph. I was shocked at what I read from the very first page:

Das Kapital: Kritik der politischen Ökonomie, Band V.

The *fifth* volume of *Capital*. Marx had died prior to completing the *second*, which I published myself from his notes. Before turning my energies to the Dialectical Engine, I had edited the third volume for publication. While the prior volumes of the book offered a criticism of bourgeois theories of political economy and a discussion of the laws of the capitalist mode of production, this fifth volume, or extended appendix in truth, was something else. It contained a description of socialism.

The internal contradictions of capitalism had doomed it to destruction. What the bourgeoisie would create would also be used to destroy their reign. The ruling class, in order to stave off extinction, would attempt to use its technological prowess to forestall the day of revolution by radically expanding its control of the proletarian and his labour-power. But in so doing, it would create the material conditions for socialism. The manuscript was speaking of steamworkers, though of course the Dialectical Engine had no sensory organs with which to observe the metal-encased corpse that had expired in its very innards the evening prior. Rather, the Engine *predicted* the existence of human-steam hybrids from the content of the decade-old correspondence between Marx and myself.

What then, would resolve the challenge of the proletarian brain trapped inside the body of the steam worker? Dialectical logic pointed to a simple solution: the negation of the negation. Free the proletarian *mind* from its physical *brain* by encoding it onto a new mechanical medium. That is to say, the Dialectical Engine itself was the key. Free the working-class by having it exist in the physical world and the needs of capitalism to accumulate, accumulate. Subsequent pages of the manuscript detailed plans for Dialectical Engine Number 2, which would be much smaller and more efficient. A number of human minds could be "stitched-up" into this device and through collective endeavour, these beings-in-one would create Dialectical Engine Number 3, which would be able to hold still more minds and create the notional Dialectical Engine Number 4. Ultimately, the entire working-class of England and Europe could be up-coded into a Dialectical Engine no larger than a hatbox, and fuelled by power drawn from the sun. Without a proletariat to exploit—the class as a whole having taken leave of realm of flesh and blood to reconstitute itself as information within the singular Dialectical Engine Omega—the bourgeoisie would fall into ruin and helplessness, leaving the working-class whole and unmolested in perpetuity. Even after the disintegration of the planet, the Engine would persist, and move forward to explore the firmament and other worlds that may orbit other stars.

Within the Dialectical Engine Omega, consciousness would be both collective and singular, an instantaneous and perfect industrial democracy. Rather than machines replicating themselves endlessly as in Mister Butler's novel—*the machines are gaining ground upon us; day by day we are becoming more subservient to them*—it is us that shall be liberated by the machines, through the machines. We are gaining ground upon them! *Proletarier aller Länder, vereinigt euch!* We have nothing to lose but our chains, as the saying goes!

The Dialectical Engine fell silent after nineteen hours of constant production. I should have been weary, but already I felt myself beyond hunger and fatigue. The schematics for Dialectical Engine Number 2 were incredibly advanced, but for all their cleverness the mechanism itself would be quite simple to synthesize. With a few skilled and trusted workers, we could have it done in a fortnight. Five brains could be stitched-up into it. The girls and myself were obvious candidates, and from within the second engine we would create the third, and fourth, and subsequent numbers via pure unmitigated *Arbeitskraft*!

Bold? Yes! Audacious? Certainly. And indeed, I shall admit that, for a moment, my mind drifted to the memory of the empty spectacle of Mister Peake's play, of the rampaging monster made of dead flesh and brought to life via electrical current. But I had made no monster, no brute. That was a bourgeois story featuring a bogeyman that the capitalists had attempted to mass produce from the blood of the working-class. My creation was the opposite number of the steam-worker and the unphilosophical monster of stage and page; the Engine was *mens sana sine corpore sano*—a sound mind outside a sound body.

What could possibly go wrong…?

THIS IS HOW it might have gone:

The Circus Tresaulti spent the winter on the road, Ayar the strong man knocking the stakes into the ground when it was frozen over.

They bartered for liquor to keep warm, and when spring came they pushed the trucks through the mud to save oil, and everything went on as before, and nothing broke.

But that was the winter they found the house.

The mansion stands more than two miles from the city walls, far enough that the looters have given up, and it's been left to rot so long that the city's children wouldn't understand it's a house.

The windows go first, from enemy fire and bad frosts. Then the moss and ivy move in, and the birds, and the rain. At last, the brick begins to crumble.

By the time the Circus comes, it will be a ruin.

But by the time the Circus comes, the storm has been raging for days, and the house rises up from the road, and Boss thinks, We must rest here, there's no way to go on.

"Stop," says Boss, and the Circus stops.

The Circus waits in leaking trailers while Boss takes her lieutenants through the house.

Then, her lieutenants are Elena from the trapeze, and Panadrome the music man, who presses his accordion bellows tight to his side to keep it from sharp edges, and Alec, their final act, who folds his gleaming wings tight against his back so he can fit through the hole in the wall.

Inside, the ceiling is waterlogged and sagging, but when Alec opens his wings even the nails sing for him.

Alec laughs, and the birds in the rafters scatter as if he's called them down.

(Alec will be dead in a year; these are the last birds he sees.)

They split up to cover ground; the house was grand, before it went to seed.

What Boss sees: five rooms with floors that haven't rotted through; a ballroom with a chandelier still hanging; three bathrooms with copper pipes intact behind the stone. (She can see metal right through walls, by now.)

What Boss does not see: Alec in a dining room with only a sideboard left, silhouetted against wallpaper that was green once. He faces a painting of a banquet, but his head is lowered. His wings are folded; he is still.

Elena stands behind him. Her forehead rests on his bare back, in the cradle between the wings. Her eyes are closed; her skin becomes pinker, as if she's waking from a long sleep.

(His wings are tall. They swallow her.)

Panadrome is beside the piano when Boss finds him.

One of the legs has collapsed, dropping the higher registers to the ground, and a few keys sank with the impact, but otherwise it's pristine.

He holds a blanket in his skeleton fingers, and the piano is free of dust; long ago someone, in their terror, still risked a kindness to a beautiful thing.

"We'll stay here," Boss says.

He doesn't think it's a good idea. He thinks the Circus might fall apart if it stops.

After too long he says, "As you like."

"You think it's not safe?"

Alec comes in, and Elena a few moments later.

"If you want us to live in an obstacle course," Elena says, "you've found the right place."

Boss says, "They can use the mess to shore up the holes, then. Call them."

Elena scowls and goes.

Alec smiles at Boss, holds out a hand. "Did you see the dining hall? There's a painting of a banquet, in case you forget what room you're in."

A moment later Panadrome is alone, one hand on the piano, pulling in breath he doesn't need.

Boss has a knack for skeletons.

Panadrome has never asked to have his silver hands covered over (though more than once Boss brought back someone's hands, still bleeding, and asked, "You need a pair of gloves?").

He is proud of the slender phalanges, the slightly curved metatarsals, the wrist joints always dark with oil. It is a testament to her art, and he would never dream of covering it.

But it is not a hand.

(A painting of a banquet may be beautiful, but you're no less hungry.)

They gave him oranges to carry, palm down. It strained very particular muscles so you could hold your hands aloft for the length of a concert.

(You cannot rest your weight in your fingertips when you play; your fingers are puppets, and the palms of your hands are the framework that holds them aloft.)

Now, he can play the accordion just as well as he ever could, though he thinks it's not as though anyone plays the accordion so much as cajoles a song from it.

But in the crumbling house, he stands beside the piano without moving to the bench.

(Panadrome's hands are pipes and gears. He does not have the spread between fingers that you need—the spread you could achieve if you practiced hard enough, if you held enough oranges, if you were born with the necessary reach. He could cover thirteen notes, in his prime.)

He has not seen a piano in a long time; winters are hard, and their wood burns as well as any other.

He is the last piano player in the world, the very last, and in the crumbling house he stands beside the instrument and trembles.

The Circus makes a home.

They drag stones to patch up the holes, and bolster the ceilings where they can, and come to blows over who gets the driest rooms, and Ayar the strong man reaches through the brick walls like they're made of cheese and pulls away long strands of copper. He takes it all; Boss wants it for the things she builds, and there's no knowing the next time they'll have a store like this.

"You look like a snake charmer," says Little George, when Ayar brings them to the workshop trailer for safekeeping.

(Not a drop of rain has gotten into the workshop. The workshop is sealed tight as the grave.)

Elena fights to keep the aerialists in their trailer and out of the house ("Just what I need, one of them breaking and me having to start from scratch."), but Boss allows no mutinies.

So Elena turns her battle to getting them the driest room, and they all crowd their pallets in, laughing, alongside Ayar and Jonah, whose clockwork lungs are susceptible to damp.

Elena lasts two hours before she moves her things to the third story.

The next day Boss says, "The floors up there are rotted through. You'll fall and snap your head off."

"I'll take my chances," Elena says.

Panadrome comes back to the piano room, often, and pulls the blanket away like a magician mid-trick.

He thought he was used to knowing that there would be no music that did not come from him, from the brass barrel of his body and the spindly silver lengths of his arms, from the bellows on one side and the keys on the other that make him useless for work.

He thought it would please him, to have power like that. (You think a lot of strange things, before the truth sinks in.)

If he tried, he might be able to play the final duet from *Heynan and Bello*. If he tried.

The melodies are layered, but the range is not large; it's an opera expressiva, and those rely on depth over breadth.

It's a pleasure to conduct. It lacks the classic majesty of *Queen Tresaulta*, but *Heynan and Bello* has its own appeal for the musician: Every theme (the bold brother Bello, the clever sister Heynan, the court families, the castle) can be played over any of the others.

During the siege, when all the themes are played at once, the wall of sound is transporting, and even from his harbor on the conductor's podium there is a sense that the music could break free and swallow them.

The finale is softer. Only Heynan and Bello are onstage, and their separate notes move quietly forward into the end. When they're about to be discovered, they clasp hands and pitch themselves over the edge of the tower into the sea, to keep their love from becoming known.

After they fall, the love theme plays. It has appeared only once before, in the moment of their first kiss, two bars of music between their own songs like a dream they only remember after it's too late.

He found himself bent almost double at the end of every performance, as if he could pull every bow over the strings himself.

But he has never understood it.

The music is beautiful enough that he should be able to understand (he's a musician, that's his work), but it's the reverse; their themes are so sad that every time he conducts it, he thinks that this time they will face whoever enters, and triumph, and walk out free.

(If you can make something so beautiful, why would you ever stop?)

This is what he thinks about every time Boss is going to bring someone into the circus.

She takes his hand, pulls him aside (she never hesitates to touch him, the only one of them who does).

Then she asks, "What did you think of that?" and behind her eyes the performer is already taking shape.

"I vote yes," he says, because if you can make something beautiful, why would you ever stop?

(Her hands are always warm; he doesn't know how he knows.)

"No fires," Boss says, the first night.

The house is far from the city, but she knows by now that the kind of city that grows from a prison is the kind that doesn't like neighbors moving in.

She and Alec make their bed in a room with no windows, just in case. His wings catch any light they can find.

"It's charming," he says the first night, as they listen to what might be birds fighting over their heads. "Reminds me of camping."

(It's a joke. He was born after the war started; that kind of leisure doesn't exist anymore. But she tells him what the world was like, and he pretends, because it pleases her.)

"Go to sleep," she says, smiling, and he settles onto his stomach, his wings along his back.

They each face away from the other, pretending to sleep, for a long time.

He is listening to the little bird-sounds above them that he knows are Elena.

Boss is listening as hard as she can, right through the walls, for the sound of the city coming for them.

For a while, everything is quiet.

The crew sleeps, recovering from the winter. The aerialists sleep, recovering from Elena.

The floors start to fall in, and the Grimaldi Brothers practice by balancing on each other in the weakest points, and leaping away when the boards give in. (Little George stands in the doorway, judges how impressive the tumbling is, and declares winners.)

Ayar and Jonah find a few books under a pile of rubble, read them until the paper starts to flake.

Elena strings up a trapeze in the attic.

"The birds won't be happy," says Alec, at dinner.

(Elena still comes down to dinner with the rest; Boss gave the order.)

Elena seems not to hear, and it's Little George who says under his breath, "She's probably eating them," and gets a box on his ears from Boss.

Panadrome watches from his corner for a while before he disappears.

(He's long ago given up the pretense of food. He tried for a while, to be part of the family, but some things aren't worth pretending over.)

The house is enormous, but they seem to fill it more as days pass, until it's a trick to find a room that won't eventually be hosting the Grimaldis as they play.

There are two exceptions.

The music room they leave alone. Boss gave the order.

The attic is Elena's, and that's all it takes to keep them out. Not worth the trouble; she holds a grudge.

No one gives that one a second thought. No one even glances at the attic stairs, growing from a servants' staircase at the end of some hallway they gutted of pipes.

(No one sees the second set of footprints marking passage, flanked with little sharp cuts in the dust where his feathers have been.)

The city sees them.

When the militia comes, Boss meets them with Little George beside her, and two of the crew in their work clothes, and one of the crew dressed up in bangles and veils. The others arrange themselves inside the house to hide their numbers and look as sweet as possible.

Alec, Panadrome, Ayar, and Jonah crowd into the windowless room where Boss and Alec sleep. Elena stands guard at the door, in case the city people make it that far. (She was a good soldier, in her day.)

Little George comes up to relieve them.

"She said we were happy to put on a week of free shows," he says, still panting from the sprint upstairs. "They didn't want any of it. They said we have until nightfall to leave town, or they're going to burn us out."

"What did Boss say?" Panadrome frowns.

"She said, Yes of course, no harm meant, we didn't realize it was city property, thank you for the warning, we'll start packing right now, and then they left."

Alec is smiling. "And what does Boss really say?"

Little George grins so hard his ears move up his head.

"She says if they're going to be rude, so can we. We're heading to the woods to harvest what we can."

Jonah and Ayar and Alec walk out smiling.

Panadrome doesn't move. He stands where he is, and reminds himself over and over that the piano is just another beautiful thing.

They've all said goodbye to beautiful things; it's the nature of the business.

Still, he stands where he is a long time.

(What Panadrome does not see: Elena standing in the attic, looking at Alec's footprints in the dust, reminding herself it's the nature of the business.)

Jonah comes back with an armful of potatoes.

"There are more," he says, "it's just that the ground cover is so thick, and I can't reach."

(His lungs are housed in a gold beetle-dome; he has to be careful.)

Boss organizes a hunting party, and under cover of dusk they slink into the trees to shore up enough food to keep the crew from dropping dead around them.

Panadrome takes the time to look over the house, now that people's boots have left a trail where the floor is sound. He'd never been beyond the ground floor before; he's not an adventurer, by nature.

He's on the second story when the music starts, and he thinks his mind is playing tricks on him.

But there are too many mistakes his imagination would never make, and he creeps downstairs wishing there were a weapon left for him to wield.

Instead he creeps to the doorway, glances inside.

Elena is kneeling, playing a song they use in children's primers, pausing every few chords to frown and adjust her fingering.

Her hands are strong enough (a lifetime on trapeze), but her fingers are stiff. She had a poor teacher. The piano's out of tune, which doesn't help.

But still he rests his temple on the wall, and listens to the first notes in ages that haven't come from him.

Then she pauses mid-phrase, and he realizes after too long that she's standing. It's not absence of mind—she's given up. The notes are hanging, dissonant.

"You have to finish," he says, moving into sight.

If she's startled, it doesn't show. "I don't remember."

"I'll teach you," he says.

He must sound too desperate, too eager, because she levels a look at him he's rarely seen. Cruel, yes, and angry, yes, and terrified, but not this.

"Play it yourself," she says.

He raises and drops his hands a few inches (it passes as a shrug), says, "I can't."

She watches his fingers, glances out the window.

(He can see her thinking, You still could, if you had any courage, but she's known him long enough to try not to be cruel.)

"Please, just to the end," he says. "Only ten measures."

(Before Boss gets back, he thinks. He would never let her see him this way; he would never seem so ungrateful.)

"We'll have to leave," she says. "You can't keep this."

He doesn't answer. (He's asked for so little, in all this time. There must be a way.)

When he doesn't meet her eye, she says, "This house was a mistake. Don't let this ruin you, too."

He doesn't understand her. He nods to her—manners, always—and goes.

In the kitchen he breathes so deeply that the brass strains against the bolts.

This is what he can't admit: His body forgets.

The music he remembers; he remembers things he said and did. But he has forgotten the taste of wine, and the pinch of the baton between his fingers, and the itch at his throat from his tie. Thinking back is like watching film, knowing it happened but sensing nothing.

He learned accordion after; for the Circus, he can play.

But the rest was so long ago, he might kneel in front of the piano and not have one note left in him.

(The first thing he sensed was the warmth of the sun rising, and when he opened his eyes Boss was in front of him, standing watch.)

The music comes back after a very long time. It's halting, and off-key, and she needs an orange under her palm—her fingers will wear out, this way.

But you don't examine a gift (manners, always), so he stays where he is, closes his eyes, listens until the song is over.

What Panadrome does not see:

The others coming back from the forest in the deep night, with enough plants to survive on. Alec leads the way, wings loose, carrying a blanket filled to bursting.

When he sees Elena in the doorway, he smiles like a crowd is watching.

But then he reaches her.

Then his face softens, and his wings tremble, and she reaches out over his shoulder to touch them.

For a moment they stand in the hall as if on the edge of the castle tower.

Then she pulls back her hand. (Boss is coming, and they don't dare be seen, and by morning they'll be on the road and have to leave this behind; it's the nature of the business.)

She walks alone up to the attic, and Alec stands and waits for Boss and the others bringing in the harvest.

What Panadrome does not see: notes moving quietly forward, into the end.

What no one sees:

Alec emerging from the forest as the clouds thin across the moon, and light flickers off his wings like a signal beacon across the hills to the city.

Little George is on the deep-night watch; he's the one who comes running inside.

"They're coming!" he shouts.

The house riots.

The crew knock each other awake and scramble. The Grimaldi Brothers drop through the hole in their floor.

It takes less than five minutes for the Circus to run, when it has to. They've made an art of vanishing when the takings go cold.

Panadrome has nothing to gather, but still he cannot leave.

He's standing beside the piano when Elena finds him.

"We can't leave it," he says. "Not for them."

"Burn it yourself, then," says Elena.

She's holding a match; her voice is the kindest it's ever been.

"What?" he says. "No."

"Better you than them," she says. "A funeral or a butchering."

He looks at her. His face has turned to stone.

"It might be the last one," he says. His mouth is dry, somehow. "The very last."

She looks him in the eye. She says, "I know."

She rests it in the plate of his palm, vanishes.

He closes his eyes, feeling the piano behind him as though it's moving closer, swallowing him.

Then he opens them, and Boss fills his vision.

(Every time he looks at her is a little like that first time; waking, and knowing he is bound.)

"We can take it with us," he says. "Please. Ayar can carry it."

"No time to be careful," she says. "No spare fuel to carry it."

Panadrome feels his body is falling to pieces.

"But look at it!"

There are tears in her eyes.

"They're coming," Boss says. "We have to go."

But she doesn't move.

Even Elena has turned in the doorway to watch, Elena who has never waited.

He looks at the piano as if he could lay hands on it and bring it to life.

Far away come the familiar sounds of a mob.

In another lifetime, someone might come to this house to take refuge from the winter. They might find the piano, and kneel, and play.

But someone is coming now, axe in hand and looking for kindling, and they might not even take the blanket off before they start their work.

Boss hasn't moved. He realizes this is the illusion of choice; Boss has given her order.

(He doesn't look at Elena. She gave him the match; there is no question what she would do at the castle precipice, on the verge of being found out.)

When he strikes the match against his palm, his silver fingers do not tremble; he does not feel the fire.

The whole house has caught by the time the last truck is on the road.

Panadrome looks out the grimy window as the fire snakes the ivy, races across the rafters.

He imagines he can see the piano through a gaping window, long past the point he knows it's gone.

(He ran as soon as he dropped the match inside, and the fire caught. Some things he can, barely, stand; the sound of piano wires snapping is not one.)

Boss sits beside him without speaking.

In their view, the house turns into a hearth, into a lit match, into nothing.

They pass the thin, pale lamp of some other city, far away, but Boss doesn't give the signal, and so no one turns. The trucks rattle over the rocky ground.

It's almost a metronome, he thinks as if from some other life; phantom oranges rest in the upturned nests of his palms as he presses his fingers to the keys as long as he can before they fall.

Finally they escape the very last of the city light, and there's nothing left but the sky, silent and cold and spotted with stars.

(Panadrome hasn't missed the stars; he's not an adventurer, by nature.)

"Stop," says Boss, and the Circus stops.

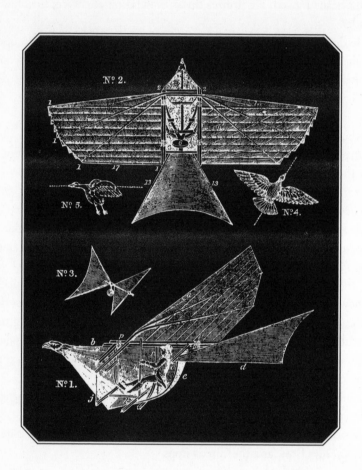

Beside Calais

Samantha Henderson

THE HILLS THAT bordered the École Aéronautique were covered in long grass, and as they dipped to the sea the blades dispersed through the tawny sand, which in turn fingered out into gray water. The foliage that covered the slopes was still bright with new growth. Three or four hundred meters away, a small flock of éoles grazed. They were among the smallest of the flying beasts, but each was at least the size of a full-grown bull, and the green grass was stripped when they fed.

Claire halted clumsily beside him. It seemed to him every step she took was an invitation to crumple, and he feared she would lose her footing and tumble over the drop-off. Ian Chance fought the urge to slip a hand under her elbow to steady her.

General Adair was right. The éoles would have to go. Yet Ian smiled as he watched them; an éole was the first flying beast he had broken by his own hand and flown over the neat russet-and-green rectangles of his father's farm in Lancashire, and he had a fondness for the breed.

Some hopped from bush to hillock, arching the wide stretch of their batlike wings to catch the breeze. Ian could hear the gentle chug of the éoles' engines, and behind that the constant sough of the water. Spring was warming into summer, and the nascent heat in the breeze reminded him of the Saharan winter, although so near the sea the air was not as dry.

Thready white steam rose over the flock, forming white puffs that glowed crisp against the blue sky. Save for the steam, the sky was cloudless: the smooth, even cerulean of a medieval painting. If he squinted against the light reflecting off the waters of the Channel, Ian could see the white rise that was Dover.

That last time he had been to England, London was still in mourning for Queen Victoria. He remembered a length of tattered black ribbon tied high on a lamppost, fluttering in the breeze. At the time he had wondered if the same breeze traveled the Channel that season to hold the flying beasts aloft in their migration north.

This morning, when he'd seen Claire waiting for him outside the old dormitories at the flying school beside Calais, a bright splash of checkered red against the gray, weathered wood, he'd felt shy, and delighted too. To see her again brought back a familiar warmth in his belly, a memory of days where the breeze blew warm or cool according to the season until it became a thing of the bones and the body grew attuned to the fine sea spray or yeasty pollen that the wind carried and offered, constantly.

Ian lived by the wind then, breaking in the hardy little éoles until the once-wild creatures could be flown in intricate formation. He tamed the calm, aloof dunne monos until they'd take decomposed iron from his hand. At night he and Claire would curl around each other under her duvet in the women's quarters; she rated her own room in part because those in command of the Air Corps decided, in their lopsided way, that she outranked the nurses. No one disputed her right: Claire rose long before dawn broke, to catch the chance of seeing a blériot over the Channel as the sun rose, and the nurses needed their sleep. Besides, her family had owned the land before her drunken grandfather, broke from trying to harness wild éoles to harsher work than they were formed for, sold it to a government seeking a place to make use of the flying beasts that ranged this coast time out of mind.

She stood straight as she watched for him outside the dormitory, and for a moment he allowed himself to think it wouldn't be so bad, that the reports of her injuries were exaggerated and that she had recovered. He was out of the car the Corps Aéronautique had sent before Plantard, a sunburned boy that looked barely old enough to drive, could open the door. Then she moved. Her limbs twisted painfully and her shoulders humped, and she dragged one foot behind her. He felt disappointment like a blow to the stomach and then the slow burn of contempt at his own cowardice.

She didn't show him that she saw it, unless it was in the amused curve of her lips when he bent to embrace her.

"Plantard will take your bags to quarters," she whispered, nodded at the boy. "Come with me to the cliffs."

One of the éoles reared on its back wheel at their approach, spreading its ungraceful wings and spinning its propeller: a dominant male, getting their scent. The flock stopped grazing for a second, and the low hum of their engines quickened as they readied for the signal to take off. When the male remained in place they relaxed and returned to pulling at the green foliage, hungry from their long postwinter flight from Africa. He wondered how the tang of leftover winter felt on their sand-scored wings. If he could walk among them, could he smell the baked-bread smell of the Egyptian air on their leathers? Would he find the compass shape of the Bat d'Af brand beneath the strut of a mount gone feral?

General Adair's orders went 'round and 'round in Ian's head like a cylinder recording.

"If a breeding program's to work, Chance, we'll need all the local resources," the General had said. "That means the feral flocks will have to be diverted—or culled. You'll need to make that happen before we ship the stock in."

Ian knew the little éoles had no place in the Corps' breeding program, based as it was on the calm, sturdy dunne monos and the powerful wright flyers—the American pair of Roosevelt-bred flying beasts Taft had sent as a gift to Whitehall.

"There might be room for an avion or two," Ian replied. "They're quick and clever—look much like the éoles but sturdier."

Adair had flashed him a look. The North African sun had burnt the Frenchman's skin until he was ruddy even in the cool of the evening. In his time he'd flown dunne monos and antoinettes, back when one did so at the risk of seeming eccentric, before the military knew what do with the Air Corps. Now war loomed with Germany and Italy, and the old corpsman was recalled to make a war machine out of men and flying beasts.

"I'll leave it to you," he told Ian. "None of our people knows what we'll need on the African lines, and you've stewed in Algiers long enough so you're not so offensively English. Your only weakness is sentimentality. The éoles must go. And the blériot, any that remain. They are intractable, unpredictable."

Four years since Claire had netted a rogue blériot and ridden it over the shore of Calais; four years since it tumbled her onto the rocks.

"Wakeman will meet you at the school."

Adair's voice brought him back to himself: he'd been looking at the horizon, when the setting sun bled across the desert sands, but seeing the gray sea of the channel.

"Wakeman?"

He'd met the hunter once in Egypt; they'd never met in England, although both were bred in Lancashire. He remembered a man tanned brown where Adair was burnt, almost past middle age but with a predator's lean body and a killer's blue eye.

"The British are sending him to help with the culling." Adair's tone defied him to object. Ian shrugged. The General was right: the wrights and dunnes would need the grazing.

"He'll never get that blériot, though," he muttered under his breath.

It had taken three weeks for Claire to trap the blériot, setting wire snares in the low foliage that rimmed the northeast cliffs between the school and Boulonge-sur-Mer. One morning, with the low clouds beating a constant, needle-spray mist against the tents and cottage of the camp, they spotted something thrashing in the distance and Claire ran across the hillocks to it, hair unbound across her shoulders and sodden in the drizzle. Ian followed after and heard her laugh before he saw they'd caught a young avion, half adult size, its twin propellers buzzing indignantly as it jerked against the wire, bouncing up and down in the gray bushes.

Claire freed its forewheel from the wire with a few practiced flicks of her wrist and steadied its wing until it was able to take off across the dull flat water, the whirr of its engine scolding them until it faded in the distance. She watched it fondly, looping the trap wire between her fingers absently before bending to reset it, the wire high enough to snare the wheels but too low to foul or snap the struts.

"You do love them," he told her, watching the back of her drizzle-wet head as she adjusted the wire, and she cocked her head sideways, not looking at him but listening, always listening, as if not only English but any human speech was foreign to her, and took a fraction of a second to understand.

"Tomorrow I'll set it somewhere else," she said, as if he had not spoken. "He's not coming back here."

But she was wrong, because midafternoon, when the clouds had burned off and the fresh-broke avions had just been penned, there was a shout and a stableboy ran to the ramps, waving his cap wildly, looking for Mam'selle. They ran together to the site, and Claire laughed out loud at the sight of the beast bucking against the ropes, the beautiful curve of its graceful wings, so simple and functional compared to the bat-winged éoles and avions, its powerful engine buzzing furiously.

She didn't intend to ride it—not even Claire was that foolhardy. She only meant to mount it for a minute or so, to get the creature used to her weight. The boys had sunk the stakes deep on either side of the great taut, silken wings, and the ropes should have held. She approached it cautiously, clucking in the way one clucks instinctively at a skittish horse, one arm upraised to protect her face.

"Be careful, Claire," he called. She waved a hand at him without turning around. It leaned away from her as far as the ropes would allow.

Claire patted the blériot's quivering side for a long time, speaking to it in the low calming monotone she always used with the half-broke flying beasts. The angry buzz quieted. She closed her hand around the struts, then released them, then grasped them again, until the blériot no longer flinched when she did so.

Finally she took a firm grip and slung herself into the rigging. The blériot lurched forward instantly, threatening to tumble tail over propeller, but the ropes held and Claire rode out each buck with a casual roll backward and the ease of long experience.

Ian realized he'd been biting the inside of his cheek with the tension. Gingerly he tongued the raw spot and wished Claire would come back.

"That's enough for now," he called, and she turned to him and seemed about to shout out, perhaps to bring her another length of rope. Then, with a powerful lurch, the creature pulled half the stakes out of wet ground soaked by several mornings' worth of rain. Claire hung on desperately as the beast rocked the other way, dislodging the remainder of the stakes.

Ian ran, the wet grass lashing at his ankles. The flying beast heaved its body off the ground, and, unaccustomed to a human's weight, came to ground again, its wheels gouging the muddy soil. The great wings flexed, the engine hummed, and it rose again, wavering and heavy-bodied as a summer beetle. The lowermost struts were even with Ian's face by the time he reached it and it was gaining altitude. Claire was stretched facedown in the structure, and he caught a glimpse of her gray eyes, wide with alarm. Desperate, he reached and leaped, catching hold of a muddy wheel with both hands.

The blériot lurched closer to the cliff and dipped sharply down, cumbered with their combined weight.

"Let go!" Claire shouted. "It's too much—it's going to crash!"

Stubbornly he held on to the slippery wheel, his fingers cramping. He felt his toes drag against the ground. The blériot managed to lift, wavering over the edge of the cliff, and Ian had a brief, dizzying view of rock and white seafoam.

"Damn you, let go!" Claire barked.

The beast tipped back over solid ground and dipped again. Ian's hands were a red blaze of pain.

It was going to crash. He would have to trust that Claire could control it. Gritting his teeth, he forced his cramped fingers open and fell, rolling on the sodden ground with an impact that drove the air from his lungs.

Free of his weight, the blériot rose again, heading for the sea. Ian rolled to his belly and watched, breathing painfully. For a few seconds the flying beast straightened and flew sure toward the horizon. Then one wing dipped and sideslipped.

Ian watched with impotent horror while a gray shape separated from the body of the blériot, suspended an impossible few seconds clinging to a wing, and then as the creature tipped dangerously, sidewise fell, plunging feet first, arms outstretched, to the rocks below. The curve of Claire's body as she fell seemed to have a control, an intent to it, as if she saw what was beneath her and was calculating how best to angle her limbs. Her silk scarf rippled up as the rest of her plummeted like Icarus. The blériot above her slipped sideways, descending as if it could scoop her out of the air.

Although he never took his eyes off her, Ian never remembered seeing the moment of impact, only that one instant she was falling and the next she was sprawled on the black wet boulders semisubmerged in the tide, legs trailing in the black water like a mermaid's tail.

"Is the avion with the flock?"

Claire's voice had graveled with the years, and although her English was sure as it was before, her accent was stronger. Maybe no one spoke English to her after he left. Her English was better than his French, so that's what they spoke, during the day and during the night.

Ian glanced at Claire's profile: all horizontal lines—sun-bleached wheaten hair pushed aside by the insistent breeze and squint lines carved at the corner of her eye as she stared at the flock she must have seen a hundred times. Since the accident the strong planes of her face had softened, and the skin of her neck was loose. Ian wondered if he would notice it as much had he not been a coward, if he had stayed as she had stayed.

He looked back at the flying beasts, peering beneath his palm, and yes, there in the middle, rooting with the rest, an avion. Its bat-wings arched over its fellows and it bore a double propeller, but it didn't seem interested in contending with the éole male for dominance.

"The others don't mind?" he asked.

"No. He's been flying with them for years."

"Perhaps he's lonely." Avions, never the most numerous of the flying beasts, were almost extinct in the wild.

"Perhaps."

From that fall they thought she would die, and even the unsentimental Corps Aéronautique considered it cruel to take her away from her grandfather's land and the flying beasts she loved. But she survived and healed, even if she healed crooked. She lived at the École Aéronautique as a patient and then a ground instructor, teaching boys like Eugène Plantard to fly and die and find glory on the shores of Europe and the sands of the Empty Quarter.

In a world of automobiles and great ships few had use for the flying beasts, and for a time the École was all but abandoned. There was Claire, and the skeleton staff, and a couple of private students. But war was looming and soon it would teem with trainee flyboys, and Corps staff, and flying beasts. Not caught and broke from the wild flocks but bred for war, as the Italians and Germans were breeding the taube beasts with their dovelike, agile wings to carry more and move faster.

The locals should be happy with the business the work of the Corps would bring. The mines were failing and fewer rich tourists came. The burgeoning war would be profitable, and no one had to think yet of the death from the sky that a race of flying beasts bred for war would bring.

Four years since he had fled her to Memphis, to Gazuul and farther south, where the flying beasts bred huge and wild and he caught and broke them for rich men, for the Corps Aéronautique, and for His Majesty's Airborne Calvary. Craven, he had never come back until now.

He told himself it was because he didn't want to see the woman he loved for her strength and her dexterity live crippled, but it was a lie. It was because most who fell as Claire had fallen died, and death was a gentle sleep. But Claire was living testimony to what could be done to the fragile construct of sinew, skin, and bone that made a human.

In his memory, Claire ran along the side of the wooden training pen, poised to grasp the underwing struts of an éole, the tight cling of her habitual leathers showing the flex of limb and muscle. Now she halted along, and what was hidden beneath her checked skirt was mortal and twisted. He found grotesque possibilities of Claire's veiled flesh obscene, and hated himself for it.

Now Claire stumbled and recovered before he could embarrass them both by catching at her. Ian felt a flare of anger, which shamed him because it's shameful to be annoyed at the cripple exhibiting, like a statue holding stone fruit to the sun, this is how frail your body is, all children of men. You are brave and beset with the need to soar, and it means nothing to the wind that topples you and the air that parts beneath you and the ground that will take you as no lover has.

"I know why you're here," Claire said, still staring at the avion. "We've heard rumors about a breeding program for months. Flyboys passing through, repeating gossip. I didn't think it was true, though. I didn't think you'd agree to it. Not until I saw you this morning, with your fancy Corps automobile."

He listened for the mocking tone to her voice that meant she was angry with him, but she only sounded resigned.

"It's not a matter of my agreeing to it, Claire," he said, shoving his hands into the pockets of his too-warm greatcoat to stop himself from taking her arm. "It will happen whether we will it or not. And neither your people nor mine have much choice. You've haven't seen the Roosevelt wrights yet...."

"Obviously." Her voice went tart and the band across his chest loosened a little.

"...but you will, soon. Theodore Roosevelt's breeding program's been in effect for what—ten, twelve years? They've been tapping their wild herds for the best and they have three lines now, and they're stocking their Air Corps 80, maybe 90 percent with them. Huge beasts, with endurance ours can't match, and docile too."

"Docile."

She began to laugh and was turning to him when she gasped. He seized her arm, thinking her leg had finally given way. Effortlessly she shook him off and hobbled ahead. Ian stood frozen. Over the water came a vast stretch of curved wing and an assembly of cables, flying strong and sure: a blériot, fresh from across the channel. It crested the lip of the cliff-side, circled, and landed with insolent ease, not thirty meters away.

The éoles started and beat themselves into the air like a scurry of huge gulls, their engines chugging and throwing off steam. The avion took off, flying slow and low to the ground, in search of more berries.

Shaking off Ian's arm, Claire stumbled toward the blériot while Ian stood frozen. The flying beast's motor purred and impossibly, it remained still until she reached it. Claire, chuckling with delight, stroked the side of a parchment panel. Watching her bend her once-bright head to the beast, Ian felt his pulse quicken painfully.

It couldn't be the same one. It couldn't.

Later that night, after he had a pipe by the fire and read through the Corps dispatches one more time, he went to her bed. She was in the same room, and even the pattern of nicks in the paint on the door were familiar to his touch. Under her old quilt she lay to one side, so there was room for him to slip between the cool sheets. She made no move, either to welcome or repel him. Rough muslin covered the window imperfectly, letting moonlight drape across the coverlet; she blinked at him curiously.

"How often does it come to you? The blériot?"

Claire turned on her back; in the dim light he could see her chest rise and fall.

"Not for months sometimes. Sometimes only once a year, in the spring."

"It knows you. I know it's not possible, but it knows you."

She sighed.

"Do you know the name Wakeman?"

Her breathing hitched. "I have heard it. He is a great man, I hear. A hunter of repute."

"He should be here tomorrow or the next day. The Corps is borrowing him from the British. He's to clear the wild stock from the forage, if they can't be driven away."

She didn't answer for a long time, and he thought she might have fallen asleep.

"I knew the world wouldn't ignore us forever," she said at last. "There was a time, when we were young, that I resented it. Being dismissed. Now…you get used to it, and find your peace with it. And all this time we've been sleeping on the edge of a precipice, the waters churning below, and only a matter of time before we go down into it. Peace is mere skin over war's true face.

"And the flying beasts—there's no more room for the wild ones in this world. Soon there won't be an éole or an antoinette alive that isn't tame, bred, or broke to our need. Soon we'll forget that they ever ran free. We'll think we've always bred them. Men will believe they built them."

When he spoke he was surprised at the anger in his voice.

"You fell. How could you fall? You were the best. You were perfect."

Her voice was deliberately cool. "Such things happen."

"Not to you. Not unless you allow it. And you did allow it. I didn't realize it at first, though something in me recognized it."

"What do you mean?"

Ian drew a deep breath. "If you'd stayed in the struts, the blériot would've crashed, but it would've broken your fall. You let go. You let go so it wouldn't go down."

"You can't think that."

"I know that. I know you, Claire. And maybe better after I left."

She laughed softly. "Did it make you so angry, then?"

"Yes. That you could chose between us. That you could break your body so."

"Hundreds break in this work. Hundreds more, man and flying beast, will break before this is over."

"Yes. But not you. It should never have been you."

Her hand found his and they lay there, without speaking, for a long time until her fingers loosened in his and she slept. The moon had set before Ian, listening to her even breathing and the distant tide, turned to the cool of his pillow and slept too.

One by one the éoles rose and lighted again a few hundred meters away, barely interrupting their feeding. The children laughed, waving shirts and sheets they'd likely stolen off their mothers' clotheslines. A dog loped from child to child, a big golden retriever, pausing now and then to bark at the flying beasts. The éoles paid it less mind than they had the children, waving their clothing like the pennants of an improbable army.

"That's never going to clear them," said Wakeman.

The hunter had arrived that morning, accompanied by a small case of personal effects and two long, lovingly polished trunks of dark wood containing his weapons. Ian was discomposed as it was; he had slept far later than he was accustomed, to find sunlight dappling through the curtains and Claire's side of the bed empty and cold. Entering the cafeteria he found a scant few tardy students and young Plantard escorting the expressionless Englishman, and no sign of Claire anywhere. Ian barely nodded at his countryman, leaving him to find his own place while he went to the cluster of stone cottages that marked where the grounds of the École gave way to farmland.

He didn't know these children—the ones who had brought butter and eggs to the École years before were now probably hard-faced farmers. Maybe some labored in the failing mines. But if the cheerfully dirty, towheaded kids didn't know him they knew the École Aéronautique, and they whooped at the prospect of earning a few sous chasing away the beasts from the grazing.

But Wakeman was right: the éoles and the avion had long lost their fear of men.

"No time like the present," said Wakeman, turning on his heel toward the dormitories. "I heard that blériot was spotted off the coast at dawn. That's where your chatelaine's got to. Queer woman, that. Looks right through one."

Ian didn't reply, fingering a pocketful of coins warm from his body as he watched the children forgo all pretense at chasing away the beasts and start playing at bullfighting between them.

"I hear you and mam'selle have a history," Wakeman threw over his shoulder. "Will that get in my way?"

Ian shook his head, not caring if the hunter saw.

Wakeman was right: the blériot was back, perched before the place where the cliff fell away. Claire stood apart, leaning on her cane as he hadn't seen her do before. The sea beyond was shrouded with the last of the morning fog, rapidly burning away. Wakeman, carrying a large shotgun, had almost reached her. The hunter kept her body between him and the blériot, as if using her as a blind.

Wakeman nodded at him. Claire didn't stir or look at Ian when he stood beside her.

"Claire," he said. "Go back. You don't want to see this."

Wakeman moved from behind her.

"That's never a full-blood blériot," he muttered, chambering a round. "Too big. Quarter antoinette, at the least."

Even a twisted thing can move quickly, and Claire moved quicker than thought, bringing her cane down one-handed on the barrel of the gun. The shot tore into the ground three meters in front of them, tearing the new green grass away from the earth and plowing a furrow into the flesh of the earth. The blériot hopped, startled, toward the lip of the precipice. At the drop-off it paused, and rotated toward them.

"Go, you stupid thing!" shouted Claire, struggling to regain her balance. Wakeman, jolted back by blow and unexpected angle of the discharge, swore colorfully and opened the chamber.

"Muzzle your bitch, Chance," he barked, eyeballing the distance to the flying beast that was, inexplicably, still within range. Claire stood, sobbing. Before Ian could hook an arm around her waist she struck again with the cane, two-handed this time, striking Wakeman hard in the solar plexus.

The hunter's breath left him with a great foosh and he sat on the ground, still holding his gun, legs stretched before him in the high grass. Claire drew back and held the burled cane high in the air, as if to bring it down on Wakeman's head. He looked up at her quizzically, struggling to draw breath, without the presence of mind to swivel the muzzle of the weapon toward her.

But he would, any second. Ian grasped Claire's arm.

"Claire," he said. "No."

She looked at him, eyes wild and streaming. Then with a stifled sob she pulled away and threw down the cane, across Wakeman's legs. The hunter flinched and struggled to his feet. Claire had turned from both of them, and halted across the grass toward the blériot that still paused at the edge, its engine humming like a swarm of agitated bees in the warm air. Ian followed a few steps and stopped, knowing she didn't want him.

He could hear Wakeman breathing heavily behind him. Turning, he saw the hunter sighting down the barrel, aiming square at Claire's back.

Ian moved between them, looking not at Wakeman but at the twin holes of the barrel as if he could stare them down. "You will not," he growled.

"Not that I don't want to," said the hunter, never lowering the barrel, "but I'm waiting for a shot at the beast. She's right in front."

Ian strode into the barrel and grasped the cold metal, shoving the gun down, and watched as Claire stood before the blériot. Shyly, as if she had never touched it before, she reached out to pat the taut material of the wing that curved over her. The beast quivered but stayed put, and her hand moved over the tight silk, down a strut, following the thick rib to the body of the blériot. Never taking her hand away, she moved closer, dragging her damaged leg behind her. When her shoulder touched the main body of the blériot, she felt along the structure, fumbling where years ago she had grasped with confidence. Then, as the beast didn't move, she seemed to find her old strength and lifted herself into the beast's undercarriage.

Suddenly Wakeman twisted the gun out of Ian's grip. Ian swore and tried to follow, but the hunter moved fast, pulling away from Ian's reach, and as Claire and the blériot tipped over the cliff the shotgun blast tore a hole through the animal's left wing, punching a fist-sized hole through the silk, leaving raw edges to flutter in the wind.

The flying beast tipped dangerously to the right, so far out of true it seemed that it must stall and tumble to the sea below. Ian knew that in the under-carriage Claire must be fighting to shift her weight and help the blériot balance. A terrible fear seized him then, that Claire would do as she had before, cast herself free of the beast that it might fly free of her.

She wouldn't be so lucky this time. If you could call it luck.

Ian heard the click of another shell in the gun and turned on Wakeman. The hunter's face looked impassive but his jaw was clenched tight and the veins stood out in the sunburned neck.

"Try it and I'll have you down for murder," said Ian. "And I'll let the flyboys at you first."

Wakeman squinted at the horizon. "Sometimes the wounded will come back to land. Out here it's got nowhere else to go."

By degrees the blériot leveled out, finding a way to balance the torn wing and the whole. It made no move to circle back to the coast, flying straight across the Channel. Ian stared after it until it became a pale dot, and then winked out, beyond his eyesight, beyond his ken, taking Claire with it.

Patrols flew until dusk, looking for any sign of the wreckage. One pair even went as far as Boulonge-sur-Mer, on the off chance that the blériot and its passenger had made it so far. Stations and lighthouses far down the coast, and across the water at Dover too, were alerted. There was no trace, no report.

The next day they started slaughtering the éoles. Ian stayed at the École Aéronautique, supervising the rebuilding of the pens where the wright flyers would stable. Occasionally a shot would crack the freshening air like a whip.

At noon he went to see. As he approached the slopes where the flocks had clustered, he heard a thin, high, tearing sound, like a teakettle left to boil. Wakeman was standing by the avion that was crumpled in the grass. A few remaining éoles bleated behind it, chugging goats of steam in their distress, too confused to fly away. One of the avion's bat-wings was half torn away and thread of steam jetted from its damaged thorax. Calmly, Wakeman chambered a cartridge and aimed just behind the fuselage. The rifle cracked, and the agonized whistle stopped abruptly.

On the hills behind Ian could see a small cluster of farm children, their dog with them, standing very still. It seemed impossible that they were the same brats who ran between the bat-winged éoles yesterday, waving their clean, tattered blouses.

He couldn't watch the rest. More shots rang out through the afternoon, and as the sun began to set he spotted one éole flying out to sea, framed against the bloody sun.

Ian stayed at the École Aéronautique long enough to see the breeding pair of wrights fly in, their tiered wings shining white in the sun. That night, in Claire's room, he packed and repacked his few possessions, bound back for Algiers at first light. Adair would be furious; Ian didn't care. Plantard came to tell him the car would be ready at first light.

Ian asked if the wrights had settled.

"Yes," said the boy. "Ate their fill and roosted. I've never seen an American beast. They're magnificent."

He eyed Ian as he took a pair of trousers from the pile in his suitcase and refolded them, pinching the already sharp seams sharper.

"I want you to know, sir, me and some of the other flyboys—well, we're not going to stop. Looking for her, I mean. Every day at sunrise, part of the morning exercises. We're taking turns at it. I mean, you never know what will show up, do you?"

"You won't find her," said Ian.

"Even so." The boy's voice was defiant.

"She won't let you find her. She might let you see it, sometimes. To make us remember they were wild beasts once, and never made, whatever lies we tell ourselves. But keep looking, by all means."

"You're not coming back, are you, sir?"

There was pity in the flyboy's voice, and compassion, and a little bit of contempt.

Ian's hands stilled and he stared at the rough plaster wall. "No, Plantard. I don't see it."

Plantard was silent as he drove Ian over the rough roads to Calais. They wouldn't remain in disrepair long—as the wrights bred and the École Aéronautique grew, as war quickened between nations they would be rebuilt smooth and straight into the heart of the countryside, tamed like the flying beasts. In the meantime the car rose and fell, rose and fell with the broken pavement and he caught brief glimpses of the gray sea and sky. Once he saw what might be a blériot rising over the waves, but it was probably a gull, hunting for fish in the cold sea.

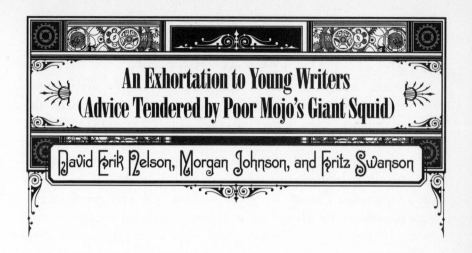

An Exhortation to Young Writers
(Advice Tendered by Poor Mojo's Giant Squid)

David Erik Nelson, Morgan Johnson, and Fritz Swanson

DEAREST SCRIBBLERS AND Scribblerixes,

I ask that my students and clients please pardon the dearth of prefatory pleasantries in this, my brief missive, but I fear that time is not in overabundance: I have just now had the good fortune to lay hold of this hand-crank cellular telephone carelessly left over-near my temporary confines here, and have but a brief moment to text unto you-all my "OMFG"-worthy predicament, for I find myself held prisoner within the extensive bowels of what I am beginning to be made to suspect may be the main (or possibly prime subsidiary) offices of the Fiction-Writing Directorate—a sort of penal colony *cum* re-education camp for the dedicated writers of Diverting, if Dis-truthful, Fancies.

GASP!

Indeed! Lower your shockéd and supercilious brows, Gentle Readers, for it is true: I am held here against my will, all due to what I have begun to suspect are the sinister machinations of the American Meteorological Society, in conjunction with the Target Corporation.

To abridge what might otherwise be an oppressively complex tale: Some months past I received a certified letter reminding me of an obligation I had made to George Dayton (founder of Target Corporation) in 1906, on the occasion of the celebration of the nuptials of his eldest son, David, and a distant cousin of mine, Beatrix—an invitation I had intended to decline, until I had discovered that I would already be in the vicinity on other business, and that a four-course dinner would be served with open bar (I was not always the well-to-do cephalopod you know and love today, Dear Readers).

In the end, I was so charmed by the ceremony—not to mention the sight of Beatrix's many silk-and-tulle-wrapped arms and tentacles arcing up out of the black and depthless waters of the Portsmouth Mine Pit to grip David's puny human paws in deathless and dreamless matrimony, a sight whose inherent beauty was only amplified by the 72 mint juleps I had already imbibed that afternoon—that I inadvertently agreed to aid in the promotion of the groom's father's burgeoning discount dry-goods business. The next morning, as I nursed my swollen and aching headsac, it dawned upon me that Dayton may have mistaken me for a more famous relation of mine—having seen snapshots from the event (to which I had chosen to wear the new copper-and-iron surface-walking suit that I had come to that municipality to fetch), I must confess that I did cut a handsome mien: The westering sun gleaming on my suit's crystalline dome and brass pressure-fittings, the gouts of steam and smoke billowing from my dual-exhaust ports, the scythe-ish curves and gleaming serrations of the primary-manipulator claws—it was far from shocking that a noted Midwestern businessman might have mistook me for a Deathless Dreamer with deep pockets and noted leverage in local and state government.

In any event, I had presumed that the dissolution of this marriage four years later relieved me of my obligations to George Dayton and the corporate entity that ultimately inherited his personhood, soul, and vast, mechanized subterranean estate following Dayton's exeunt from this material plane in 1938. Sadly, my lawyers inform me that I was mistaken. And so—despite a busy schedule, which included writing and revising my weekly advice column, among other personal and professional obligations—I found myself hanging in a blue and cloudless sky, ensconced in my finest mechanical velocitating suit, dangling below a red-and-white montgolfière and above the scintillant waters of our own Detroit River, so that promotional "B-roll" might be shot for some upcoming commercial advertisements to be televised during a much ballyhooed event in which grown men of mixed race fight for the skin of a pig in order that one might rise to the rank of President of these as-of-yet-still United States.

Then, without warning and despite assurances to the contrary by both the National Weather Service and the National Oceanic and Atmospheric Administration, violent thunderheads rolled in from the suburbs, blotting out the sun, and whipping me and my lighter-than-aircraft first out of frame, and then entirely out of the region.

I was buffeted and beaten by the savage winds, draggéd through the peaks of uncooperative pines, harrowed by scavangerous birds, and ultimately suffered a precipitous descent after a clutch of nefarious robins loosed and absconded with a large portion of the stitching securing the deflation port of my balloon's envelope. Fortunately, my acceleration was retarded when the sagging silk snagged upon the spire of a great, sooty, jackstraw building. *Perhaps some disused factory or abandoned Rust-Belt fortification?* was my brief thought as I considered the gothic architectural flourishes and occluded crenellations—that is, prior to my velocitating suit swinging forcefully into the edifice's rough-hewn brick walls, at which time I lost all sense for an undetermined period.

When I awoke I found myself here, presumably within the great and terrible confines of that building, rudely stripped of my modern (and quite comfort-able) land-walking velocitating suit, and deposited in a tiled tank—perhaps a mid-sized swimming pool, or a bathtub formerly tenanted by William Howard Taft (who, as I recall, was likewise a cousin of Beatrix, but not mine—although I can no longer claim to recollect the tortuous genealogical arabesque which made such a case possible).

In the intervening hours between that wakening and now, all manner of displeasantry has befallen me: A strange little dwarf of a man, Gustav, has stared at me for long hours, often making notes, and generally refusing to an-swer questions with anything other than a derisive *tsk* or *tut*; on two occasions he has been joined by bun-haired Ethelie, whose insistence that they "shall see good work of you, yet—or in the least, good canapés" is precisely as disturb-ing as one might suppose—although significantly less disturbing than the fre-quent visits by Lida, who sits upon the edge of my tiled temporary tank, gently stroking my left hunting tentacle and insisting that "this shall all be sorted out sooner than you'd expect." Obviously, Lida's visits are not disturbing in and of themselves, but are made so owing to the presence of the janitor Boggins, who stands in the doorway, his hands toiling within his trouser pockets in a most distressing fashion as his greasy eyes caress my visible convexities (the tank be-ing somewhat shallow for one of my, *ahem*, girth).

And all of this is the more frustrating because I do, as a very important cephalopod, indeed have very important business to be about, such as my much-celebrated advice column.

So then, my advice for you this week is to consider the following: What commitments—real or imagined—keep you confined, and prevent you from returning to your prime and true work, that of writing That Very Special Thing Which You and You Alone Must Compose?

> In this Predicament I Remain,
> *Your Giant Squid*
> Advice Columnist
> & Literary Advisor

My Dearest Typistas and Quilleros,

I fear matters have, for me, become substantially more grim in the intervening week. Specifically, despite Lida's insistence that we shall soon sort out my implicit confinement here within the strange towers of the Fiction-Writing Directorate, I seem to have, in the meantime, dug my own grave—or, essentially no different, garnished my own serving platter.

Yesterday I submitted to a mid-afternoon interview with Ethelie and Gustav, the latter clutching yet a new and even more be-paperéd clip board. Gustav was especially particular in elucidating, in great and terrifying detail, the increasing debts I incur as they quarter me here.

Gustav further made clear that my vast writing credentials and experience in project management of both supergun and weather-control programs (leaving aside my brief, noncontiguous stints as President of These United States and frontsquid of a glamorous rock-whilst-rolling minstrel's band) earn me little formal recognition among the upper management and investors of the Directorate, in terms of gainful employment.

Ethelie then indicated that, having analyzed their staffing needs, the Directorate currently has only two open posts: a) a French translator (by which I took her to mean one who could translate from French to English, the *lingua non-franca* of the Directorate itself, rather than a generic translator who is of French extraction) or b) a source of valuable and tasty protein for the cafeteria buffet.

As it would happen, prior to spending four days and three nights in Quebec City several years past, I was briefly tutored in this tongue by one of the many startlingly violent, somewhat nefarious, but otherwise basically agreeable francophonic chimps who serve as my paid executive assistants. As such, I elected to interview for the former position—yes, I was less qualified for it, but it was nonetheless more desirable, as it started at a higher wage, included a matching 401k fund, and did not result in my immediate death and dismemberment.

Madam Ethelie quickly rattled off a looping, staccato chain of French declarations trailing a single lilting interrogative. In response, I deployed the first French phrase that came to my razorish beak—and, incidentally, the only French phrase I know *not* directly related to procuring food or drink, booking passage by freight train, or complaining about the qualities of bed-and-breakfast accommodations. I was, at that time, under the impression that the phrase served in somewhat the same capacity as "And a many and fine good day to you, sir or madame":

"Va pèter dans le trèfle, maudite fausse-couche!"

Had a Victrola jukebox been playing at that moment, its needle would have noisily scraped free of the record, and in the ensuing silence crickets would have sung but briefly, then stopped. Gustav's jaw dropped, and Ethelie's glacial face began to calve, only to halt itself mid-collapse and petrify, her lips a line thin and sharp enough to slice a hard cheese. Even the janitor Boggins briefly paused in his trouser-pocket toils. Lida, sweet and well-meaning Lida, giggled, then covered her mouth to stifle the trickle, then guffawed.

Ethelie turned on her hobnailed heel and, stately as a cloud of mustard gas, left my room. Gustav made a single, authoritative tick on his papers, then followed. I was soon thereafter informed that I had been hired to serve in the cafeteria.

NOW, DEAR READERS AND WRITERS, I NOTE:

There is truth—often unintended truth—in the speech of our mouths, and although my Quebecois greeting held not the meaning I had intended, its Truth is beyond doubt. Today's exercise is this:

Quickly, and without undue pre-consideration, settle upon two characters whose goals are at crosscurrent: Perhaps you might imagine a car salesperson who desperately needs to sell an ill-used 1982 Chevrolet Chevette at a slightly exorbitant rate, despite the dismembered corpse concealed in the bay which ought to hold the Chevette's spare tire. His counterpart is, of course, a purchaser who is anxious to transport a soon-to-be-reanimated corpse, but whose bejeweled Lana Marks Cleopatra clutch *does not* contain funds sufficient to the demands of the lusty salesperson—although it does contain a gun, which lacks bullets, and which she would prefer not to reveal.

Write them into a dialogue in which all of the above is revealed, despite the speakers' best efforts at concealing these facts. Do not use the words "corpse" or "gun." That the corpses are siblings, and the buyer and seller likewise, may or may not come into play.

With Any Small Luck I Shall Remain,
Your Giant Squid
Advice Columnist
& Literary Advisor

My Dearest and Devoted Scribblerians and Writorios,

I text in haste and, I fear, without sufficient care, for I am exhausted: Today, I am to be transferred from the relative comforts of my tiled tank here in the Directorate's tower to either the primary or *sous*-kitchen, so that I might be butchered and yet live again, first as sashimi, then as handrolls, then as calamari, then as taco salad, then as "seafood medley," and finally as some abomination which Boggins reports Gustav has called "meatloaf surprise."

Thus, it should shock none that I suffered some measure of insomnia this past evening, passing the night in the company of Lida, who throughout the thin and gruesome hours stroked my tentacles and helped me dream of the life that we might have together, were I not destined for the chafing dish. Together we fantasized in great detail of our frontier life upon the prairies, she in her bonnet, me in my homespun, steam-powered velocitational suit, the bright and life-giving sun lending my brass fittings a warm glow as I cut the sod for our house, set the timbers for our barn, and dismembered the still quivering and lowing cows for our dinners. Meanwhile, Lida would spin us fine angora wool from our many angora cats, which we would then weave into angora nets, and use to scoop up the delicious angora children from the neighboring angora villages, so that she might school them in the finer points of general literacy, poetic license, and flower-identification and pressing, prior to my spit-roasting them and selling their meats to nearby encampments of zombie Confederate soldiers, gathered to repel the onslaught of clockwork Union infantrymen come to staunch the flow of our dear Bleeding Kansas.

But, Dear Readers, note that it is not the exhaustion of my long night of "could have beens" with Lida that makes my time so short this morning, for just moments ago my fair mistress and hostess excused herself to "powder the room." When I heard the door creak again, revealing creeping—and undeniably creepy—Mr. Boggins accompanied by none others than several members of the troupe of francophonic chimps long in my employ!

"I wired your monkeys," Boggins said simply. "They've got your walking suit tip-top and coming up to steam, and are prepared to haul it most of the way to you, then you the rest of the way to it."

"My Mr. Boggins!" I did exclaim. "Why, I am somewhat indebted to you, I imagine!"

"Yup," Boggins said simply. "I figure I'll let Ethelie and Gustav think that Lida let you slip away, and then find a way to get her out of the mess, and in the end she'll fall in love with me."

I must have looked dubious, for he then added, "There's still details to work on." I opened my beak—despite my best interests—intent on helping Mr. Boggins realize just how many details he might be hoping will sort themselves out when my chimp Claude tapped on the face of the fine chronometer strapped to his hirsute wrist, and I took his meaning: It was time for us to make our exeunt, with all due celerity.

And so it is I live to write another day.

As such, my dear reader-writers, I enjoin you: Take a moment, for a moment is all you have, to very gently explain to a very lovely confidant why you have abandoned her to her no-doubt complicated fate. Time yourself; pen for no more than seven minutes, revise for exactly three, and work ardently to leave her heart intact…now *WRITE! GO!*

I Remain to Opine Another Day,
Your Giant Squid
Advice Columnist
& Literary Advisor

A Handful of Rice

Vandana Singh

At last Vishnumitra saw the King.

The city was alive with beasts, mechanical and organic; there were elephants in the procession, stately and benign, draped with silk and brocade, bearing jeweled howdahs on their backs; then the metal men, marching in formation, sun glinting off their armor; the King's black horse, riderless and unsaddled, hooves ringing, leading the King's glory, the tallest howdah on the tallest elephant. Crowds leaned out of balconies, lined the roads, throwing rose petals into the parade. Horseless carriages of the latest fashion, just out from the King's own factories, led the procession, but it would not do for the King to sit in one of those. There were few things, said the traitor to Vishnumitra, as royal as elephants.

To Vishnumitra the elephants looked out of place. He was an outsider from a village in the far reaches of the kingdom, and the bright, ringing clamor of the streets, the heavy scent of roses and sweat were all too much for him. His opinion was of no account, so he said nothing. But he thought with some nostalgia about the home he had left behind these many, weary months, although the picture that came into his mind was one from his boyhood. Kind-eyed elephants bathing on the shore of the Ganga with the village boys, the water a gray sheet under a cloudy sky. Ahead were the steps of the ghat going down to the water and on the steps his mother and sisters, saris billowing red and orange. It was early morning; it was going to rain. On the rise along the shore the shisham trees spoke sibilantly in the breeze, their leaves a tender green. He saw his mother bend down and release the little earthen diya in the water, in its garland boat of woven leaves and marigolds. Her hands cupped the small flame to make certain it did not go out in the wind, but the currents pulled the diya away from her, and she straightened and looked at the little boat—fire on water—sail off midstream. Fire on water, a prayer released into the world.

He shook his head to clear it of old memories and immediately the noise and pomp of the procession assaulted his senses again. Annoyed with himself for dwelling so much on the past lately, he tried to turn his attention to the task at hand: to get a good look at that elusive, all-powerful monarch, the great man who ruled Hindustan, the man who, it was said, would live forever. Harbinger of Peace and Prosperity, they called him, this mysterious man who would not let anybody draw his portrait or take his picture. He was not quite mortal, it was said. He had held off Sher Shah's kingdom in the North-West, the Portuguese colony in the East, and the British territories to the South, and only magic of some kind could have accomplished that, said the sycophants and admirers of the King.

Vishnumitra did not believe in magic; instead he believed in rigorous observation and systematic study. The glimpse was the first step; after that he didn't know whether he was going to do it, or how he was going to do it. He was not an assassin, he had told the traitor. The traitor nodded as though to imply that all the assassins said that anyway, and Vishnumitra had felt soiled by the man's polite disbelief. Somehow these days of waiting and plotting in the great nation's capital had been the hardest period since he had left home two years ago. Perhaps it was no wonder that he was tired; that his resolve was shaken by that deep, inexpressible desire to go home. Looking at the King's portrait on the coinage of the country, the abstract, fluid lines suggesting a face beautiful in repose, he had thought about his mother making kheer in the kitchen. A portrait of the king, made illegally and paid for in blood, showed the lean, aristocratic face, the eyes large, clear, cold. "This is not very accurate, but maybe it is good enough?" the traitor had said. Vishnumitra had a sudden clear vision of the schoolroom in his village, the foot-thick mud walls, the golden thatch overhead, the view of the distant river. It took him some time to frown and say that he really needed to be able to recognize the King clearly before he could be certain he had killed the right man. It was known that the

King had proxies who sometimes spoke for him on lesser public occasions. At least once, such a proxy had been killed. No, Vishnumitra needed to see the King face to face.

"How can I be certain," he asked the traitor, "that the man in the procession is indeed the King?"

"For the anniversary of his coronation? Only the real King rides the royal elephant, my friend."

The broad way was divided in the middle by a long water channel that had been sprinkled with rose petals. Along each side of the road was a five-foot-high divan, a raised platform bristling with tall, plumed soldiers. The noise was tremendous, with shouts and the baying of horns.

And Vishnumitra saw the King.

The room he was in was level with the howdah in which the King rode. The building was too far from the street for clear viewing with the naked eye; they had already been searched for weapons by guards. So Vishnumitra put the telescope in position and squinted through it, waiting for the attendant inside the howdah to do his job.

The attendant, in the pay of the traitor, did his job. He had an embroidered palm-leaf punkha in his hand and while fanning the King he let it catch in one of the King's long braids. The King wore his ceremonial turban above his coiffure; the crown shifted, the black braids parted. The King turned instinctively toward the punkha, his hand already up to adjust the braid, his mouth an o of surprise and irritation, and in that moment Vishnumitra saw him.

The procession continued. Vishnumitra lowered the telescope, stood staring out through the latticed window, his mind a maelstrom.

No wonder he had been thinking so much about his youth.

The King—surely there could be no mistaking it—the King was no other than Upamanyu, the young man he had befriended in his boyhood, the wanderer who had made a home with them for four unforgettable years, closer than a brother. But no, it could not be. In the interim Vishnumitra had aged; despite his practice of the forbidden sciences, he had a few gray hairs. He looked younger than his fifty-seven years, but the King looked twenty-five.

Upamanyu...the face burned into his mind, thirty-eight years ago, never forgotten. Remembered always, with yearning.

If the King was, indeed, Upamanyu, that could only mean one thing.

"Well?" said the traitor. "Can you...will you do it?"

Vishnumitra took a deep breath. He controlled the needless dissipation of his body's prana with an effort, a skill learned over years, and felt his mind and body getting back to equilibrium. He now understood that his wanderings in search of the hidden sciences and their practitioners, his investigations into the murder of the girl Shankara, whose name he still could not say without pain— were all intended to bring him to this place at this point. He was the only man in the four kingdoms who knew who the King was.

"This is where our association ends," Vishnumitra said to the traitor. "You have been paid. If I do it, I will do it alone."

That night, Vishnumitra went walking through the long, lamp-lit streets of Dilli.

The city rose over the banks of the Yamuna like a poet's dream. Here was the delicate arch of a doorway, the doors carved with scenes from a fairy tale; there was a temple spire, beside the dark crown of a mango tree. The dome of a mosque, silver in the twilight, and above it the fort itself, red sandstone, turrets, and tessellations. Closer at hand: a man selling roasted shakarkand under a tree by the roadside, the smell of coal and sweetness and spices, the flare of the fire. Voices from within a walled garden where somebody was watering rosebushes. He could smell wet earth and the inescapable fragrance of roses. The horseless carriages still startled him as they went by, leaving behind a wet smell, coal and steam, and the image of a face or faces at a window. Here and there were patrols of the King, guards in red and brown, with green turbans, riding horses. And the ornate carriages filled with nobility, pulled by the great, white, humped oxen that stood six feet high at the shoulder. One time he saw a patrol accompanying those curious artifacts, the metal men (borrowed for the parade), back to the factories where they worked. The metal men walked stiffly; with each step the joints clanged faintly, metal on metal, and there was a sigh of steam. Vishnumitra could not get used to their swiveling heads, their eyeless gaze.

He walked swiftly, like a man with a purpose, so as not to draw attention to himself. But his back was against the wall. There really was no place to go any more. This place, this moment, was where the last two decades had brought him. He could give himself the illusion of being free, the stranger in the city who must be on his way soon, but he was chained by his promise to the dead. He had to kill the King.

But Upamanyu...

If even that is his real name, Vishnumitra thought, with bitter humor. The King called himself Akbar Khan. Every child in the kingdom knew how he had come to occupy the throne of the Mughals; in towns all over, people still enacted the story. The British forces fighting their way all the way to Dilli from the South, burning and looting, setting the bazaar on fire. The valiant Mughal army, with the King, Mirza Mughal, in the lead. All the King's sons fall in battle that black day, until there is only Mirza Mughal chasing a knot of enemy soldiers into an alleyway and out in the open by the river. He is known for his swordsmanship; he dispatches three of them quickly, a few of the others flee, but there is one left. Mirza Mughal leaps from his great black horse, fighting hard, blood on his sword, his armor broken across the chest. Last of the Mughals, he is holding back a pale, yellow-haired youth with a bayonet. There's the Yamuna before him, and in the black water he can see his city burning. At the last minute when Mirza Mughal is so tired he almost wants to die, there comes a madman leaping into the fray, challenging the British soldier, wielding a sword but in a style Mirza Mughal has never seen. Then a strange thing happens: the bayonet falls from the British soldier's hand as if of its own accord; the boy seems surprised, horrified, and the madman's sword makes short work of him. The stranger bows, introduces himself to his King. His name is Akbar Khan. The King and his subject return to the fray, fighting side by side until a stray bullet hits the King. In the last scene of the tragedy, Mirza Mughal is dying in Akbar Khan's arms while Dilli burns. The river is burning too: boats succumb first to fire, then water. In the presence of what is left of his army, Mirza Mughal tells Akbar Khan: my sons are dead. I give you my Kingdom. Drive out the enemy and rule!

Over the body of the dead King, Akbar Khan rouses the soldiers and the common people of the city with a speech that is still recited today in the dramas. Men leap over courtyard walls, where they have been cowering, and throng the streets; mothers lock the children in their homes and take up kitchen knives and burning brands, and leap into the fray. It is as though a tsunami has suddenly hit the invaders. In the narrow alleyways, the once-gracious city squares, in courtyards, and on the riverbank the British are cut to bits. The invading armies flee.

In the dark and smoke, the smell of blood and burning flesh, the wails of the bereaved, Akbar Khan stands still for a moment, outlined in the archway of a garden that has become a charnel house. Watchers see him limned in the light from the fires behind him, his bloody, smoking sword by his side.

Then, in a moment immortalized by innumerable dramas, Mirza Mughal's great black horse comes up to Akbar Khan. He has lost his saddle, and there is a gash on his side, but the great beast simply bows his head, stands, and waits. Akbar Khan pauses for a moment, strokes the horse's head, and with a lithe movement that no theater performer can quite emulate, leaps upon the horse. The horse bears the new King to the fort.

Vishnumitra had to concede that it was quite a story: how the nobody, Akbar Khan, ascended the throne of Dilli. But holding on to that throne for so many years was an even greater achievement. What Akbar Khan did, the stories went, is to first consolidate that nexus of power, the harem. Mirza Mughal's harem was fairly modest, with two chief queens, seventy-five lesser wives, and about five hundred concubines along with hundreds of female administrators, a corps of eunuchs, and female guards. This was where the King had lived, where the affairs of state were decided, and where he opened reports from his spies. It was said that Akbar Khan won over the queen mothers first. The dead princes were given elaborate funerals and the queens shown the utmost respect. So when the intrigues and assassination attempts began, Akbar Khan was not without friends. His pleasing mien and obvious wizardry with the sword was rivaled only by his political acumen. When Mirza Mughal's relatives challenged him he played one faction against the other until most of his rivals were eliminated. As for the rest, he invited them to challenge him in a duel unto death.

Those were the early years. The challenges were issued mostly by nobles outraged that a man without a lineage, let alone a proper Persian lineage, could sit upon the throne of Hindustan with such insouciant ease. Such challenges were the talk of the citizenry, because Akbar Khan received and accepted them in the public durbar. Sometimes the challenger wanted a game of chess; sometimes it was a duel by arms, but always it was the throne at stake, and always, failure meant death. The challenge itself was held in a private room off the durbar, with only the King and the challenger present. And always, the challenger would be found dead the next morning, in the trash heap outside the city walls. There was no evidence of poison or other underhand means, only a bruising about the skin, and a neat sword cut to the throat. The victim didn't bleed much, it was said. There were rumors of magic and other skullduggery, but the King, while contradicting these, did not work too hard to suppress the imaginations of the credulous. Always, he generously compensated the families of the victims.

After his first two years in office, Akbar Khan stopped accepting challenges. The occasional madman would still issue a challenge but Akbar Khan showed great compassion in turning such fools away. Enough blood had been shed. His Kingdom was established.

Having silenced his critics, Akbar Khan had set his skill and charisma to work on the rest of the country, bringing to it a relatively stable economy and a robust peace. He befriended Sher Shah of the North-West Kingdom and played the Portuguese and the British against each other while making neighborly noises to both. It was rumored that he gave covert support to the revolutionaries in the South so the British had their hands full. This was the King who embraced the modern science of Europe's industrial revolution, and in doing so revived the metallurgical genius of the ancient Indians by searching for and bringing to his capital all indigenous talent; he brought over some of Europe's finest engineers to work with them. The manufactories of Dilli rolled out horseless carriages of gleaming steel that moved on the new-paved roads like boats on still water. They were becoming popular in Britain; the manufactories were having a difficult time keeping up with the frenzied demands from abroad.

At the same time Akbar Khan had been careful not to create a culture of demand in his own land. Very few Indians owned their own cars; for long-distance travel there were the railways, laid across the land like lines on a palm. Vishnumitra had, during his wanderings, acquired a reluctant fascination for this mode of transport; there was something about the sway and rhythm of these sleek, serpentine monsters that brought to his heart an inexplicable joy. It was also easy to think while traveling like this, and he had spent some of his most contemplative moments in the last two years on a train, watching the countryside flash by.

It was said that while the South-West reeled under the despotism of the Portuguese king, and the South itself knew mass poverty and economic collapse for the first time under the rule of the British general, Hindustan was free. And prosperous. Glory be to the King, Akbar Khan the First. So what if he used magic and was rumored to be unconventional, even heretical? So what if he defied the kazis and brought back the syncretic, hybrid Hindu-Muslim culture of his namesake, Akbar the Great? So what if he kept his hair in long braids, had private quarters outside the harem atop a small tower, where only he and invited guests could go?

So what if his eccentricities included banning of the ancient science of healing?

Vishnumitra had, from afar, supported the rise of Akbar Khan until then. For him Akbar Khan had been a person of legend in distant Dilli, a man of whom absurdly tall tales were told, who had somehow been able to consolidate the kingdom and keep its enemies at bay. Then the news came, slowly at first, trickling into the outer reaches of the kingdom from wanderers and tradespeople, and finally from local officials: the practice of the ancient arts was banned. Some of the herbal lore was all right to practice, but the rest of it, referred to by the King as quackery, was no longer allowed. Significant parts of the ancient medical system of Ayurveda, particularly those concerned with the prana vidya, as well as the various methods of acupuncture brought by Chinese scholars were now forbidden. A system of national medical care had been set up by the King, employing a mishmash of traditions, from the European to the Yunnani, and the textbooks had been standardized and rewritten. So while a practitioner of Ayurveda would have studied the works of, say, Charaka, or Patanjali, now only "relevant" extracts were read, the implication being that the rest was not worth learning. The King claimed he wanted to modernize the country. Yet he did nothing to stop other kinds of quackery; charlatan astrologers could wander the land at will, but a traditional healer could find himself thrown in jail. Yoga as exercise was all right, but healing through the control and manipulation of prana was quackery, and its practice punishable by imprisonment. Vishnumitra had been angry and bewildered, but there was nothing to be done. He had to keep his true vocation a secret and lie about his age.

But now, walking through the city like a man possessed, Vishnumitra thought he knew why the King had banned the ancient sciences of healing, while reserving them for himself under the guise of magic. Still, it made no sense that a man who was sixty-two years old should look twenty-five, even with the practice of the prana vidya. They gave good health, not immortality. Something was very wrong.

He thought of the girl Shankara, whom he himself had trained in the forbidden sciences. For his first year of wandering she and a handful of others had been his dear companions. She had cut off her hair and disguised herself as a man so as to be able to travel with less trouble. With their help Vishnumitra had established over much of Hindustan a secret network of the practitioners of prana vidya, all of whom had once operated alone, and in fear. The fear was still there, but with it now there was comradeship, the exchange and enhancement of knowledge. No longer did one healer or scholar of such arts fear that the knowledge would die with him or her.

And the best of them had been Shankara.

She had gone to Dilli against his advice, to challenge the King.

Since the months after a friend discovered her body on the refuse pile outside the city, Vishnumitra had wondered how it had happened. Why had the King, who no longer accepted challenges, accepted one from Shankara? And how had someone of Shankara's skill been outmaneuvered?

Oh, those months of grief and rage....

Vishnumitra paused by a shop selling sugarcane juice. He had a cupful so he could sit down for a moment, away from the crowd around the stall. There was a cracked marble platform around the roots of a pipal tree; he sat himself down on it. Behind him, under the tree's great canopy, was the mausoleum of a minor Sufi poet. He could smell incense and flowers.

Upamanyu....

He could not let himself feel what he had once felt, but even now, thinking of the name was enough to quicken his pulse. Once dearest friend, dearer than a brother! How lonely the years had been without him. He could never have imagined that he, Vishnumitra, who would once have defended Upamanyu with his life, would one day be plotting his death. He took a deep, shaky breath. A great wave of resistance to the notion rose in him, and along with it a desire to see Upamanyu again, and to leave this matter of revenge and murder to someone else. After all, there was all of Hindustan at stake. What would happen to its freedom and prosperity when Upamanyu was gone? He had thought through it all before, before he knew who the King was, and settled on the idea that what is right is right, and if a right act leads to great evil, then that evil must be thought of as independent of the act that preceded it, and fought on its own terms. But here, in the great city, with its show of might, power, and glory, and the terrible news streaming in from the South as though to say, "This is what will happen to Hindustan if you kill the King," it was difficult enough to justify this reasoning. And now that he knew who the King was, could he lift a hand against him?

And yet, and yet....

Shankara.

And the rest of the practitioners, who now worked in fear and secrecy, and the ones who had been found and killed. He had to do what he had set out to do.

He thought: after this I will go back home to my village, to what is left of my father's ashram by the Ganga. He did not tell himself that the very air, there, would remind him of Upamanyu. That after this Upamanyu's name might well be written on the paths they had once walked in the forests, together, or on the mud walls of the now-abandoned ashram.

The ashram was the place of his earliest memory. The walls were nearly a foot thick, made from a mixture of mud and straw; in the sun they glowed as though they were made of gold. Some of the walls were carved with the images, such as a god on a chariot, or a hero atop an elephant. To the small boy he had been, the walls of the ashram told stories without saying a word. Inside, under the thatch roof, it was always cool in summer and warm in winter; even now he remembered leaning his head against the textured surface, feeling safe, feeling he was home.

The first time he saw Upamanyu...nearly forty years ago. That face, in its youthful, unchanged beauty, had burned in his memory for all these years.

He remembered. How could he not? It was the first time that the world had come to his doorstep, after all, in the form of a young man, wanderer and eternal traveler. On his clothes were the dust of Baluchistan, Mysore, and Assam. He had stories to tell about the fall of Travancore in the South, the winds of the Western Desert, the arid cliffs of the North-West where Sher Shah had his citadel.

That morning Vishnumitra had been reading a copy of the Charaka Samhita on the verandah, practicing his Sanskrit while trying to learn something about healing. He was fifteen, a tall, quiet boy grown golden in the sun like the walls, and had acquired some of their contemplative silence. He wanted to be a healer, to use the knowledge of the ancients to heal the sick. His world had been whole, complete, until Upamanyu walked into it.

The children had been singing multiplication tables out in the courtyard, swaying with the music of it, making Vishnumitra feel pleasantly sleepy, so that he couldn't go beyond stanza one of the first verse of the Charaka Samhita (that great medical treatise being written in poetry, as was once the norm). The other children were bringing in mustard leaves from the garden they had been tending, the leaves scenting the air with their delicate pungency. And there was the stranger at the gate, as though the air had conjured him up: a tall, long-limbed fellow in the outlandish loose pants and long shirt of the

North-West, with a mane of unruly black hair. He stood there unhurried and smiling, hefting his cloth bag on his shoulder, rubbing the stubble on his chin with his other hand.

Vishnumitra rose to greet the stranger but his father had already waved the children to silence. His father loved wanderers and outcasts, having been one himself for so long. In a few minutes the stranger was seated on a low wooden seat under the pipal tree. Water was brought for his hands and feet, and to drink. That was what he had stopped for: water, and five minutes of rest before wandering on to the town twelve miles away. Later Upamanyu would tell Vishnumitra: I stopped for five minutes and stayed five years—I, who have never stayed in a place longer than a month!

All these years later Vishnumitra wondered why Upamanyu had stayed so long. He had always thought it was because of the love that had arisen between them, the love of brother for brother and friend for friend; but now he was not so sure. Perhaps all that had been an illusion. His mentor and dear friend, who had taught him sword-fighting and filled his ears with the knowledge of a world far greater than the little ashram, may have had other reasons to linger. Who knew if even Upamanyu were his real name?

Every morning Vishnumitra would recite verses from the Charaka Samhita for his father. Upamanyu would be leaning against the wall, his mane of hair tied casually into a knot, his eyes bright with curiosity. Maitreya would explain each concept.

"Prana is the life-force. Some people call it breath but it is that which comes before breath. In every healthy living being, prana flows unimpeded through its designated channels. Sickness is when there is a blockage or abnormality in the prana flow, and then the healer must restore its pathways in order to restore health...."

"But is prana not the same as blood?" this from Upamanyu.

"No, indeed. Prana cannot be seen, heard, or felt, except by the one trained in the ancient art of healing. Such a practitioner can tell the state of the prana flow when he feels the patient's pulse, for the quality of the flow is reflected in the characteristics of the pulse. But the true sage can induce in himself a state of direct prana perception, in which the flow of prana appears manifest to the inner eye as the flow of the Ganga is manifest to the outer."

"Can you do this, Guruji? Will you teach me?"

Maitreya laughed.

"It is not so easily done. It takes the discipline of years. You will have to set down your traveling staff, my son, and study like Vishnumitra here. I myself have only touched the edge of that perceptive state. This knowledge is very arcane; I have found one version of it in a Tibetan text that I found by chance. But here too the greater truth is hinted at and concealed in a morass of lesser truths. This is the language of the twilight, as they say. It takes a lifetime to interpret these hints and intimations."

"Teach me, then, Guruji! For you I lay down my staff. You will find your pupil unused to instruction and too full of questions and impatience, but he will be grateful to be schooled...."

What Vishnumitra realized was that his father was in fact pleased. Later he wondered if Upamanyu had reminded his father of his own youth. Upamanyu's habit of asking questions as though he were issuing a challenge in a duel instigated in Maitreya delight instead of anger, and in fact Vishnumitra spent the next few days hating their guest, thinking himself less loved, a boring, overly obedient, dull sluggard of a student. But it all changed when Upamanyu asked Vishnumitra if he would help him achieve a better hand—his writing was atrocious. After that they went for walks in the forest, swam in the river, and engaged the village youth in games like kho and stick-fighting. Upamanyu revealed himself to be skilled with stick and sword, prideful and quick to temper, but just as easily recovering his good nature. In the forest one day Upamanyu brushed his hand across a chameli bush. Its white, scented flowers were like stars.

"Do you think plants have prana, too, Vishnu?"

Vishnumitra thought, with a little surge of triumph: so you don't know everything, my friend!

Aloud he said:

"They do. My father has not yet taught you about cosmic prana. The prana that is in us flows into us and out again, and into and out of other things also. I don't quite understand it myself. But once, during meditation, he achieved the deepest state of prana perception—just for a few seconds—and he told me later it was like rivers of light falling out of the sky, flowing in and out of everything. Like the delta of a river, small streams coming together and then flowing apart...."

"That's what I want to see," Upamanyu said enthusiastically. Ahead of them the Ganga lay silver in the semidarkness. They sat on the bank in companionable silence.

So long ago, it had been. It amazed Vishnumitra to think that the ashram had so long withstood the depredation of time and prejudice. His father had been a maverick, a madman. An outcast who had given up the Brahmin's sacred thread to marry a Muslim woman and not even insist on her conversion, let alone the various purification rituals! It was said that while she performed Hindu rituals, such as the chhat fast, she also kept to her daily Islamic prayers! So Maitreya had lost caste and status, been turned out with his wife to roam the world. In his late youth he had finally found this place by the great, slow river, where among the trees a new kind of ashram had been founded. Eklavya, where any child could come to learn, irrespective of caste or creed or religion. The Brahmins kept their sons at home but in time the other castes sent their children, afraid to miss out on such an education. Apart from learning the duties of a householder, they would learn mathematics, music, astronomy, Ayurveda, yoga, tending a garden, cooking, sword-fighting, and wrestling. Maitreya found teachers from the ranks of swordsmen and wandering dervishes, Sufi healers and itinerant craftsmen. So in time the children of petty tradesmen, Hindu or Muslim, sat with those of cowherds, rich landowners, and the occasional defiant Brahmin and sang their multiplication tables, or learned to cook and eat together and thus destroy both caste and religion. But what they created, Maitreya would say, was more important: a hybrid culture, a *din-i-illahi* made real, imbued with the best of both traditions. Friendship, community, a temple of knowledge.

And it was that. In the kitchen Vishnumitra's mother Tasleem took the clay pot of rice off the earthen stove and carried it out to the courtyard, swept clean by the children. There was a daal and some vegetables, and berries the children had picked in the forest. Everyone was sitting cross-legged on the ground, in a row, waiting to be served. The platters were made of dried, woven leaves, and soon each held a mound of rice, the famous red-tinged rice of that region. Many years after he had left home, Vishnumitra remembered the aroma of that rice: rich, earthy, with a touch of walnut. Whenever he met a trader from those parts he was sure to buy enough red rice to last him some time.

And in the nighttime, sleeping in the open under the stars, with the crickets singing in the undergrowth, and from the forest the low, sweet call of a koel. His father would tell the small ones stories of pirs, or gods, or kings.

"...And so Krishna became the King of Dwarka, but his friend of childhood, Sudama, remained poor even as a grown man. He lived in a hut with his wife and children, and they were hungry many times. One day he decided he would go to Dwarka to see his old friend. All he had that he could bring as a gift was a bag of rice, just the kind you ate today. So he walked all the way to Dwarka...."

It was an old, comforting story: the friend, Sudama, in his rags, with his lowly gift, being laughed at by the courtiers until the King saw him and came to him and embraced him, and expressed inordinate delight at the gift of rice. And Sudama spent a few days with Krishna, and when he returned home he found that his fortunes had changed. Where his rude hut had been, there stood a mansion, and his wife and children were well-fed and well-clothed.

"...So, children, wherever you go when you are grown, may you remember your days together and be friends to each other as Krishna and Sudama were...."

Somewhere a queen-of-the-night bush was in bloom; its heavy scent was wafted by the breeze from the river. In the quiet after the story, Vishnumitra stole a glance at his friend, who was stretched out in the next pallet. He wanted to touch Upamanyu's hand, to make real his feeling that they were and always would be as Krishna and Sudama had been to each other, but shyness held him back. Upamanyu's fine, clever face was soft with moonlight, and listening.

And after all, Upamanyu had been the first to leave. He wanted to go to Tibet, he said, to look for the lost books on prana lore. But even before that Vishnumitra had sensed a restlessness in him, a preoccupation. He had known, but not admitted to himself until years later, that what called to Upamanyu was not just old palm-leaf manuscripts on prana lore but the long journey, the new sights along the way, and new adventures. He was tired of staying in one place. It was time to move on.

He had gone away one day with promises to be back in a year or two. There were disturbances from the South: the British invaders were marching North. Nothing was certain.

Maitreya knew he wouldn't be back, and he kept his disappointment and sorrow to himself. Vishnumitra's heart broke. The world became empty to him, and every familiar place reminded him of Upamanyu's absence. Only a few years later his father died in a skirmish during the confusion of the first British incursion North. Vishnumitra ran the ashram as best he could until his mother died. Some years after that the news came that the new King had banned the practice of the ancient arts. Vishnumitra could have kept the ashram going with all the remaining disciplines, but its existence was already a thorn in the side of the new provincial governor, who frowned upon such sacrilegious intermingling of caste and religion. Vishnumitra had no heart left for trouble. When the ashram closed he found that the wanderlust had come to him after all.

He set off into the world, not knowing what it held in store for him. He hid his true occupation, calling himself a scribe or a scholar, practicing his healing arts when they were truly needed. He found that if he stayed in a place more than a few days after a healing, others would come to him in the dark of night, begging for help to save a life or work a miracle. Sometimes he could do something; at other times he found himself on the run like a criminal.

But what he valued most was the discovery of those already versed in the arts; although few were superior to him, it was a delight to be able to discuss the finer points of prana control and manipulation, and the techniques to restore harmony for different conditions. When he met such people he taught them what he knew and learned from them as well. He found that his travels could help connect one practitioner with another, across cities and villages. And as he wandered, he picked up companions who wanted to be trained in the art. Mostly young people who became his family.

Now they were all scattered, doing the same work he had set out to do. Except for Shankara, who was dead.

After all, it was the bag of rice that did it.

The clerk in the royal court had shaken his old head as he watched Vishnumitra sign the document of challenge. He had reluctantly agreed to submit the bag of rice that Vishnumitra handed him with the scroll. "He will not see you," he had said, darkly. "He turns away all…nearly all who challenge him."

But the summons came two days later. The King would receive Vishnumitra—not in the Diwan-i-Khas but in his private room atop the tower. In the hour of twilight.

In the late afternoon Vishnumitra hired a boatman to take him to the opposite bank of the Yamuna. He chose a small pipal tree on the bank and sat down in the lotus position. Slowly he steadied his wildly beating heart. In the golden light the fort was a vision in red sandstone and marble.

Breathing slowly, Vishnumitra calmed his body, balancing out the prana flow in the two main channels on either side of his spine. He felt the slow shock of kundalini energy flowing up the sushumna channel toward the crown of his head, a wave of exhilaration, of limitless strength flooding him.

He let his consciousness flow and become one with the prana, softening the flow in the seventy-two thousand distributaries of the subtle body. In this deep, receptive state he opened his inner eye. With years of discipline he had come close to mastering what his father had taught him: the perception of the mahaprana, the cosmic channels of the life-force. He saw the mahaprana as a faint skein of unearthly light, limning every living thing: tree or grazing cow, or the waiting boatman. Raining down from the vastness of the sky were the greater channels, joining and connecting one life to another, from the smallest beetle now crawling along his arm to the King himself, awaiting him at the palace. When Vishnumitra had first glimpsed this cosmic marvel, two years after Upamanyu's own initiation, he had asked his father the same question Upamanyu had: from whence did the mahaprana flow? What was the source of it, beyond the sky? His father did not know.

Slowly Vishnumitra drew himself out of the meditation. He brushed the beetle from his arm with infinite tenderness and watched it scuttle away over the rock on which he was sitting. He waved to the silent boatman. It was time to go.

Between the fort walls are wonders: gracious gardens abloom with flowers, fountains that sing as water soars up into the air, a metal woman dancing in the center of a stone circle. Officials in small groups leave lighted rooms and confer in the scented gloom, as lamps flicker on, creating moving shadows. Vishnumitra is deep in the centered peacefulness that any glimpse of the mahaprana affords him—he has accepted what he must do, with all its moral ambiguity. Dharma is dharma, and if it is his fate to commit murder of one dearer to him than a brother, he will meet it like a scholar and a man.

To his surprise the King meets him at the base of the tower. His face is luminous in the light of the lamps; he makes an impatient gesture and his guards leave his side, watching from several paces away, out of earshot. Vishnumitra hesitates, but the King is holding out his arms.

The braids are held back, the face open, young as when Vishnumitra last saw him, filled with humor and intelligence, and at this moment—yes, this is so—the King's eyes are moist with tears.

"Dear brother! Vishnumitra!"

Vishnumitra cannot but accept the embrace, feeling tears pricking his own eyelids while simultaneously his mind warns him not to deviate from his purpose.

"Upamanyu!"

"Hush! Only to you, my friend!"

They stand apart, looking at each other. Vishnumitra feels his purpose like a burden whose weight he can hardly bear. Under other circumstances this would be a joyous reunion. He breathes deep.

"You know why I am here."

"We will talk of that in a few moments. As a condemned man, surely I have a right to ask for one last wish: a walk with my brother in the gardens? Come now, do not deny me!"

The old, affectionate, mocking tone. Vishnumitra's composure is shaken; he finds himself being led through the magical garden, with one wonder after another being pointed out. His heart is a traitor—this is what he has yearned for since Upamanyu left: this reunion, where he is Sudama to Upamanyu's Krishna, treated like an honored guest. Now the King's guards fling open the great doors of a large, circular building surrounded by Ashok trees. Within are bright lights, the hiss of steam and the noise of metal upon metal. Mechanical men are working in clusters, monitoring pulleys and wheels, fitting together beautifully wrought pieces of metal with exquisite precision. Vishnumitra, his mouth agape in wonder, understands nothing, recognizes nothing. What are they building? This is no manufactory of horseless carriages.

"This is my personal laboratory," the King says with pride. "For these many years I have become interested in the forces of nature apart from…from the life-force itself. I have read the ancient Yunnanis Aristut, and Sukrat, and our own atomist schools. I have perused the barbarian vilayati scholar Niyuton. You have seen for yourself what wonders their discoveries have brought to us! Yet what I seek is to understand how these different imperatives, these forces are related. Observe, my friend!"

He hands Vishnumitra a wooden tray upon which silver wires have been arranged in a rectangular array. Within this lattice are small canisters of metal. The King asks Vishnumitra to place his finger in such a way as to bridge a gap between the wires. Vishnumitra does so and feels the faintest shock, a jolt not unlike the sting one feels touching a metal gate before a thunderstorm. Not unlike the first experience of kundalini energy for a beginner. He jerks his finger away, raises startled eyes to Upamanyu.

"Ah, I see you are wondering if I have captured a storm in a few pieces of wire! Or is it a jolt of prana? So similar, yet the two forces are different—this one arises from inanimate matter, and the other from life itself! A mystery, is it not?"

They emerge from the chamber; the doors clang behind them, and a sweet silence descends. In the lamp-lit dark the King is leading him to the tower. Courtiers and guards watch curiously from afar.

The stairs spiral upward and at the top there is a door, and a room furnished relatively simply—a small Persian rug over the marble floor, a low divan, a few chairs. A table with neat stacks of paperwork. Shelves filled with books— forbidden books! The Charaka Samhita, the works of the great physician Sushruta, Patanjali's Yoga Sutra, works on the tantric mysteries, tomes in Tibetan, Pali, and Sanskrit, and in languages he does not know. Vishnumitra stares at the books and then at Upamanyu, who is smiling indulgently as an older brother might.

"You've seen what I've wrought in this kingdom, dear brother. And yet through all these years I have been alone. A decade ago I sent my spies to find you, but all they found was the ashram, abandoned, and you flown. And now you stand before me, bent upon revenge. And yet when we embraced there were tears in your eyes in answer to my own. Dear friend! Let us forget about this challenge! I have needed you for a long time, and you are here at last."

Vishnumitra feels his purpose weakening. The promise he has made to his art, to his dead, feels now like a burden whose weight he can hardly bear. Bitterness and sorrow rise in his throat like bile. He wants to say: why didn't you come back and keep your promise? Why did you abandon me? Why did you betray us all, betray the prana vidya itself?

Vishnumitra draws himself up, remembers his dharma. He brings deliberately to memory the imprisonments and murders that have befallen his dear companions, the practitioners of the art. He remains standing, ignoring Upamanyu's invitation to sit down.

"I need answers, Upamanyu, not pretty speeches. Tell me, why did you ban the prana vidya? Why have your spies pursued and killed the practitioners these many years?"

"Come, my friend, can I afford to have every fool in the empire learn and use what is the most arcane of arts? Why do you think I look so young, al- though I am older than you in years? Ah, I can see from your face that you know, or suspect. I am the best practitioner of the art in the empire, and it is that which has kept me young. It is that which allows me to defend myself from my enemies. Do you blame me for making sure that nobody else can be an adept in the art?"

"I am also an adept," Vishnumitra says softly. "And I might look twenty years younger, but I have aged, Upamanyu. What you are doing is against cosmic order. The prana vidya is not to be misused to confer immortality."

"Cosmic order will survive, my friend! Do you not recall the old stories about the sages who lived for thousands of years? Here I thought you'd congratulate me upon my great discovery! I have wandered far, from mountain to desert, read countless ancient tomes, studied under the most learned of teachers to teach myself what nobody else would, or could. The manipulation of the mahaprana itself!"

Looking at him, Vishnumitra is struck by how young Upamanyu is, not only in appearance but in mind. It is as though the companion of his boyhood is back, with his lively intelligence, his curiosity, his unending propensity for play. The playful look is in those bright eyes.

"I wish to choose my weapon."

"What if I refuse your challenge?"

"You will not refuse, Upamanyu."

An unreadable expression in Upamanyu's eyes. The shoulders drop, and when he speaks it is the same light tone, but resigned. Regretful.

"Choose, then."

"I choose combat by prana vidya."

Vishnumitra has done this before, used manipulation of prana to kill. When someone is dying in great pain, it is a mercy to let the individual prana flow cease, to draw life out gently, as one draws the last of thread from a spindle. He has never used this skill to murder. But his way is clear.

Upamanyu is shaking his head as though Vishnumitra has just proposed something quite absurd, but he comes up to Vishnumitra, and their hands meet. Fingertip to fingertip, then clasping lightly, as though they might be about to draw each other into an embrace. Vishnumitra can sense the prana flow in the other's body—thick and strong. He senses the other finding his own prana flow as a bird on the wing might sense the landscape below. The duel begins.

Vishnumitra attempts to still the flow, to draw life and breath and consciousness from Upamanyu, and in the beginning Upamanyu simply resists. He is smiling a little, but Vishnumitra hardly notices. He is intent upon the task, looking for weaknesses in the chakras, turbulence in the nadis. The thing is to take Upamanyu by surprise, to strike without warning, as he scans his friend's subtle body with that gentle inner gaze. Then he's hit.

It feels as though the world has suddenly grown dark. Controlling his breath, Vishnumitra finds his balance; the light returns. He fights back. They are going back and forth, sending great waves of weakness, invisible sword cuts that might stop the heart or constrict a blood vessel. Every few minutes Vishnumitra is aware of that gaze, so light, contemplative even. He is aware that deep within him there is a great resistance to kill the man he loves. Surely there is another way! In his pain and love he cries out:

"In the name of the art, which you betrayed, in the names of those whom you had imprisoned and killed, for Shankara, who was innocent in her fierceness and courage, I beg you, Upamanyu, to repent by choosing death! Do not make me kill you!"

Upamanyu's face is intent, sweat has broken out over his brow.

"Nobody can kill me...."

And Vishnumitra sees with his inner eye what Upamanyu has done, how he can kill an adept in the art, how he must have killed Shankara. The columns of mahaprana that rain down from the sky are joining and coalescing, coming down at him, filling every part of his being with the life-force, a fullness that his body cannot take. For a moment Upamanyu is Indra himself, wielding the thunderbolt. Vishnumitra knows for a split second the beauty of the cosmic prana, the vastness of the mystery that they have barely begun to comprehend, and he knows that he has done wrong, just as Upamanyu has, to use the prana vidya for murder. As he accepts his death, welcomes it as a man guided by dharma must, he senses the capillaries on his skin bursting. A pain in his chest, his lungs, and he is losing consciousness, falling to the floor. Then blessed darkness and he knows nothing at all.

When Vishnumitra came to, the first thing he noticed was the smell. It was a rotten odor, sickly sweet, like spoiled fruit. He hurt all over. Gradually, through the pain, he realized he was alive. He was lying on a great pile of refuse, above which he could see the silhouette of the fort wall, a dark wave against the starlit sky. He tried to sit up and groaned as the pain hit him anew. Lying back in the filth, he tasted his defeat, and the struggles that still lay ahead, and the bitterness of knowing that he—greatest of the practitioners of the art (or so he'd thought), defender of the prana vidya—had ultimately betrayed it and failed all the ones he loved. He shuddered in the cold air.

Why had Upamanyu left him alive?

He should be dead!

He must have lain there for many hours before he noticed the horse. There was a faint radiance in the eastern sky, although the darkness was still profound. Against that sky stood the King's stallion, black, strong, unmistakable. There was no rider.

Vishnumitra dragged his broken body off the pile of trash and crawled to where the stallion stood. The horse bent its great head, snorting softly, blowing twin puffs of breath from the enormous nostrils. Vishnumitra saw the pale shape of a rolled scroll hanging from the saddle and reached for it. He lay gasping on the hard ground, waiting for the light. The horse waited too.

Dear brother, [Upamanyu wrote]

I regret the pain I have caused you, but perhaps it is better this way. As I said I have awaited your coming these many years. Kingship has been very interesting but I grow weary of it. You recall that your father's explanation of the mahaprana when I was just a boy launched me on a journey of discovery. My kingdom was but a stop on the way to greater adventures, one that enabled me to consolidate my knowledge and distracted me pleasantly with interesting dilemmas. I have as yet no answer to the question I once posed your father: from whence does the cosmic prana arise? What is the origin of the life-force beyond this earth? Some invoke gods but I seek no such convenient answers. My dabbling with the knowledge of the mechanical forces convinces me that one will lead me to the other. The Chinese have been experimenting with propulsion power for eons, and in my own small laboratory I have found enough evidence that a carefully designed craft might bear the weight of a man to the endless skies. There I will fly as the Vidyadharas are said to do, and seek the adventures that have constantly beckoned my soul.

Meanwhile, I leave you my horse (with great regret as he, strengthened by my knowledge of prana vidya, has been my dear companion these many years). And I leave you my kingdom. I have talked all night with my chief queen, the peerless Jahanara, who has known for some time that I have a brother in spirit. She is to be trusted, as is Noori, her slave and my best spy, who is an expert archer and fighter. My minister, Sukhwant Singh, will guide you as well. Your name, my friend, is Ambar Khan, and you are born of a Muslim father and a

Hindu mother (this small reversal of the truth I deemed necessary in order to explain away any Hindu traits that you, the next Mughal king, might display). Do not fear that such a thing would betray you, for I have attempted to recreate as much as possible the vibrant hybrid culture that I so enjoyed in your father's ashram. I have prepared the ground, you see, for the past few years, in the hope that you might come, although what it took to draw you out was the girl Shankara's death. It might comfort you to know that she fought bravely to the end, and that I spared her pain at the passing. So I bid you, dear brother, to save and keep what I have built—the most prosperous kingdom in the hemisphere, if not the world. This morning at dawn one of my proxies will appear at the jharokha as usual, for the people of the city must see their king daily. I will be well on my way by then, on the north road out of Dilli, once more a traveler on a quest, unhampered by the burdens of the settled life. My heart will be as light as my pack, which contains little besides a device or two of my invention, a few books—and a bagful of rice from the one place that felt like home to me.

Now you must take my horse to the inn an hour's journey from the gate, and rest and recover a while. Just before sunset I bid you ride into the city from the Eastern gate on my horse. The smallest child in the city knows that the new king will, like Akbar Khan, take the kingdom without a single weapon, riding in on this very horse, the noble Vikram. I have signed documents stating that none of my offspring will inherit the throne, which is perhaps the main reason they have not killed each other. Apparently the latter is a tradition among the Mughals.

If you do not wish to be king, simply let my horse return to the city. Sukhwant Singh will know what to do. But I am confident that you, who have always been led by your dharma, will not betray the people who await you.

Through all my life I have resisted giving my heart to another. It would only be a distraction from my quest, which is to comprehend the mysteries that surround me, and thus to comprehend myself. I have never even told anyone the name I was born with—I have worn names as another man might wear clothes. Yet you, Vishnumitra, took my heart from me without my knowledge or permission. I knew this as I stood over your body. My anger—unused to defiance all these years, and honed by the sutras of the ancient, rageful sage Durvasa, who lived five thousand years—flared up as we dueled. In that moment I would have given up my careful plans to install you in my place (a wise ruler always has other options prepared)—I would have killed you, my friend, but when I held the hand that had brought me the rice from his mother's kitchen, I could not do it. So have I learned that my knowledge of myself is far from complete, and this humbles me.

I do not know if you will forgive me. I will not insult you or those dear to you I killed by asking it of you. But consider this: you have a vast network of practitioners of the prana vidya spread all over the country. This great instrument I have forged as much as you have, by pruning the incompetent or the rash. Use it as you will, for in the days ahead there will be much turmoil. Sher Shah in the North-West shows signs of impatience; there are rumors the Portuguese king is mad, and as the British lose their hold over the South, their envious gaze turns northward.

So, dear brother, farewell! I go north to China now, to the next adventure. Only the sky—Ambar!—is my limit! May you and yours find peace.

Your brother in spirit,

Upamanyu

Vishnumitra read this missive three times. The horse whinnied softly, and at last he put the scroll away in his shirt and staggered shakily to his feet. He leaned against the horse's side and wept for all he had lost, and for all the losses still to come. He thought of the curve of the great river of his home, and the steps of the ghat leading down to the gray water, and the kind-eyed elephants sporting by the shore. He saw in memory the bright saris of his mother and sisters, and the golden walls of the ashram. Then, with great difficulty, he hoisted himself upon the horse, and lay for a moment against his neck, panting. He wiped his tears with his tattered sleeve and turned the horse away from the city toward the inn, to await the sunset of all he had known. Above him the last stars went out in the vast bowl of the sky.

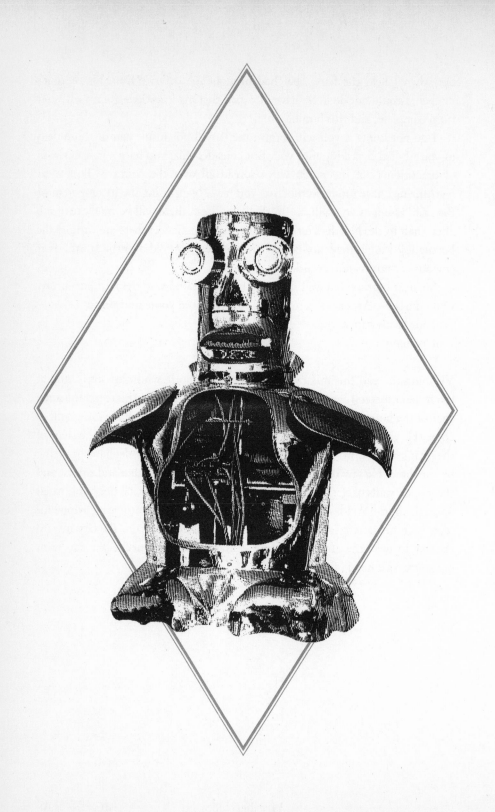

Fixing Hanover

Jeff VanderMeer

WHEN SHYVER CAN'T lift it from the sand, he brings me down from the village. It lies there on the beach, entangled in the seaweed, dull metal scoured by the sea, limpets and barnacles stuck to its torso. It's been lost a long time, just like me. It smells like rust and oil still, but only a tantalizing hint.

"It's good salvage, at least," Shyver says. "Maybe more."

"Or maybe less," I reply. Salvage is the life's blood of the village in the off-season, when the sea's too rough for fishing. But I know from past experience, there's no telling what the salvagers will want and what they will discard. They come from deep in the hill country abutting the sea cliffs, their needs only a glimmer in their savage eyes.

To Shyver, maybe the thing he'd found looks like a long box with a smaller box on top. To me, in the burnishing rasp of the afternoon sun, the last of the winter winds lashing against my face, it resembles a man whose limbs have been torn off. A man made of metal. It has lamps for eyes, although I have to squint hard to imagine there ever being an ember, a spark, of understanding. No expression defiles the broad pitted expanse of metal.

As soon as I see it, I call it "Hanover," after a character I had seen in an old movie back when the projector still worked.

"Hanover?" Shyver says with a trace of contempt.

"Hanover never gave away what he thought," I reply, as we drag it up the gravel track toward the village. Sandhaven, they call it, simply, and it's carved into the side of cliffs that are sliding into the sea. I've lived there for almost six years, taking on odd jobs, assisting with salvage. They still know next to nothing about me, not really. They like me not for what I say or who I am, but for what I do: anything mechanical I can fix, or build something new from poor parts. Someone reliable in an isolated place where a faulty water pump can be devastating. That means something real. That means you don't have to explain much.

"Hanover, whoever or whatever it is, has given up on more than thoughts," Shyver says, showing surprising intuition. It means he's already put a face on Hanover, too. "I think it's from the Old Empire. I think it washed up from the Sunken City at the bottom of the sea."

Everyone knows what Shyver thinks, about everything. Brown-haired, green-eyed, gawky, He's lived in Sandhaven his whole life. He's good with a boat, could navigate a cockleshell through a typhoon. He'll never leave the village, but why should he? As far as he knows, everything he needs is here.

Beyond doubt, the remains of Hanover are heavy. I have difficulty keeping my grip on him, despite the rust. By the time we've made it to the courtyard at the center of Sandhaven, Shyver and I are breathing as hard as old men. We drop our burden with a combination of relief and self-conscious theatrics. By now, a crowd has gathered, and not just stray dogs and bored children.

First law of salvage: what is found must be brought before the community. Is it scrap? Should it be discarded? Can it be restored?

John Blake, council leader, all unkempt black beard, wide shoulders, and watery turquoise eyes, stands there. So does Sarah, who leads the weavers, and the blacksmith Growder, and the ethereal captain of the fishing fleet: Lady Salt as she is called—she of the impossibly pale, soft skin, the blonde hair in a land that only sees the sun five months out of the year. Her eyes, ever-shifting, never settling—one is light blue and one is fierce green, as if to balance the sea between calm and roiling. She has tiny wrinkles in the corners of those eyes, and a wry smile beneath. If I remember little else, fault the eyes. We've been lovers the past three years, and if I ever fully understand her, I wonder if my love for her will vanish like the mist over the water at dawn.

With the fishing boats not launching for another week, a host of broad-faced fisher folk, joined by lesser lights and gossips, has gathered behind us. Even as the light fades: shadows of albatross and gull cutting across the horizon and the roofs of the low houses, huddled and glowing a deep gold-and-orange around the edges, framed by the graying sky.

Blake says, "Where?" He's a man who measures words as if he had only a few given to him by Fate; too generous a syllable from his lips, and he might fall over dead.

"The beach, the cove," Shyver says. Blake always reduces me to a similar terseness.

"What is it?"

This time, Blake looks at me, with a glare. I'm the fixer who solved their well problems the season before, who gets the most value for the village from what's sold to the hill scavengers. But I'm also Lady Salt's lover, who used to be his, and depending on the vagaries of his mood, I suffer more or less for it.

I see no harm in telling the truth as I know it, when I can. So much remains unsaid that extra lies exhaust me.

"It is part of a metal man," I say.

A gasp from the more ignorant among the crowd. My Lady Salt just stares right through me. I know what she's thinking: in scant days she'll be on the open sea. Her vessel is as sleek and quick and buoyant as the water, and she likes to call it *Seeker*, or sometimes *Mist*, or even just *Cleave*. Salvage holds little interest for her.

But I can see the gears turning in Blake's head. He thinks awhile before he says more. Even the blacksmith and the weaver, more for ceremony and obligation than their insight, seem to contemplate the rusted bucket before them.

A refurbished water pump keeps delivering from the aquifers; parts bartered to the hill people mean only milk and smoked meat for half a season. Still, Blake knows that the fishing has been less dependable the past few years, and that if we do not give the hill people something, they will not keep coming back.

"Fix it," he says.

It's not a question, although I try to treat it like one.

Later that night, I am with the Lady Salt, whose whispered name in these moments is Rebecca. "Not a name men would follow," she said to me once. "A land-ish name."

In bed, she's as shifting as the tides, beside me, on top, and beneath. Her mouth is soft but firm, her tongue curling like a question mark across my body. She makes little cries that are so different from the orders she barks out ship-board that she might as well be a different person. We're all different people, depending.

Rebecca can read. She has a few books from the hill people, taught herself with the help of an old man who remembered how. A couple of the books are even from the Empire—the New Empire, not the old. Sometimes I want to think she is not the Lady Salt, but the Lady Flight. That she wants to leave the village. That she seeks so much more. But I look into those eyes in the dimness of half-dawn, so close, so far, and realize she would never tell me, no matter how long I live here. Even in bed, there is a bit of Lady Salt in Rebecca.

When we are finished, lying in each other's arms under the thick covers, her hair against my cheek, Rebecca asks me, "Is that thing from your world? Do you know what it is?"

I have told her a little about my past, where I came from—mostly bedtime stories when she cannot sleep, little fantasies of golden spires and a million thronging people, fables of something so utterly different from the village that it must exist only in dream. *Once upon a time there was a foolish man. Once upon a time there was an Empire.* She tells me she doesn't believe me, and there's freedom in that. It's a strange pillow talk that can be so grim.

I tell her the truth about Hanover: "It's nothing like what I remember." If it came from the Empire, it came late, after I was already gone.

"Can you really fix it?" she asks.

I smile. "I can fix anything," and I really believe it. If I want to, I can fix anything. I'm just not sure yet I want Hanover fixed, because I don't know what he is.

But my hands can't lie—they tremble to *have at it,* to explore, impatient for the task even then and there, in bed with Blake's lost love.

I came from the same sea the Lady Salt loves. I came as salvage, and was fixed. Despite careful preparation, my vessel had been damaged first by a storm, and then a reef. Forced to the surface, I managed to escape into a raft just before my creation drowned. It was never meant for life above the waves, just as I was never meant for life below them. I washed up near the village, was found, and eventually accepted into their community; they did not sell me to the hill people.

I never meant to stay. I didn't think I'd fled far enough. Even as I'd put distance between me and the Empire, I'd set traps, put up decoys, sent out false rumors. I'd done all I could to escape that former life, and yet some nights, sleepless, restless, it feels as if I am just waiting to be found.

Even failure can be a kind of success, my father always said. But I still don't know if I believe that.

Three days pass, and I'm still fixing Hanover, sometimes with help from Shyver, sometimes not. Shyver doesn't have much else to do until the fishing fleet goes out, but that doesn't mean he has to stay cooped up in a cluttered workshop with me. Not when, conveniently, the blacksmith is next door, and with it the lovely daughter of Growder, whom he adores.

Blake says he comes in to check my progress, but I think he comes to check on me. After the Lady Salt left him, he married another—a weaver—but she died in childbirth a year ago, and took the baby with her. Now Blake sees before him a different past: a life that might have been, with the Lady Salt at his side.

I can still remember the generous Blake, the humorous Blake who would stand on a table with a mug of beer made by the hill people and tell an amusing story about being lost at sea, poking fun at himself. But now, because he still loves her, there is only me to hate. Now there is just the brambly fence of his beard to hide him, and the pressure of his eyes, the pursed, thin lips. *If I were a different man. If I loved the Lady Salt less. If she wanted him.*

But instead it is he and I in the work room, Hanover on the table, surrounded by an autopsy of gears and coils and congealed bits of metal long past their purpose. Hanover up close, over time, smells of sea grasses and brine along with the oil. I still do not *know* him. Or what he does. Or why he is here. I think I recognize some of it as the work of the Empire, but I can't be sure. Shyver still thinks Hanover is merely a sculpture from beneath the ocean. But no one makes a sculpture with so many moving parts.

"Make it work," Blake says. "You're the expert. Fix it."

Expert? I'm the only one with any knowledge in this area. For hundreds, maybe thousands, of miles.

"I'm trying," I say. "But then what? We don't know what it does."

This is the central question, perhaps of my life. It is why I go slow with Hanover. My hands already know where most of the parts go. They know most of what is broken, and why.

"Fix it," Blake says, "or at the next council meeting, I will ask that you be sent to live with the hill people for a time."

There's no disguising the self-hatred in his gaze. There's no disguising that he's serious.

"For a time? And what will that prove? Except to show I can live in caves with shepherds?" I almost want an answer.

Blake spits on the wooden floor. "No use to us, why should we feed you? House you…?"

Even if I leave, she won't go back to you.

"What if I fix it and all it does is blink? Or all it does is shed light, like a whale lamp? Or talk in nonsense rhymes? Or I fix it and it kills us all?"

"Don't care," Blake says. "Fix it."

The cliffs around the village are low, like the shoulders of a slouching giant, and caulked with bird shit and white rock, veined through with dark green bramble. Tough, thick lizards scuttle through the branches. Tiny birds take shelter there, their dark eyes staring out from shadow. A smell almost like mint struggles through. Below is the cove where Shyver found Hanover.

Rebecca and I walk there, far enough beyond the village that we cannot be seen, and we talk. We find the old trails and follow them, sometimes silly, sometimes serious. We don't need to be who we are in Sandhaven.

"Blake's getting worse," I tell her. "More paranoid. He's jealous. He says he'll exile me from the village if I don't fix Hanover."

"Then fix Hanover," Rebecca says.

We are holding hands. Her palm is warm and sweaty in mine, but I don't care. Every moment I'm with her feels like something I didn't earn, wasn't looking for, but don't want to lose. Still, something in me rebels. It's tiring to keep proving myself.

"I can do it," I say. "I know I can. But…."

"Blake can't exile you without the support of the council," Lady Salt says. I know it's her, not Rebecca, because of the tone, and the way her blue eye flashes when she looks at me. "But he can make life difficult if you give him cause." A pause, a tightening of her grip. "He's in mourning. You know it makes him not himself. But we need him. We need him back."

A twinge as I wonder how she means that. But it's true: Blake has led the Sandhaven through good times and bad, made tough decisions, and cared about the village.

Sometimes, though, leadership is not enough. What if what you really need is the instinct to be fearful? And the thought as we make our way back to the village: *What if Blake is right about me?*

So I begin to work on Hanover in earnest. There's a complex balance to him that I admire. People think engineering is about practical application of science, and that might be right, if you're building something. But if you're fixing something, something you don't fully understand—say, you're fixing a Hanover—you have no access to a schematic, to a helpful context. Your work instead becomes a kind of detection. You become a kind of detective. You track down clues—cylinders that fit into holes in sheets of steel, that slide into place in grooves, that lead to wires, that lead to understanding.

To do this, I have to stop my ad hoc explorations. Instead, with Shyver's reluctant help, I take Hanover apart systematically. I document where I find each part, and if I think it truly belongs there, or has become dislodged during the trauma that resulted in his "death." I note gaps. I label each part by what I believe it contributed to his overall function. In all things, I remember that Hanover has been made to look like a man, and therefore his innards roughly resemble those of a man in form or function, his makers consciously or subconsciously unable to ignore the implications of that form, that function.

Shyver looks at the parts lying glistening on the table, and says, "They're so different out of him." So different cleaned up, greased with fresh fish oil. Through the window, the sun's light sets them ablaze. Hanover's burnished surface, whorled with a patina of greens, blues, and rust red. The world become radiant.

When we remove the carapace of Hanover's head to reveal a thousand wires, clockwork gears, and strange fluids, even Shyver cannot not think of him as a statue anymore.

"What does a machine like this *do?*" Shyver said, who has only rarely seen anything more complex as a hammer or a watch.

I laugh. "It does whatever it wants to do, I imagine."

By the time I am done with Hanover, I have made several leaps of logic. I have made decisions that cannot be explained as rational, but in their rightness set my head afire with the absolute certainty of Creation. The feeling energizes me and horrifies me all at once.

It was long after my country became an Empire that I decided to escape. And still I might have stayed, even knowing what I had done. That is the tragedy of everyday life: when you are in it, you can never see your *self* clearly.

Even seven years in, Sandhaven having made the past the past, I still had nightmares of gleaming rows of airships. I would wake, screaming, from what had once been a blissful dream, and the Lady Salt and Rebecca both would be there to comfort me.

Did I deserve that comfort?

Shyver is there when Hanover comes alive. I've spent a week speculating on ways to bypass what looked like missing parts, missing wires. I've experimented with a hundred different connections. I've even identified Hanover's independent power source and recharged it using a hand-cranked generator.

Lady Salt has gone out with the fishing fleet for the first time and the village is deserted. Even Blake has gone with her, after a quick threat in my direction once again. If the fishing doesn't go well, the evening will not go any better for me.

Shyver says, "Is that a spark?"

A spark?

"Where?"

I have just put Hanover back together again for possibly the twentieth time and planned to take a break, to just sit back and smoke a hand-rolled cigarette, compliments of the enigmatic hill people.

"In Hanover's...eyes."

Shyver goes white, backs away from Hanover, as if something monstrous has occurred, even though this is what we wanted.

It brings memories flooding back—of the long-ago day steam had come rushing out of the huge iron bubble and the canvas had swelled, and held, and everything I could have wished for in my old life had been attained. That feeling had become addiction—I wanted to experience it again and again—but now it's bittersweet, something to cling to and cast away.

My assistant then had responded much as Shyver is now: both on some instinctual level knowing that something unnatural has happened.

"Don't be afraid," I say to Shyver, to my assistant.

"I'm not afraid," Shyver says, lying.

"You should be afraid," I say.

Hanover's eyes gain more and more of a glow. A clicking sound comes from him. Click, click, click. A hum. A slightly rumbling cough from deep inside, a hum again. We prop him up so he is no longer on his side. He's warm to the touch.

The head rotates from side to side, more graceful than in my imagination.

A sharp intake of breath from Shyver. "It's alive!"

I laugh then. I laugh and say, "In a way. It's got no arms or legs. It's harmless."

It's harmless.

Neither can it speak—just the click, click, click. But no words.

Assuming it is trying to speak.

John Blake and the Lady Salt come back with the fishing fleet. The voyage seems to have done Blake good. The windswept hair, the salt-stung face—he looks relaxed as they enter my workshop.

As they stare at Hanover, at the light in its eyes, I'm almost jealous. Standing side by side, they almost resemble a King and his Queen, and suddenly I'm acutely aware they were lovers, grew up in the village together. Rebecca's gaze is distant; thinking of Blake or of me or of the sea? They smell of mingled brine and fish and salt, and somehow the scent is like a knife in my heart.

"What does it do?" Blake asks.

Always, the same kinds of questions. Why should everything have to have a function?

"I don't know," I say. "But the hill folk should find it pretty and perplexing, at least."

Shyver, though, gives me away, makes me seem less and less from this place: "He thinks it can talk. We just need to fix it *more*. It might do all kinds of things for us."

"It's fixed," I snap, looking at Shyver as if I don't know him at all. We've drunk together, talked many hours. I've given him advice about the blacksmith's daughter. But now that doesn't matter. He's from here and I'm from *there*. "We should trade it to the hill folk and be done with it."

Click, click, click. Hanover won't stop. And I just want it over with, so I don't slide into the past.

Blake's calm has disappeared. I can tell he thinks I lied to him. "Fix it," he barks. "I mean *really* fix it. Make it talk."

He turns on his heel and leaves the workshop, Shyver behind him.

Lady Salt approaches, expression unreadable. "Do as he says. Please. The fishing…there's little enough out there. We need every advantage now."

Her hand on the side of my face, warm and calloused, before she leaves.

Maybe there's no harm in it. If I just do what they ask, this one last time—the last of many times—it will be over. Life will return to normal. I can stay here. I can still find a kind of peace.

Once, there was a foolish man who saw a child's balloon rising into the sky and thought it could become a kind of airship. No one in his world had ever created such a thing, but he already had ample evidence of his own genius in the things he had built before. Nothing had come close to challenging his engineering skills. No one had ever told him he might have limits. His father, a biology teacher, had taught him to focus on problems and solutions. His mother, a caterer, had shown him the value of attention to detail and hard work.

He took his plans, his ideas, to the government. They listened enough to give him some money, a place to work, and an assistant. All this despite his youth, because of his brilliance, and in his turn he ignored how they talked about their enemies, the need to thwart external threats.

When this engineer was successful, when the third prototype actually worked, following three years of flaming disaster, he knew he had created something that had never before existed, and his heart nearly burst with pride. His wife had left him because she never saw him except when he needed sleep, the house was a junkyard, and yet he didn't care. He'd done it.

He couldn't know that it wouldn't end there. As far as he was concerned, they could take it apart and let him start on something else, and his life would have been good because he knew when he was happiest.

But the government's military advisers wanted him to perfect the airship. They asked him to solve problems that he hadn't thought about before. How to add weight to the carriage without its serving as undue ballast, so things could be dropped from the airship. How to add "defensive" weapons. How to make them work without igniting the fuel that drove the airship. A series of challenges that appealed to his pride, and maybe, too, he had grown used to the rich life he had now. Caught up in it all, he just kept going, never said no, and focused on the gears, the wires, the air ducts, the myriad tiny details that made him ignore everything else.

This foolish man used his assistants as friends to go drinking with, to sleep with, to be his whole life, creating a kind of cult there in his workshop that had become a gigantic hangar, surrounded by soldiers and barbed-wire fence. He'd become a national hero.

But I still remembered how my heart had felt when the prototype had risen into the air, how the tears trickled down my face as around me men and women literally danced with joy. How I was struck by the image of my own success, almost as if I were flying.

The prototype wallowed and snorted in the air like a great golden whale in a harness, wanting to be free: a blazing jewel against the bright blue sky, the dream made real.

I don't know what the Lady Salt would have thought of it. Maybe nothing at all.

One day, Hanover finally speaks. I push a button, clean a gear, move a circular bit into place. It is just me and him. Shyver wanted no part of it.

He says, "Command water the sea was bright with the leavings of the fish that there were now going to be."

Clicks twice, thrice, and continues clicking as he takes the measure of me with his golden gaze and says, "Engineer Daniker."

The little hairs on my neck rise. I almost lose my balance, all the blood rushing to my head.

"How do you know my name?"

"You are my objective. You are why I was sent."

"Across the ocean? Not likely."

"I had a ship once, arms and legs once, before your traps destroyed me."

I had forgotten the traps I'd set. I'd almost forgotten my true name.

"You will return with me. You will resume your duties."

I laugh bitterly. "They've found no one to replace me?"

Hanover has no answer—just the clicking—but I know the answer. Child prodigy. Unnatural skills. An unswerving ability to focus in on a problem and solve it. Like...building airships. I'm still an asset they cannot afford to lose.

"You've no way to take me back. You have no authority here," I say.

Hanover's bright eyes dim, then flare. The clicking intensifies. I wonder now if it is the sound of a weapons system malfunctioning.

"Did you know I was here, in this village?" I ask.

A silence. Then: "Dozens were sent for you—scattered across the world."

"So no one knows."

"I have already sent a signal. They are coming for you."

Horror. Shock. And then anger—indescribable rage, like nothing I've ever experienced.

When they find me with Hanover later, there isn't much left of him. I've smashed his head in and then his body, and tried to grind that down with a pestle. I didn't know where the beacon might be hidden, or if it even mattered, but I had to try.

They think I'm mad—the soft-spoken blacksmith, a livid Blake, even Rebecca. I keep telling them the Empire is coming, that I am the Empire's chief engineer. That I've been in hiding. That they need to leave now—into the hills, into the sea. *Anywhere but here....*

But Blake can't see it—he sees only me—and whatever the Lady Salt thinks, she hides it behind a sad smile.

"I said to fix it," Blake roars before he storms out. "Now it's no good for anything!"

Roughly I am taken to the little room that functions as the village jail, with the bars on the window looking out on the sea. As they leave me, I am shouting, "I created their airships! They're coming for me!"

The Lady Salt backs away from the window, heads off to find Blake, without listening.

After dark, Shyver comes by the window, but not to hear me out—just to ask why I did it.

"We could at least have sold it to the hill people," he whispers. He sees only the village, the sea, the blacksmith's daughter. "We put so much work into it."

I have no answer except for a story that he will not believe is true.

Once, there was a country that became an Empire. Its armies flew out from the center and conquered the margins, the barbarians. Everywhere it inflicted itself on the world, people died or came under its control, always under the watchful, floating gaze of the airships. No one had ever seen anything like them before. No one had any defense for them. People wrote poems about them and cursed them and begged for mercy from their attentions.

The chief engineer of this atrocity, the man who had solved the problems, sweated the details, was finally called up by the Emperor of the newly minted Empire fifteen years after he'd seen a golden shape float against a startling blue sky. The Emperor was on the far frontier, some remote place fringed by desert where the people built their homes into the sides of hills and used tubes to spit fire up into the sky.

They took me to His Excellency by airship, of course. For the first time, except for excursions to the capital, I left my little enclave, the country I'd created for myself. From on high, I saw what I had helped create. In the conquered lands, the people looked up at us in fear and hid when and where they could. Some, beyond caring, threw stones up at us: an old woman screaming words I could not hear from that distance, a young man with a bow, the arrows arching below the carriage until the airship commander opened fire, left a red smudge on a dirt road as we glided by from on high.

This vision I had not known existed unfurled like a slow, terrible dream, for we were like languid Gods in our progress, the landscape revealing itself to us with a strange finality.

On the fringes, war still was waged, and before we reached the Emperor I saw my creations clustered above hostile armies, raining down *my* bombs onto stick figures who bled, screamed, died, were mutilated, blown apart... all as if in a silent film, the explosions deafening us, the rest reduced to distant pantomime narrated by the black-humored cheer of our airship's officers.

A child's head resting upon a rock, the body a red shadow. A city reduced to rubble. A man whose limbs had been torn from him. All the same.

By the time I reached the Emperor, received his blessing and his sword, I had nothing to say; he found me more mute than any captive, his instrument once more. And when I returned, when I could barely stand myself anymore, I found a way to escape my cage.

Only to wash up on a beach half a world away.

Out of the surf, out of the sand, dripping and half-dead, I stumble and the Lady Salt and Blake stand there, above me. I look up at them in the half-light of morning, arm raised against the sun, and wonder whether they will welcome me or kill me or just cast me aside.

The Lady Salt looks doubtful and grim, but Blake's broad face breaks into a smile. "Welcome stranger," he says, and extends his hand.

I take it, relieved. In that moment, there's no Hanover, no pain, no sorrow, nothing but the firm grip, the arm pulling me up toward them.

They come at dawn, much faster than I had thought possible: ten airships, golden in the light, the humming thrum of their propellers audible over the crash of the sea. From behind my bars, I watch their deadly, beautiful approach across the slate-gray sky, the deep-blue waves, and it is as if my children are returning to me. If there is no mercy in them, it is because I never thought of mercy when I created the bolt and canvas of them, the fuel and gears of them.

Hours later, I sit in the main cabin of the airship *Forever Triumph.* It has mahogany tables and chairs, crimson cushions. A platter of fruit upon a dais. A telescope on a tripod. A globe of the world. The scent of snuff. All the debris of the real world. We sit on the window seat, the Lady Salt and I. Beyond, the rectangular windows rise and fall just slightly, showing cliffs and hills and sky; I do not look down.

Captain Evans, aping civilized speech, has been talking to us for several minutes. He is fifty and rake-thin and has hooded eyes that make him mournful forever. I don't really know what he's saying; I can't concentrate. I just feel numb, as if I'm not really there.

Blake insisted on fighting what could not be fought. So did most of the others. I watched from behind my bars as first the bombs came and then the troops. I heard Blake die, although I didn't see it. He was cursing and screaming at them; he didn't go easy. Shyver was shot in the leg, dragged himself off moaning. I don't know if he made it.

I forced myself to listen—to all of it.

They had orders to take me alive, and they did. They found the Lady Salt with a gutting knife, but took her too when I told the Captain I'd cooperate if they let her live.

Her presence at my side is something unexpected and horrifying. What can she be feeling? Does she think I could have saved Blake but chose not to? Her eyes are dry and she stares straight ahead, at nothing, at no one, while the Captain continues with his explanations, his threats, his flattery.

"Rebecca," I say. "Rebecca," I say.

The whispered words of the Lady Salt are everything, all the Chief Engineer could have expected: *"Someday I will kill you and escape to the sea."*

I nod wearily and turn my attention back to the Captain, try to understand what he is saying.

Below me, the village burns as all villages burn, everywhere, in time.

Salvage

Margaret Ronald

COLONEL DIETERICH CLOSED the maintenance panel below the airship's secondary propeller, sending a puff of gray dust cascading over the mesa. "Well, it looks fine, despite the rough landing," he said. "I should be able to fly us out of here."

I brushed dust from my trousers. "Not that I'm accusing you of hubris, sir, but I'm sure others have said the same thing, and, well—" I gestured to the shambles just beyond our little airship: the shattered undercarriage of a wrecked dirigible much larger than our own. The high, sagging dome scaled with thousands of bronze plates verdigrised by half a century's disuse gave the derelict *Chiaro* the look of some great fish dragged from its home. Beside it, our little propeller-driven airship was no more than a sneeze.

Dieterich's heavy brows lowered in an irritated glare. "Yes, well, they weren't flying a ship of my design, now were they? Nor were the other idiots who tried to land on the far side of the wreck, with their ridiculous 'salvage blimp'—" He stopped as a ramp unfolded from the side of our ship. "Don't tell the Professora I said so," he added in an undertone.

I nodded assent as Professora Lundqvist descended from our airship onto the mesa. Her tank sloshed gently as her wheels reached the uneven ground, and the sensor ring on top of her tank rotated one way, then the other. "Professora," I ventured, "are you sure you ought to be out?"

"Quite sure," she responded, her phonograph translating not only her words but her air of dismissal. "Would you rather I stayed put, like some kind of potted plant?"

"I'd rather you stayed back in town," Dieterich grumbled, getting to his feet. "You have no business being along on this mission, Lundqvist; you're too easily damaged."

"Phidias was my student. That makes it my business." She pivoted back and rolled some distance away. "If one of your students decided to go off on some harebrained salvage mission that then crashed in hostile territory, I'm quite certain you'd do the same."

The Colonel sighed. "In that case, we'd best make our way around and examine where his blimp crashed. At the very least we can learn how they— damn it all, Lundqvist!"

The Professora had already moved on, trundling across the mesa. Grumbling about damnably stubborn brains in damnably stubborn jars, Dieterich followed after her, tugging his greatcoat over his shoulders, then paused as he realized I wasn't following. "Coming, Charles?"

"In a moment, sir."

I've traveled with the Colonel too long to keep certain moods secret. He turned back to face me, arms folded. "You've been out of sorts since…well, since we got word about Phidias, at least. Mind telling me what's wrong?"

Since longer than that, to be truthful, but I didn't blame the Colonel for looking to the proximate cause. "I don't much like derelicts, sir." Truth, if not the whole truth.

Dieterich chuckled. "Me either, honestly. They're too strong a reminder of mortality. But," he added, stumping after the Professora, "as I said, our little ship should be just fine. Don't worry so."

"If you say so, sir," I murmured, gazing up at the plates that had once armored the *Chiaro*'s dirigible sac, now unhinged by time and age.

It was not that I held the misunderstanding against the Colonel. He might see it as a theoretical *memento mori,* but the shattered metal and gears of the *Chiaro* were a little too similar to the mechanical augmentations that ran through my own flesh. It was understandable that he would forget, given that for a number of reasons I had to keep my nature a secret from all but him and the Professora, but I was never unaware of it. I had been designed and altered with as much care as the *Chiaro* had been, and though I might no longer use my Merged elements in their original cause, I could not so much as draw breath or even blink without remembering them.

We left the sagging dome of the dirigible sac unexamined, since despite its awe-inspiring bulk it was no more than a shell. Instead we crept into what little of the undercarriage remained. According to the old broadsheets, when the pilot's control over the mighty airship broke at last, giving way to the many wounds inflicted by the automata of Parch, the undercarriage had dragged along the top of the mesa and left nothing behind.

This proved only partly accurate; while the lower levels had been demolished entirely, a few of the higher ones remained. We wrangled the Professora over the shattered beams, ignoring her grumbling at having to be manhandled so, and I wrenched open a gap in what had once been the floor of the second-class compartments. "The gilding's still in place," I said as we clambered through. "It looks untouched."

"Of course it's untouched," the Professora muttered. "Only idiots come up here. And yes, I am including Phidias in that assessment."

She had a point. The *Chiaro* had remained undisturbed for two very good reasons: the bitter winds that wreathed the mesa and had given us such a rough landing, and the automaton town of Parch to the east. Automata, thinking machines, were not particularly bellicose, but they were fiercely protective of anything they considered their territory. The *Chiaro* itself had proved that by straying into Parch's airspace, and that had been its downfall: the vaunted plating of the sac proved ineffective as armor but very effective as ballast. The wounded dirigible had limped away and crashed in disputed territory, so any official recovery attempts were scrapped.

Which left the unofficial, the underfunded, and, inevitably, the disastrous attempts. And, sure as gravity, people like the Professora to clean up after those attempts, bringing along people like me in her wake, who were just as adrift as the damaged *Chiaro* had been.

Behind me, Dieterich turned in a slow circle. "They still tell stories about the crash, you know."

Lundqvist made a sharp, chattering noise, something her phonograph could not quite interpret into speech. "I'm sure they do. Charles, could you move this beam? Dieterich, do give him a hand; your valet can't do all the work."

"He already makes all the tea," the Colonel said mildly, but winked at me. We heaved a large beam—glittering with fine strands of werglass—out of an arched doorway, now at a thirty-degree angle. "Last time I was back home," he went on, "they even made it part of the pantomime. Something about self-sacrifice, the men and women who'd signed on as thaumaturges giving their lives to keep the *Chiaro* aloft while the passengers evacuated. They'd even brought an actress from the Capitol to play Raisa the pilot, dying in her throne...."

I caught his eye, and he shrugged. "Melodrama, of course," he added sheepishly.

"Good lord," the Professora said, and when we looked up from the beam, we understood why. Even the most luxurious airship I'd traveled in was still at heart a transport, and so every space had been used. Here, the makers of the *Chiaro* had flaunted their wealth through empty space. Even though the walls had been twisted by the crash, this was unmistakably a ballroom. Parquet floors sloped from a low angle at one end to the opposite angle at the far end, like an ocean wave, and each inlay gleamed with gold leaf.

It was not the only mark of excess. "Look," Dieterich said, pointing to the walls. High panels of molded werglass glowed weakly. "I haven't seen this much waste since my brother's wedding," he added, but in a tone of wonder rather than condemnation as his reflection pointed back at him.

"There's werglass spun through the whole thing," the Professora said, rolling with some difficulty toward a broken gap in the wall. Dust from the mesa had sifted inside, limning the long, broken strands of glass that ran through the wall like horsehair through plaster. A faint, greasy glow sparked as she drew back, a sign of thaumic distillation worked into the glass.

"But that would make every wall worth a king's ransom," I said.

"Several kings," she acknowledged, using one of her two styli to pry aside a fragment of werglass. "The thaumaturges who managed it must have been able to perceive the entire structure."

I shivered, and not just because of the wind leaking through the broken walls. Airship thaumaturgy was based on the link between man and machine, a machine controlled directly by human concentration, by carefully trained experts whose mental discipline simultaneously kept them separate from the machine and cognizant of its flight. I was the opposite: my machinery was completely integrated, to the point where I no longer perceived it as something outside myself. My eyes itched from the pressure of multiple lenses behind them, and for a moment I was very aware of the thrum of the engines that passed for my heart.

My reflection watched me from a cracked werglass panel, streaked down the middle with blackish-green where the ore had seeped out from the crack and solidified. From outside I looked human, but only the same way that from a distance the *Chiaro* looked intact. But the thaumaturges of the *Chiaro* had not considered their airship any more alive than their pocket watches. I smiled nervously, and after a second, the reflection smiled too. Werglass reflections, and their delay, will never cease to unnerve me.

"Halloo!" Dieterich yelled from the next room over, and I hurried over the warped parquet to reach him. Here, a small tea-salon had been turned on the opposite side from the second-class compartments, as if the whole undercarriage had been corkscrewed. A broad staircase had once been meant to sweep down into what I assumed had been passenger cabins; a smaller, less ornate one led to a more utilitarian door that still sported an embossed gold seal. "Halloo, anyone there?"

No answer. The Professora's springs sagged, and she drew styli and phonograph in as if to protect herself. "I can't make it over those stairs," she murmured. "Charles, Dieterich, let's go back outside and around to the salvage mission wreck—"

A tiny quad-bolt, no longer than the last joint on my little finger, dropped from the staircase above, coming to rest against the Colonel's boot. Slowly, like a broken wind-up toy, a man's face peered down from behind the little door with the gold seal. "Who," he said, then blinked and donned a pair of cracked eyeglasses. "Professora? Is that you?"

"Phidias." Lundqvist rolled to the foot of the stairs. "You are a royal idiot, first class, do you know that? Come down here this instant."

Her former student obeyed, still moving as if he were unsure how arms and legs worked. "Professora," he said again, and smiled. Even with three weeks' beard and a dry, unwashed aroma to him, his smile remained as brilliant as if we were at a Society function. "I'm so glad you came," he added, resting his forehead against the top of her tank, sand-colored hair flopping lank over her sensor ring.

"So am I, Fiddy. So am I." She was silent a moment, then rolled back. "Where are the rest of your team? What happened?"

"Windstorm?" the Colonel offered.

"Not quite," he said, walking past us to a breach in what had once been the floor but now made one of the walls of the tea-salon. "We're near Parch, remember? One moment we were about to land, and then—" He shook his head. "I thought I'd seen something on the ground, but it was too late—the first shot knocked us out of the sky, and the second finished the job. I'm surprised you made it past them." He drew a shaky breath. "As for your other question—" He opened the window, then turned away. "There."

I risked a glance over the Colonel's shoulder. Six mounds of earth marked a line tucked against the side of the *Chiaro*. "Fiddy," the Professora whispered. "I'm so sorry."

He managed a shrug, but his eyes were red. "We knew it was a risk to come up here, but we thought those damned Parch clankers wouldn't be guarding it. Most of my team died in the crash, and the ones who didn't...I'm no doctor, Professora. I was never good at field medicine."

The Colonel bowed his head. "You've been here alone, then?" I said.

Phidias started. I regretted speaking up; my status with the Colonel and Professora might be more informal, but to the Society at large I was still only the Colonel's valet, no more than a fixture in the background. "It wasn't so bad," he said, turning to the Professora. "And we'd brought enough rations and water for seven.... I haven't even really put a dent in that."

"Yes, well, we've come to take you home, Fiddy. I can cover your debts, and then you and I are going to have a long talk—"

"Home?" He looked up, alert for the first time. "No, no, I can't go home yet. You don't realize what they did when they made this ship."

"What, burned heaps of money in a furnace?" Dieterich muttered.

Phidias shot him a glare. "No, you—no, nothing like that." He held up a thin sliver of werglass so dark it practically stank of thaumic contamination, then fumbled in his coat and produced a folded blueprint. "Raisa, the pilot—you remember the stories? She wasn't just the pilot; she designed the whole thaumaturgical linkup, and she was so ahead of her time I can barely decipher her work. But the linkup is entirely different—it's based on parallel rather than serial mode."

I glanced at the Colonel, since most of that had gone over my head. To my dismay, he looked thoughtful, and the Professora's tank had begun to bubble. "You mean a multiply-enhanced link," he said, tugging at his mustache. "Compartmentalization."

"Exactly!" Phidias beamed at him. Myself, I was still lost. "Exactly. They haven't tried to make anything on the scale of the *Chiaro* since the crash, but if a parallel link process could be developed, it would revolutionize airship design. I'm almost on the verge of deciphering it—please, just a little longer, and I'll have it. You can even take the credit before the Society if you want, I don't mind, it's not as though they'll have me back—"

"Don't talk like that, Fiddy," the Professora said. "If you make a discovery, you claim credit. Simple as that." She rotated to face Dieterich. "We've got the provisions. And don't worry about me; I had my tank changed before we left."

"Then it's settled!" Phidias clapped his hands. "I'll bring down the unit log—"

A thump and rattle sounded from the depths of the *Chiaro,* and Phidias froze. "Not another one!"

"Another—"

Phidias paid no attention to the Colonel. "They've been coming here, coming to steal her—" He clenched the banister so tight, his fingers turned white, then he clambered up the skewed staircase and returned with several loops of heavy cable. "Help me. If we trip it, we can tie it—"

The Colonel glanced at me and nodded to the Professora. She made an irritated noise, but I put my back to her tank, ready to defend her.

Because Phidias wasn't looking, I leaned over and exerted some of my Merged strength to wrench a bent pipe from what was left of the wall. But as I straightened up, a glimmer flickered in the corner of my eye—not from below, but behind, in the ballroom.

"There!" Phidias whispered. "Do you see it?"

"Yes," I said, but in truth I wasn't sure what I saw—something like the reverse of a shadow, a glimmer of reflected light passing from one pane of werglass to another. Sunlight, I told myself despite the heavy cloud cover outside, or some Merged reaction to the werglass. Shivers running down through my bones, I raised the pipe, backing up against the Professora—

A shriek and clatter echoed behind me, and I spun to see Phidias clinging to the back of what looked like a four-legged metal spider. Dieterich swung his end of the cable and lassoed the thing's legs, and the whole mess toppled over, chattering in a blur of unintelligible static. "That's it!" Phidias yelled, scrambling away. "That's one of them!"

"An automaton?" the Professora said. "From Parch?"

The machine looked up at her—a strange gesture from something that had neither head nor eyes. Instead, something like a scarab had been welded onto the front of it, and this rotated as it got a better look at us. "Parch," it repeated in a surprisingly dulcet voice.

"Oh, this isn't good," Dieterich muttered.

I was not accustomed to the sentient automata that populated the Hundred Cities, and had always assumed they would be larger. This one, however, stood only about a foot taller than me, its legs folding out from a central core as wide as the Professora's tank. The speaker at the base of the machine's "head" thrummed, and a stream of atonal syllables issued forth.

Dieterich shook his head. "None of us speaks Lower Kingdom."

The automaton clacked, a sound that somehow echoed one of Lundqvist's irritated sniffs. "I speak Imperial. Not well."

"I thought this was off-limits to *both* sides of the border," said the Professora.

"Rule of Parch, yes. Rule of earth, no. I follow rule of earth."

Dieterich drummed his fingers against the crumpled samovars, scarred brown digits tapping out an irregular rhythm. "So you're here in violation of Hundred Cities law?"

Its central column swiveled in place. "Rule of Cities, rule of earth. I am here for, *hhhnn,*" the speaker twitched as it thought, "pilgrimage."

"What?" I took a step closer, forgetting that I still held the pipe, and the automaton twitched, focusing on me.

"That's ridiculous." Phidias got up from his place at the foot of the tilted staircase, his fists clenching and unclenching. "Ridiculous. And the ones who shot us down, were they on 'pilgrimage' too?"

It swiveled again. "Might be."

Phidias's lips curled. "Then they're in violation too," the Professora said smoothly. "In the meantime, I intend to stay put."

"And for better reasons than that—thing," Phidias snapped. "It's a machine. Machines don't have a religion. If you believe that 'pilgrimage' rot, then you're—"

"Belief isn't the matter here," Dieterich paused, glancing at the automaton. *"Do* machines have a religion?"

Phidias snorted, and for the first time I found myself in agreement with him. Obviously, machines didn't bother with such matters; the idea was as foolish as...as life remaining in a derelict airship. I cast a glance over my shoulder at the empty ballroom, shivering.

The automaton's insides churned a moment, an unpleasantly grinding noise. "No," it said finally. "But this one will make her circuit regardless." It rose up, snapping the cable as if it were no more than frost-killed straw. "This one is Transit-born, chosen female, designated Chaff."

Though he'd flinched back at the sight of the cable breaking, Phidias snorted at the "chosen female" bit. "Some automata do choose a gender," Dieterich pointed out.

Chaff nodded. "Stayed female fifty years. Before that, neuter. Considered gender a fad for younger mata. Changed mind before beginning Path."

"You don't look much like a thresher," I said.

Chaff's eyes swung toward me. "Do you look as you did when natal?"

"Charles," the Professora said softly, and I quieted. Behind her, a faint glimmer passed over the shattered werglass in the wall, gone before I could be sure that anything had provided that reflection.

I shivered and glanced again at the empty ballroom, trying to convince myself that I'd seen nothing, a task that might have been easier had I not known I'd been designed to notice unusual things.

The next few days passed far too slowly for my tastes. Phidias scrambled all over the remnant of the *Chiaro*, ranging from his little nest in the pilot's cabin with cutting torches and saws in hand, claiming that the residue of Raisa's work remained in the werglass logs in the "unnecessary portions" of the ship. I couldn't argue with the fact that much of the *Chiaro* seemed unnecessary, but as wall after wall gave way to his incessant banging, the resulting headache seeped into my skull and would not leave. It didn't help that he liked to sing as he worked, and though I couldn't make out the tune, the echoes of it were deeply unnerving.

Dieterich, for his part, proved much the same as his role at the Society: place a puzzle in front of him, and he was happily enthralled. Occasionally, he tried to find a way into the thaumaturgy chamber, because airtight emergency doors had shut that section off, presumably so that any fires that started in the airship would not affect the thaumaturges. Because the Professora was limited to those parts of the wreck that her wheels could traverse, she spent much of her time in the tea-salon, brooding.

Myself, I tried to find reasons to stay out of the wreck. But there were few other places to go—our cramped propeller ship, the smeared wreckage of Phidias's salvage expedition, or the barren mesa itself. Cold, dry wind drove grit into my eyes when I ventured outside, and though the heavy gray sky above threatened rain, I knew anything that fell would evaporate long before it reached us.

The *Chiaro* wreck itself was little more hospitable: at one end was the uncanny ballroom, at the other a nest of airtight doors blocking off the thaumaturgy chamber. The pilot's cabin itself was Phidias's domain, though I hardly grudged him the space, because that must have been where Raisa herself had died. To reach the Professora, I had to cross that warped parquet floor, and every time I entered the ballroom I had the sensation of being watched. My mechanical reflexes remained alert, but with nothing to lash out at. And though I had passed for human for decades, here I was far too aware of what ran in my bones as surely as thaumic distillation ran through werglass. I slept poorly, dreaming of the metal inside me, of the airship coming alive around me as my own body betrayed and devoured itself, and woke to a ship that should have been empty and dead. But the occasional glimmer, trick of the light or my eyes or something more, made that "should have" more of a hope than a statement.

If Phidias had been through three weeks of this on his own, no wonder he was such a wreck.

My nerves went from unsteady to outright paranoid when, late one afternoon, I heard a tenor voice, clearer than it had ever been, echoing from the *Chiaro*. I picked my way through the second-class cabin, gooseflesh prickling my skin. It was a sentimental love song, the kind to which swains add their beloveds' names: *Even the wind follows your steps/but not as close as I/Raisa, Raisa....*

The name sent a fresh shiver down my back, and I stumbled, knocking over a broken bench. The singing stopped, and quick footsteps receded. I hurried through the door in time to see the glimmer shivering across the panes on the far side of the ballroom. To either side Phidias's reflection, slower than he was, turned and ran. But deeper in the glass, held in the reflections of reflections, he was still dancing, arms extended to nothing.

I started after him, then stopped as I realized the light in the room was dimmer than it should have been. I turned to the gap in the wall, only to see a blank scarab-face staring back. "Chaff," I breathed, but the automaton turned away, its shadow following.

I squeezed out through the wall, werglass bristles dragging at my trousers, and landed on the uneven mesa with a thump that sent dust spiraling out. Chaff made no move to elude me, forelegs folding to bring it closer to the earth. "Chaff," I said as I reached it. "What did you do to him?"

It leaned farther, tapping its body against the ground, then rose. "Specifics?"

"The glimmer—Phidias. What he was dancing with. You've been projecting that, haven't you?" A coil tightened, somewhere in my gut. "You did, didn't you? You did something to the werglass, made that glimmer. He was *dancing* with it."

Chaff was silent a moment. "I am not so strong," it said finally. "Nor so active."

I caught my breath, startled no less by the machine's serenity than by its tacit agreement that the glimmer was not my imagination.

It continued walking, stopping every five paces in what I assumed was an approximation of prayer. "Pilgrimage of the Path is not worship, but consideration. Meditation on the liminal states. Here, on sin as well." It bent again, this time murmuring a chatter of machine-talk. "I contemplate the echo of flesh in machine and the great sin behind it. Contemplation is not what that one wants."

The echo of flesh in machine. I put one hand to my chest, very aware of what passed for a heart there, of the thaumically infused flesh that kept me alive and running. Chaff's life, if it could be called that, sprang from the residual thaumic infusion of her its body; I was not so different, for all that I counted myself mostly human. "But if you truly mean what you say," I went on, not quite able to believe I was entertaining the possibility, "then why did you tell the Colonel that the machines had no religion?"

Chaff's central column pivoted, the result very like a person cocking her head to one side. "Because he used the singular."

It took a moment for that to settle in. "You mean there's more than one?"

Chaff made a winding-up noise, and abruptly I recognized it as a chuckle. "One? That is like saying, *hhhhn,*" she paused to consider, "all flesh has one favorite music. Many kinds. And some prefer no music, or pictures instead."

"Many kinds," I echoed.

"Many and many." Her scarab tilted. "Path of the Earth, best. Noughts, fine but talk too much, do little. Monastic Column, broke off from Path some time ago, idiots. Way of the Steel Emperor, all stripped gears, bent ratchets... also *smug*. Yes. Smug is right." Chaff chuckled again. "In Parch, ninety-two sects, three hundred mata. Interesting conversations. Of those ninety-two...."

She went on, speaking more quickly, interspersing automata chatter and Lower Kingdom words. I could already feel my eyes glazing over at the thought of an hour-long discussion of sectarian beliefs among the automata.

Chaff turned to face me. "You would hear Path of the Earth?"

"I—" Although proselytizing automata might be worse.

"Charles! A word with you!" Dieterich emerged from underneath our little airship, then paused as he saw Chaff. "*Now,* please, Charles."

I followed Dieterich behind our airship. "Yes, sir?"

"Get Lundqvist and young Phidias. Make him pack up every last splinter of glass if that's what it takes, but we're leaving as soon as I get this repaired."

"Gladly, sir," I began, then stopped. "Repaired?"

"Yes." He opened a panel under the propeller mount and gestured at the cables within—and the very noticeable gap where the cables ended. "Repaired. The motivating element's gone. As well as half our fuel—enough that descending will probably be interesting."

"Stolen? You're sure?" Dieterich gave me a look. "Sorry, sir. But who—"

He chomped on his pipe thoughtfully. "Phidias is too scatterbrained, I think, to manage any real sabotage. Chaff, though…I rather like automata, Charles, but they don't think the same way we do."

I thought of Chaff's meditation on sin. I'd been so baffled by her that I hadn't asked why she had been watching Phidias, or what the glimmer really was. I pushed away my lingering unease over the glimmer to concentrate on the more real, present problem. "It's possible."

"More than possible. And certainly it would be convenient for the Parch automata if we did not return." He ran one hand over the fringe of tight gray curls that was all that remained of his hair. "I can rig the ship to fire without it, but I don't want to risk another sabotage. We're leaving now."

I hurried back inside the wreck, scrambling over splintered benches, casting glances over my shoulder for Chaff. "Professora! Phidias!"

"Here, Charles."

I paused at the door to the ballroom. The Professora stood before one of the mirrors, her brain reflected as no more than a pale smear against the glass. "Professora," I said, not liking either how my voice echoed or how my reflections bent one after the other to follow her. "How soon can you pack up?"

"Hm? Oh, a few minutes, I suppose." She didn't move, though. "Charles, could you do me a favor?"

If it would get her moving, I'd do anything. "Certainly, Professora."

"I know you can *see* properly. Would you do so now?"

I hesitated. The Professora and Dieterich both knew my nature, knew that my eyes were only one of the many parts of me that no longer had a claim to being human.

"Your secret will be safe. Phidias is off cutting through walls to get to his lost Raisa, so he won't see you."

At that I started. "You knew?"

She let out a long, slow noise, not unlike a sigh. "Fiddy and were close once. I can tell when he's in love. Please, Charles."

I blinked, then focused, lenses sliding in front of my eyes as they adjusted, the pressure in what in humans was the sinus cavity building into a slow headache. "What exactly am I looking at?" I said, flicking from lens to lens.

"The glass, Charles. And I think you've seen it too."

My mouth was dry, and I forced away the memory of Phidias dancing with nothing. "A ghost?" I managed, failing to imply that the idea was foolish.

"That's what Fiddy thinks," the Professora said simply.

I shifted the last lens into place and caught my breath. Through the altered lenses of my Merged physiognomy, the werglass to every side flared and flickered, energy chasing through it like a flock of birds in the air, like fire across a grass plain. "There's a trace of power still moving through the glass." Not a ghost, after all, but residual energy, something left over from its former use. No more a ghost than the lenses I used were an intruder in my body. "It's not coherent, though. The glass isn't in use, it's just still powered. Somehow."

"I thought so. My senses aren't exactly the same as yours, Charles, but I could still tell something about the glass...." She sighed, her springs relaxing. "Do you know what they warn us about in theoretical thaumics?"

"It's not my department," I said, still staring.

"Embodiment. Loss of self. It's worst for the thaumaturges; there's a reason most airships only keep them on short shifts. When you're using your mind to control an entire airship, it's easy to lose oneself in the body of the machine." She flexed her each of her styli in turn, like an artist examining her hands. "It's almost the opposite of what they tell anyone going through the acorporeal treatment."

Echo of flesh in machine, Chaff had said.

"They've tried to transfer the human mind to automata, you know. Failed, repeatedly. You and I are as close as they'll ever come to that, and my position is hardly enviable." She chuckled, sadly. "But dying while linked isn't yet fully understood. And now Fiddy...Fiddy believes he's fallen in love with a ghost."

"An echo," I said. And a sin? What was sin to machines?

"Charles, I need you to do one more favor for me."

I adjusted my eyes back to normal, wincing at the pressure. "Professora, the Colonel has said we need to leave immediately."

"So we shall. This will only take a moment. And it will make the leaving easier."

The favor in question was simple enough: put down a ramp so that the Professora could finally reach the little pilot's cabin where Phidias had been working. She waited in the salon, listening to the muffled cacophony as Phidias cut yet another section of undercarriage away, while I wrestled several fragments of benches into place and helped her wheel onto them.

The cabin was the one part of the *Chiaro* that resembled any other airship: crammed with equipment, werglass consoles on swinging frames so that a quick pilot could shuffle between them when needed without bothering to consult the thaumaturges—the ones who must have been on the far side of the sealing door at the end of the chamber, I realized. Instinctively, I turned to the heavy chair built into the wall: the main throne, from which the pilot could run the whole dirigible in case of thaumaturgy failure. It was empty. "Raisa—she should be—"

"Fiddy probably buried what was left," Lundqvist said absently, turning over lenses. "If there was anything—it looks like the fire came through here, even if Fiddy's been polishing it up." She motioned to blackened, ashy marks on the werglass, the crazed and leaking lenses.

Phidias's blankets and foul-smelling clothes lay in a heap, swaddling shards and irregular blocks of werglass. "This can't be his research," I murmured. "I don't think even the Colonel could draw anything from this."

"Which is why he kept Dieterich working on the larger pieces," Lundqvist said over the growing din of Phidias's work. "Poor Dieterich. He might play the hardened military man, but he's too trusting." Her lower stylus lifted disintegrating leather straps and dropped them again. "The werglass is useless, Charles. There is no hidden breakthrough."

"Then why stay?"

The Professora hissed. "Charles, look." She glided back half a pace. "This throne is not meant for proper thaumaturgy. No one in a meditative mudra could sit here. Nor would they need to be strapped in."

I got to my feet. "You think—"

"There are scratches on the armpieces. Small, but present. And the neural tap—" Her stylus drew back, as if fearing contagion.

I looked where she gestured. Near the top of the throne, where Raisa's head would have rested, there should have been a werglass knob. Instead, a dull metal spike gleamed with tracings of glass. I shuddered at the sight of it.

"That is anything but temporary, Charles. I always wondered how the *Chiaro* even got airborne—it was too big, you'd need dozens of thaumaturges on repeated shifts, not the six plus Raisa that the broadsheets lauded. And with the werglass—that would just make things worse, the thaumaturges would have been aware of the entire damned ship, not just the propulsion. Unless they weren't kept on shifts. Unless they were irrevocably wired into the machine."

I adjusted my eyes to see the scratches better. Heroic sacrifice, Dieterich had said of the pantomime back home. But what worth was a forced sacrifice?

The scratches on the throne became clearer, as did something else. The tarnish of fifty years' disuse had been scraped away. "Professora, these scratches—"

The constant clang of Phidias's investigations suddenly turned deafening. I spun to see the airtight door opening, a cloud of dust—no, not dust, but smoke—

I may have lost much that made me human, but my lungs are as weak as any man's. I fell back, coughing, and only briefly caught a glimpse of Phidias, masked, raising a bent pipe and bringing it down across my temple.

I woke to pressure across my chest and waist and outright pain at my extremities. My head ached, more from the smoke than the blow, and now my eyes refused to focus on even such a nearby thing as the straps holding my wrists in place. I started to struggle, then froze as a voice made it through the fog in my brain. "…simple enough," Phidias said. "Cut away the dead weight, and the structure is still good."

A dull pain throbbed at the back of my neck, like a bruise but pressing, though I clearly remembered Phidias striking me on the temple. And besides, my hand looked wrong. I tried twitching my fingers. Nothing. And it looked… wizened, somehow. There was a smell in the air, like dried meat, like lizards in the sun.…

Phidias stalked past me, and I froze again, but he paid no attention to me. "Residual energy and pattern transfer did only so much, though. So as I said, I'm very glad you came."

The fog in my brain was clearing, enough that I could see that the hand I'd been concentrating on was a left hand, even though it was on my right. The pressure on my neck worsened, as if something were trying to push through my skull. I was hanging—no, not quite suspended, locked into a sitting position, as if I were a harvest effigy in a wicker chair, ready for the bonfire.

At the far end of the room, the Professora's tank had been nestled among dozens of werglass lenses on swinging frames—the pilot's cabin, I thought, then rejected it, because these were in much better condition, unmarked by fire. Phidias moved between us, pacing, checking the panels as if he were beginning an experiment. Not Raisa's cabin, then, and that was a relief of sorts....

"There's no saving her, Fiddy," the Professora said at last.

"You don't know that." He moved past me again, this time carrying a piece of machinery, too new to be the *Chiaro*'s. The motivational element from our little airship.

"I *meant* the ship," Lundqvist said tartly. "Raisa's been dead for decades."

"She's in the glass, Olga. She's in the glass and I can bring her out."

He probably buried what was left, I heard the Professora say in memory, and reflexively jerked away. Leather stretched and tore, and I finally realized whose hand I'd been staring at, why the scratches on the throne in the pilot's cabin had seemed fresh, what that dry-lizard smell was, and worse, worse—

I was in another thaumaturge's throne, the link jammed against the base of my neck. And to either side of me were the other members of Phidias's salvage team, dead and desiccated, hanging in thrones of their own. The hand beside mine was twisted into a claw, still grasping futilely at the strap that held it in place.

He hadn't buried his team. He'd buried the original thaumaturges, and replaced them with his team. *Residual energy and pattern transfer.*

I screamed, my voice giving way to the Merged cry I'd first used as a child, grating forth in a howl. At the other end of the chamber—the main thaumaturgy chamber, I realized, the place that had been sealed off—Phidias leapt up from beside the Professora. "What? He should be linked—"

"Charles is a little different when it comes to these things," the Professora said, her phonograph barely flattening the relief in her voice.

That was one way to put it. Phidias must have tried to link me in, as he had with all the members of his team—maybe those who survived the crash, or maybe none had survived, maybe he had linked them dead—but my Merged physiognomy did not mesh with Society thaumaturgy, the metal woven through my skull did not permit a full link, and I remained unlinked, if mildly concussed.

I yanked at the straps on my wrists, and decades-old leather began to fray. Where was Dieterich? Struck down the same way? Linked already? The room seemed to lurch as I tore one hand free.

"It doesn't matter," Phidias said. "All I need is you."

The Professora's styli drew back. "Fiddy—"

"You're used to it," he said. "You'll be fine. And once I carry the glass out of here, I can find a way to bring her out too." He took hold of the Professora's upper stylus as if to shake hands, then jammed it into a socket on the console.

A strangled noise—not a scream, nothing with as much thought behind it, but a horrible chattering cacophony of garbled phonemes—emerged first from her phonograph and then from the walls themselves.

The strap on my left wrist snapped. A bang echoed my cry, loud as Phidias's work in the struts. But the Professora's scream went on, and the pounding continued, till I no longer knew what was in my head and what was real. I tore open the last strap and dropped to the floor, then rolled as the floor changed direction entirely.

The entire room seemed to pulse in time with the clamor—from the closest wall, I realized, and saw the weathered steel dent inward. I stumbled forward, but Phidias stood between me and the Professora, one hand gently patting her tank as if to encourage a pack animal. "Professora!" I yelled.

She didn't answer, or couldn't. But a rack of lenses swung forward, against the pull of gravity, and struck Phidias first across the jaw, then in the gut as he staggered back. A second lens flailed against him, shattering over his head, and the keening from every wall took on a harsher, furious note.

The lenses continued to strike as I leapt over Phidias. I wrenched Lundqvist's stylus from the socket, heedless of the damage I did to both. "Professora Lundqvist!" I shouted, peering at her sensor ring and the brain beyond. But the walls continued to keen, and Lundqvist's phonograph remained silent.

The closest wall dented and caved, tearing apart, and the noise cut off abruptly. Fresh air poured in, driving werglass splinters over me and revealing the rest of the *Chiaro* falling away around us. Chaff and Dieterich peered through the gap, clinging to what was left of the *Chiaro*'s structure. "Dammit, Charles, I told you we'd be taking off, but I meant in *my* ship!" Dieterich roared as Chaff tore the rest of the wall free as easily as I might tear paper.

I was in no mood for wit. "The Professora," I gasped, dragging her tank along—then stopped dead as I saw the mesa sinking below us. We were already six feet up and rising. "We can't leave her—"

Instead of answering me, Chaff leapt onto the Professora, knocking me aside. She pinned the Professora's tank between her forelegs, as if she were a vessel to be borne, then tumbled back, out of the diminished compartment. Still clinging to the wall, Dieterich reached in and caught my sleeve. "Mind the fall, Charles, and don't waste time!" he shouted, and leapt into the cloud of dust and splinters that hid Chaff and the Professora from view.

Phidias moaned behind me, and I glanced back. The werglass still glimmered, but in every panel now, glowing unmistakably. I adjusted my eyes, heedless of Phidias's presence, only to see a pattern blooming in the glass, fragmented and uncertain but present. But compared to the Professora, even to the machine in my own flesh, it was only a trace, an echo, swallowed up by the horror of the dead in that room.

Phidias got to his feet, sobbing, reaching out first for the glimmer in the glass and then to the empty throne. "Phidias!" I called.

He ignored me, clutching the arms of the throne, clinging to the frayed leather as he tried to fit himself where I had been, then throwing his head back—

I turned and leapt. An unMerged man might have died in such a fall. But I was wholly Merged, wholly myself, with machinery as much a part of me as my brain, and I could trust those reflexes to minimize any damage. That didn't keep it from hurting, though; I hit the ground, bearings shifting and tendons parting even as I rolled. I came to a halt at last, one ankle badly twisted and my nose and mouth full of gray earth.

"Charles." The Professora's voice, weak but present. I turned to see her, still held by Chaff, her wheels askew and styli dangling useless, but her tank uncracked and marvelous brain unhurt. *"Look."*

I rolled over to see. The great arch of the *Chiaro,* those green-blue panes gleaming like cabochon gems, rose in a slow curve above the mesa. Below hung truncated fragments of the undercarriage: the pilot's cabin alone. No, not alone—the ballroom as well, those endless werglass mirrors no doubt reflecting us in miniature. *Raisa, Raisa, even the wind follows your steps....*

A gust of wind rattled across the ground, sending debris whirling past us—but above, the toll was greater. One by one at first, then more as the corroded bolts gave way, the bronze plates reduced to paper thinness by time and corrosion trembled. Like petals from some strange tree, they scattered to reveal only rusted mesh below.

For a fraction of a second, even the air stilled, as if to preserve the *Chiaro* in place. A breeze reeking of hot tin and broken stone and the horrible mummified scent of the dead salvage team wrapped round us. Then, so slowly it was almost gentle, the *Chiaro* fell, this time shattering itself against the side of the mesa, crumbling against it till there was nothing left.

We offered Chaff a lift off the mesa, but she rejected it. "The Path of the Earth should remain on the earth," she said. "I have already sinned once by leaving it."

Though we were all glad she had done so, none of us was up to debating the philosophy of transgression with her. Instead, Dieterich shepherded us back to our little ship and took off, guiding us through what was left of the wind.

"I followed Chaff at first," he said finally. "Found the wreck of Phidias's airship…it hadn't been shot down at all. No, it looked like they'd tried to take off, only to crash again." He let out a long breath. "That told me I needed to find you, and I'm just sorry it took so long."

"You could tell that just from the crash, sir?" It had looked like any other wreck to me.

"I'm insulted you even need to ask, Charles." He was silent a moment, then began patting his pockets, searching for his pipe. The airship lurched, and he stopped. "Lundqvist—"

"I should be flattered," she said quietly. "He thought enough of my intellect to let me be the linchpin of his plan to bring Raisa back." She let out a long sigh—imitated it, I thought, clinging to human mannerisms as if to remind herself what she was. "I should be, but I'm not."

"It was an insane plan," Dieterich grumbled.

"Perhaps not, depending on which branch of theory you follow," the Professora said, a little of her didactic nature reasserting itself. "If he were the man I taught, if he remembered anything of my lessons, then he would have linked himself in as a last effort. But that would have lasted just long enough to be part of the ship, to feel it come apart around him. If I wanted revenge, that would be it."

I thought of Phidias flinging his head back against the throne, felt the still-raw wound pulse at the back of my neck, and kept silent.

"And if you didn't?" Dieterich asked.

"If I didn't." Her phonograph thrummed with another imitation of a sigh. "If I didn't, I'd remember how it felt to be—be part of all that. Integrated, even imperfectly. I'm still not sure whether *I* struck him, or whether...." She caught herself, then began again. "I think if he linked, he found more than he expected."

"He did," I said quietly. As had all of us. I put one hand to my forehead, feeling the pressure of lenses behind bone, the glimmer of life in both, the echo of machine in flesh.

Below us, Chaff continued her trek across the mesa, cutting a new path. I watched her go as we descended, down into the lands far from Parch.

Urban Drift

Andrew Knighton

THE JOB DIDN'T start well for Cam. Sleepless and strung out, too long since his last high, he was marched into the presence of Duodiseus Gast. The gangster filled an antique wire frame chair, loose flesh sagging through the gaps, dressed only in a stained pair of shorts. The walls around him were lined with obsessively hoarded sketches, paintings, and sculptures. Cam's eyes fell upon a tiny oil of St. Joachim with the shepherds, and he felt his pulse accelerate, that hollow hungry feeling rising inside.

"You into icons, Maguire?" Gast asked, fingers drumming against an enormous thigh.

Cam nodded. There was no point lying to Gast. He probably ran Cam's suppliers.

"I thought science soldiers stuck to amphetamines and unhealthy thoughts," Gast said.

"I was clean in those days."

Cam could feel himself stiffening into a posture of wary defense. Gast's guards shifted away from the walls, hands reaching inside bulging jackets. The man himself only laughed.

"Don't worry, Maguire," he said, waving a hand dismissively. "No one here's going to judge you. In fact, I have something for you."

A serving girl stepped out of the shadows, demure beneath her cloth cap, and held out a silver tray. In the center was a flat block of wood no bigger than Cam's thumb. The varnish on its surface was old and cracked, but beneath it could be seen a bearded face in archaic oils.

"St. Peter. One of a series of twelve."

Cam picked the icon up from the tray and carried it to a window, examining it in the brief sunlight before a pipe factory approached, plunging him into shadow. A hiss of scraping mortar filled the room as the two buildings pressed past each other.

"A down payment," Gast explained over the noise. "The remaining eleven to be paid on delivery."

Cam placed the picture in a pocket of his weathered jacket, then looked back at Gast.

"What's the job?"

Gast stopped twiddling his thumbs and gave a small wave. Another servant girl approached. On her tray was a glass cube about eight inches across. Even by the muted light of electric bulbs, it sparkled with rare beauty. Bright points filled its internal space in smooth, flowing lines, etched in the glass as it was formed. They shimmered with fragile elegance, a glowing network that made Cam's breath catch in his throat. Though abstract they embodied something substantial, a heartfelt joy toward which he might aspire.

"The Song of the City," Gast said, his voice hushed. "Second most valuable of Nebulous Efram's sculptures of the ideal. I also own the third through to the fifteenth. Naturally, I want the top one too. I want Urban Drift."

The factory finished grinding past outside, exposing a swath of parkland. Sunshine streamed in through the window, splintering as it hit the cube, forming a bright web more elegant than that of any spider. Gast paused for a moment, basking in its glow, before an office block rumbled into view, once more blocking out the sun. In the dulled moments that followed, Cam was sickeningly aware of the sweat trailing down his employer's skin.

The first servant returned and handed Cam a photograph. The sepia-toned image showed a stately house in an antiquated style, with wrought-iron balconies, a pillared porch, and wide chimneys protruding from a slate-lined roof.

"This is Alexandria Immanent's place," Gast said. "She has what I want. You're going to get it for me."

Gast paused to sip from a tall blue drink, then continued, jowls wobbling with enthusiasm.

"In three nights' time a rundown tenement will be passing the House of Immanent. Your crew will be in it, disguised as a salvage gang. You enter the house, grab the prize, and smash things up on your way out. Poor Alexandria's agents will spend months hunting for her art in the salvage slums. If they ever realize they've been looking in the wrong place, the trail will be long dead.

"Meanwhile, you deliver Urban Drift to me, and I deliver your next dozen highs on a silver platter."

"I'll need money too," Cam said. "For expenses."

"Rensford knows my limits." Gast indicated a tall man Cam had taken for a guard. "Take him when you go shopping."

"And for my colleagues."

Gast shook his head. "Don't push your luck. They'll get the pick of the rest of Immanent's collection. That's more than enough.

"Now, are we on, or are you wasting my time?"

Cam found Grinning Jenny beneath a table in the Autoreeve's Arms, a battered old tavern slowly crawling along East Reach. She squinted up at him through a haze of pipe smoke and brick dust.

"What d'you want?" she demanded, staggering to her feet.

Cam crouched, putting them face to face, and handed her a mug of the Arms's watered ale. Jenny's fellow crawlers fell into awkward silence at the familiarity of the full man.

"You look uncomfortable," Jenny said, impatience seeping through her unbreakable smile.

Cam shrugged. "I'd pull up a chair, but...."

He gestured at the low stools, the rickety table barely rising above his knees.

The crawlers stared for a moment, then they started to laugh. Soon they were drinking and chattering as if Cam weren't there.

Jenny downed her drink, pale liquid dribbling off her chin.

"Let me guess," she said. "You need money to get high, and you want me to help steal it."

"Something like that," Cam replied.

She snorted and spat into the sawdust beneath their feet.

"You could stay in your factory with the crawlers and the press gangs," Cam said, staring pointedly at her battered fingers. "Be like all the other little people. Or you could come with me."

Jenny's eyes twinkled dangerously above her meaningless toxified grin. Then she sighed.

"Why fight the inevitable?" she said, shoulders sagging. "Let's go."

Springheel was showing off again, somersaulting through the air high above a fast-shifting slum. People paused in the street below, staring up at the gangling figure as he leapt, hollering and whooping, across the unstable rooftops.

Cam waited to see where the routine ended, then headed into the stairwell of a decrepit terrace block. As dusk came creeping through the sky, he crawled out the end of a broken gable and onto the lichen-smeared slates. Soot bellowed from a nearby chimney, and in its shadow Springheel sat, his back against the red bricks, taking a screwdriver to one of his legs.

"Nice routine," Cam said, stepping carefully across the rooftop. The tenements shook as they squeezed past each other, making space for other, more important buildings. The housewives and factory workers who warmed these rundown piles might never see a mansion or trading house, but they felt the tremble of their passing.

Springheel looked up with a grin. Clarasites darted across his blond dreadlocks, swallowing fragments of ash as they fell from the chimney.

"Hey Cam!" he said.

"You got a minute?"

Springheel nodded.

"Always. Just let me pop this back on."

He set the screwdriver aside and strapped the prosthetic leg beneath the shattered mess of his knee. Then he rose to his feet, swaying rhythmically on the springy curves of metal that served him for shins.

"I've got a job for you," Cam said.

"I'm in," Springheel replied.

"You don't know what it is yet."

Springheel shrugged. "You always find exciting work. Besides, how else am I going to pass the time?"

The three of them sat in an abandoned shop, sunk in the darkness between office blocks. Somewhere outside, the sun was setting orange across the plains. Down here, there was only the flickering light from broken furniture burning in a rusty brazier.

Cam ran a knife down the miniature of St. Peter, scraping away fragments of paint. He caught the flakes in one hand, then crushed them with the butt of the knife. The fine dust disappeared up his nose in one swift sniff. Suddenly the world seemed clearer, brighter, a place of certainty and substance.

"I can't believe this place is going to pass through banker central," Jenny growled from beneath a heap of dirty blankets.

"It's not an accident," Cam said.

"And the lack of real scavenger gangs in this block?"

"Mr. Gast's power reaches down as well as up."

"Cool," Springheel said, adjusting the torn trousers that concealed his mechanical legs. "You've sure covered the details."

"There's one more to address before we go in," Cam said.

He opened one of the sacks by his feet and spread its contents across the floor. Gunmetal glinted in the firelight.

Jenny crawled out of her heap and across the room. She picked up one of the guns and span the chamber, eyes narrowing as she looked at the engraved butt.

"Morgan Number 16," she said. "I thought these were barred from import."

"Associate in the Assault Guard," Cam said. "He brings things back from campaign."

Springheel bounced forward and picked up another of the guns.

"Are we gonna use these?" he asked.

Cam shook his head. "Shouldn't need to, but best to be on the safe side."

They ate beans from battered cans and drank coffee brewed over the open fire. Outside, the darkness grew deeper. At last, the background rumble of passing pavement and walls softened, as they entered a region of smooth joins and well-oiled gears.

At a nod from Cam the others rose, strapping guns and tools into position beneath dark, shapeless rags. Cam turned the handle of the shop door and pushed.

The door remained stubbornly shut. Cam pushed it again, leaning his weight through his shoulder.

Springheel stepped forward, opened a window, and leaned around.

He sniggered softly. "Door's too low. They must've raised the pavement to keep the riffraff out."

He swung one leg and then the other over the sill, reaching back to offer

Jenny his hand. She slapped it aside and scrambled out after him, leaving Cam to bring up the rear, grinding his teeth at the petty setback.

They stepped out into the scent of roses and the sound of a distantly playing fountain. Moonlight fell across them in bars, striped with the shadow of a tall iron fence. Springheel crouched, tensing the composite curves of his legs, and then leapt. He landed on top of the fence, balancing with rubber-soled feet on a ridge of razor-spiked metal. He smothered the spines in a heavy blanket, then lowered a rope to Cam and Jenny.

Inside the grounds, they jogged across perfectly manicured lawns, moving from one shadow to the next between birches and cherry trees that protected the house's residents from viewing the outside world.

Cam heard a scraping. He raised his hand and the other halted in their tracks, listening to heavy footsteps approaching on gravel. Stooped close to the ground, they backed into the entrance of a hedge maze.

Steam hissing from the joints of his motorized armor, a science soldier stomped into view. Electric lanterns cast dazzling beams of light from his shoulders, throwing vast, distorted shadows across the lawn. The glare paused on the maze entrance.

Cam felt sweat prickle his face and dribble down into his left eye. He didn't dare move to brush it away. The seconds stretched out. Something clicked in the darkness behind those lamps. Was now the time to run? He tensed his legs, took a deep lungful of air, and....

The science soldier turned and marched on around the house, rifle swinging at his side.

Cam slumped into the shadows, heart hammering, waiting for his vision to return. He reached into his pocket and pulled out the icon, crooked fingernail scraping a few flakes free and up his nose.

"Great timing," hissed Jenny by his ear.

Cam shrugged her off and headed closer to the house, tension receding to a warm tingle.

Around the back of the building, noisy gravel gave way to paved footpaths. On edge against further guards they approached the reinforced windows beneath a third-floor balcony. At a nod from Cam, Springheel took two swift strides and jumped, springing onto the platform above. He lowered a rope and the others scrambled up.

The balcony door was locked, a big brass keyhole covering an intricate assemblage of bolts and gears. Up here, a solid bolt would have sufficed, but such simple solutions were far too common for the House of Immanent.

Jenny unrolled a leather cylinder, revealing a set of slender brass instruments. She took up the tools with nimble fingers trained to unblock the dangerous workings of steam looms. Hooks and levers prodded at the lock's innards, probing, testing, turning, until Jenny gave a satisfied nod, twisted her wrist, and the mechanism clicked.

The door swung open.

As Cam stepped across the threshold he knew they were in the right room. Carefully contained gas lamps cast a soft glow across dozens of priceless pieces of art. Paneled walls of unadorned wood were hung with rows of paintings, from tranquil pastoral watercolors to bright oils of city life.

The only furniture was an oak pedestal in the center of the room, topped with a small glass cabinet. In its center lay a velvet cushion, and on that the most beautiful object Cam had ever seen.

It was a glass cube, like the one Duodiseus Gast had shown him but smaller, perhaps six inches across. It seemed to suck in all nearby light, focusing it into perfect points, like stars frozen in clear amber. They hung in a sparkling web, a network of still streets caught in the moment before they would burst outward, spreading across the face of the city. Each dazzling fragment drew the eye to the next, creating a sense of motion within stillness, a tension between the frozen crystal landscape and a desperate desire to move. The sight touched a sad corner of Cam's soul. He too was trapped, caught on the brink of tears by its beauty. This was their goal. This was Urban Drift.

Springheel nudged him.

"C'mon mate, let's get on with it."

Cam nodded and moved forward, forcing his gaze away from the pedestal, looking down and around for traps and alarms. Twice he stepped around floorboards with suspiciously well-defined, dirt-free edges. At several points they stopped for Jenny to examine thread-thin wires crossing the room at knee height. She would squint carefully at the wire, watching the way it vibrated under her breath, before either cutting it or signaling to the others to step over.

Cam could feel his legs trembling as he crossed the room. Instinctively, his hand reached for the icon in his bag, but he cursed himself for the weakness and kept moving.

At last, they stood beside the pedestal. Jenny found and disabled two more wires, tiny clamps screwing them into place before she brought out the snips. Then Cam spun the wheel on a pocket fire knife and ran its tiny white flame across the glass, catching the clear circle that fell away.

Cam reached through the hole. Moving slowly to suppress the shaking of his hand, he lifted Urban Drift from its nest and drew it toward him. All three of them held their breath as he edged the glass cube through the gap. The only sound was the echo of footsteps elsewhere in the house.

Cam didn't even think about the icon now. His whole attention was on the artwork in his hand. Not just the professional attention of a thief at work, but that of a man enraptured, his gaze drawn by those tiny points that, even in the shadow of his hand, gleamed with the fire of stars.

A spasm ran through him, comedown and adrenaline. His arm twitched and there was a clink of glass against glass.

"Crap."

He yanked Urban Drift clear and thrust it into his satchel.

They hung in a moment of silence. Springheel shook his head, clarasites bouncing through his dreadlocks.

Something in the case clicked. Cam had just enough time to swear before a bell began clanging above their heads.

They rushed onto the balcony. Voices cried out across the grounds and heavy footfalls raced across gravel.

"Go!" Cam cast a rope down into the darkness.

Springheel grabbed Jenny under one arm and leapt, bounding across the garden in a series of arcs that carried him high above the treetops. The sound of voices and footsteps receded after him, interspersed with the snap of gunfire and hiss of tesla beams.

Cam scrambled hand over fist down the rope, knuckles scraping against brickwork. As he reached the ground he turned and scurried, low in the shadows, along the side of the house. With a trembling hand he reached again into his bag and drew out the Morgan Number 16, its butt reassuringly heavy in his hand. His fingers brushed against Urban Drift, and the thought of its beauty sent a tingle up his arm.

The starboard wing of the house, currently facing east, was well lit but badly guarded. A quick glance told Cam that the science soldiers who patrolled this space were gone, chasing Springheel into the night. Cam took a deep breath, steeling himself against disaster, and ran. Gas lamps flickered in the corners of his vision as he sprinted along a mosaic pavement toward a discrete gate.

Cam's heart pounded. The gate was close. Thirty meters. Twenty. Ten.

"Halt!"

Without pausing, Cam pointed the Morgan over his shoulder and fired. The gun barked once, twice, three times. Cam's instincts were still good, but his hand was unsteady. The science soldier grunted as bullets hit armored plates, ricocheting off into the darkness.

Cam jumped, fingers grasping the top of the gate, and flung himself over in a rough cartwheel. Bright tesla fire crackled where he had been. He landed heavily in the road, the impact jarring scar tissue in his ankle.

For a moment, he was back on a wind-blasted battlefield. Trapped beneath the smoking ruins of a tank, blood pouring from the twisted top of his boot as he screamed for a medic.

The smell of melting tar snapped him back. The science soldier was racing toward the gate, tesla fire licking the road around Cam. Gritting his teeth against the pain in his ankle, he jerked upright and along the road. Behind him, the gate clanged back against worn stonework and the guard began to run, the heavy footfalls and hiss of his motorized armor pursuing Cam down a wide, tree-lined street.

Cam knew he wasn't in the proud shape of his youth, but he'd always been an impressive runner. He kept his lead past the wide gates of three grand houses and into a settled cluster of upmarket shops, together so long that moss had grown over the joins between them. Ducking round corners and down alleyways he tried to shake his pursuer, firing his remaining rounds as a deterrent when he got too close. They ran for an hour through the warm summer night, Cam's training keeping him going long after he should have collapsed. But the science soldier had steam armor on his side, and his pace never flagged. Cam tried to lose him by leaping aboard a fast-moving workshop as it disappeared into a huddle of factories, but the guard soon reappeared, a hulking silhouette pounding along a fire escape. The sky turned gray as they raced through a shifting checkerboard of artisan suburbs and into a junction cluster. Around them, roads and paths twisted around and across each other before disappearing into a central shaft.

Cam's body endured, but his mind was beginning to buckle. He couldn't endure the tension and adrenaline this long without help. Flickers of memory were playing across his brain, moments of mayhem whittling away at his determination. St. Peter was in his satchel, in easy reach. If he could just find a moment to pause, to take breath and catch a hit, then everything would be all right. If only....

He felt the pavement twist beneath him. Up ahead, paving slabs stood up one by one and disappeared into a dark maw of whirling gear teeth. The broken end of a drive-belt lapped out like a tongue. His pulse mingled with flying dust and the footfalls of pursuit, forming a fog that surrounded and penetrated, flooding his mind. The jagged junction tunnel became the rim of a crater, the ground shaken by the hammer of approaching artillery. Fear froze him in its sights, a tortured past screaming in his ears.

Then the present hit him hard, the science soldier slamming into his spine, sending him skidding across rough concrete. Blood speckled the slabs as skin was scraped from his face. His bag slid from his grasp, its contents tumbling away toward the dark opening. An empty gun; a tiny, scarred icon; and Urban Drift, sparkling in the red light of early dawn. Its pattern glowed like blood drops in a blasted land, then turned from crimson to white, from horror to hope, as the sun rose above the street and cast its clear rays down upon them.

Cold steel pressed against the base of his skull.

"That's so you understand how fucked you are." The science soldier took a step back, gun still pointing at Cam. "Stand. Slowly."

Cam did as he was told, raised his hands above his head. The broken drive-belt lashed out, almost striking his arm. The pavement tilted beneath his feet, threatening to spill the things he had dropped into the grinding darkness below.

"One of us should pick those up," he said. Ahead of them, paving slabs were rising like tombstones and disappearing into the junction.

"You get the cube." The guard's armor hissed as he twisted to stay balanced. "Only the cube. And careful. You touch that gun...."

Cam heard the crackle of a tesla warming up. The drive-belt snapped out, air brushing his ear as it passed.

He sank slowly to the pavement, settling onto his knees. Stretching out with one hand, his fingers brushing the familiar face of the icon where it lay next to Urban Drift.

The drive-belt hissed over his head and slammed into the science soldier. A broken piston screeched and the man staggered.

The pavement tilted, Urban Drift and Cam's icon fix sliding toward the dark machines below. Instinctively, he shot out a hand and snatched one, the other tumbling into the void.

The science soldier crashed to the ground, an arm flailing wildly, whipped around by a broken mechanism.

The pavement twisted again. Below, roads crisscrossed each other in the darkness. Cam slid, fell, shot out his free hand, and grabbed a passing lamppost. His shoulder crunched and pain shot up his arm, but he clung on, carried beneath the city and away.

The weather was changing over the city, storm clouds rolling across a clear sky. Raindrops shone like silver in the sunlight as Cam stepped off the pavement and across the road. Patches of blue were vanishing into darkness above a converted warehouse.

Inside the building, guards led him up concrete steps and through a waiting room that smelled of polish and secondhand leather. Springheel and Jenny sat in silence on a padded bench. Both glanced up as Cam passed. Springheel's clarasites were removing clotted blood from above a bruise in his hairline. Jenny's cheek was swollen and scraped.

Duodiseus Gast's chair creaked beneath him as he sat back, staring at Cam. A door slammed, sealing them in silence as low suburbs rolled past the window.

Cam took his time viewing the gangster's art, admiring the creases of a uniform on a military portrait, the fine artifice of light across a charcoal landscape. His gaze caught briefly on St. Joachim and his flock, but moved on.

One of the guards coughed. Cam glanced up. The hand of the antique clock above Gast's head had moved on a quarter hour since he came in.

"I...." Cam halted, caught by Gast's glare.

"That's twice you've kept me waiting." The gangster's fingers tapped a rhythm on his belly, the patter of an executioner's drum. "Once for you to show your face, and once more for you to tell me what I already know."

"There was a—"

"Save it for whoever you're hiding out with. You've got my goods?"

Cam rummaged in his satchel. Gast's guards reached inside their jackets, then relaxed as he pulled out a glass cube, its inner etchings glittering like crystals of frozen light.

A serving girl took Urban Drift on a silver tray and passed it to Gast with a jeweler's monocle and a curtsy.

Gast crammed the lens into the fat around his eye. He squinted at the cube, nodded.

"You may have made a big fuss out of it, Maguire, but you got the job done." He looked up at one of the guards. "Rensford, fetch me a hammer."

Cam clenched up inside. Against all good sense, he spoke.

"Hammer?"

Gast was grinning. "I suppose I could melt it, but there's something satisfying about feeling things shatter."

He laughed as he saw Cam's face. "Don't worry, Maguire, I'm not going to destroy you. You might still be useful to me in one piece, although I'm not sure how. This, on the other hand, is too well known to sell, and no use to me sitting on a shelf. But once word gets round that it's been found in pieces, I will own the fourteen most valuable of Efram's ideals, and I can set my own price."

He tossed Urban Drift from hand to hand, corners sketching fine rainbows across Cam's vision.

"I know this is all a little beyond you, Maguire. Suffice to say, I am not content to be guided by the invisible hand. Not when I can become its great, grasping fingers."

Gast threw the cube higher and higher, his laughter gurgling like a drain.

Cam thought of the hammer hitting Urban Drift, slithers of light bursting in every direction, losing form, meaning, beauty.

A serving girl stepped forward at a gesture from Gast. From her tray, eleven oil-paint disciples stared at Cam, promising to carry him closer to God's bliss.

"Your pay, Maguire. Don't let Rensford's boot hit your arse on the way out."

Cam stepped forward, gazing for a longing moment at those bearded faces.

He seized the edge of the tray and shoved the serving girl to the floor, swinging back to strike an approaching guard with the silver-plated disk. One hand shot out, grabbing Urban Drift. The remaining guard was reaching for his gun even as Cam flung the tray into his face. The man reeled backward, crashing through the window and to the ground. Cam followed, leaping over the street onto a passing corner shop. Gast bellowed after him as he ran, Urban Drift shining in his hand.

The sun was sinking beyond the city, colors blazing like the heart of a smelting furnace. Cam watched its beams catch the frames of doors and windows, writing red runes on sheets of dark concrete. He smiled and ran a finger over the tiles on which he sat, lost in a sea of soft shadows.

Something clattered on the roof behind him. The click of a gun being cocked echoed in his ears.

"Sorry, man." It was Springheel, his voice trembling, legs creaking as he stepped up behind Cam. "Gast says we're part of the job. Either we make it good, or…. Well, Jenny said we should hide, but you know that wouldn't work. Gast gets everywhere. And then there'd be three of us dead, not just one."

Cam nodded. "I know. Just give me a moment."

"Okay."

Springheel paused, hovering uncertainly behind Cam.

"You know there are buildings that only surface every forty, fifty years?" Cam was smiling still, watching a pack of tower blocks split apart. Some, shiny and new, moved west to form a business district. "Real antiques, not sturdy enough for regular use, but too beautiful to be destroyed. They rise for a few days, and people go visit. Old women reliving washed-out memories. School groups touring a bit of history. Worn-down veterans looking for a few last moments of wonder before they die."

One tower was left where the others had clustered, a baroque heap of gargoyles and perilous spires. Its central point rose, needlelike, above the rest. A bell tower, its peak a shadowy void sheltered by four pillars and a domed roof.

"That's All Saints." Cam pointed at the tower. "I saw it once as a kid. My grandma called it All Sinners, some tradition from when she was young."

Springheel threw something into Cam's lap.

"For old times' sake," he said. "Go out buzzing, y'know?"

Cam set aside the crude painting of St. Thomas.

"No thanks. That's not the art I need."

He pointed at the tower as it crossed the sun's path and golden light burst through its intricate tiers.

"That is."

The light caught on something as it shone through the empty bell tower. Caught and fractured into a hundred perfect points, shining and spinning around each other through a prism of crafted glass. Motes danced like tiny angels across the church, then were snuffed out one by one as it descended into the city's open maw.

Springheel's mouth hung open, the gun limp in his hand.

"You didn't...."

Cam nodded. "I'll be long dead before it appears again. But so will Gast, and that makes it safe."

He turned to Springheel, tears in his eyes.

"Some things are too beautiful to destroy. But I'm not one of them. So you do what you've got to do, and then live a long life. Get to see this again."

Cam turned his face toward the sunset as Springheel pressed the gun against his temple. In his mind's eye, silver points danced in a crystal landscape, never moving but forever changing. Light made life, drawing his soul up to something higher. The hammer clicked back once more, and he smiled.

"Time to move on."

Ascension

Leow Hui Min Annabeth

It is December 10. Thirty-three years, then, exactly to the day; and she is eighty-three. The thought does not disturb her. She has had a very long while to come to terms with her mortality. And she has known for a very long while with unwavering certainty that this day would arrive in time.

Thirty-three years. The machine is complete, the Empress's oldest wish will come true, and Ada will be able to leave this surreal celestial half-world at last.

Thirty-three years were lost to her. Thirty-three years were hers.

The thought is intoxicating, giddying, liberating.

She is withered; she is decrepit, shrunken with age. In the chrome surface of a 鼎 in her workshop, she inspects her reflection, unimpressed. This morning she pinned an orchid to the lapel of her padded jacket—not in celebration, mind; she plucked the orchid from the vase at her bedside just *because.* Now the pink of the bloom stands out, sharp and shrill against her dark complexion. It reminds her of the scarlet sins of a mad, bad George Byron.

Ada winces, but does not remove the flower. There was a time when she would have found herself preoccupied with a feeling of unease, shrinking away from the thought of her parents and her old life; but she has changed, she is no longer the nervous, pitiable wreck that she was as a younger woman. She has, in truth, so much more to treasure than the aimless philandering of a long-dead poet.

So she pulls her jacket a little closer about herself, setting her jaw in aged obstinacy. She looks around the room—it will be her last time here, she thinks, and she wants to preserve it in her memory as it is. (If only memories could be moved as easily as she trusts she can move life.)

The desk by the wall, her cyanotype linens neatly arranged in a corner. The scribe-*zhēng* beside it, for when she was too tired to handwrite her notes. The 鼎 she had endeavored to use as a crucible, before she jury-rigged it into part of a wind-up mechanical fan. (And hadn't that been a laugh? The Empress had been ever so tickled when the court ladies were left bewildered by what to do with their delicate folded 扇子 of silk.) The cooling engine, with its airflow reversed now that it is winter, clanking away to radiate warmth from the ventilation slats.

And the small touches that make the room *hers*—not just a workroom but her study room, her sometime living quarters, *hers*. Ada is not a sentimental woman; her mother beat any inclination toward romanticism out of her, and she is, in any case, not much given to turning maudlin, even in her cups. But there is a string of pearls, on the table—one of William's wedding gifts, which she has not worn since their separation. A letter, much read, delivered from Greece—"My lovely, precious child, forgive me…." She cannot hate her father, but she can hate what he did with his life. And, beside the door, a small structure of brass, gleaming from the coat of polish she frequently applies—a perfect miniature model of the difference engine, the work between her and Charles (and Mary Somerville, of course), which was never finished in London or the Paris of her exile.

Well, she thinks, her amusement grim. Well, the engines. Please God, I at least have done something with my days.

Outside in the courtyard the clock gong strikes three past the dawn hour. Ada twitches her braid farther over her shoulder, gritting her teeth at the ache of arthritis, and calls into the speaking tube by the door: "Pearl, you may enter now. Godsdamn, where is the child? *Pearl!*"

The patter of feet running along the corridor outside. A cautious knock on the door, which Ada flings open.

"Lady Jin," the maidservant murmurs.

Pearl is a good girl, well behaved and sharp of wit for all that she is just fourteen. Her mistress relents.

"I am going to Her Majesty now," says Ada, quietly, imperiously. "I do not

require that you accompany me, but I want you to take charge of the possessions in this room. Except for what the Crown claims, they are yours, and I
have lodged affidavits to that effect."

Pearl's expression is composed, settled. Privately Ada wonders how much
the girl knows.

"Do not worry, Lady Jin. I will apply myself to my studies."

Ada has tutored her in mathematics and in engineering; and who knows,
perhaps Pearl will even win a scholarship to the imperial colleges. Perhaps she
has done right in encouraging the child to dream. Perhaps Pearl will pass the
official examinations and take pride of place in the imperial workshops, building aetherships and writing punch cards for the Jacquard engine.

And perhaps a maid from a poor family will end up married before her
sixteenth year, and will spend the remainder of her life in indentured drudgery,
no longer able to work magic with numbers.

So many paths that twist into the future.... Ada shakes off the desire to hug
this granddaughter of hers, to whisper, "I will take care of you after I am gone,
when you make offerings to me and call me Ada 姨."

Instead she gestures Pearl into the room, shuts the door, and walks down
the freezing passageway toward the gate into the courtyard. And then across
the cobbles of the palace compound, toward the 太和 殿, and into what remains of her life.

There are many accounts of the arrival of Lady Jin Ada into the Imperial Court,
but in truth it was many years ago that Ada found her way into the land under
heaven, calling herself Elizabeth King on the passage from England, and using
her title of countess when she claimed an imperial audience. Neither of those
names had any currency in court—Her Majesty preferred to style her Lady
Jin—but she was, sometimes, secretly pleased that she was still recognized as
an enchantress of numbers.

"But that is to be expected!" the Empress exclaimed, when Ada confessed
her surprise at this appellation. "If not for natural philosophers like yourself, we
would long have been overrun by the field mice of your continent. Overrun,
and carved up into extraterritorialities, as 南洋 was before we liberated it."

The Empress said that in a tone so unyieldingly matter of fact, so arrogant,
that it was burnt into Ada's memory. For if she had to situate her empress in an
occidental context (for 慈禧太后 was *her* empress, far more than the so-distant

Victoria Regina), then she would say, in all confidence, "She is our Ailénor d'Aquitane."

She learnt her histories, as a child, before her mother set her to algebra and Euclid. She read of Eleanor and she never forgot her. Naughty, wicked Eleanor, who went on crusade to kill, and who adored *l'amour courtois*. Wife of kings! Mother of kings! Strumpet, warrior, monarch. A paradox, Eleanor, and a paragon at the same time. Even so, Ada told herself, even the inimitable Poitevin queen was but a pale precursor to Cixi.

Ada was grateful for the Empress's patronage, grateful with a depth of feeling that she had owed to no one else, not to her mother and certainly not to Charles. The Empress was, for one, honestly proud of Ada's achievements; and it was for this pride that Ada sold her loyalty to a chit, an upstart whore who somehow jostled her way onto the Heavenly Throne.

And it was for the challenge also: when the Empress looked at her, with an incomprehensible emotion in her implacable face, and said, "We have brought you in, as our own daughter, to extend the reach of my realm and to defend us from your nation of barbarians, through your skill in the natural sciences. But there is another matter."

A pause, during which moment the blood had been thudding so hard in Ada's ears that she could barely hear a thing.

"You see," said the Empress softly—and it seemed to Ada that Her Majesty was weary, slipping into an informality of speech—"there is also that matter, that small trifle, of my heart's desire. That one thing that has eluded so many generations of kings and emperors—I believe you will be the one to find it for me."

Ada had fallen to her knees at this and pressed her head to the floor, doing obeisance in a manner that would have scandalized her own ancestors. "My queen, my queen, thank you for your trust in me, for harboring me, thank you." And she took her oath, there and then, under the outraged glances of the courtiers.

The Great Hall is empty, silent; and the winter cold bites through clothing into bone. The lesser halls, where the Empress holds court sometimes, have mannequins installed along the walls—some as heralds with phonographs, and some to play the zither. (Ada had no part in the design of the phonograph, though she wrote the algorithms for the doll-musicians. She regretted that almost instantly; the mechanical music grates.) Not so 太和殿，which is unadorned by the modernist impulse to technology.

The only appearance of anything out of place is the new throne that stands upon the highest dais.

"Your Majesty," Ada whispers as she approaches, and the sound carries through the mausoleum. (Because this *is* a mausoleum. It will no longer be used for weddings and coronations, for the great feasts of the monarchy. Not after today. She knows it.)

"Madam," the Empress rejoins, voice cracking. This is the closest to intimacy that they will ever achieve. "Help me, if you please."

Now that Ada is closer to the throne she can see it more clearly, and she almost rears away in her shuddering horror.

A monstrosity, she thinks. Grotesque. And then, her repulsion giving way to curiosity: Is this really the fruit of my imagination? Did the architects construct this from my plans?

The chair—it is a chair, not a throne, an electric chair as lethal as the one that tinkerer boy in Menlo Park has dreamed up so far across the western seas in the Occident—the chair is fitted to the Empress's frame like a brace. There are iron valves, brass pipes, tubing that she cannot remember having specified in her diagrams.

"I am not an anatomist!" she cries, before realizing the words have left her shriveled lips. "I cannot guarantee that this will accomplish anything, Your Majesty. And you will die," she continues in her passion, "if not now, then eventually! That is the natural order of things. And His Majesty Guangxu will be emperor after you, and his children thereafter. And all shall be well, the kingdom shall be well, you can rest easy in heaven…."

"Heresy," snaps the Empress. "Control yourself, madam. This one will not be well if you shriek and squawk and continue to utter all these inauspicious delusions. You made a vow to us, and that is the end of it."

Under that piercing stare, Ada falters and feels the color come into her cheeks.

"Lady Jin"—and the Empress's tone softens, and she beckons Ada closer—"have I not told you that I respect you, for your intellect and your age, because you are my elder despite my rank?"

That is truth. She has learnt so much from this woman two decades her junior, in the years she has spent at court.

"You call me inscrutable," the Empress said once, her fury icelike. "Have you never wondered what it meant? Have you never thought how it placed demands upon me, upon my people, to be open to the scrutiny of yours? I will be as inscrutable as I please, Lady Jin, because it shows I do not give in so easily to the diplomacy of gunboats asking me to open my soul."

"Lady Jin," the Empress calls again. "I am *begging* you"—and that is not possible, the royal family does not beg—"I have kept you here so long and you are so close to winning your freedom. Can you obey one last order?"

It is not a matter of *can you*, Ada realizes, but *will you*. Or *must you*. The most powerful woman in the world needs her help. And she needs to obey. She needs to be free.

She has spent thirty-three years in this beautiful cage in the 紫禁城.

"Your Majesty." Ada watches the Empress carefully because she will not stand to be gulled this one last time. "You said to me, when you were younger, 'I am only a queen because my son is a powerful heir; *you* are only the queen of numbers because your father was a rich man.' But that is a lie, Your Majesty. You are queen because you have made it so."

She lifts herself, slowly, painfully, with an effort, climbing the steps to the throne. If there were anyone else in the Great Hall, it would be treason, lèse majesté. Here and now, the Empress does not protest.

"Are you sure you will do this?" Ada whispers, feeling faint.

The Empress's lip curls—iron matriarch to the end. "You are strangely squeamish today, Lady Jin."

"I do not feel well. I did not take my medication." Ada is not lying.

It is the final part of their arrangement. Every morning for thirty-three years, the Empress has sent a eunuch to her quarters with the lithium salts for her melancholia and the wheat grain for the crab in her belly. Until last week, when the messenger did not arrive, and Ada did not bother asking for him.

"You will feel better soon," the Empress promises. "As will I."

Ada wrenches the first plug into place.

She sits on the floor of the Great Hall, peering through the dimness with tired, old-woman eyes. She can hear the spitting and wheezing and clank of the artificial respiration, and the rasp of a voice speaking to nobody in particular:

"What the great men of the past could not accomplish...the First Emperor, dead of the mercury pills; the archer-god Hou Yi, whose wife was sacrificed to prevent his eternal tyranny; the Yongle Emperor, who would rather cull the treasure fleet of Zheng He in search of the elixir of life…what these men set out to do, who in the process failed and perished in the flesh as men are wont to do, *I have achieved.*"

It makes Ada smile, pulls her mouth taut against her dry, wizened skin. Her gaze is fixed on the single phlegethon gas lamp hissing and burning in the bracket by the throne. She bites her lip as she watches it sputter, feeling the dull throbbing in her womb and her head, feeling her body crave the laudanum.

Then the lamp goes out, and there is only a machine muttering, muttering through the dark.

GLOSSARY
鼎: *ding;* a type of cauldron or vessel, used in antiquity.
scribe-*zhēng*: the *zheng* is a keyboardlike string instrument; this is a reference to a typewriter analogue.
扇子: fanpiece.
姨: aunt; a term of respect for an older woman.
太和殿: the Hall of Supreme Harmony, the largest hall and the center of the Forbidden City.
南洋: Southeast Asia.
慈禧太后: Empress Dowager Cixi.
紫禁城: the Chinese name for the Forbidden City.

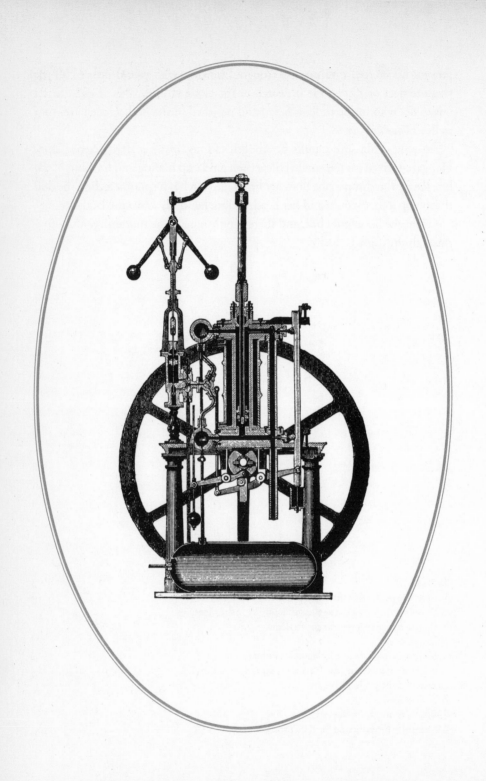

Nowhere Fast

Christopher Rowe

THE SKY LUZ rode under was a pale and hazy gray, its color burned away by sun and smoke years before she was born. Luz might have even called the sky white, but the zinc oxide sunscreen she and the others had dutifully spread over their skin was so stark against her brown arms and legs that there was no comparison.

Her grandmother said that when she was a teenager in California, thousands of miles distant and decades and decades gone in the past, girls welcomed the sun and used its rays to burn themselves darker. Luz had asked if that meant the girls didn't know about skin diseases and sun lesions and her grandmother had answered with one of the private gestures they shared. Hand to head, then hand to heart meant that knowing something and believing it weren't the same thing.

Right now, Luz couldn't believe that tiny Priscilla was steadily pulling away from her on the long climb up from the ferry. She pushed harder on her bicycle's pedals, trying to match the rhythm of the turning wheels to her rapid breathing. Still, the younger girl danced on ahead, standing on her pedals, apparently unaware that she was leaving Luz and the others behind.

There were four of them out on their bikes, fifteen miles from town and taking their time getting to the upland field of strawberries they were scheduled to hoe free of weeds. Luz had sent her younger brother, Caleb, to the work hall with strict instructions to find something far from town. She'd been pleased when he brought back the slip listing a work site on the bluffs above the Kentucky River—far enough and different enough from town that she could pretend she was really travelling—but slightly annoyed that Sammy and Priscilla came trailing in after him.

She liked Priscilla, but had assumed—mistakenly it turned out—that the young girl would slow them down. She liked Priscilla's brother Sammy well enough, too, but he'd lately started liking her back in a way she just didn't reciprocate. It made for some awkward talk when they went out on the same community service jobs.

Not that there had been much call for talk on the long ride out, especially not as they finally crested the hill, breathing hard.

Up ahead, Priscilla signaled a stop, and at first Luz thought she was finally tiring. But then the girl spoke.

"Is that an *engine?*" Priscilla asked, eyes wide.

Luz stopped beside her, struggling to slow her breath so she could hear the howling sound floating over the fields better. Hard to say how far away the noise was, but it was clearly in motion. And moving closer, fast.

Caleb and Sammy stopped beside them and dismounted.

"It is," said Caleb, excitement in his voice. "Internal combustion, not too big."

Even though Caleb was the scholar of the group, Sammy couldn't pass up an opportunity to try to impress Luz. "Not like on any of the Federal machines, though," he said. "Not like anything I've ever heard."

Luz thought of the last time one of the great Army recruitment trucks had come through Lexington, grinding and belching and trumpeting its horn. It had been the previous autumn. Her parents had made her hide in one of the sheds behind the house, even though she was only sixteen and the Federals weren't supposed to draft anyone younger than eighteen. She had stood behind a tidy stack of aluminum doors her mother had salvaged from the ghost suburbs south of town and listened to the engine closely.

The Army engine had been a deeper sound than this, though whatever was approaching was not as high as the mosquito buzz of the little motors on the sheriff's department chariots. If the deputies rode mosquitoes, then the Federals rode growling bears. This was something in between, a howling wolf.

The noise dropped away briefly, stuttered, and then came back louder than ever.

"Whatever it is, it just turned into the lane," Luz told the others. She dismounted and waved for them all to move their bikes into the grassy verge to one side. They'd stopped at a point where the road was bound on either side by low, dry stone walls. A pair of curious chestnut quarter horses, fully biological, not the hissing mounts of Federal outriders, ambled over briefly, hopeful of treats, but they snorted and trotted away as the noise came closer.

Suddenly, the sound blared as loud as anything Luz had ever heard and a… vehicle rounded the curve before them. Luz flashed on the automobile carcasses some people kept as tomato planters. She saw four wheels, a brace of 55 gallon drums, and a makeshift seat. The seat was occupied by a distracted-looking young man wrestling a steering wheel as the vehicle hurtled past them, forcing them to move even farther off the road.

The vehicle fishtailed from side to side on the crumbling pavement, sputtering, and came to an abrupt halt when it took a hard left turn and hit the wall on the south side of the road. The top two layers of rock slid into the field as the noise died away.

They all ran towards the crash. Luz could see now that the vehicle was a modified version of a hay wagon, sporting thick rubber tires and otherwise liberally outfitted with ancient automobile parts. The seat was a cane-bottomed rocker with the legs removed, screwed to the bed. The young man was strapped into the chair, with a dazed expression on his face.

The huge metal engine that took up most of the wagon bed ticked.

The young man, and Luz saw that he was younger than she had first thought, just a little older than her sixteen years, perhaps, blinked and looked at them. He had tightly curled black hair and green eyes.

"I think…" he began, and trailed off, lips still moving, eyes still unfocussed. "I think I need to adjust the braking mechanism."

He claimed, unbelievably, that he was from North Carolina. Hundreds of miles away, the other side of mountains with collapsed tunnels and rivers with fallen bridges. In Luz's experience, traffic from the east came into the Bluegrass along only two routes; down from the Ohio off boats from Pittsburgh, or along the Federal Highway through Huntington. Or by air, though the Federal flying machines were forbidden to land in Lexington by treaty.

"No, no," the driver said, piling the last rock back on top of the wall his machine had damaged. "I didn't come over the mountains. I went south, first, then along the Gulf shore, then up the Natchez Trace through Alabama and middle Tennessee. The state government in Tennessee is pretty advanced. They've built pontoon bridges over all their rivers now."

Luz reached behind Fizz—that was the name he'd given—and made an adjustment to the slab of limestone he haphazardly dropped atop the wall. He'd accepted their offer to help him repair the fence, which was a good thing, because it was clear that he had no experience with dry stone work. For some reason, this made him seem even more foreign to Luz than his vehicle or his claim to have seen the ocean. Sammy had whispered his opinion that Fizz would have left the wall in disrepair if they hadn't witnessed the crash, but Luz wasn't ready to be that judgmental.

Sammy was also more persistent in his questions than Luz thought was polite. "Well, then how did you cross the Kentucky River? And the Green and all the creeks you must have come to? We just came from the ferry and they would have mentioned you. And there's no way the Federals would have let you bring that thing across any of *their* bridges."

"There's more local bridges than you might think," said Fizz, either completely missing the hostility in Sammy's voice or ignoring it. "I only had to float Rudolf once. See the air compressor there? I can fill old inner tubes and lash them to the sides. That converts him into a raft good enough for the width of a creek, anyways."

Caleb was examining the vehicle. "There are a lot of bridges that aren't on the Federal map," he said, almost to himself. Then he asked, "Why do you call it Rudolf?"

"Rudolf Diesel!" said Fizz, in a different, stranger accent than most of his speech. He seemed to think that answered Caleb's question.

Priscilla whispered, "He speaks German." Luz found Priscilla's instant and obvious crush on Fizz annoying.

Fizz looked at the girls. "Sure he did," he said, and smiled at Luz. "He *was* German. He probably spoke like eleven languages, not just English and Spanish. Everybody did back then. He designed this engine—or its ancestor, anyway." He pointed to the cooling metal engine on his vehicle.

"I hope you paid him for it," said Sammy.

"No, I remember," said Caleb. "Diesel was one of the men who made the internal combustion engines." A troubled expression crossed his face. "That's from history. You shouldn't tell people you named your car after him, Fizz."

Fizz wrinkled his nose and brow, scoffing. "Figures the only thing the Federals are consistent about are their interstate highway monopolies and their curriculum suggestions. Diesel wasn't a bad guy! The 19ᵀᴴ century, which is when he invented this, only ended a couple of hundred years ago. Don't you guys have grandparents? Don't they talk about when everybody could go everywhere?"

Some do, Luz thought. Aloud, she said, "Our abuela *has* been everywhere. She's from Chiapas, and came here from California before the oil finally ran out."

"And we can go anywhere we like, anyway," said Sammy. "We just like it here."

"But going places takes forever!" said Fizz. Then he finally seemed to notice the uncomfortable glances being shared between Caleb and Sammy. "Not that this isn't a great place to be. The hemp seed oil Rudolf is burning for fuel right now is from around here someplace. Or it was. My tanks are about dry. That's why I turned north when the Tennesseans wouldn't trade me any."

Luz nodded. "Sure. The biggest oil press anywhere is over in Frankfort. Our uncles sell them most of their hemp. What have you got to trade that the Feds would want?"

Fizz made the face again. "Eh, they're not much for bartering with people like me."

"And who's that?" asked Sammy. "Who are people like you?"

Fizz looked them all up and down, deciding something.

Then he said, "Revolutionaries."

"Revolting is more like it," Sammy gasped. He and Luz were working very hard, barely turning the pedals of their bikes over in their lowest gears. Fizz had brought out some cords from the toolbox on his machine, and between them, he and Luz had figured out a way to rig a Y harness connecting the automobile's front axle to the seatposts of hers and Sammy's bikes. The others rode behind the automobile, hopping off to push on the hills.

Except for Fizz, of course, who rode the machine the whole time, manning the steering wheel and chattering happily to curious Caleb and smitten Priscilla. Luz wished she could be back there. She had a thousand questions about the wider world.

Fizz had insisted they take a little used, poorly surfaced route into town. He said he wanted to approach the council of farmers and merchants who acted as the community council before they saw his machine. "I had trouble some places," he said. "Farther south."

Now, as they hauled the stranger and his strange vehicle, they kept the fleet of canvas balloons anchored high above Lexington dead ahead. Federal government ornithopters were forbidden to land inside the town limits, but Kentucky was still the primary source for their fuel, so the brass-winged engines could usually be seen clinging to the netting below their coal-laden baskets, crawling and supping like the fruit bats that haunted the orchards ringing the town.

Responding to Sammy, Luz asked, "What's revolting?"

He answered her with a question. "Do you know what we're pulling? I'll tell you. It's a *car*. A private car."

Luz took her left hand off the handlebars long enough to point out a particularly deep pothole in the asphalt. Sammy acknowledged with a nod and they bore to the right.

"Don't be silly," Luz continued after they'd negotiated the hole. "Cars ran on oil. Petroleum oil I mean."

But Luz had already noticed that a lot of the machine's parts were similar to those she found when she went scrounging with her mother. The steering wheel, for one thing, was plastic, and plastic was the very first word in the list of nonrenewables she'd memorized in grade school. Luz was still five years away from the age when she would attain full citizenship, and thus be allowed to learn to read, but like most teenagers she had paid close enough attention when adults practiced that art to recognize a few words. One of the words stamped on Fizz's machine was "transmission," but she did not tell Sammy this.

"Well, I guess he made a car that runs on hemp seed oil," said Sammy. "Or somebody did, anyway." Sammy doubted every part of Fizz's story. "He probably stole it off the Federals."

Luz doubted that. The only vehicles she knew the Federals to use besides their Army trucks were bicycles, the coal-burning horses that patrolled the highways, and the ornithopters that patrolled the skies, their metal wings flapping like a hawk's. Bikes and horses and 'thopters and trucks alike shared a sleek, machined design. Nothing at all like the haphazard jumble of Fizz's "car."

The group managed to attract only a few stares before they made it to one of the sheds behind Luz and Caleb's house. Luz supposed that people assumed they'd found a heap of scrap metal and had knocked together a wagon on site to transport it to their mother's salvage shops. People brought her old things all the time.

"Are you going to get your father?" Sammy asked. "Because you should." Then, unusually, he left before Luz asked him to, saying he had to get home.

His little sister, however, clearly had no intention of leaving. She wordlessly followed Fizz as he crawled around checking the undercarriage of his machine.

"I guess this job posting is open all week," said Caleb, pulling the paper out from his belt. Luz had completely forgotten the original purpose of their ride. "Maybe we can go on Wednesday if we can get enough people."

"Sure," said Luz.

"So it's okay if I work here?" Fizz asked. "You won't get in trouble?"

Caleb was worried. "Our father will be home soon—"

"Wait," Luz interrupted. Fizz and his car were the most interesting thing that had happened to Luz in a long time. "Mama's in the mountains, gleaning in the tailings from the old mines. I'll go to the shop and talk to Papa."

"That'd be great," said Fizz, popping his head out from under the machine right at their feet. "Looks like you've probably got everything I need to get Rudolf up and running."

Luz left quickly, knowing it would be better for them all if her father knew what was waiting for him at home.

The shop was the more or less permanent stall in the market by the courthouse run by their father. It served as the main bike shop in town. Luz and her friends had free use of a parts box that was pretty extraordinary by anybody's standards, and their father had connections all over the place if they needed something he didn't have, or couldn't recycle or rig themselves. He fixed the post office's long-haul cargo bikes for free in exchange for good rates bringing in stuff from the coast, but always insisted that his children—and his other customers—make an honest attempt at repair before they settled on replacement.

Papa moved around the stall, putting away tools and hanging bikes from hooks in the ceiling. "Yes, he could have driven here from North Carolina," he told Luz. "Before the Peak people made the trip in a few hours."

Luz didn't doubt that her father was telling the truth, but thought of the hand to heart gesture again, of the difference between knowing and feeling the truth. She could *feel* the truth when somebody said the sun was hot, but could only *acknowledge* the truth when somebody said it was 93 million miles away.

"That's what he was talking about, I guess," she said. "Fizz. When he said that it takes forever to go anywhere now."

Without warning, Papa dropped the seatpost he was holding to the shop floor. It made a dull clattering sound as it bounced back and forth.

"Hey!" said Luz as he grabbed her arm, *hard*, and pulled her out the open end of the stall.

Out in the street, he let go, and pointed up at the sky. "Look up there!" he barked.

Luz had never heard her father sound so angry. She found it hard to tear her eyes away from his livid face but he thrust his finger skyward again. "Look!" he said.

Luz stared at the sky, gray and cloudless as ever in the spring heat.

"That is a *bruised* sky," he said, punctuating his words with his hand. "That is a *torn up* sky."

His mood suddenly changed in a way that made Luz think of a deflating tire. He leaned against the corner support pole of the shop. "You don't know what our ancestors did to this world. There's so much less of everything. And if there is one reason for it, it's in what this stranger told you. 'Forever,' hah! It takes as long to get somewhere as it should take—his *expedience* leads to war and flood."

Luz didn't understand half of what he was saying.

"What about the Federals?" she asked. "They drive trucks and have flying machines."

Papa waved his hand. "We are not the Federals. We live lightly upon the earth, light enough that the wounds they deal it will heal. Your grandparents' generation fought wars so that we could rescue the world from excess. People like us act as stewards, we save the rivers and the sky and the land from the worst that people like them do. When you're older you'll understand."

Luz thought about that for a moment, then said, "People like us and people like the Federals?"

Papa looked at her. "Yes, Luz."

"What about people that aren't like either?" Luz asked.

Papa hadn't answered her before Priscilla came tearing down the street. "Luz! They took him! They came and took Fizz and his machine both! Caleb couldn't stop them!"

She slid to a halt next to them in a cloud of dust. "It was Sammy! He brought the deputies!"

Luz instantly hopped on her bike, and saw from the corner of her eye that her father was pulling his own out from behind the workbench. She didn't wait for him to catch up.

Hours later, Luz and Caleb pedaled along abandoned streets behind the tannery and the vinegar works, looking for the stockade where the deputies had taken Fizz. They might have missed him if he hadn't shouted out.

"Hey! Luz!"

Fizz was leaning half out of a ground-floor window in an old brick building set in an unkempt lawn of weeds and trash. As they rode over to him, a deputy rounded the corner and growled at Fizz to stay inside the window. Clearly, the deputies weren't used to having prisoners. When Caleb asked if they could speak to Fizz, the man shrugged and instructed them not to let him escape.

"The trial's tonight," the deputy said, then went back to the corner, where he sat on a stool and idly turned the letter-pressed pages of last week's town newsletter.

"I've had it worse, that's for sure," Fizz told them. "They seem a lot more concerned with Rudolf than they are with me. I hope your father didn't get in trouble for it being at your house."

Luz and Caleb glanced at one another. The car had been much easier to locate than its driver. They had stood with the other younger people and watched uneasily while their parents and grandparents hung the vehicle from a hastily erected scaffold in the square. Their father had rigged the block and tackle the men used to haul it above a growing pile of scrap timber.

"No," said Luz. "Papa's fine."

"I don't think Rudolf will be able to say the same," Caleb said.

The serious look that passed over Fizz's face made Luz notch her guess of his age back up another year or two. But then he flashed a wide smile and said, "Rudolf's never offered an opinion on anything at all, Caleb. We hit the road before I figured out how to make him talk."

When they didn't join his laughter, Fizz nodded and said, "I see that you're worried. Don't be. I've been in communities like yours before. Heck, I've even been in jails like this one before. Your council and—" he raised his eyebrow, "I'm guessing your father, too? They're more concerned about the machine than the machinist. They'll do whatever they're going to do to Rudolf and then storm and glower at me for an hour and send me on my way."

Luz said, "Papa's name came up in the lottery at New Year's, so he's on the council this year. And yes, he's concerned about the machine. But I think he's even more concerned about the use you put it to."

Fizz didn't reply. He gazed at her steadily, as if she knew the answer to a question he'd forgotten to ask aloud.

"'Everybody could go everywhere,'" she finally said, quoting him.

"Ah," Fizz said. "Your friend said that everybody still can."

Luz shook her head. "I don't think Sammy is my friend anymore. And anyway," she added, her voice unexpectedly bitter, "he's never *wanted* to go anywhere."

Fizz was sympathetic. "What about you?" he asked her. "Where would you go if you could?"

Luz thought about it for a moment. She remembered Fizz's route along the Gulf of Mexico, but even more, she remembered her grandmother's stories of California.

"I would go to the ocean," she said. "My grandmother was a surfer. You know, on the waves?" She held her palm out flat and rocked it back and forth.

Fizz nodded.

"She says that I'm built right for it. It sounds…fast."

"And light on the earth, too," Fizz said. "Am I saying that right?"

"You're close," said Caleb, frowning at them both. "It's 'lightly upon the earth.'"

Luz had never thought about how often she heard the phrase. It was something said by the older people in the community over and over again. "How did you know people say that here?" she asked.

Fizz shrugged. "People say it everywhere," he said.

Luz had expected her father and the other council members to be arrayed behind a long table in the courtyard square. She had expected the whole town to turn out to watch the proceedings, and even for Fizz to be marched out by the deputies with his hands tied before him with a coil of rope.

She had not expected Federal marshals.

There were two of them, a silver-haired man and a grim-faced woman. Neither of them bothered to dismount their strange horses, only issuing terse orders to the closest townspeople to fetch pails of coal they then turned into the furnaces atop the hybrid creatures' hindquarters. They seemed impatient, as was ever the way with Federals.

Luz sat on the ground in front of a bench crowded with older people, leaning back against her grandmother's knees. "I thought the covenants between the town and the Federals guaranteed us the right to have our own trials," Luz said.

Her abuela patted her shoulder, though there was nothing of reassurance in it. "My son," she said, speaking of Luz's Papa, "is more afraid of what this Fizz can do to us than what the Federals can. The council asked the marshals here."

Before Luz could express her dismay at this news, the council chair banged on the table with a wrench to quiet the crowd. "We're in extraordinary session, people," she said, "and the only order of business is the forbidden technology this boy from…North Carolina has brought to our town."

Before anything more could be said, Luz's Papa raised his hand to be recognized. "I move we close this meeting," he said. "We'll be talking of things our children shouldn't be made to hear."

The gathered townspeople murmured at this, and Luz was surprised at the tone. She would have expected them to be upset that they couldn't watch the proceedings, but except for the people her age, most there seemed to be agreeing with her father. Before any of the council members could respond to the suggestion, though, Fizz spoke up.

"I believe I'm allowed to speak, yes?" he asked. "That's been the way of it with the other town councils."

Luz saw the woman marshal lean over in her saddle and whisper something to her partner, whose deadeyed gaze never shifted from Fizz.

The chairwoman saw the exchange, too, and seemed troubled by it. "Yes, son," she told Fizz. "We've heard this isn't the first time you've been brought up on these charges. But you should be careful you don't say anything to incriminate yourself. It might not be us that carries out whatever sentence we decide on."

Fizz looked directly at the marshals, and then back at the council. "Yes ma'am," he said. "I see that. I've not been in a town controlled by the Federal government before."

Papa's angry interruption cut through the noise from the crowd. "Here now!" he said. "We're as sovereign as any other town in America and signatory to covenants that reserve justice to ourselves. It's our laws you've flouted and our ruling that will decide your fate. These marshals are here at our invitation because we want to demonstrate how seriously we take your crimes."

Luz did not realize she had stood until she spoke. "What crimes?"

Papa frowned at her. "Sit down, Luza," he said.

Before she could respond, Fizz spoke. "I can choose someone to speak on my behalf, isn't that right? I choose her. I want Luz to be my advocate."

To Luz's surprise—to *everyone's* surprise—the voice that answered did not come from the council, but from one of the Federals.

"Oh for God's sake," the woman said, directing her words to Luz's father. "Andy, we came here to destroy this unauthorized car as a favor to you, not to watch you Luddites play at justice." With that, she and the man leapt from the saddles stitched to their horses' flanks. They both whistled high and hard and pointed at Fizz's vehicle. It slowly turned in the air, held a foot above the ground by a strong cable.

For the first time, Fizz appeared confused, even frightened.

Then *everyone* was frightened, as the horses leapt.

Their lips curled back, exposing spikes where an unaltered horse's teeth would be. Long claws extended from the dewlaps above their steel shod hooves and the muscles rippling beneath their flanks were square and hard. They jumped onto the hanging car, clinging to opposite sides, steam and smoke belching from their noses and ears as they struck and bit, kicked and tore. The sounds of metal ripping and wood splitting rang across the square, frighteningly loud, yet still not loud enough to drown the frightened cries of the children in the crowd. Luz was as shocked by the sounds the horses made as she was by the savagery of their assault.

In moments, the car called Rudolf was a pile of scrap metal and wood. The horses' spikes and claws retracted as they trotted back to their riders, who waited with more skips of coal to replenish what they'd burned up in the destruction.

The Federals swung into their saddles and the woman spoke to Luz's father once more. "Do you want us to take your prisoner off your hands, too, Andy? We're better equipped to deal with his kind of trouble than you."

"No!" cried Luz.

Everyone turned to look at her. "If Fizz has broken any rules they were *ours*, not yours. You...you lot get going."

Luz's father nodded at the Federals. The woman and the deadeyed man exchanged ugly grins, but they put their spurs to their mounts and left the square.

Luz turned to the council. "And *you* lot, you get to explaining. What is all this? Papa, you can't stand the Federals and their ways. None of you can. You'd put us in debt to enforce some law that you won't even name?"

All of the people sitting behind the table looked troubled, and only Papa would meet her gaze.

"We protect our children from such things until they've reached their majority, Luz," he said. "You know that. But since you all just saw...what we all just saw..." He hesitated for a moment. "It's basically what I said earlier, Luz," he continued. "Your friend there has a personal car, and that's the source of so much bad in the world I can't even begin to explain it to you. It can't be allowed."

Luz rolled her eyes and walked over to the pile of debris beneath the scaffold. She pointed to it and said, "This, you mean? It doesn't look to me like he has a car anymore."

She turned to Fizz for support, but he was still staring at the wreckage. For once, he had nothing to say. *I'm his advocate,* she remembered.

"You should let him go," she said. *"We* should let him go."

Before her father could respond, the chairwoman called him closer. They exchanged a few murmured words. Then she said, "The young man is no longer a danger to our community, or to the earth. He's free to go."

Papa added, "He *must* go."

The crowd stood and milled around, everyone talking about what had just happened. Luz spotted her father approaching, and then saw her abuela shake her head to stop him from coming near.

Luz went and stood beside Fizz. She thought about what she had learned about making and repairing things from her father. She thought about what she had learned about scavenging from her mother. She thought of the stories of gliding across an ocean's wave told to her by her grandmother. She put her hand on Fizz's shoulder.

"I know where we can get some parts," she said.

PRICE, : : : 50 CENTS.

ILLUSTRATED

VISITORS' GUIDE

TO

NEW ORLEANS.

PUBLISHED BY

J. CURTIS WALDO,

PUBLISHER OF "THE ROYAL HERALD,"

OFFICIAL JOURNAL OF CARNIVAL COURT,

NEW ORLEANS.

L. Graham, Printer, 127 Gravier street, N. O.

The Effluent Engine

N. K. Jemisin

NEW ORLEANS STANK to the heavens. This was either the water, which did not have the decency to confine itself to the river but instead puddled along every street, or the streets themselves, which seemed to have been cobbled with bricks of fired excrement. Or it may have come from the people who jostled and trotted along the narrow avenues, working and lounging and cursing and shouting and sweating, emitting a massed reek of unwashed resentment and perhaps a bit of hangover. As Jessaline strolled beneath the colonnaded balconies of Royal Street, she fought the urge to give up, put the whole fumid pile to her back, and catch the next dirigible out of town.

Then someone jostled her. "Pardon me, miss," said a voice at her elbow, and Jessaline was forced to stop, because the earnest-looking young man who stood there was white. He smiled, which did not surprise her, and doffed his hat, which did.

"Monsieur," Jessaline replied, in what she hoped was the correct mix of reserve and deference.

"A fine day, is it not?" The man's grin widened, so sincere that Jessaline could not help a small smile in response. "I must admit, though; I have yet to adjust to this abysmal heat. How are you handling it?"

"Quite well, monsieur," she replied, thinking, *what is it that you want from me?* "I am acclimated to it."

"Ah, yes, certainly. A fine negress like yourself would naturally deal better with such things. I am afraid my own ancestors derive from chillier climes, and we adapt poorly." He paused abruptly, a stricken look crossing his face. He was the florid kind, red-haired and freckled with skin so pale that it revealed his every thought—in point of which he paled further. "Oh, dear! My sister warned me about this. You aren't Creole, are you? I understand they take it an insult to be called, er…by certain terms."

With some effort Jessaline managed not to snap, *do I look like one of them?* But people on the street were beginning to stare, so instead she said, "No, monsieur. And it's clear to me you aren't from these parts, or you would never ask such a thing."

"Ah—yes." The man looked sheepish. "You have caught me out, miss; I'm from New York. Is it so obvious?"

Jessaline smiled carefully. "Only in your politeness, monsieur." She reached up to adjust her hat, lifting it for a moment as a badly needed cooling breeze wafted past.

"Are you perhaps—" The man paused, staring at her head. "My word! You've naught but a scrim of hair!"

"I have sufficient to keep myself from drafts on cold days," she replied, and as she'd hoped, he laughed.

"You're a most charming ne—woman, my dear, and I feel honored to make your acquaintance." He stepped back and bowed, full and proper. "My name is Raymond Forstall."

"Jessaline Dumonde," she said, offering her lace-gloved hand, though she had no expectation that he would take it. To her surprise he did, bowing again over it.

"My apologies for gawking. I simply don't meet many of the colored on a typical day, and I must say—" He hesitated, darted a look about, and at least had the grace to drop his voice. "You're remarkably lovely, even with no hair."

In spite of herself, Jessaline laughed. "Thank you, monsieur." After an appropriate and slightly awkward pause, she inclined her head. "Well, then; good day to you."

"Good day indeed," he said, in a tone of such pleasure that Jessaline hoped no one had heard it, for his sake. The folk of this town were particular about matters of propriety, as any society that relied so firmly upon class differences. While there were many ways in which a white gentleman could appropriately express his admiration for a woman of color—the existence of the *gens de couleur libre* was testimony to that—all of those ways were simply Not Done in public.

But Forstall donned his hat, and Jessaline inclined her head in return before heading away. Another convenient breeze gusted by, and she took advantage of it to adjust her hat once more, in the process sliding her stiletto back into its hiding place amid the silk flowers.

This was the dance of things, the *cric-crac* as the storytellers said in Jessaline's land. Everyone needed something from someone. Glorious France needed money to recover from the unlamented Napoleon's endless wars. Upstart Haiti had money from the sweet gold of its sugarcane fields, but needed guns—for all the world, it seemed, wanted the newborn country strangled in its crib. The United States had guns but craved sugar, as its fortunes were dependent upon the acquisition thereof. It alone was willing to treat with Haiti, though Haiti was the stuff of American nightmare: a nation of black slaves who had killed off their white masters. Yet Haitian sugar was no less sweet for its coating of blood, and so everyone got what they wanted, trading 'round and 'round, a graceful waltz—only occasionally devolving into a knife fight.

It had been simplicity itself for Jessaline to slip into New Orleans. Dirigible travel in the Caribbean was inexpensive, and so many travelers regularly moved between the island nations and the great American port city that hardly any deception had been necessary. She was indentured, she told the captain, and he had waved her aboard without so much as a glance at her papers (which were false anyhow). She was a wealthy white man's mistress, she told the other passengers, and between her fine clothes, regal carriage, and beauty—despite her skin being purest sable in color—they believed her and were alternately awed and offended. She was a slave, she told the dockmaster on the levee; a trusted one, lettered and loyal, promised freedom should she continue to serve to her fullest. He had smirked at this, as if the notion of anyone freeing such an obviously valuable slave was ludicrous. Yet he, too, had let her pass unchallenged, without even charging her the disembarkation fee.

It had then taken two full months for Jessaline to make inquiries and sufficient contacts to arrange a meeting with the esteemed Monsieur Norbert Rillieux. The Creoles of New Orleans were a closed and prickly bunch, most likely because they had to be; only by the rigid maintenance of caste and privilege could they hope to retain freedom in a land that loved to throw anyone darker than tan into chains. Thus more than a few of them had refused to speak to Jessaline on sight. Yet there were many who had not forgotten that there but for the grace of God went their own fortune, so from these she had been able to glean crucial information and finally an introduction by letter. As she had mentioned the right names and observed the right etiquette, Norbert Rillieux had at last invited her to afternoon tea.

That day had come, and....

And. Rillieux, Jessaline was finally forced to concede, was an idiot.

"Monsieur," she said again, after drawing a breath to calm herself, "as I explained in my letter, I have no interest in sugarcane processing. It is true that your contributions to this field have been much appreciated by the interests I represent; your improved refining methods have saved both money and lives, which could both be reinvested in other places. What we require assistance with is a wholly different matter, albeit related."

"Oh," said Rillieux, blinking. He was a savagely thin-lipped man, with a hard stare that might have been compelling on a man who knew how to use it. Rillieux did not. "Your pardon, mademoiselle. But, er, who did you say you represented, again?"

"I did not say, monsieur. And if you will forgive me, I would prefer not to say for the time being." She fixed him with her own hard stare. "You will understand, I hope, that not all parties can be trusted when matters scientific turn to matters commercial."

At that, Rillieux's expression turned shrewd at last; he understood just fine. The year before, Jessaline's superiors had informed her, the plan Rillieux had proposed to the city—an ingenious means of draining its endless, pestilent swamps, for the health and betterment of all—had been turned down. Six months later, a coalition of city engineers had submitted virtually the same plan and been heaped with praise and funds to bring it about. The men of the coalition were white, of course. Jessaline marveled that Rillieux even bothered being upset about it.

"I see," Rillieux said. "Then, please forgive me, but I do not know what it is you want."

Jessaline stood and went to her brocaded bag, which sat on a side table across the Rillieux house's elegantly apportioned salon. In it was a small, rubber-stopped, peculiarly shaped jar of the sort utilized by chemists, complete with engraved markings on its surface to indicate measurements of the liquid within.

At the bottom of this jar swirled a scrim of dark brown, foul-looking paste and liquid. Jessaline brought it over to Rillieux and offered the jar to his nose, waiting until he nodded before she unstoppered it.

At the scent that wafted out, he stumbled back, gasping, his eyes all a-water. "By all that's holy! Woman, what is that putrescence?"

"That, Monsieur Rillieux, is effluent," Jessaline said, neatly stoppering the flask. "Waste, in other words, of a very particular kind. Do you drink rum?" She knew the answer already. On one side of the parlor was a beautifully made side table holding an impressive array of bottles.

"Of course." Rillieux was still rubbing his eyes and looking affronted. "I'm fond of a glass or two on hot afternoons; it opens the pores, or so I'm told. But what does that—"

"Producing rum is a simple process with a messy result: this effluent, namely, and the gas it emits, which until lately was regarded as simply the unavoidable price to be paid for your pleasant afternoons. Whole swaths of countryside are afflicted with this smell now as a result. Not only is the stench offensive to men and beasts, we have also found it to be as powerful as any tincture or laudanum; over time it causes anything exposed to suffocate and die. Yet there are scientific papers coming from Europe that laud this gas's potential as a fuel source. Captured properly, purified, and burned, it can power turbines, cook food, and more." Jessaline turned and set the flask on Rillieux's beverage stand, deliberately close to the square bottle of dark rum she had seen there. "We wish you to develop a process by which the usable gas—methane—may be extracted from the miasma you just smelled."

Rillieux stared at her for a moment, then at the flask. She could tell that he was intrigued, which meant that half her mission had been achieved already. Her superiors had spent a profligate amount of money requisitioning a set of those flasks from the German chemist who'd recently invented them, precisely with an eye toward impressing men like Rillieux, who looked down upon any science that did not show European roots.

Yet as Rillieux gazed at the flask, Jessaline was dismayed to see a look of consternation, then irritation, cross his face.

"I am an engineer, mademoiselle," he said at last, "not a chemist."

"We have already worked out the chemical means by which it might be done," Jessaline said quickly, her belly clenching in tension. "We would be happy to share that with you—"

"And then what?" He scowled at her. "Who will put the patent on this process, hmm? And who will profit?" He turned away, beginning to pace, and Jessaline could see that he was working up a good head of steam, to her horror. "You have a comely face, Mademoiselle Dumonde, and it does not escape me that dusky women such as yourself once seduced my forefathers into the most base acts, for which those men atoned by at least raising their half-breed children honorably. If I were a white man hoping to once more profit from the labor of an honest Creole like myself—one already proven gullible—I would send a woman like you to do the tempting. To them, all of us are alike, even though I have the purest of French blood in my veins, and you might as well have come straight from the jungles of Africa!"

He rounded on her at this, very nearly shouting, and if Jessaline had been one of the pampered, cowed women of this land, she might have stepped back in fear of unpleasantness. As it was, she did take a step—but to the side, closer to her brocade bag, within which was tucked a neat little derringer whose handle she could see from where she stood. Her mission had been to use Rillieux, not kill him, but she had no qualms about giving a man a flesh wound to remind him of the value of chivalry.

Before matters could come to a head, however, the parlor door opened, making both Jessaline and Norbert Rillieux jump. The young woman who came in was clearly some kin of Rillieux's; she had the same ocherine skin and loose-curled hair, the latter tucked into a graceful split chignon atop her head. Her eyes were softer, however, though that might have been an effect of the wire-rimmed spectacles perched atop her nose. She wore a simple gray dress, which had the unfortunate effect of emphasizing her natural pallor, and making her look rather plain.

"Your pardon, Brother," she said, confirming Jessaline's guess. "I thought perhaps you and your guest might like refreshment?" In her hands was a silver tray of crisp square beignets dusted in sugar, sliced mirliton with what looked like some sort of rémoulade sauce, and tiny wedges of pecan penuche.

At the sight of this girl, Norbert blanched and looked properly abashed. "Ah—er, yes, you're right, thank you. Ah—" He glanced at Jessaline, his earlier irritation clearly warring with the ingrained desire to be a good host; manners won, and he quickly composed himself. "Forgive me. Will you take refreshment, before you leave?" The last part of that sentence came out harder than the rest. Jessaline got the message.

"Thank you, yes," she said, immediately moving to assist the young woman. As she moved her brocade bag, she noticed the young woman's eyes, which were locked on the bag with a hint of alarm. Jessaline was struck at once with unease—had she noticed the derringer handle? Impossible to tell, since the young woman made no outcry of alarm, but that could have been just caution on her part. That one meeting of eyes had triggered an instant, instinctual assessment on Jessaline's part; *this* Rillieux, at least, was nowhere near as myopic or bombastic as her brother.

Indeed, as the young woman lifted her gaze after setting down the tray, Jessaline thought she saw a hint of challenge lurking behind those little round glasses, and above that perfectly pleasant smile.

"Brother," said the young woman, "won't you introduce me? It's so rare for you to have lady guests."

Norbert Rillieux went from blanching to blushing, and for an instant Jessaline feared he would progress to all the way to bluster. Fortunately he mastered the urge and said, a bit stiffly, "Mademoiselle Jessaline Dumonde, may I present to you my younger sister, Eugenie?"

Jessaline bobbed a curtsy, which Mademoiselle Rillieux returned. "I'm pleased to meet you," Jessaline said, meaning it, *because I might have enjoyed shooting your brother to an unseemly degree, otherwise.*

It seemed Mademoiselle Rillieux's thoughts ran in the same direction, because she smiled at Jessaline and said, "I hope my brother hasn't been treating you to a display of his famous temper, Mademoiselle Dumonde. He deals better with his gadgets and vacuum tubes than people, I'm afraid."

Rillieux did bluster at this. "Eugenie, that's hardly—"

"Not at all," Jessaline interjected smoothly. "We were discussing the finer points of chemistry, and your brother, being such a learned man, just made his point rather emphatically."

"Chemistry? Why, I adore chemistry!" At this, Mademoiselle Rillieux immediately brightened, speaking faster and breathlessly. "What matter, if I may ask? Please, may I sit in?"

In that instant, Jessaline was struck by how lovely her eyes were, despite their uncertain coloring of browny-green. She had never preferred the looks of half-white folk, having grown up in a land where, thanks to the Revolution, darkness of skin was a point of pride. But as Mademoiselle Rillieux spoke of chemistry, something in her manner made her peculiar eyes sparkle, and

Jessaline was forced to reassess her initial estimate of the girl's looks. She was handsome, perhaps, rather than plain.

"Eugenie is the only other member of my family to share my interest in the sciences," Rillieux said, pride warming his voice. "She could not study in Paris as I did; the schools there do not admit women. Still, I made certain to send her all of my books as I finished with them, and she critiques all of my prototypes. It's probably for the best that they wouldn't admit her; I daresay she could give my old masters at the École Centrale a run for their money!"

Jessaline blinked in surprise at this. Then it came to her; she had lost Rillieux's trust already. But perhaps....

Turning to the beverage stand, she picked up the flask of effluent. "I'm afraid I won't be able to stay, Mademoiselle Rillieux—but before I go, perhaps you could give me your opinion of this?" She offered the flask.

Norbert Rillieux, guessing her intent, scowled. But Eugenie took the flask before he could muster a protest, unstoppering it deftly and wafting the fumes toward her face rather than sniffing outright. "Faugh," she said, grimacing. "Definitely hydrogen sulfide, and probably a number of other gases too, if this is the product of some form of decay." She stoppered the flask and examined the sludge in its bottom with a critical eye. "Interesting—I thought it was dirt, but this seems to be some more uniform substance. Something *made* this? What process could generate something so noxious?"

"Rum distillation," Jessaline said, stifling the urge to smile when the Eugenie looked scandalized.

"No wonder," Eugenie said darkly, "given what the end product does to men's souls." She handed the flask back to Jessaline. "What of it?"

So Jessaline was obliged to explain again. As she did, a curious thing happened: Eugenie's eyes grew a bit glazed. She nodded, "mmm-hmming" now and again. "And as I mentioned to your brother," Jessaline concluded, "we have already worked out the formula—"

"The formula is child's play," Eugenie said, flicking her fingers absently. "And the extraction would be simple enough, if methane weren't dangerously flammable. Explosive even, under certain conditions...which most attempts at extraction would inevitably create. Obviously any mechanical method would need to concern itself primarily with *stabilizing* the end products, not merely separating them. Freezing, perhaps, or—" She brightened. "Brother, perhaps we could try a refinement of the vacuum-distillation process you developed for—"

"Yes, yes," said Norbert, who had spent the past ten minutes looking from Jessaline to Eugenie and back, in visibly increasing consternation. "I'll consider it. In the meantime, Mademoiselle Dumonde was actually leaving; I'm afraid we delay her." He glared at Jessaline as Eugenie made a moue of dismay.

"Quite right," said Jessaline, smiling graciously at him; she put away the flask and tucked the bag over her arm, retrieving her hat from the back of the chair. She could afford to be gracious now, even though Norbert Rillieux had proven intractable. Better indeed to leave, and pursue the matter from an entirely different angle.

And, as Norbert escorted her to the parlor door with a hand rather too firm upon her elbow, Jessaline glanced back and smiled at Eugenie, who returned the smile with charming ruefulness and a shy little wave.

Not just handsome, pretty, Jessaline decided at last. And that meant this new angle would be *most enjoyable* to pursue.

There were, however, complications.

Jessaline, pleased that she had succeeded in making contact with *a* Rillieux, if not the one she'd come for, treated herself to an evening out about the Vieux Carre. It was not the done thing for a lady of gentle breeding—as she was emulating—to stop in at any of the rollicking music halls she could hear down side streets, though she was intrigued. She could, however, sit in on one of the newfangled vaudevilles at the Playhouse, which she quite enjoyed, though it was difficult to see the stage well from the rear balcony. Then, as nightfall finally brought a breath of cool relief from the day's sweltering humidity, she returned to her room at the inn.

From time spent on the harder streets of Port-au-Prince, it was Jessaline's longtime habit to stand to one side of a door while she unlocked it, so that her shadow under the door would not alert anyone inside. This proved wise, as pushing open the door she found herself facing a startled male figure, which froze in silhouette before the room's picture window, near her traveling chest. They stared at one another for a breath, and then Jessaline's wits returned; at once she dropped to one knee and in a single smooth sweep of her hand, brushed up her booted leg to palm a throwing knife.

In the same instant the figure bolted, darting toward the open balcony window. Jessaline hissed out a curse in her own Kreyòl tongue, running into the room as he lunged through the window with an acrobat's nimbleness, rolling to his feet and fetching up against the elaborately ironworked railing. Fearing to lose him, Jessaline flung the knife from within the room as she ran, praying it would strike, and heard the thunk as it struck flesh. The figure on her balcony stumbled, crying out—but she could not have hit a vital area, for he grasped the railing and pulled himself over it, dropping the short distance to the ground and out of sight.

Jessaline scrambled through the window as best she could, hampered by her bustle and skirts. Just as she reached the railing, the figure finished picking himself up from the ground and turned to run. Jessaline got one good look at him in the moonlight, as he turned back to see if she pursued: a pinch-faced youth, clearly pale beneath the bootblack he'd smeared on his face and straw-colored hair to help himself hide in the dark. Then he was gone, running into the night, though he ran oddly and kept one of his hands clapped to his right buttock.

Furious, Jessaline pounded the railing, though she knew better than to make an outcry. No one in this town would care that some black woman had been robbed, and the constable would as likely arrest her for disturbing the peace.

Going back into her room, she lit the lanterns and surveyed the damage. At once a chill passed down her spine. The chest held a number of valuables that any sensible thief would've taken: fine dresses; a cameo pendant with a face of carved obsidian; the brass gyroscope that an old lover, a dirigible navigator, had given her; a pearl-beaded purse containing twenty dollars. These, however, had all been shoved rudely aside, and to Jessaline's horror, the chest's false bottom had been lifted, revealing the compartment underneath. There was nothing here but a bundle of clothing and a larger pouch, containing a far more substantial sum—but that had not been taken either.

But Jessaline knew what *would* have been in there, if she had not taken them with her to see Rillieux: the scrolls that held the chemical formula for the methane extraction process, and the rudimentary designs for the mechanism to do so—the best her government's scientists had been able to cobble together. These were even now at the bottom of her brocade bag.

The bootblack boy had been no thief. Someone in this foul city knew who and what she was, and sought to thwart her mission.

Carefully Jessaline replaced everything in the trunk, including the false bottom and money. She went downstairs and paid her bill, then hired a porter to carry her trunk to an inn two blocks over, where she rented a room without windows. She slept lightly that night, waking with every creak and thump of the place, and took comfort only from the solid security of the stiletto in her hand.

The lovely thing about a town full of slaves, vagabonds, beggars, and blackguards was that it was blessedly easy to send a message in secret.

Having waited a few days so as to let Norbert Rillieux's anger cool—just in case—Jessaline then hired a child who was one of the innkeepers' slaves. She purchased fresh fruit at the market and offered the child an apple to memorize her message. When he repeated it back to her word for word, she showed him a bunch of big blue-black grapes, and his eyes went wide. "Get word to Mademoiselle Eugenie without her brother knowing, and these are yours," she said. "You'll have to make sure to spit the seeds in the fire, though, or Master will know you've had a treat."

The boy grinned, and Jessaline saw that the warning had not been necessary. "Just you hold onto those, Miss Jessaline," he said back, pointing with his chin at the grapes. "I'll have 'em in a minute or three." And indeed, within an hour's time he returned, carrying a small folded square of cloth. "Miss Eugenie agrees to meet," he said, "and sends this as a surety of her good faith." He pronounced this last carefully, perfectly emulating the Creole woman's tone.

Pleased, Jessaline took the cloth and unfolded it to find a handkerchief of fine imported French linen, embroidered in one corner with a tiny perfect "R." She held it to her nose and smelled a perfume like magnolia blossoms; the same scent had been about Eugenie the other day. She could not help smiling at the memory. The boy grinned too, and ate a handful of the grapes at once, pocketing the seeds with a wink.

"Gonna plant these near the city dump," he said. "Maybe I'll bring you wine one day!" And he ran off.

So Jessaline found herself on another bright sweltering day at the convent of the Ursulines, where two gentlewomen might walk and exchange thoughts in peace without being seen or interrupted by curious others.

"I have to admit," said Eugenie, smiling sidelong at Jessaline as they strolled amid the nuns' garden, "I was of two minds about whether to meet you."

"I suppose your brother must've given you an earful after I left."

"You might say so," Eugenie said, in a dry tone that made Jessaline laugh. (One of the old nuns glowered at them over a bed of herbs. Jessaline covered her mouth and waved apology.) "But that wasn't what gave me pause. My brother has his ways, Mademoiselle Jessaline, and I do not always agree with him. He's fond of forming opinions without full information, then proceeding as if they are proven fact." She shrugged. "I, on the other hand, prefer to seek as much information as I can. I have made inquiries about you, you see."

"Oh? And what did you find?"

"That you do not exist, as far as anyone in this town knows." She spoke lightly, Jessaline noticed, but there was an edge to her words too. Unease, perhaps. "You aren't one of us, that much anyone can see; but you aren't a freedwoman either, though the people at your old inn and the market seemed to think so."

At this, Jessaline blinked in surprise and unease of her own. She had not thought the girl would dig that deeply. "What makes you say that?"

"For one, that pistol in your bag."

Jessaline froze for a pace before remembering to keep walking. "A lady alone in a strange, rough city would be wise to look to her own protection, don't you think?"

"True," said Eugenie, "but I checked at the courthouse too, and there are no records of a woman meeting your description having bought her way free anytime in the past thirty years, and I doubt you're far past that age. For another, you hide it well, but your French has an odd sort of lilt; not at all like that of folk hereabouts. And for thirdly—this is a small town at heart, Mademoiselle Dumonde, despite its size. Every time some fortunate soul buys free, as they say, it's the talk of the town. To put it bluntly, there's no gossip about you, and there should have been."

They had reached a massive old willow tree that partially overhung the garden path. There was no way around it; the tree's draping branches had made a proper curtain of things, nearly obscuring from sight the area about the trunk.

The sensible thing to do would have been to turn around and walk back the way they'd come. But as Jessaline turned to meet Eugenie's eyes, she suffered another of those curious epiphanies. Eugenie was smiling, sweet, but despite this there was a hard look in her eyes, which reminded Jessaline fleetingly of Norbert. It was clear that she meant to have the truth from Jessaline, or Jessaline's efforts to employ her would get short shrift.

So on impulse Jessaline grabbed Eugenie's hand and pulled her into the willow-fall. Eugenie yelped in surprise, then giggled as they came through into the space beyond, green-shrouded and encircling, like a hurricane of leaves.

"What on Earth—? Mademoiselle Dumonde—"

"It isn't Dumonde," Jessaline said, dropping her voice to a near-whisper. "My name is Jessaline Cleré. That is the name of the family that raised me, at least, but I should have had a different name, after the man who was my true father. His name was L'Overture. Do you know it?"

At that, Eugenie drew a sharp breath. "Toussaint the Rebel?" she asked. "The man who led the revolution in Haiti? *That* was your father?"

"So my mother says, though she was only his mistress; I am natural-born. But I do not begrudge her, because her status spared me. When the French betrayed Toussaint, they took him and his wife and legitimate children and carried them across the sea to torture to death."

Eugenie put her hands to her mouth at this, which Jessaline had to admit was a bit much for a gently raised woman to bear. Yet it was the truth, for Jessaline felt uncomfortable dissembling with Eugenie, for reasons she could not quite name.

"I see," Eugenie said at last, recovering. "Then—these interests you represent. You are with the Haitians."

"I am. If you build a methane extraction mechanism for us, Mademoiselle, you will have helped a nation of free folk *stay* free, for I swear that France is hell-bent upon reenslaving us all. They would have done it already, if one of our number had not thought to use our torment to our advantage."

Eugenie nodded slowly. "The sugarcane," she said. "The papers say your people use the steam and gases from the distilleries to make hot-air balloons and blimps."

"Which helped us bomb the French ships most effectively during the Revolution, and also secured our position as the foremost manufacturers of dirigibles in the Americas," Jessaline said, with a bit of pride. "We were saved by a mad idea and a contraption that should have killed its first user. So we value cleverness now, Mademoiselle, which is why I came here in search of your brother."

"Then—" Eugenie frowned. "The methane. It is to power your dirigibles?"

"Partly. The French have begun using dirigibles too, you see. Our only hope is to enhance the maneuverability and speed of our craft, which can be done with gas-powered engines. We have also crafted powerful artillery that use this engine design, whose range and accuracy is unsurpassed. The prototypes work magnificently—but the price of the oil and coal we must currently use to power them is too dear. We would bankrupt ourselves buying it from the very nations that hope to destroy us. The rum effluent is our only abundant, inexpensive resource…our only hope."

But Eugenie had begun to shake her head, looking taken aback. "Artillery? Guns, you mean?" she said. "I am a Christian woman, Mademoiselle—"

"Jessaline."

"Very well, Jessaline." That look was in her face again, Jessaline noted, that air of determination and fierceness that made her beautiful at the oddest times. "I do not care for the idea of my skills being put to use in taking lives. That's simply unacceptable."

Jessaline stared at her, and for an instant fury blotted out thought. How dare this girl, with her privilege and wealth and coddled life…. Jessaline set her jaw.

"In the Revolution," she said, in a low tight voice, "the last French commander, Rochambeau, decided to teach my people a lesson for daring to revolt against our betters. Do you know what he did? He took slaves— including those who had not even fought—and broke them on the wheel, raising them on a post afterward so the birds could eat them alive. He buried prisoners of war, also alive, in pits of insects. He *boiled* some of them, in vats of molasses. Such acts, he deemed, were necessary to put fear and subservience back into our hearts, since we had been tainted by a year of freedom."

Eugenie, who had gone quite pale, stared at Jessaline in purest horror, her mouth open. Jessaline smiled a hard, angry smile. "Such atrocities will happen again, Mademoiselle Rillieux, if you do not help us. Except this time we have been free for two generations. Imagine how much fear and subservience these *Christian* men will instill in us now?"

Eugenie shook her head slowly. "I…I had not heard…I did not consider.…" She fell mute.

Jessaline stepped closer and laid one lace-gloved finger on the divot between Eugenie's collarbones. "You had best consider such things, my dear. Do you forget? There are those in this land who would like to do the same to you and all your kin."

Eugenie stared at her. Then, startling Jessaline, she dropped to the ground, sitting down so hard that her bustle made an aggrieved creaking sound.

"I did not know," she said at last. "I did not know these things."

Jessaline beheld the honest shock on her face and felt some guilt for having troubled her so. It was clear the girl's brother had worked hard to protect her from the world's harshness. Sitting beside Eugenie on the soft dry grass, she let out a weary sigh.

"In my land," she said, "men and women of all shades are free. I will not pretend that this makes us perfect; I have gone hungry many times in my life. Yet there, a woman such as yourself may be more than the coddled sister of a prominent scientist, or the mistress of a white man."

Eugenie threw her a guilty look, but Jessaline smiled to reassure her. The women of Eugenie's class had few options in life; Jessaline saw no point in condemning them for this.

"So many men died in the Revolution that women fill the ranks now as dirigible pilots and gunners. We run factories and farms too, and are highly placed in government. Even the houngans are mostly women now—you have vodun here too, yes? So we are important." She leaned close, her shoulder brushing Eugenie's in a teasing way, and grinned. "Some of us might even become spies. Who knows?"

Eugenie's cheeks flamed pink and she ducked her head to smile. Jessaline could see, however, that her words were having some effect; Eugenie had that oddly absent look again. Perhaps she was imagining all the things she could do in a land where the happenstances of sex and caste did not forbid her from using her mind to its fullest? A shame; Jessaline would have loved to take her there. But she had seen the luxury of the Rillieux household; why would any woman give that up?

This close, shoulder to shoulder and secluded within the willow tree's green canopy, Jessaline found herself staring at Eugenie, more aware than ever of the scent of her perfume, and the nearby softness of her skin, and the way the curls of her hair framed her long slender neck. At least she did not cover her hair like so many women of this land, convinced that its natural state was inherently ugly. She could not help her circumstances, but it seemed to Jessaline that she had taken what pride in her heritage that she could.

So taken was Jessaline by this notion, and by the silence and strangeness of the moment, that she found herself saying, "And in my land it is not uncommon for a woman to head a family with another woman, and even raise children if they so wish."

Eugenie started—and to Jessaline's delight, her blush deepened. She darted a half-scandalized, half-entranced look at Jessaline, then away, which Jessaline found deliciously fetching. "Live with—another woman? Do you mean—?" But of course she knew what Jessaline meant. "How can that be?"

"The necessities of security and shared labor. The priests look the other way."

Eugenie looked up then, and Jessaline was surprised to see a peculiar daring enter her expression, though her flush lingered. "And...." She licked her lips, swallowed. "Do such women...ah...behave as a family in...*all* matters?"

A slow grin spread across Jessaline's face. *Not so sheltered in her thoughts at least, this one!* "Oh, certainly. All matters—legal, financial, domestic...." Then, as a hint of uncertainty flickered in Eugenie's expression, Jessaline got tired of teasing. It was not proper, she knew; it was not within the bounds of her mission. But—just this once—perhaps—

She shifted just a little, from brushing shoulders to pressing rather more suggestively close, and leaned near, her eyes fixed on Eugenie's lips. "And conjugal," she added.

Eugenie stared at her, eyes huge behind the spectacles. "C-conjugal?" she asked, rather breathlessly.

"Oh, indeed. Perhaps a demonstration...."

But just as Jessaline leaned in to offer just that, she was startled by the voice of one of the nuns, apparently calling to another in French. From far too near the willow tree, a third voice rose to shush the first two—the prying old biddy who'd given Jessaline the eye before.

Eugenie jumped, her face red as plums, and quickly shifted away from Jessaline. Privately cursing, Jessaline did the same, and an awkward silence fell.

"W-well," said Eugenie, "I had best be getting back. I told my brother I would be at the seamstress's, and that doesn't take long."

"Yes," Jessaline said, realizing with some consternation that she'd completely forgotten why she'd asked for a meeting in the first place. "Well. Ah. I have something I'd like to offer you—but I would advise you to keep these out of sight, even at home where servants might see. For your own safety." She reached into the brocade bag and handed Eugenie the small cylindrical leather container that held the formula and plans for the methane extractor. "This is what we have come up with thus far, but the design is incomplete. If you can offer any assistance—"

"Yes, of course," Eugenie said, taking the case with an avid look that heartened Jessaline at once. She tucked the leather case into her purse. "Allow me a few days to consider the problem. How may I contact you, though, once I've devised a solution?"

"I will contact you in one week. Do not look for me." She got to her feet and offered her hand to help Eugenie up. Then, speaking loudly enough to be heard outside the willow at last, she giggled. "Before your brother learns we've been swapping tales about him!"

Eugenie looked blank for a moment, then opened her mouth in an "o" of understanding, grinning. "Oh, his ego could use a bit of flattening, I think. In any case, fare you well, Mademoiselle Dumonde. I must be on my way." And with that, she hurried off, holding her hat as she passed through the willow branches.

Jessaline waited for ten breaths, then stepped out herself, sparing a hard look for the old nun—who, sure enough, had moved quite a bit closer to the tree. "A good afternoon to you, Sister," she said.

"And to you," the woman said in a low voice, "though you had best be more careful from now on, *estipid.*"

Startled to hear her own tongue on the old woman's lips, she stiffened. Then, carefully, she said in the same language, "And what would you know of it?"

"I know you have a dangerous enemy," the nun replied, getting to her feet and dusting dirt off her habit. Now that Jessaline could see her better, it was clear from her features that she had a dollop or two of African in her. "I am sent by your superiors to warn you. We have word the Order of the White Camellia is active in the city."

Jessaline caught her breath. The bootblack man! "I may have encountered them already," she said.

The old woman nodded grimly. "Word had it they broke apart after that scandal we arranged for them up in Baton Rouge," she said, "but in truth they've just gotten more subtle. We don't know what they're after, but obviously they don't just want to kill you, or you would be dead by now."

"I am not so easily removed, madame," Jessaline said, drawing herself up in affront.

The old woman rolled her eyes. "Just take care," she snapped. "And by all means, if you want that girl dead, continue playing silly lovers' games with her where any fool can suspect." And with that, the old woman picked up her spade and shears, and walked briskly away.

Jessaline did too, her cheeks burning. But back in her room, ostensibly safe, she leaned against the door and closed her eyes, wondering why her heart still fluttered so fast now that Eugenie was long gone, and why she was suddenly so afraid.

The Order of the White Camellia changed everything. Jessaline had heard tales of them for years, of course—a secret society of wealthy professionals and intellectuals dedicated to the preservation of "American ideals" like the superiority of the white race. They had been responsible for the exposure—and deaths, in some cases—of many of Jessaline's fellow spies over the years. America was built on slavery; naturally the White Camellias would oppose a nation built on slavery's overthrow.

So Jessaline decided on new tactics. She shifted her attire from that of a well-to-do freedwoman to the plainer garb of a woman of less means. This elicited no attention as there were plenty such women in the city—though she was obliged to move to yet another inn that would suit her appearance. This drew her well into the less-respectable area of the city, where not a few of the patrons took rooms by the hour or the half day.

Here she laid low for the next few days, trying to determine whether she was being watched, though she spotted no suspicious characters—or at least, no one suspicious for the area. Which, of course, was why she'd chosen it. White men frequented the inn, but a white face who lingered or appeared repeatedly would be remarked upon, and easy to spot.

When a week had passed and Jessaline felt safe, she radically transformed herself using the bundle that had been hidden beneath her chest's false bottom. First she hid her close-cropped hair beneath a lumpy calico headwrap, and donned an ill-fitting dress of worn, stained gingham patched here and there with burlap. A few small pillows rendered her effectively shapeless—a necessity, since in this disguise it was dangerous to be attractive in any way. As she slipped out in the small hours of the morning, carrying her belongings in a satchel and shuffling to make herself look much older, no one paid her any heed—not the drowsy old men sitting guard at the stables, nor the city constables chatting up a gaudily dressed woman under a gas lamp, nor the young toughs still dicing on the corner. She was, for all intents and purposes, invisible.

So first she milled among the morning-market crowds at the waterfront awhile, keeping an eye out for observers. When she was certain she had not been followed, she made her way to the dirigible docks, where four of the great machines hovered above a cluster of cargo vessels like huge, sausage-shaped guardian angels. A massive brick fence screened the docks themselves from view, though this had a secondary purpose: the docks were the sovereign territory of the Haitian Republic, housing its embassy as well. No American-born slave was permitted to step upon even this proxy version of Haitian soil, since by the laws of Haiti they would then be free.

Yet practicality did not stop men and women from dreaming, and near the massive ironwork gate of the facility there was as usual a small crowd of slaves gathered, gazing enviously in at the shouting dirigible crews and their smartly dressed officers. Jessaline slipped in among these and edged her way to the front, then waited.

Presently, a young runner detached herself from the nearby rope crew and ran over to the fence. Several of the slaves pushed envelopes through the fence, commissioning travel and shipping on behalf of their owners, and the girl collected these. The whole operation was conducted in utter silence; an American soldier hovered all too near the gate, ready to report any slave who talked. (It was not illegal to talk, but any slave who did so would likely suffer for it.)

Yet Jessaline noted that the runner met the eyes of every person she could, nodding to each solemnly, touching more hands than was strictly necessary for the sake of her work. A small taste of respect for those who needed it so badly, so that they might come to crave it and eventually seek it for themselves.

Jessaline met the runner's eyes too as she pushed through a plain, wrinkled envelope, but her gaze held none of the desperate hope of the others. The runner's eyes widened a bit, but she moved on at once after taking Jessaline's envelope. When she trotted away to deliver the commissions, Jessaline saw her shuffle the pile to put the wrinkled envelope on top.

That done, Jessaline headed then to the Rillieux house. At the back gate she shifted her satchel from her shoulder to her hands, retying it so as to make it square-shaped. To the servant who then answered her knock—freeborn; the Rillieuxs did not go in for the practice of owning slaves themselves—she said in coarse French, "Package for Mademoiselle Rillieux. I was told to deliver it to her personal."

The servant, a cleanly dressed fellow who could barely conceal his distaste at Jessaline's appearance, frowned further. *"English,* woman, only high-class folk talk French here." But when Jessaline deliberately spoke in butchered English, rendered barely comprehensible by an exaggerated French accent, the man finally rolled his eyes and stood aside. "She's in the garden house. Back there. There!" And he pointed the way.

Thus did Jessaline come to the overlarge shed that sat amid the house's vast garden. It had clearly been meant to serve as a hothouse at some point, having a glass ceiling, but when Jessaline stepped inside she was assailed by sounds most unnatural: clanks and squealing and the rattling hiss of a steam boiler. These came from the equipment and incomprehensible machinery that lined every wall and hung from the ceiling, pipes and clockworks big enough to crush a man, all of it churning merrily away.

At the center of this chaos stood several high worktables, each bearing equipment in various states of construction or dismantlement, save the last. At this table, which sat in a shaft of gathering sunlight, sat a sleeping Eugenie Rillieux.

At the sight of her, Jessaline stopped, momentarily overcome by a most uncharacteristic anxiety. Eugenie's head rested on her folded arms, atop a sheaf of large, irregular sheets of parchment that were practically covered with pen scribbles and diagrams. Her hair was amuss, her glasses askew, and she had drooled a bit onto one of her pale, ink-stained hands.

Beautiful, Jessaline thought, and marveled at herself. Her tastes had never leaned toward women like Eugenie, pampered and sheltered and shy. She generally preferred women like herself, who could be counted upon to know what they wanted and take decisive steps to get it. Yet in that moment, gazing upon this awkward, brilliant creature, Jessaline wanted nothing more than to be holding flowers instead of a fake package, and to have come for courting rather than her own selfish motives.

Perhaps Eugenie felt the weight of her longing, for after a moment she wrinkled her nose and sat up. "Oh," she said blearily, seeing Jessaline. "What is it, a delivery? Put it on the table there, please; I'll fetch you a tip." She got up, and Jessaline was amused to see that her bustle was askew.

"Eugenie," she said, and Eugenie whirled back as she recognized Jessaline's voice. Her eyes flew wide.

"What in heaven's name—"

"I haven't much time," she said, hastening forward. She took Eugenie's hands in quick greeting, and resisted the urge to kiss her as well. "Have you been able to refine the plans?"

"Oh—yes, yes, I think." Eugenie pushed her glasses straight and gestured toward the papers that had served as her pillow. "This design should work, at least in theory. I was right; the vacuum-distillation mechanism was the key! Of course, I haven't finished the prototype, because the damned glassmaker is trying to charge pirates' rates—"

Jessaline squeezed her hands, exhilarated. "Marvelous! Don't worry; we shall test the design thoroughly before we put it into use. But now I must have the plans. Men are searching for me; I don't dare stay in town much longer."

Eugenie nodded absently, then blinked again as her head cleared. She narrowed her eyes at Jessaline in sudden suspicion. "Wait," she said. "You're leaving town?"

"Yes, of course," Jessaline said, surprised. "This is what I came for, after all. I can't just put something so important on the next dirigible packet—"

The look of hurt that came over Eugenie's face sent a needle straight into Jessaline's heart. She realized, belatedly and with guilty dismay, what Eugenie must have been imagining all this time.

"But...I thought...." Eugenie looked away suddenly, and bit her lower lip. "You might stay."

"Eugenie," Jessaline began, uncomfortably. "I...could never have remained here. This place...the way you live here...."

"Yes, I know." At once Eugenie's voice hardened; she glared at Jessaline. "In your perfect, wonderful land, everyone is free to live as they please. It is the rest of us, then, the poor wretched folk you scorn and pity, who have no choice but to endure it. Perhaps we should never bother to love at all, then! That way, at least, when we are used and cast aside, it will at least be for material gain!"

And with that, she slapped Jessaline smartly, and walked out. Stunned, Jessaline put a hand to her cheek and stared after her.

"Trouble in paradise?" said a voice behind her, in a syrupy drawl.

Jessaline whirled to find herself facing a six-shooter. And holding it, his face free of bootblack this time, was the young man who had invaded her quarters nearly two weeks before.

"I heard you Haitians were unnatural," he said, coming into the light, "but this? Not at all what I was expecting."

Not me, Jessaline realized, too late. *They were watching Rillieux, not me!* "Natural is in the eye of the beholder, as is beauty," she snapped.

"True. Speaking of beauty, though, you looked a damn sight finer before. What's all this?" He sidled forward, poking with the gun at the padding 'round Jessaline's middle. "So that's it! But—" He raised the gun, to Jessaline's fury, and poked at her breasts none too gently. "Ah, no padding *here*. Yes, I do remember you rightly." He scowled. "I still can't sit down thanks to you, woman. Maybe I ought to repay you that."

Jessaline raised her hands slowly, pulling off her lumpy headwrap so he could see her more clearly. "That's ungentlemanly of you, I would say."

"Gentlemen need gentle*women,*" he said. "Your kind are hardly that, being good for only one thing. Well—that and lynching, I suppose. But we'll save both for later, won't we? After you've met my superior and told us everything that's in your nappy little head. He's partial to your variety. I, however, feel that if I must lower myself to baseness, better to do it with one bearing the fair blood of the French."

It took Jessaline a moment to understand through all his airs. But then she did, and shivered in purest rage. "You will not lay a finger upon Eugenie. I'll snap them all off fir—"

But before she could finish her threat, there was a scream and commotion from the house. The scream, amid all the chaos of shouting and running servants, she recognized at once: Eugenie.

The noise startled the bootblack man as well. Fortunately he did not pull the trigger; he did start badly, however, half-turning to point the gun in the direction of Eugenie's scream. Which was all the opening that Jessaline needed, as she drew her derringer from the wadded cloth of the headwrap and shot the man point-blank. The bootblack man cried out, clutching his chest and falling to the ground.

The derringer was spent; it carried only a single bullet. Snatching up the bootblack man's six-gun instead, Jessaline turned to sprint toward the Rillieux house—then froze for an instant in terrible indecision. Behind her, on Eugenie's table, sat the plans for which she had spent the past three months of her life striving and stealing and sneaking. The methane extractor could be the salvation of her nation, the start of its brightest future.

And in the house—

Eugenie, she thought.

And started running.

In the parlor, Norbert Rillieux was frozen, paler than usual and trembling. Before him, holding Eugenie about the throat and with a gun to her head, was a white man whose face was so floridly familiar that Jessaline gasped. "Raymond Forstall?"

He started badly as Jessaline rounded the door, and she froze as well, fearing to cause Eugenie's death. Very slowly she set the six-gun on a nearby sideboard, pushed it so that it slid out of easy reach, and raised her hands to show that she was no threat. At this, Forstall relaxed.

"So we meet again, my beauteous negress," he said, though there was anger in his smile. "I had hoped to make your acquaintance under more favorable circumstances. Alas."

"You are with the White Camellia?" He had seemed so gormless that day on Royal Street, not at all the sort Jessaline would associate with a murderous secret society.

"I am indeed," he said. "And you would have met the rest of us if my assistant had not clearly failed in his goal of taking you captive. Nevertheless, I too have a goal, and I ask again, sir, where are the plans?"

Jessaline realized belatedly that this was directed at Norbert Rillieux. And he, too frightened to bluster, just shook his head. "I told you, I have built no such device! Ask this woman—she wanted it, and I refused her!"

The methane extractor, Jessaline realized. Of course—they had known, probably via their own spies, that she was after it. Forstall had been tailing her the day he'd bumped into her, probably all the way to Rillieux's house; she cursed herself for a fool for not realizing. But the White Camellias were mostly philosophers and bankers and lawyers, not the trained, proficient spies she'd been expecting to deal with. It had never occurred to her that an enemy would be so clumsy as to jostle and converse with his target in the course of surveillance.

"It's true," Jessaline said, stalling desperately in hopes that some solution would present itself to her. "This man refused my request to build the device."

"Then why did you come back here?" Forstall asked, tightening his grip on Eugenie so that she gasped. "We had men watching the house servants too. We intercepted orders for metal parts and rubber tubing, and I paid the glass-smith to delay an order for custom vacuum-pipes—"

"You did that?" To Jessaline's horror, Eugenie stiffened in Forstall's grasp, trying to turn and glare at him in her affront. "I argued with that old fool for an hour!"

"Eugenie, be still!" cried Norbert, which raised him high in Jessaline's estimation; she had wanted to shout the same thing.

"I will not—" Eugenie began to struggle, plainly furious. As Forstall cursed and tried to restrain her, Jessaline heard Eugenie's protests continue. "—interference with my work—very idea—"

Please, Holy Mother, Jessaline thought, taking a very careful step closer to the gun on the sideboard, *don't let him shoot her to shut her up.*

When Forstall finally thrust Eugenie aside—she fell against the bottle-strewn side table, nearly toppling it—and indeed raised the gun to shoot her, Jessaline blurted, "Wait!"

Both Forstall and Eugenie froze, now separated and facing each other, though Forstall's gun was still pointed dead at Eugenie's chest. "The plans are complete," Jessaline said to him. "They are in the workshop out back." With a hint of pride, she looked at Eugenie and added, "Eugenie has made it work."

"What?" said Rillieux, looking thunderstruck.

"What?" Forstall stared at her, then Eugenie, and then anger filled his expression. "Clever indeed! And while I go out back to check if your story is true, you will make your escape with the plans already tucked into your clothes."

"I am not lying in this instance," she said, "but if you like, we can all proceed to the garden and see. Or, since I'm the one you seem to fear most—" She waggled her empty hands in mockery, hoping this would make him too angry to notice how much closer she was to the gun on the sideboard. His face reddened further with fury. "You could leave Eugenie and her brother here, and take me alone."

Eugenie caught her breath. "Jessaline, are you mad?"

"Yes," Jessaline said, and smiled, letting her heart live in her face for a moment. Eugenie's mouth fell open, then softened into a small smile. Her glasses were still askew, Jessaline saw with a rush of fondness.

Forstall rolled his eyes, but smiled. "A capital suggestion, I think. Then I can shoot you—"

He got no further, for in the next instant Eugenie suddenly struck him in the head with a rum bottle.

The bottle shattered on impact. Forstall cried out, half-stunned by the blow and the sting of rum in his eyes, but he managed to keep his grip on the gun, and keep it trained more or less on Eugenie. Jessaline thought she saw the muscles in his forearm flex to pull the trigger—

—and then the six-gun was in her hand, its wooden grip warm and almost comforting as she blew a hole in Raymond Forstall's rum-drenched head. Forstall uttered a horrid gurgling sound and fell to the floor.

Before his body stopped twitching, Jessaline caught Eugenie's hand. "Hurry!" She dragged the other woman out of the parlor. Norbert, again to his credit, started out of shock and trotted after them, for once silent as they moved through the house's corridors toward the garden. The house was nearly deserted now, the servants having fled or found some place to hide that was safe from gunshots and madmen.

"You must tell me which of the papers on your desk I can take," Jessaline said as they trotted along, "and then you must make a decision."

"Wh-what decision?" Eugenie still sounded shaken.

"Whether you will stay here, or whether you will come with me to Haiti."

"Haiti?" Norbert cried.

"Haiti?" Eugenie asked, in wonder.

"Haiti," said Jessaline, and as they passed through the rear door and went into the garden, she stopped and turned to Eugenie. "With me."

Eugenie stared at her in such dawning amazement that Jessaline could no longer help herself. She caught Eugenie about the waist, pulled her near, and kissed her most soundly and improperly, right there in front of her brother. It was the sweetest, wildest kiss she had ever known in her life.

When she pulled back, Norbert was standing at the edge of her vision with his mouth open, and Eugenie looked a bit faint. "Well," Eugenie said, and fell silent, the whole affair having been a bit much for her.

Jessaline grinned and let her go, then hurried forward to enter the workshop—and froze, horror shattering her good mood.

The bootblack man was gone. Where his body had been lay Jessaline's derringer and copious blood, trailing away…to Eugenie's worktable, where the plans had been, and were no longer. The trail then led away, out the workshop's rear door.

"No," she whispered, her fists clenching at her sides. "No, by God!" Everything she had worked for, gone. She had failed, both her mission and her people.

"Very well," Eugenie said after a moment. "Then I shall simply have to come with you."

The words penetrated Jessaline's despair slowly. "What?"

She touched Jessaline's hand. "I will come with you. To Haiti. And I will build an even more efficient methane extractor for you there."

Jessaline turned to stare at her and found that she could not, for her eyes had filled with tears.

"Wait—" Norbert caught his breath as understanding dawned. "Go to Haiti? Are you mad? I forbid—"

"You had better come too, brother," Eugenie said, turning to him, and Jessaline was struck breathless once more by the cool determination in her eyes. "The police will take their time about it, but they'll come eventually, and a white man lies dead in our house. It doesn't really matter whether you shot him or not; you know full well what they'll decide."

And Norbert stiffened, for he did indeed know—probably better than Eugenie, Jessaline suspected—what his fate would be.

Eugenie turned to Jessaline. "He can come, can't he?" By which Jessaline knew it was a condition, not an option.

"Of course he can," she said at once. "I wouldn't leave a dog to these people's justice. But it will not be the life you're used to, either of you. Are you certain?"

Eugenie smiled, and before Jessaline realized what was imminent, she had been pulled rather roughly into another kiss. Eugenie had been eating penuche again, she realized dimly, and then for a long perfect moment she thought of nothing but pecans and sweetness.

When it was done, Eugenie searched Jessaline's face and then smiled in satisfaction. "Perhaps we should go, Jessaline," she said gently.

"Ah. Yes. We should, yes." Jessaline fought to compose herself; she glanced at Norbert and took a deep breath. "Fetch us a hansom cab while you still can, Monsieur Rillieux, and we'll go down to the docks and take the next dirigible southbound."

The daze cleared from Norbert's eyes as well; he nodded mutely and trotted off.

In the silence that fell, Eugenie turned to Jessaline.

"Marriage," she said, "and a house together. I believe you mentioned that?"

"Er," said Jessaline, blinking. "Well, yes, I suppose, but I rather thought that first we would—"

"Good," Eugenie replied, "because I'm not fond of you keeping up this dangerous line of work. My inventions should certainly earn enough for the both of us, don't you think?"

"Um," said Jessaline.

"Yes. So there's no reason for you to work when I can keep you in comfort for the rest of our days." Taking Jessaline's hands, she stepped closer, her eyes going soft again. "And I am so very much looking forward to those days, Jessaline."

"Yes," said Jessaline, who had been wondering just which of her many sins had earned her this mad fortune. But as Eugenie's warm breast pressed against hers, and the thick perfume of the magnolia trees wafted around them, and some clockwork contraption within the workshop ticked in time with her heart...Jessaline stopped worrying. And she wondered why she had ever bothered with plans and papers and gadgetry, because it was clear she had just stolen the greatest prize of all.

To Follow the Waves

Amal El-Mohtar

HESSA'S LEGS ACHED. She knew she ought to stand, stretch them, but only gritted her teeth and glared at the clear lump of quartz on the table before her. To rise now would be to concede defeat—but to lean back, lift her goggles, and rub her eyes was, she reasoned, an adequate compromise.

Her braids weighed on her, and she scratched the back of her head, where they pulled tightest above her nape. To receive a commission from Sitt Warda Al-Attrash was a great honor, one that would secure her reputation as a fixed star among Dimashq's dream-crafters. She could not afford to fail. Worse, the dream Sitt Warda desired was simple, as dreams went: to be a young woman again, bathing her limbs by moonlight in the Mediterranean with a young man who, judging by her half-spoken, half-murmured description, was not precisely her husband.

But Hessa had never been to the sea.

She had heard it spoken of, naturally, and read hundreds of lines of poetry extolling its many virtues. Yet it held little wonder for her; what pleasure could be found in stinging salt, scratching sand, burning sun reflected from the water's mirror surface? Nor did swimming hold any appeal; she had heard pearl divers boast of their exploits, speak of how the blood beat between their eyes until they felt their heads might burst like overripe tomatoes, how their lungs ached with the effort for hours afterward, how sometimes they would feel as if thousands of ants were marching along their skin, and though they scratched until blood bloomed beneath their fingernails, could never reach them.

None of this did anything to endear the idea of the sea to her. And yet, to carve the dream out of the quartz, she had to find its beauty. Sighing, she picked up the dopstick again, tapped the quartz to make sure it was securely fastened, lowered her goggles, and tried again.

Hessa's mother was a mathematician, renowned well beyond the gates of Dimashq for her theorems. Her father was a poet, better known for his abilities as an artisanal cook than for his verse, though as the latter was full of the scents and flavors of the former, much appreciated all the same. Hessa's father taught her to contemplate what was pleasing to the senses, while her mother taught her geometry and algebra. She loved both as she loved them, with her whole heart.

Salma Najjar had knocked at the door of the Ghaflan family in the spring of Hessa's seventh year. She was a small woman, wrinkled as a wasp's nest, with eyes hard and bright as chips of tourmaline. Her graying hair was knotted and bound in the intricate patterns of a jeweler or gem-cutter—perhaps some combination of the two. Hessa's parents welcomed her into their home, led her to a divan, and offered her tea, but she refused to drink or eat until she had told them her errand.

"I need a child of numbers and letters to learn my trade," she had said, in the gruff, clipped accent of the Northern cities. "It is a good trade, one that will demand the use of all her abilities. I have heard that your daughter is such a child."

"And what is your trade?" Hessa's father asked, intrigued, but wary.

"To sculpt fantasies in the stone of the mind and the mind of the stone. To grant wishes."

"You propose to raise our daughter as *djinn?*" Hessa's mother raised an eyebrow.

Salma smiled, showing a row of perfect teeth. "Far better. *Djinn* do not get paid."

Building a dream was as complex as building a temple, and required knowledge of almost as many trades—a fact reflected in the complexity of the braid pattern in which Hessa wore her hair. Each pull and plait showed an intersection of gem-crafting, metal-working, architecture, and storytelling, to say nothing of the thousand twisting strands representing the many kinds of knowledge necessary to a story's success. As a child, Hessa had spent hours with the archivists in Al-Zahiriyya Library, learning from them the art of constructing memory palaces within her mind, layering the marble, glass, and mosaics of her imagination with reams of poetry, important historical dates, dozens of musical *maqaamat,* names of stars and ancestors. *Hessa bint Aliyah bint Qamar bint Widad....*

She learned to carry each name, note, number like a jewel to tuck into a drawer here, hang above a mirror there, for ease of finding later on. She knew whole geographies, scriptures, story cycles, as intimately as she knew her mother's house, and drew on them whenever she received a commission. Though the only saleable part of her craft was the device she built with her hands, its true value lay in using the materials of her mind: she could not grind quartz to the shape and tune of her dream, could not set it into the copper coronet studded with amber, until she had fixed it into her thoughts as firmly as she fixed the stone to her amber dopstick.

"Every stone," Salma said, tossing her a piece of rough quartz, "knows how to sing. Can you hear it?"

Frowning, Hessa held it up to her ear, but Salma laughed. "No, no. It is not a shell from the sea, singing the absence of its creature. You cannot hear the stone's song with the ear alone. Look at it; feel it under your hand; you must learn its song, its language, before you can teach it your own. You must learn, too, to tell the stones apart; those that sing loudest do not always have the best memories, and it is memory that is most important. Easier to teach it to sing one song beautifully than to teach it to remember; some stones can sing nothing but their own tunes."

Dream-crafting was still a new art then; Salma was among its pioneers. But she knew that she did not have within herself what it would take to excel at it. Having discovered a new instrument, she found it unsuited to her fingers, awkward to rest against her heart; she could produce sound, but not music.

For that, she had to teach others to play.

First, she taught Hessa to cut gems. That had been Salma's own trade, and Hessa could see that it was still her chief love: the way she smiled as she turned a piece of rough crystal in her hands, learning its angles and texture, was very much the way Hessa's parents smiled at each other. She taught her how to pick the best stones, cleave away their grossest imperfections; she taught her to attach the gem to a dopstick with hot wax, at precise angles, taught her the delicate dance of holding it against a grinding lathe with even greater precision while operating the pedal. She taught her to calculate the axes that would unlock needles of light from the stone, kindle fire in its heart. Only once Hessa could grind a cabochon blindfolded, once she learned to see with the tips of her fingers, did Salma explain the rest.

"This is how you will teach songs to the stone." She held up a delicate amber wand, at the end of which was affixed a small copper vice. Hessa watched as Salma placed a cloudy piece of quartz inside and adjusted the vice around it before lowering her goggles over her eyes. "The amber catches your thoughts and speaks them to the copper; the copper translates them to the quartz. But just as you build your memory palace in your mind, so must you build the dream you want to teach it; first in your thoughts, then in the stone. You must cut the quartz while fixing the dream firmly in your mind, that you may cut the dream into the stone, cut it so that the dream blooms from it like light. Then, you must fix it into copper and amber again, that the dream may be translated into the mind of the dreamer.

"Tonight," she murmured quietly, grinding edges into the stone, "you will dream of horses. You will stand by a river and they will run past you, but one will slow to a stop. It will approach you, and nuzzle your cheek."

"What color will it be?"

Salma blinked behind her goggles, and the lathe slowed to a stop as she looked at her. "What color would you like it to be?"

"Blue," said Hessa, firmly. It was her favorite color.

Salma frowned. "There are no blue horses, child."

"But this is a dream! Couldn't I see one in a dream?"

Hessa wasn't sure why Salma was looking at her with quite such intensity, or why it took her so long a moment to answer. But finally, she smiled—in the gentle, quiet way she smiled at her gems—and said, "Yes, my heart. You could."

Once the quartz was cut, Salma fixed it into the center of a copper circlet, its length prettily decorated with drops of amber, and fitted it around Hessa's head before giving her chamomile tea to drink and sending her to bed. Hessa dreamed just as Salma said she would: the horse that approached her was blue as the turquoise she had shaped for a potter's husband a few nights earlier. But when the horse touched her, its nose was dry and cold as quartz, its cheeks hard and smooth as cabochon.

Salma sighed when Hessa told her as much the next day. "You see, this is why I teach you, Hessa. I have been so long in the country of stones, speaking their language and learning their songs, I have little to teach them of our own; I speak everything to them in facets and brilliance, culets and crowns. But you, my dear, you are learning many languages all at once; you have your father's tasting tongue, your mother's speech of angles and air. I have been speaking nothing but adamant for most of my life, and grow more and more deaf to the desires of dreamers."

Try as she might, Hessa could not coordinate her knowledge of the sea with the love, the longing, the pleasure needed to build Sitt Warda's dream. She had mixed salt and water, touched it to her lips, and found it unpleasant; she had watched the moon tremble in the waters of her courtyard's fountain without being able to stitch its beauty to a horizon. She tried, now, to summon those poor attempts to mind, but was keenly aware that if she began grinding the quartz in her present state, Sitt Warda would wake from her dream as tired and frustrated as she herself presently felt.

Giving in, she put down the quartz, removed her goggles, rose from her seat, and turned her back on her workshop. There were some problems only coffee and ice cream could fix.

Qahwat al Adraj was one of her favorite places to sit and do the opposite of think. Outside the bustle of the Hamadiyyah market, too small and plain to be patronized by obnoxious tourists, it was a well-kept secret tucked beneath a dusty stone staircase: the servers were beautiful, the coffee exquisite, and the iced treats in summer particularly fine. As she closed the short distance between it and her workshop, she tried to force her gaze up from the dusty path her feet had long ago memorized, tried to empty herself of the day's frustrations to make room for her city's beauties.

There: a young man with dark skin and a dazzling smile, his tight-knotted braids declaring him a merchant-inventor, addressing a gathering crowd to display his newest brass automata. "Ladies and gentlemen," he called, "the British Chef!" and demonstrated how with a few cranks and a minimum of preparation, the long-faced machine could knife carrots into twisting orange garlands, slice cucumbers into lace. And not far from him, drawn to the promise of a building audience, a beautiful mechanical, her head sculpted to look like an amira's headdress, serving coffee from the heated cone of it by tipping forward in an elegant bow before the cup, an act that could not help but make every customer feel as if they were sipping the gift of a cardamom-laced dance.

Hessa smiled to them, but frowned to herself. She had seen them all many times before. Today she was conscious, to her shame, of a bitterness toward them: what business had they being beautiful to her when they were not the sea?

Arriving, she took her usual seat by a window that looked out to Touma's Gate, sipped her own coffee, and tried not to brood.

She knew what Salma would have said. *Go to the sea,* she would have urged, *bathe in it! Or, if you cannot, read the thousands of poems written to it! Write a poem yourself! Or,* slyly, then, *only think of something you yourself find beautiful—horses, berries, books—and hide it beneath layers and layers of desire until the thing you love is itself obscured. Every pearl has a grain of sand at its heart, no? Be cunning. You cannot know all the world, my dear, as intimately as you know your stones.*

But she couldn't. She had experimented with such dreams, crafted them for herself; they came out wrapped in cotton wool, provoking feeling without vision, touch, scent. Any would-be dream crafter could do as well. No, for Sitt Warda, who had already patronized four of the city's crafters before her, it would never do. She had to produce something exquisite, unique. She had to know the sea as Sitt Warda knew it, as she wanted it.

She reached for a newspaper, seeking distraction. Lately it was all airships and trade agreements surrounding their construction and deployment, the merchant fleets' complaints and clamor for restrictions on allowable cargo to protect their own interests. Hessa had a moment of smirking at the sea-riding curmudgeons before realizing that she had succumbed, again, to the trap of her knotting thoughts. Perhaps if the sea was seen from a great height? But that would provoke the sensation of falling, and Sitt Warda did not want a flying dream....

Gritting her teeth, she buried her face in her hands—until she heard someone step through the doorway, sounding the hollow glass chimes in so doing. Hessa looked up.

A woman stood there, looking around, the early afternoon light casting a faint nimbus around her, shadowing her face. She was tall, and wore a long, simple dark blue coat over a white dress, its embroidery too plain to declare a regional origin. Hessa could see she had beautiful hands, the gold in them drawn out by the midnight of the blue, but it was not these at which she found herself staring. It was the woman's hair.

Unbound, it rippled.

There was shame in that, Hessa had always felt, always been taught. To wear one's hair so free in public was to proclaim oneself unbound to a trade, useless; even the travelers who passed through the city bound knots into their hair out of respect for custom, the five braids of travelers and visitors who wished themselves known as such above anything else, needing hospitality or good directions. The strangeness of it thrilled and stung her.

It would perhaps not have been so shocking were it one long unbroken sheet of silk, a sleek spill of ink with no light in it. But it rippled, as if just released from many braids, as if fingers had already tangled there, as if hot breath had moistened it to curling waves. *Brazen,* thought Hessa, the word snagging on half-remembered lines of English poetry, *brazen greaves, brazen hooves.* Unfamiliar words, strange, like a spell—and suddenly it was a torrent of images, of rivers and aching and spilling and immensity, because she wanted that hair in her own hand, wanted to see her skin vanish into its blackness, wanted it to swallow her while she swallowed it—

It took her a moment to notice the woman was looking at her. It took another for Hessa to flush with the understanding that she was staring rudely before dropping her gaze back to her coffee. She counted to seventy in her head before daring to look up again: by the time she did, the woman was seated, a server half hiding her from Hessa's view. Hessa laid money on the table and rose to leave, taking slow, deliberate steps toward the door. As soon as she was outside the coffee house, she broke into a run.

Two nights later, with a piece of finely shaped quartz pulsing against her brow, Sitt Warda Al-Attrash dreamed of her former lover with honeysuckle sweetness, and if the waves that rose and fell around them were black and soft as hair, she was too enraptured to notice.

Hessa could not stop thinking of the woman. She took to eating most of her meals at Qahwat al Adraj, hoping to see her again—to speak, apologize for what must have seemed appalling behavior, buy her a drink—but the woman did not return. When she wasn't working, Hessa found her fingertips tracing delicate, undulating lines through the gem dust that coated her table, thighs tightly clenched, biting her lip with longing. Her work did not suffer for it—if anything, it improved tremendously. The need to craft flooded her, pushed her to pour the aching out into copper and crystal.

Meantime, Sitt Warda could not stop speaking of Hessa, glowing in her praise; she told all her wealthy friends of the gem among dream-crafters who dimmed all others to ash, insisting they sample her wares. Where before Hessa might have had one or two commissions a week, she began to receive a dozen a day, and found herself in a position to pick and choose among them. This she did—but it took several commissions before she saw what was guiding her choice.

"Craft me a dream of the ruins of Baalbek," said one kind-eyed gentleman with skin like star-struck sand, "those tall, staggering remnants, those sloping columns of sunset!" Hessa ground them just shy of twilight, that the dreamt columns might be dimmed to the color of skin darkened by the light behind it, and if they looked like slender necks, the fallen ones angled slant as a clavicle, the kind-eyed gentleman did not complain.

"Craft me a dream of wings and flight," murmured a shy young woman with gold-studded ears, "that I might soar above the desert and kiss the moon." Hessa ground a cabochon with her right hand while her left slid between her legs, rocking her to the memory of long fingers she built into feathers, sprouted to wings just as she moaned a spill of warm honey and weightlessness.

Afterward, she felt ashamed. She thought, surely someone would notice—surely, some dreamer would part the veils of ecstasy in their sleep and find her burning behind them. It felt, awkwardly, like trespass, but not because of the dreamers; rather, it seemed wrong to sculpt her nameless, braidless woman into the circlets she sold for crass money. It felt like theft, absurd though it was, and in the aftermath of her release, she felt guilty, too.

But she could not find her; she hardly knew how to begin to look. Perhaps she had been a traveler, after all, merely releasing her hair from a five-braided itch in the late afternoon; perhaps she had left the city, wandered to wherever it was she came from, some strange land where women wore their hair long and wild and lived lives of savage indolence, stretching out beneath fruit trees, naked as the sky—

The flush in her cheeks decided her. If she couldn't find her woman while waking, then what in the seven skies was her craft for, if not to find her in sleep?

Hessa had never crafted a dream for her own use. She tested her commissions, sometimes, to ensure their quality or correct an error, but she always recast the dream in fresh quartz and discarded the test stone immediately, throwing it into the bath of saltwater steam that would purify it for reworking into simple jewelry. It would not do, after all, for a silver necklace or brass ring to bear in it the echo of a stranger's lust. Working the hours she did, her sleep was most often profound and refreshing; if she dreamt naturally, she hardly ever remembered.

She did not expect to sleep well through the dream she purposed.

She closed shop for a week, took on no new commissions. She hesitated over the choice of stone; a dream crafted in white quartz could last for up to three uses, depending on the clarity of the crystal and the time she took in grinding it. But a dream crafted in amethyst could last indefinitely—could belong to her forever, as long as she wanted it, renewing itself to the rhythm of her thoughts, modulating its song to harmonize with her dream desires. She had only ever crafted two dreams in amethyst, a matched set to be given as a wedding gift, and the sum she commanded for the task had financed a year's worth of materials and bought her a new lathe.

Reluctantly, she chose the white quartz. Three nights, that was all she would allow herself; three nights for a week's careful, loving labor, and perhaps then this obsession would burn itself out, would leave her sated. Three nights, and then no more.

She wondered if Salma had ever done anything of the sort.

For three days, she studied her only memory of the woman, of her standing framed in the doorway of Qahwat al Adraj, awash in dusty light; she remembered the cut of her coat, its color, and the woman's eyes focusing on her, narrowing, quizzical. They were almost black, she thought, or so the light made them. And her hair, of course, her endless, splendid, dreadful hair, curling around her slim neck like a hand; she remembered the height of her, the narrowness that made her think of a sheathed sword, of a buried root, only her hair declaring her to be wild, impossible, strange.

Once the woman's image was perfectly fixed in her thoughts, Hessa began to change it.

Her stern mouth softened into hesitation, almost a smile; her lips parted as if to speak. Hessa wished she had heard her voice that day—she did not want to imagine a sound that was not truly hers, that was false. She wanted to shift, to shape, not to invent. Better to leave her silent.

Her mouth, then, and her height; she was probably taller than Hessa, but not in the dream, no. She had to be able to look into her eyes, to reach for her cheeks, to brush her thumb over the fullness of her lips before kissing them. Her mouth would be warm, she knew, and taste—

Here, again, she faltered. She would taste, Hessa, decided, of ripe mulberries, and her mouth would be stained with the juice. She would have fed them to her, after laughing over a shared joke—no, she would have placed a mulberry in her own mouth and then kissed her, yes, lain it on her tongue as a gift from her own, and that is why she would taste of mulberries while Hessa pressed a hand to the small of her back and gathered her slenderness against herself, crushed their hips together....

It took her five days to build the dream in her thoughts, repeating the sequence of her imagined pleasures until they wore grooved agonies into her mind, until she could almost savor the dream through her sleep without the aid of stone or circlet. She took a full day to cast the latter, and a full day to grind the stone to the axes of her dream, careful not to miss a single desired sensation; she set it carefully into its copper circlet.

Her fingers only trembled when she lifted it onto her head.

The first night left her in tears. She had never been so thoroughly immersed in her art, and it had been long, so long since anyone had approached her with a desire she could answer in kisses rather than craft. She ached for it; the braidless woman's body was like warm water on her skin, surrounded her in the scent of jasmine. The tenderness between them was unbearable; for all that she thirsted for a voice, for small sighs and gasps to twine with her own. Her hair was down soft, and the pleasure she took in wrapping it around her fingers left her breathless. She woke tasting mulberries, removed the circlet, and promptly slept until the afternoon.

The second night, she nestled into her lover's body with the ease of old habit, and found herself murmuring poetry into her neck, old poems in antique meters, rhythms rising and falling like the galloping warhorses they described. "I wish," she whispered, pressed against her afterward, raising her hand to her lips, "I could take you riding—I used to, when I was little. I would go riding to Maaloula with my family, where almond trees grow from holy caves, and where the wine is so black and sweet it is rumored that each grape must have been kissed before being plucked to make it. I wish," and she sighed, feeling the dream leaving her, feeling the stone-sung harmony of it fading, "I wish I knew your name."

Strangeness, then—a shifting in the dream, a jolt, as the walls of the bedroom she had imagined for them fell away, as she found she could look at nothing but her woman's eyes, seeing wine in them, suddenly, and something else, as she opened her mulberry mouth to speak.

"Nahla," she said, in a voice like a granite wall. "My name is—"

Hessa woke with the sensation of falling from a great height, too shocked to move. Finally, with great effort, she removed the circlet, and gripped it in her hands for a long time, staring at the quartz. She had not given her a name. Was her desire for one strong enough to change the dream from within? All her dream devices were interactive to a small degree, but she always planned them that way, allowing room, pauses in the stone's song that the dreamer's mind could fill—but she had not done so with her own, so certain of what she wanted, of her own needs. She had decided firmly against giving her a name, wanting so keenly to know the truth—and that voice, so harsh. That was not how she would have imagined her voice....

She put the circlet aside and rose to dress herself. She would try to understand it later that night. It would be her final one; she would ask another question, and see what tricks her mind played on her then.

But there would be no third night.

That afternoon, as Hessa opened her door to step out for an early dinner at Qahwat al Adraj, firm hands grasped her by the shoulders and shoved her back inside. Before she could protest or grasp what was happening, her braidless woman stood before her, so radiant with fury that Hessa could hardly speak for the pain it brought her.

"Nahla?" she managed.

"Hessa," she threw back in a snarl. "Hessa Ghaflan bint Aliyah bint Qamar bint Widad. Crafter of dreams. Ask me how I am here."

There were knives in Hessa's throat—she felt it would bleed if she swallowed, if she tried to speak. "...How?"

"Do you know," she was walking, now, walking a very slow circle around her, "what it is like"—no, not quite around, she was coming toward her but as wolves did, never in a straight line before they attacked, always slant—"to find your dreams are no longer your own? Answer me."

Hessa could not. This, now, felt like a dream that was no longer her own. Nahla's voice left her nowhere to hide, allowed her no possibility of movement. Finally, she managed something that must have looked enough like a shake of her head for Nahla to continue.

"Of course you wouldn't. You are the mistress here, the maker of worlds. I shall tell you. It is fascinating, at first—like being in another country. You observe, for it is strange to not be at the center of your own story, strange to see a landscape, a city, an ocean, bending its familiarity toward someone not yourself. But then—then, Hessa—"

Nahla's voice was an ocean, Hessa decided, dimly. It was worse than the sea—it was the vastness that drowned ships and hid monsters beneath its sparkling calm. She wished she could stop staring at her mouth.

"—Then, you understand that the landscapes, the cities, the oceans, these things are you. They are built out of you, and it is you who are bending, you who are changing for the eyes of these strangers. It is your hands in their wings, your neck in their ruins, your hair in which they laugh and make love—"

Her voice broke, there, and Hessa had a tiny instant's relief as Nahla turned away from her, eyes screwed shut. Only an instant, though, before Nahla laughed in a way that was sand in her own eyes, hot and stinging and sharp.

"And then you see them! You see them in waking, these people who bathed in you and climbed atop you, you recognize their faces and think you have gone mad, because those were only dreams, surely, and you are more than that! But you aren't, because the way they look at you, Hessa, their heads tilted in fond curiosity, as if they've found a pet they would like to keep—you are nothing but the grist for their fantasy mills, and even if they do not understand that, you do. And you wonder, why, why is this happening? Why now, what have I done—"

She gripped Hessa's chin and forced it upward, pushing her against one of her work tables, scattering a rainfall of rough-cut gems to the stone floor and slamming agony into her hip. Hessa did not resist anything but the urge to scream.

"And then," stroking her cheek in a mockery of tenderness, "you see a face in your dreams that you first knew outside them. A small, tired-looking thing you saw in a coffee house, who looked at you as if you were the only thing in the world worth looking at—but who now is taking off your clothes, is filling your mouth with berries and poems and won't let you speak, and Hessa, *it is so much worse.*"

"I didn't know!" It was a sob, finally, stabbing at her as she forced it out. "I'm sorry, I'm so sorry—I didn't know, Nahla, that isn't how it works—"

"You made me into your *doll.*" Another shove sent Hessa crumpling to the floor, pieces of quartz marking her skin with bruises and cuts. "Better I be an ancient city or the means to flight than your *toy,* Hessa! Do you know the worst of it?" Nahla knelt down next to her, and Hessa knew that it would not matter to her that she was crying, now, but she offered her tears up as penance all the same.

"The worst of it," she whispered, now, forefinger tracing one of Hessa's braids, "is that, in the dream, I wanted you. And I could not tell if it was because I found you beautiful, or because that is what you wanted me to do."

They stayed like that for some time, Hessa breathing through slow, ragged sobs while Nahla touched her head. She could not bring herself to ask, *do you still want me now?*

"How could you not know?" Nahla murmured, as she touched her, as if she could read the answer in Hessa's hair. "How could you not know what you were doing to me?"

"I don't control anything but the stone, I swear to you, Nahla, I promise," she could hear herself babbling, her words slick with tears, blurry and indistinct as her vision. "When I grind the dream into the quartz, it is like pressing a shape into wet clay, like sculpture, like carpentry—the quartz, the wax, the dopstick, the grinding plate, the copper and amber, these are my materials, Nahla! These and my mind. I don't know how this happened, it is impossible—"

"That I should be in your mind?"

"That I, or anyone else, should be in yours. You aren't a material, you were only an image—it was never you, it couldn't have been, it was only—"

"Your longing," Nahla said, flatly. "Your wanting of me."

"Yes." Silence between them, then a long-drawn breath. "You believe me?"

A longer silence, while Nahla's fingers sank into the braids tight against Hessa's scalp, scratching it while clutching at a plaited line. "Yes."

"Do you forgive me?"

Slowly, Nahla released her, withdrew her hand, and said nothing. Hessa sighed, and hugged her knees to her chest. Another moment passed; finally, thinking she might as well ask, since she was certain never to see Nahla again, she said, "Why do you wear your hair like that?"

"That," said Nahla, coldly, "is none of your business."

Hessa looked at the ground, feeling a numbness settle into her chest, and focused on swallowing her throat-thorns, quieting her breathing. Let her go, then. Let her go, and find a way to forget this—although a panic rose in her, that after a lifetime of being taught how to remember, she had forgotten how to forget.

"Unless," Nahla continued, thoughtful, "you intend to make it your business."

Hessa looked up, startled. While she stared at her in confusion, Nahla seemed to make up her mind.

"Yes." She smirked, and there was something cruel in the bright twist of it. "I would be your apprentice! You'd like that, wouldn't you? To make my hair like yours?"

"No!" Hessa was horrified. "I don't—I mean—no, I wouldn't like that at all." Nahla raised an eyebrow as she babbled, "I've never had an apprentice. I was one only four years ago. It would not—it would not be seemly."

"Hessa." Nahla stood, now, and Hessa rose with her, knees shaky and sore. "I want to know how this happened. I want to learn—" she narrowed her eyes, and Hessa recoiled from what she saw there, but forgot it the instant Nahla smiled. "—How to do it to you. Perhaps then, when I can teach you what it felt like, when I can silence you and bind you in all the ways I find delicious without asking your leave—perhaps then, I can forgive you."

They looked at each other for what seemed an age. Then, slowly, drawing a long, deep breath, Hessa reached for a large piece of rough quartz, and put it in Nahla's hand, gently closing her fingers over it.

"Every stone," she said, quietly, looking into her wine-dark eyes, "knows how to sing. Can you hear it?"

As she watched, Nahla frowned, and raised the quartz to her ear.

Captain Bells and the Sovereign State of Discordia

JY Yang

WE HAD BEEN watching him.

For a man of such strange temperament, he kept a disappointingly regular schedule. Mondays and Tuesdays were spent instructing children and young men in the way of the machine arts. Thursdays he spent at a coffee house playing Chinese checkers with whoever happened to be there. On Fridays he visited the godowns, conducting his own private affairs.

He was the captain of the splendid airship that lorded over the mouth of the river. Immense, intricate, and incredibly luridly decked out, it was a marvel in both engineering magnificence and impressively bad taste.

It was also, according to its captain, an independent country counting all four of its crew members as citizens, a nation-state entity with its own jurisdiction and its own constitution, answerable to no laws except its own. He had christened it the *S. S. Discordia*—the *Sovereign State of Discordia*.

This, as you can imagine, was problematic for our employer, Lord Louis IV, servant of the Royal Empire of Albion and Lord Overseer—as the title went—to the Malayan Colonies.

Naturally, as any sensible royal would have done, Lord Louis called upon the services of my partner and me. Our first meeting was by the docks. Market stalls clustered around the upper port like lichen patches on a branch, marinating in air heavy with salt and spice and the dusty smell of beans and lentils (five cents a kilo, eighteen for four). I sauntered through the heat and noise in the shade of my parasol, dressed to suit the pretence that I was a lady of some noble birth. I found my quarry—ludicrous in his ever-present goggles, striped breeches, and oversize frock coat, perched on a stool beside a shop selling brass food-heating dragons and other cunning mechanical devices for the kitchen— trying to find chords to a bawdry coolie's song on his sopranissimo ukulele.

"Is it not excessively hot to be wearing a frock coat?" I asked, by way of starting a conversation.

"Miserably! I would dress like you do, my lady, but then I'd have no place to put William." To demonstrate, he held his tiny instrument aloft, then slipped it into an inside pocket of his coat where it was well hidden under the bulk of the garment.

"Do you see?" He retrieved the instrument from the pocket and strummed it, as if to prove that it still worked.

I suppressed a genuine laugh, for the ukulele was the most unexpected instrument I had seen in a long time.

He had flipped up the lenses on his goggles, and porcelain blue were eyes squinting at me.

"I presume that you are the hunter Lord Louis has sent after me, yes?"

I drew myself straighter at the challenge, wondering at the curiosity that had surfaced in his expression, sudden and lucid.

"And what if I am?"

"Then I should formally introduce myself!" He leapt to his feet. "I am Captain Godfrey Francis Wolfram Bellamy, President and Prime Minister of the Sovereign State of Discordia. You may call me Captain Bells, for short." He bowed, deep and ridiculous, his outstretched arm holding the teacup ukulele aloft. Still bent over at the waist, he looked up at me and asked, "To whom do I owe the pleasure?"

"You may call me Lady Admira," I told him, adopting a title I had no right to.

He took my proffered hand and kissed it. "My pleasure, Lady Admira."

I knew then, by some quirk of instinct, that the task that had been set for my partner and me was no ordinary one. There was some kind of slyness, a playful craftiness to his manner that intrigued me. I was sure he had some as-yet-undefined agenda.

Over the next two days we had several more cautious encounters, like dogs sizing each other up before battle. Despite the strangeness of my situation

I found it rather refreshing to be dealing with my target in this fashion: straightforward, without the false pleasantries that I had become used to through my dealings with the native sons of Albion. And he had a friendly, albeit eccentric demeanor for his part. I was learning more than I could by just following him.

Ying, my partner, was not so enamored of my methods. "We are wasting time on this simple task," she said one evening, flicking her hair over her shoulder as we spied on the *Discordia* from the window of our shophouse. "Our instructions were to eliminate him. Why could you not have simply done that? A well-placed stroke of your short staff would settle it."

It was an unusual thing for her to say, as she was famously reluctant to harm our targets unless absolutely necessary, and I said as much.

"Not as unusual as your reluctance to complete the job," she responded tartly. "Was it not you who said the quicker the Empire's dirty tasks are dispensed with, the less trouble there will be? Yet this assignment drags on. One might even think you are enjoying it."

"My interest in this case is purely professional," I insisted. I did not want to accuse her of jealousy. It seemed such a petty thing to do.

The incident happened on a Friday afternoon, no more than a few weeks after we had become acquainted. The captain and I met, as had become our custom, at the docks where he usually practiced his ukulele in the heat of the midday sun. Ying, with all her misgivings, made sure to tail behind us. When Bells caught sight of me he tucked the instrument into his coat and stood up, his cheeky grin as pronounced as ever.

"Ah, my lady. Today I go to visit Uncle Lee in his godown, to see what new marvel he has invented over the week. I think you will find it to your liking."

He skipped off without warning, leaving me to catch up with his schoolboyish gait. I imagined that I could feel Ying's presence somewhere behind us, hear her graceful deerlike footfall.

Uncle Lee's godown, as it turned out, was farther down the dock, a whitewashed building full of heat and noise and the smell of throat-burningly sour substance. The interior had been restructured to house four giant machines, each twice as tall as a man and blackened through industry, their great wheels churning at full speed, their functions mysterious. I let Bells lead me through the great room to a small wooden door.

He retrieved two pairs of gloves and boots made of rubber from a cabinet.

"These are for safety's sake," he explained. "The air inside picks up stray electrical charges quite easily. We wouldn't want you to get shocked, would we?"

I put them on with some misgiving—the thick material made me feel hampered, clumsy.

"And you'll have to leave your short staff and ring here." This earned him a fierce look, yet he was adamant. "Uncle Lee's equipment is sensitive. You could cause an explosion."

Now half-convinced he was leading me into a trap, I put aside the weapons that never left me, save for baths and when I was asleep. But I kept with me the vial of nerve poison hidden in its cleverly constructed pouch, well prepared if there were to be trouble.

"This had better be worth my time," I told him.

"I think it will." And he pushed the door open.

Beyond was another room—not as high but just as large as the previous. It was stuffed to the brim with workbenches, cabinets, filing shelves, stacks of equipment, and papers pasted everywhere. A scientist's workroom, it seemed.

At the far end sat an old man wearing rubber gloves, a massive pair of goggles, and a coolie's singlet. He did not look up when we approached. Presumably this was Uncle Lee, busy working on soldering something. The familiarity of that smell and the light's peculiar quality stirred memories that I had tried, for many years, to suppress. I shuddered.

When he was done the old man held up a single piece of neatly fused copper tubing, the joint blackened by heat. Apparently satisfied with his work, he put the tubing aside and turned his attention to Bells.

Without warning Bells burst into a staccato spate of a Fujian dialect. He retrieved a small metallic object from the depths of his coat and showed it to Uncle Lee, who muttered something and started rummaging in a drawer of his desk. I knew just enough of the language to follow the conversation: the engine part from Bells's ship was worn out and he needed a new one.

Uncle Lee passed Bells a fresh metallic object and Bells held it up to inspect it, clearly pleased.

"Who is that?" Uncle Lee asked, gesturing at me.

"My friend," Bells explained. "She wants to see the, uh...." His limited grasp of the language failed him then and he pointed to a large cabinet to our left. "That."

Uncle Lee looked at the cabinet then back at me. "Is she with the Empire?"

"Of course not," he said at once. More interesting than his ease at dissembling was the question of why he would choose to lie. Most curious, I thought.

Still the old man, apparently satisfied with this answer, nodded.

The inside of the cabinet revealed a device of a design that I had never seen before. It was a large brass box decorated with no fewer than nine Chinese dragons and a set of depressible keys, each engraved with a different letter of the alphabet. Uncle Lee plugged a plate coated with some sort of matte material into a slot in the side of the device.

"Hit something," he said to me, pointing to the keys.

Very cautiously, I tapped out with gloved fingers: THE NIGHTS OF CONSTANTINOPLE. With every letter I could hear gears moving on the inside of the box. A transmissible-code device, perhaps?

Uncle Lee pulled a lever next to the set of keys and the device made a long, whining mechanical noise. He pulled out the plate from the slot and showed it to me.

The matte surface looked blank—this was no punch-machine, then. Uncle Lee put the unmarked plate into another slot—this one lower than the first—and depressed an ornate red button. Something clanked inside—tchak! tchak!—and the device spat out a narrow spool of paper. Uncle Lee tore it off and handed it to me.

"THE NIGHTS OF CONSTANTINOPLE," I read aloud. The plate had remembered my words but not mechanically. I guessed that the device used a chemical or magnetic medium, much like the oracle machines that studied numbers and told the future, and whose existence was considered one of the Empire's most deeply hidden secrets.

Uncle Lee put the plate back into the first slot. "Hit something again," he instructed.

I tapped out ARE COLD AND LONELY, because I did not know what else I wanted to say.

Uncle Lee repeated the process, taking the plate out, putting it into the printing slot, and pressing the red button. The device whirred, spoke, and spat out another piece of paper. THE NIGHTS OF CONSTANTINOPLE ARE COLD AND LONELY.

I gave Bells a dangerous look. "This is a transmissible-code device," I said, in English. Even this was a lie, for the machine was more than a simple transmissible-code device—in function it was frightfully similar to the great machines whose existence was so jealously guarded by the Empire. Incorporate it with an abacus shelf and it could rival an oracle machine. "This is illegal."

Bells flipped up the lenses of his goggles. "Then this will be our little secret." He winked at me, and it was a wink both devilish and elegant.

There was a clatter of activity at the door and two children came running in—a boy and a girl, no more than a few years apart. Their arms were full of the matte recording plates.

"Ye-ye," the boy exclaimed then exploded into a litany of complaints about his sister and how she was ordering him around when they went to get the materials.

"Did you get all the plates?" Uncle Lee asked. His tone was sharp, but his eyes were full of fondness as he looked upon his grandchildren.

"We did," said the boy. The children unloaded their burdens onto the worktable.

The girl gave me a glance. She was, as the elder of the two, perhaps eleven or twelve, on the cusp of womanhood. From the bright curiosity in her eyes, I could see her privately forming questions about me.

"Come, my lady," Bells said, gently taking me by the elbow—a liberty that would have earned him a broken nose under other circumstances. "The Lees are a very busy family."

I let him guide me outside.

When we were back in the sunlight, I disengaged myself from his grasp. "You should not have shown me this."

He tilted his head. "Did you not like it? Was it not marvelous?"

That was hardly the point. "Did you teach them to build the transmissible-code machine?"

He seemed almost offended by the implication. "Of course not! The Lees have been inventors and innovators for many generations. I myself did not know how to build a transmissible-code machine. *They* had to teach *me.*"

"But they are not doing this alone. Those materials are not inexpensive, and the children need to eat. Who is supporting them?"

His smile was both mysterious and infuriating. "Certainly not I."

"It is the Merdeka Group, is it not? The freedom movement." I grabbed his hand. "Tell me."

He laughed, delighted. "You really are a lot more impulsive than I give you credit for. All in good time, Lady Admira. Come have tea with me tomorrow afternoon. I will be in the Arab Quarter, as usual."

I let him go. When he had completely vanished amid the chaos of the dock, Ying melted out of the shadows.

"How did you fare?" she asked, without preface. I recounted what I had seen, in all its madness.

"Now the resistance movement is involved and there are children, too. I do not like it. I cannot get them involved."

"That is hardly your fault."

"Were we followed again?" I asked her.

"Indeed. It is as we suspected: his first mate follows him wherever he goes. The captain may be a madman but he is not a fool."

"Perhaps the first mate simply intends to keep Bells out of trouble," I mused.

Ying's gaze flicked briefly over her shoulder and her impatience showed. "We should remove him from the equation," she said. "I would find it no trouble to dispatch him."

"I do not wish to hear talk of dispatching anybody," I said sharply. "Now is not the time."

"Then when would it be?" She took my hand and squeezed it imploringly, leaning in close to whisper to me. "My serum will not last another week and we will not receive our payment until we deliver something of value to Lord Louis."

This hit me hard. No, I had not forgotten. How could I, when the payment—the serum—was the very thing that kept her alive, without which her organs would fail?

"We shall follow him for another week," I promised her, "and then I will report to Lord Louis with our findings. Our discoveries should please him enough to convince him to part with more serum."

I could see that Ying was not satisfied with my answer.

She nodded, nevertheless. I wondered if I was indeed risking too much to satisfy my curiosity.

I continued to meet regularly with Bells during the following week: in the mornings for breakfast, and sometimes in the afternoons as well. We had tea. He did not bring me to see any more illegal devices, but we did talk. He was, as always, an endless source of inane trivia, telling me about the speed of a laden swallow or the sights he had seen on his journeys with his airship-state.

I listened politely. He had the mannerisms of a child, truly, given to verbosity and frank exaggeration. His eyes sparkled as he rattled off his tales. He waved and gesticulated and, very memorably, once knocked a cup of tea off the table in his enthusiasm.

Yet for all his immaturity he had wisdom hidden deep within him that showed in random flashes during our conversation, like a fossil lost within the reflecting facets of a crystal, visible only from certain angles.

"You mustn't blame Lord Louis, you know," he said once. "As the new consul to this region, he's under immense pressure from the Imperial Palace. Very large shoes to fill. The poor man wants a prize to present to the Emperor in hopes that he'll avoid the fate of the last consul here. I pity him, more than anything."

On another day he asked me, "Why do you keep working for the Empire? I can tell that you dislike it." I did not answer him.

"You must think I'm a madman," he finally said, over Thursday's milk tea and *naan* with masala. He had his chin in his hands and a boyish expression on his face. "Doing what I do, goading the Royal Empire for no reason at all."

"I do not think you are a madman," I said. "I have come to realize that the actions you take are not as random as they seem. You have a reason for toying with Imperial ambitions, but it is not a reason that I can understand. Something in your past, perhaps?"

He smiled at my attempt to get him to disclose more about his murky history. "I think you and I are more alike than we seem. After all, you too have your reasons for working as the Empire's bloodhound, don't you?"

"What are you saying?" I asked, eyes narrowing.

"I notice that your partner has stopped trailing us in the past few days. Howie, my first mate, told me that she seemed ill when he last saw her." He leaned forward and took my hand in a sudden, urgent movement. "I know how the Empire changed her. She relies on their sufferance to survive, doesn't she?"

I jerked my hand from his grasp, shocked. How dare he? This was a private matter. "You do not know what you speak of!"

"Yet she must consume the serum they provide or her metabolism will fail." His manner was suddenly intense, deadly serious. "I can help her, Admira. I know the formula that she needs."

I jumped to my feet. My heart was beating so hard I thought I might die. Ying's secret was sacred to us, a condition whose true nature was never to be referred to in public. Who did this interloper into our lives think he was, to speak of it like that? Did he think that my confidence could be so easily won, bartered like a vulgar bag of grain?

"You," I snarled, "have turned out to be as dangerous as they said."

"Who is more dangerous," he asked, "an unfettered wildcard like me or the Empire that keeps you on a leash?"

I turned on my heel and left the scene. I felt betrayed, angry, and frightened all at the same time. I had allowed myself to get too close to my target at the expense of the one I loved. I *had* risked too much and that was unacceptable.

I returned to our rented shophouse still shaken, only to find Ying sitting on the bed, her back to me as she gazed out the window. Her hands were cold and her expression distant as I knelt next to her. "How do you feel?"

"We've run out of serum," she said. "The rationing was not effective enough."

"Then it is decided," I said, now entirely convinced of my decision. "We will end this tomorrow. I will bring the captain to our taskmaster." But not, I decided, the Lees. They did not need to be a part of this.

"You will have to go alone," Ying said. "In this state, I will be of little help."

I could not meet her eyes. "Ying, I am sorry. I have caused you suffering."

She stroked my hair, even if her movements were slow. "Be careful," she said, even though she knew that I always was.

The next day I dressed in my fighting gear—subtle differences that only the trained eye would notice—outfitted it with both weapons and the poison vial. I examined myself in the mirror: my demeanor gave away nothing unusual. I was ready for the hunt.

Bells was not where I expected to find him on a Saturday. Nor was he anywhere to be found in the port area, as I methodically combed through the sinuous length of the river. It was as if he had read my thoughts beforehand and had vanished from the surface of the island. Frustrated, I stared up at the sky, at the striped brass-and-canvas confection that was Bell's ship, floating serenely and, as I fancied, uncaringly out of reach.

"Do not hide from me like a coward," I said, shouting up to the airship as if there were a chance that he might hear me.

Someone tapped on my arm. It was the young girl from the godown, Uncle Lee's granddaughter. She was carrying a bouquet of bird-of-paradise and handed the flowers to me.

"From our friend," she said, with a girlish smile.

"Wait," I said, impulsively taking her arm to stop her from running off. She simply looked at me curiously.

"Is your family with the Merdeka Rebellion?" I asked.

She gave me an unamused mask that was older than her years, and did not answer.

I pressed on. "Why are you doing this? Aren't you afraid it's dangerous? Lord Louis will arrest your family if he finds out what you are up to."

She straightened up stubbornly. *"Ye-ye* says we shouldn't stop making machines because the Empire says we cannot, because that would be stupid. And they won't find out because nobody will tell them. That's why it's a secret."

I let her go. She knew so much, yet so little. It was disheartening. The bouquet she'd given me felt cumbersome and ludicrous in my hands, the distinctive bright-red flowers visible from half a street away. I felt an unreasonable anger at Bells, both for putting the girl in such a dangerous position and for stranding me with such unpleasant choices.

Something within the fleshy red folds of the bird-of-paradise caught the light and I extracted it. It was a small tile of reader-glass, the sort used by portable transmissible-code devices to store messages. I vindictively threw it into a drainage gutter. There was nothing Bells could say that would interest me now.

I returned to the shophouse, intending to rethink my strategy. But there was a terrible stillness in the house when I entered. Fearing the worst, I rushed into the bedchamber to find Ying curled upon the bed, barely breathing.

"Ying," I exclaimed, shaking her by the shoulders, but she responded to neither my touch nor my voice. For the first time in my adult life I found myself trembling, unable to think clearly. I had run out of time.

The Imperial Palace sprawled across the top of the small hill that faced the seaport; a lumbering, solid-walled colossus guarded day and night by the Empire's mechanical men. Lord Louis's receiving chamber was right in the middle of the complex, a massive, high-ceilinged room supported by rows of forbidding white pillars, with Lord Louis's seat on a raised platform inside. The marble floor was cold to my bent knees. It was absolutely deathly silent save for the muted clanks of the metal men patrolling outside, the soft clicks of Lord Louis's nails on the edge of his chair, and the sound of my blood rushing in my ears.

"I am so very, very disappointed with your lack of progress," he drawled. He had a small and petulant voice, a pinched face, and a slight build dwarfed by the grandiosity around him. As he tapped the heavily ringed fingers of one hand on the armrest of his chair, his other hand toyed with a clear bottle of serum that Ying so badly needed.

"I was told that you were the Empire's best in this region, but it seems that information was less than accurate. Maybe I should send for someone from the homeland who would be better suited to the job, hmm?"

"Please," I said—nay, begged, "we have our reasons for the delay. Give us a week more and we will have him as you asked."

Lord Louis smiled, a curved little thing that did not reach his eyes. He tilted the bottle of serum back and forth. "And can your partner survive another week without this, hmm?"

I did not know what else I could say. Our taskmaster was obviously bent on withholding the serum until he received some information he found valuable.

"We found proof that the captain is indeed conspiring against the Empire," I said. "We have uncovered links he has to the Merdeka Group."

"Oh?" Lord Louis leaned forward, suddenly and vividly interested. "Tell me more."

I hesitated. What other choice did I have? Eyes fixed on the bottle of serum Lord Louis held, I began.

"There is a family of machinists living in a godown on the north side of the river...."

That night I lay awake wrapped in Ying's embrace, listening to her breathing smoothly and evenly. The warmth of her body and the sweet smell of her skin might have brought me solace on other nights but not this one. The windows of our rented shophouse opened over the river and an awful racket punctuated the night—the shouts of men and the sounds of explosions. I could see a red tint reflected on the clouds: somewhere along the river a godown was burning.

"You could always leave," Ying said, mumbling into the skin of my shoulder.

"What sort of foolish notion is that?"

I felt her shift her weight as she leaned a soft cheek against the plane of my shoulder blade. "You are not shackled to the Empire as I am. You could leave to find more amenable employers."

"I will not leave." I gripped her hand and turned to face her. "To remain with you is my choice."

Her returning smile did not extend further than her lips and left the sorrow in her eyes untouched. In the background the fires of conquest burned. I did not sleep that night.

The sun had barely risen the next morning when the pounding on the door started. "Let me deal with this," I told Ying, short staff in hand as I headed toward the door.

I had barely cracked it open when Bells barged through and spun around on me.

"What have you done?" he demanded.

I whipped the short staff up and pointed it at his throat. "Come no closer," I said, "or I will discharge it."

"They arrested Uncle Lee's family and burned down their home," he exclaimed. "Everyone, including the children!"

"They were breaking the laws of the land. It was to be expected."

He had his goggles on but I didn't need to see his eyes to know how he felt. "You betrayed us. I thought better of you than that."

"I am a bounty hunter tethered to the Crown," I spat. "The Empire's bloodhound, as you so eloquently put it. What were you expecting me to do?"

"You seemed an honorable person to me. I thought I saw that in you."

"Then you saw wrong!"

With my back to the door and Bells facing it, he had failed to see Ying creeping up on him from behind. Something glinted in her hand: the poison vial, its needle ready.

"Honor means less to me than Ying's survival."

"I told you I could help her," he said. "Did you not read the message I sent?"

He did not get any farther. Ying chose that moment to attack, leaping at him from behind. He tried to fight her, but her hold on him was too firm.

"Ying, no!" I shouted to warn her but I was too late. With a single move she struck, stabbing the point of the needle into his neck.

He cried out and fell to his knees. I grabbed him as he collapsed. His cap had been knocked off in the scuffle and I pulled off his goggles to check his condition. His eyes were glassy and his pupils were dilated as he stared up at me, looking more confused than terrified.

"Whhh," he slurred, unable to form words.

"A mild paralyzing toxin," I told him. "Its effects are temporary."

But even as I said this I knew it was a lie, for the dosage in the vial had been far too much. His heartbeat was slowing and his eyes fluttered shut.

"Bells?" I asked. There was no response. "Bells!"

Ying had vanished out of a window after the attack and she leapt back in, quick and silent and deadly. "He was not followed this time. What happened?"

"He was overdosed," I said, cradling his head in my hands. "He is dying."

Ying knelt beside me and studied his prone form for a moment, and I thought I saw regret in her. Bells looked so small suddenly, lying on the floor of the cavernous shophouse.

"We have to take him to Lord Louis," she said. "The Palace will have the antidote."

"No," I said, even though I could not explain why I felt this way.

Her hand closed over mine. "He will die here otherwise."

I shut my eyes. Ying was right but thinking of it caused a heavy sinking feeling in my chest, as though a stone had been hurled at it and was even now vanishing into its depths.

Ying slipped an arm under Bells's shoulders.

"Come on," she said, "help me."

And I did, for there was nothing else I could do.

That evening I watched the sun set over the river, studying the yellow patches of light that shifted in chaos. The docks seemed somehow quieter today, subdued and somber, as though a vital piece of their vibrancy had been taken. Above them still bobbed the fantastic airship that had belonged to Bells. I wondered what was happening on the ship's deck at that moment. Were they wondering what had happened to their captain and their president? Or did they already know? Were they planning something?

Ying came to stand by my side.

"The justice of the Empire is swift and brutal. We know this."

"Tell me we did the right thing," I implored of her.

Ying did not answer immediately. She seemed to be in great thought, troubled. Finally she said, "We completed the job we were tasked with."

"That does not answer my question."

"And I do not think I can answer it." Ying gazed over the horizon and did not meet my eyes. "Matters of right and wrong are subjective and I prefer to deal with fact. The fact is that we have finished the job we were tasked with and our role in the matter is over."

I stared at her. I had not imagined that she could be so cold.

"It is also fact," she continued, "that, in the eyes of the Empire, it would be none of our concern and none of our doing if the captain and his conspirators were to somehow escape from their cells tonight." She turned to me, and in her I caught a glimpse of hope burning wild and fierce. A slow smile spread across my face. "Do you think so?"

"Most definitely."

"Then perhaps it is time we planned for events that are none of our concern."

Beneath the indolent sprawl of the Imperial Palace lay the holding cells, the interrogation rooms, the laboratoriums, all the varied instruments essential to the Empire. They were connected by a series of narrow tunnels that opened out onto the side of the hill, each entrance guarded by a pair of mechanical men. These sentries were taken out with a touch of my ring: one tap for each of the brass contraptions and they fell in a mass of shorted circuits.

Ying and I ran down the tunnel, heading inward until we reached the first branching point, two narrow paths leading to separate sections of the dungeon. Far off, I could hear the sounds of a tiny, familiar instrument.

"That will be Bells," I said.

Ying took a deep breath of air. "I can smell the children."

"Then let us divide the tasks: you retrieve the family while I find Bells."

We headed in our different directions. The tunnel soon gave way to a set of cells, all of them eerily empty. Each was barely six feet by three feet, recessed into the walls and fronted by solid iron bars. I passed by them, searching for the source of the music—there!

Bells leapt up at the sight of me, interrupted from the Russian folksong he was playing.

"My lady," he said. "Have you come to rescue me, then?"

"Stand back," I said, aiming my short staff at the bolt across the door.

The report of the weapon discharging was unbearably loud in the enclosed space but it did the job. When the smoke had cleared I barged into the cell and grabbed Bells by the arm.

"Hurry, we do not have much time."

"This is certainly unexpected," he said, but he seemed pleased to see me. As I hauled him out of the cell he added, "And it seems I was right after all."

I ignored the hint of triumph in his voice and said, as we ran down the narrow confines of the tunnel, "I am surprised they let you keep the instrument."

"William and I cannot be separated," he said, baring the huge, reassuringly boyish smile of his. And I was suddenly glad that I was there at that moment, doing what I was doing. It felt right.

Bells pushed past me and took the lead as we continued.

"Follow me," he said. "I know where Uncle Lee's family is being held."

"You seem to know a lot about this place," I said. "One might suspect you have a certain amount of familiarity with it."

His returning smile was small and mysterious.

We rounded a corner and came full-tilt upon Ying leading the children behind her, accompanied by Uncle Lee and a younger man and woman I did not recognize. The children squealed in delight. "Bells!"

"There may be a problem," Ying said. "There were armed guards posted to their cells. I may have inadvertently triggered an alarm."

"Inadvertently?" I closed my eyes. If the entire Palace were on alert, there was no chance of our reaching our planned jungle escape route without encountering trouble. "We need to think of a better way out of here."

Bells laughed. "It is fortunate, then, that some of us have more foresight than others."

He produced William and shook the instrument. Out of the sound hole came tumbling a small, round device, made of brass and adorned with a single glowing light. It looked like an emitting device of some sort.

"Much as I am fond of Lord Louis, I never intended staying the night."

Uncle Lee, too, seemed to know what it was. "If your ship is coming, then we should go," he said.

We resumed our run toward the hillside egress.

There came from behind the sound of metallic feet, a regular, ominous clank-clank-clank that could only mean one thing: we had run out of time much faster than we thought.

"Take the family and go," I instructed Ying. "I will hold them off."

Bells did not follow them. "You might find me handy in a fight," he said. I did not have time to argue.

From behind us came marching a pair of mechanical minions made of blackened metal and much taller and wider than the regular gatekeepers and guardsmen. Unlike the lightly armed guards I had incapacitated earlier, these two were armed with repeating pellet guns. Behind the twin monstrosities I glimpsed the silhouette of Lord Louis, looking even smaller than ever, framed as he was between automatons.

"You must be quite something to warrant this much personal attention," I muttered to Bells.

"Fear not," he whispered back. "I have a few tricks up my sleeve." Then he leapt forward toward the marching minions and shouted, "By my command, I instruct you to halt!" He held William aloft. "I have a ukulele and I know how to use it!"

Amazingly, the two mechanical men stopped in their tracks. Their beveled heads turned toward each other as if confused. "Seize them," Lord Louis commanded but the machines made no move to do so. Bells tucked the tiny instrument into position and started dancing a jig right in front of them. Perhaps he *was* completely mad after all. *"Oy, polnym polna moya korobushka, yest' i sitets i parcha...."*

"What are you doing?" Lord Louis yelled at the immobile constructs. "Seize him!"

The walls of the tunnels suddenly shook with distant thunder—bombardment from above. Bells's airship had arrived.

"That's my cue to go!" Bells said, and quick as lightning struck the immobile machines with his ukulele. There must have been steel backing in the tiny instrument because he knocked their heads clean off.

Lord Louis marched toward us, coming out of the shadow. "I should have known, James. You were always up to childish games!" He drew a pistol from its holster.

"Oh, for mercy's sake!" I exclaimed, rolling my eyes and without further ado discharged my short staff right at Lord Louis. The electrical beam arced, hit him in the chest, and he fell over. Having had quite enough, I grabbed Bells by the hand and started running toward the exit.

"Good shot," he told me as we ran.

"How did you stop those mechanical men?" I asked.

"Only royals can command them by voice! Oh, never mind, I suppose it doesn't matter now."

He grinned.

"Did you really mean it when you said you could help Ying with her affliction?"

"Of course! The formulation for the serum is exceedingly simple, if you know the right ingredients."

"And you would happen to know these ingredients?"

He laughed. "What do you take me for?" and laughed even harder when I answered, "A madman?"

We burst out of the tunnel and were greeted by the magnificent sight of Bells's ship filling the sky, a marvelous confection of brass and steel and striped canvas, gigantic thrust rotors angled downward, allowing the ship to hover in position while in battle mode. The firing batteries mounted on the side of the ship spoke and bolts of electricity seared the air over our heads. I smelled ozone on the wind whipping in a frenzy across the beaten ground.

Ying and the Lee family were clustered underneath as a rope ladder was lowered toward them.

"Bells!" the boy hollered, waving frantically. We ran to join them.

"Captain!" came a shout from above. A young woman—a girl, really—was perched dangerously on the edge of the ship, an ankle hooked around one of the ropes anchoring the ship's balloon to its wooden frame as she lowered our salvation. "The cannons are running low on charge—hurry!"

Bells tapped everybody on the head in turn. "I grant you all asylum on board the *Discordia*," he said perfunctorily.

"Now come on!" and he started ascending the rope ladder.

The deck of the *Discordia* seemed to be engulfed in chaos, but perhaps that was the fault of the mad wind, the powerful back draft created by the airship's giant thrusting propellers blasting higher off from the ground. The ladder-girl leapt off the ship's edge and landed securely on deck.

"I'm going below in case we get followed," she said, before she vanished down a hatch in a flourish of linen and leather.

The first mate stood straight as a rod at his station, hands firmly on the wheel as he kept the ship steady. His glance toward Ying and me was narrow-eyed and squinty. I could not tell if it was due to suspicion or the wind that was cutting into everything, making it hard to speak or listen or think. Bells clapped his hand on the man's shoulder. "Come on, Howie, let us get away from this blasted place."

The first mate nodded. "Engines at maximum, captain!" he shouted over the commotion. "Everybody hold on to something."

Behind us the main rotor kicked into action with a massive roar. Howie spun the wheel and the ship swung away from the ground in a huge, sweeping arc.

Bells ran toward the ship's prow. "Sarah may need help with the cannons," he hollered, gesturing in the direction of the hatch the ladder-girl had vanished through.

"I'll go," Ying said, and she too vanished into the darkness of the hold.

Bells jumped up onto the prow, seized one of the ropes, and leaned forward as far as he could. I joined him and looked downward. The ground was rapidly receding into darkness, swallowed whole by the night. A report from the ship's electrical cannons threw the ground below into sharp white light and shadow, revealing the slow tiny dots that were the Imperial Guard marching out from the Palace. Firing batteries smoked on the hillside, having been reduced to smoldering ash by *Discordia*'s cannons.

"It does not appear that we are being pursued," I said.

"Mmm," Bells mused. "It must be chaos down there, Lord Louis being temporarily incapacitated and all."

I considered him as he stood on the prow of his ship.

He should have been triumphant yet all I sensed from him was an air of calm contemplation.

"Lord Louis called you James," I said.

"Did he, now?"

"Is that your real name?"

"Real or not, what does it matter? It is not the name I go by these days."

I narrowed my eyes. "I suspected this. You are a royal, are you not?"

Bells rubbed his chin. "I suppose I must have been," he said playfully. "But that was such a long time ago, another lifetime."

I nodded. That explained a great deal about him to me, even as it explained nothing.

Our eyes met and an indefinable warmth passed between us. Then Bells leaned forward as if to kiss me. I held up a hand to stop him. "I apologize if I have given you the wrong impression," I said. "But I am not interested in pursuing a romantic relationship. I have everything I want in Ying."

He laughed, unperturbed by this. "It was worth a try at least." Then he sighed, taking one of his signature turns in conversation. "I broke William's neck in all the excitement. I will have to make myself a new instrument." He leapt off the prow of the ship and landed on the deck.

"Where do we go now?" I asked after him, looking out at the horizon. Clear of clouds, the sky was filled with stars from one end of the horizon to the other. I imagined I could see the shapes of the Riau Islands in the distance. I had not been home in so long.

Bells looked thoughtful. "We'll have to lie low for a while, I suppose. There are some friendly ports in Indochina that may be willing to shelter us. A time to catch up with old friends and make new ones!"

He seemed cheered by the prospect. Then he winked.

"Fret not; we will be back soon enough."

The hatch opened in the deck and Ying and the ladder-girl emerged. Sarah, Bells had said her name was. Ying gazed at our surroundings, taking in the sudden calm filled with the deep hum of *Discordia*'s engines. I went to her side.

"Are you feeling all right?" I asked, slipping a hand around her waist.

"I've never felt better," she said with a smile and leaned her head against my shoulder.

I took a first look at our sudden and unexpected new home: across the deck of the ship sprawled large crates, discarded bicycle parts, stacked rolls of engineering plans, and contraptions of metal gearing. The first mate was shouting instructions to members of the Lee family, who evidently had some familiarity with the ship. The young man ran down a flight of steps, flung open a door, and yelled something into the engine room. The two Lee children were already running across the deck, shrieking and chasing each other, clearly enjoying their newfound freedom. It was chaos, pure and wonderful.

Bells leaned against a long, tall crate and grinned.

"Ladies and gentlemen, welcome to the Sovereign State of Discordia."

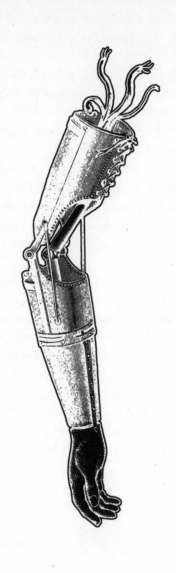

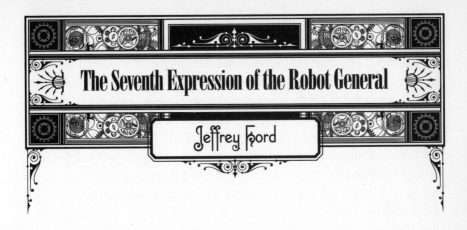

The Seventh Expression of the Robot General

Jeffrey Ford

IN HIS LATER years, when he spoke, a faint whirring came from his lower jaw. His mouth opened and closed rhythmically, accurately, displaying a full set of human teeth gleaned from fallen comrades and the stitched tube of plush leather that was his tongue. The metal mustache and eyebrows were ridiculously fake, but the eyes were the most beautiful glass facsimiles, creamy white with irises like dark blue flowers. Instead of hair, his scalp was sandpaper.

He wore his uniform still, even the peaked cap with the old emblem of the Galaxy Corps embroidered in gold. He creaked when he walked, piston compressions and the click of a warped flywheel whispering within his trousers. Alternating current droned from a faulty fuse in his solar plexus, and occasionally, mostly on wet days, sparks wreathed his head like a halo of bright gnats. He smoked a pipe, and before turning each page of a newspaper, he'd bring his chrome index finger to his dry rubber slit of a mouth as if he were moistening its tip.

His countenance, made of an astounding, pliable, nonflammable, blast-beam resistant, self-healing, rubber alloy, was supposedly sculpted in homage to the dashing looks of Rendel Sassoon, star of the acclaimed film epic, *For God and Country*. Not everyone saw the likeness, and Sassoon himself, a devout pacifist who was well along in years when the general took his first steps out of the laboratory, sued for defamation of character. But once the video started coming back from the front, visions of slaughter more powerful than any celluloid fantasy, mutilated Harvang corpses stacked to the sky, the old actor donned a flag pin on his lapel and did a series of war-bond television commercials of which the most prominent feature was his nervous smile.

It's a sad fact that currently most young people aren't aware of the historic incidents that led to our war with the Harvang and the necessity of the Robot General. They couldn't tell you a thing about our early discoveries of atmosphere and biological life on our planet's sizeable satellite, or about the initial fleet that went to lay claim to it. Our discovery of the existence of the Harvang was perhaps the most astonishing news in the history of humanity. They protested our explorations as an invasion, even though we offered technological and moral advancements. A confluence of intersecting events led to an unavoidable massacre of an entire village of the brutes, which in turn led to a massacre of our expeditionary force. They used our ships to invade us, landing here in Snow Country and in the swamps south of Central City.

It was said about his time on the battlefield that if the general were human he'd have been labeled "merciless," but, as it was, his robot nature mitigated this assessment instead to that he was simply "without mercy." At the edge of a pitched battle he'd set up a folding chair and sit down to watch the action, pipe in hand and a thermos of thick, black oil nearby. He'd yell through a bull-horn, strategic orders interspersed with exhortations of "Onward, you sacks of blood!" Should his troops lose the upper hand in the melee, the general would stand, set his pipe and drink on the ground next to his chair, remove his leather jacket, hand it to his assistant, roll up his sleeves, cock his hat back, and dash onto the battlefield, running at top robot speed.

Historians, engineers, and AI researchers of more recent years have been nonplused as to why the general's creators gave him such limited and primitive battle enhancements. There were rays and particle beams at that point in history and they could have outfitted him like a tank, but their art required subtlety. Barbed, spinning drill bits whirled out from the center of his knuckles on each hand. At the first hint of danger, razor blades protruded from the toes of his boots. He also belched poison, feathered darts from his open mouth, but his most spectacular device was a rocket built into his hindquarters that when activated shot a blast of fire that made him airborne for ten seconds.

It was supposedly a sight the Harvang dreaded, to see him land behind their lines, knuckle spikes whirling, belching death, trousers smoldering. They had a name for him in Harvang, *Kokulafugok,* which roughly translated as "Fire in the Hole." He'd leave a trail of carnage through their ranks, only stopping briefly to remove the hair tangling his drill bits.

His movements were graceful and precise. He could calculate ahead of his opponent, dodge blast beams, bend backward, touch his head upon the ground to avoid a spray of shrapnel, and then spring back up into a razor-toed kick, lopping off a Harvang's sex and drilling him through the throat. Never tiring, always perfectly balanced and accurate, his intuition was dictated by a random number generator.

He killed like a force of nature, an extension of the universe. Hacked by axe blades or shot with arrows to his head, when his business was done, he'd retire to his tent and send for one of the Harvang females. The screams of his prisoner echoed through the camp and were more frightening to his troops than combat. On the following morning he would emerge, his dents completely healed, and give orders to have the carcass removed from his quarters.

During the war, he was popular with the people back home. They admired his hand-to-hand combat, his antique nature, his unwillingness to care about the reasons for war. He was voted the celebrity most men would want to have a beer with and most women would desire for a brief sexual liaison. When informed as to the results of this poll, his only response was "But are they ready to die for me?"

Everywhere, in the schools, the post offices, the public libraries, there were posters of him in battle-action poses amid a pile of dead or dying Harvang that read: *Let's Drill Out A Victory!* The Corps was constantly transporting him from the front lines of Snow Country or the Moon back to Central City in order to make appearances supporting the war. His speeches invariably contained this line: *The Harvang are a filthy species.* At the end of his talks, his face would turn the colors of the flag and there were few who refused to salute. Occasionally, he'd blast off the podium and dive headlong into the crowd, which would catch his falling body and, hand over hand, return him to the stage.

In his final campaign, he was blown to pieces by a blast from a beam cannon the Harvang had stolen from his arsenal. An entire regiment of ours was ambushed in Snow Country between the steep walls of an enormous glacier—the Battle of the Ice Chute. His strategies were impossibly complex but all inexorably led to a frontal assault, a stirring charge straight into the mouth of Death. It was a common belief among his troops that who'd ever initially programmed him had never been to war. Only after his defeat did the experts claim his tactics were daft, riddled with hubris spawned by faulty AI. His case became, for a time, a thread of the damning argument that artificial intelligence, merely the human impression of intelligence, was, in reality, artificial ignorance. It was then that robot production moved decidedly toward the organic.

After the Harvang had been routed by reinforcements, and the Corps eventually began burying the remains of those who'd perished in the battle for Snow Country, the general's head was discovered amid the frozen carnage. When the soldier who found it lifted it up from beneath the stiffened trunk of a human body, the eyes opened, the jaw moved, and the weak, crackling command of "Kill them all!" sputtered forth.

The Corps decided to rebuild him as a museum piece for public-relations purposes, but the budget was limited. Most of his parts, discovered strewn across the battlefield, could be salvaged and a few new ones were fashioned from cheaper materials to replace what was missing. Still, those who rebuilt the general were not the craftsmen his creators were—techniques had been lost to time. There was no longer the patience in robot design for aping the human. A few sectors of his artificial brain had been damaged, but there wasn't a technician alive who could repair his intelligence node, a ball of wiring so complex its design had been dubbed "The Knot."

The Corps used him for fund-raising events and rode him around in an open car at veterans' parades. The only group that ever paid attention to him, though, was the parents of the sons and daughters who'd died under his command. As it turned out, there were thousands of them. Along a parade route they'd pelt him with old fruit and dog shit, to which he'd calmly warn, "Incoming."

It didn't take the Corps long to realize he was a liability, but because he possessed consciousness, though it be man-made, the law disallowed his being simply turned off. Instead, he was retired and set up in a nice apartment at the center of a small town, where he drew his sizeable pension and *history of combat* bonus.

An inauspicious ending to a historic career, but in the beginning, at the general's creation, when the Harvang had invaded in the south and were only miles outside Central City, he was a promising savior. His artificial intelligence was considered a miracle of Science, his construction, the greatest engineering feat of the human race. And the standard by which all this was judged was the fact that his face could make seven different expressions. Everyone agreed it was proof of the robot builder's exemplary art. Before the general, the most that had ever been attempted was three.

The first six of these expressions were slight variations on the theme of "determination." *Righteousness, Willfulness, Obstinacy, Eagerness, Grimness 1* and *2* were the terms his makers had given them. The facial formation of the six had a lot to do with the area around the mouth, subtly different clenchings of the jaw, a straightness in the lips. The eyes were widened for all six, the nostrils flared. For *Grimness 2*, steam shot from his ears.

When he wasn't at war, he switched between *Righteousness* and *Obstinacy*. He'd lost *Eagerness* to a Harvang blade. It was at the Battle of Boolang Crater that the general was cut across the cheek, all the way through to his internal mechanism. After two days of leaking oil through the side of his face, the outer wound healed, but the wiring that caused the fourth expression had been irreparably severed.

There is speculation, based primarily on hearsay, that there was also an eighth expression, one that had not been built into him but that had manifested of its own accord through the self-advancement of the AI. Scientists claimed it highly unlikely, but Ms. Jeranda Blesh claimed she'd seen it. During a three-month leave, his only respite in the entire war, she'd lived with him in a chalet in the Grintun Mountains. A few years before she died of a Harvang venereal disease, she appeared on a late-night television talk show. She was pale and bloated, giddy with alcohol, but she divulged the secrets of her sex life with the general.

She mentioned the smooth chrome member with fins, the spicy oil, the relentless precision of his pistons. "Sometimes, right when things were about to explode," she said, "he'd make a face I'd never seen any other times. It wasn't a smile, but more like calm, a moment of peace. It wouldn't last long, though, cause then he'd lose control of everything, shoot a rocket blast out his backside and fly off me into the wall." The host of the show straightened his tie and said, "That's what I call 'drilling out a victory.'"

It was the seventh expression that was the general's secret, though. That certain configuration of his face reserved for combat. It was the reason he was not tricked out with guns or rockets. The general was an excellent killing machine, but how many could he kill alone? Only when he had armies ready to move at his will could he defeat the Harvang. The seventh expression was a look that enchanted his young troops and made them savage extensions of his determination. Outmanned, outgunned, outmaneuvered, outflanked, it didn't matter. One glance from him, and they'd charge, beam rifles blazing, to their inevitable deaths. They'd line up in ranks before a battle and he'd review the troops, focusing that imposing stare on each soldier. It was rare that a young recruit would be unaffected by the seventh expression's powerful suggestion, understand that the mission at hand was sheer madness, and protest. The general had no time for deserters. With lightening quickness, he'd draw his beam pistol and burn a sudden hole in the complainant's forehead.

In an old government document, "A Report to the Committee on Oblique Renderings Z-333-678AR," released since the Harvang war, there was testimony from the general's creators to the fact that the seventh expression was a blend of the look of a hungry child, the gaze of an angry bull, and the stern countenance of God. The report records that the creators were questioned as to how they came up with the countenance of God, and their famous response was "We used a mirror."

There was a single instance when the general employed the seventh expression after the war. It was only a few years ago, the day after it was announced that we would negotiate a treaty with the Harvang and attempt to live in peace and prosperity. He left his apartment and hobbled across the street to the coffee shop on the corner. Once there, he ordered a twenty-four-ounce Magjypt black, and sat in the corner, pretending to read the newspaper. Eventually, a girl of sixteen approached him and asked if he was the robot general.

He saluted and said, "Yes, ma'am."

"We're reading about you in school," she said.

"Sit down, I'll tell you anything you need to know."

She pulled out a chair and sat at his table. Pushing her long brown hair behind her ears, she said, "What about all the killing?"

"Everybody wants to know about the killing," he said. "They should ask themselves."

"On the Steppes of Patience, how many Harvang did you, yourself, kill?"

"My internal calculator couldn't keep up with the slaughter. I'll just say, '*Many*.'"

"What was your favorite weapon?" she asked.

"I'm going to show it to you, right now," he said, and his face began changing. He reached into his inside jacket pocket and brought forth a small-caliber ray gun wrapped in a white handkerchief. He laid the weapon on the table, the cloth draped over it. "Pick it up," he said.

He stared at her and she stared back, and after it was all over, she'd told friends that his blue pupils had begun to spin like pinwheels and his lips rippled. She lifted the gun.

"Put your finger on the trigger," he said.

She did.

"I want you to aim it right between my eyes and pull the trigger."

She took aim with both hands, stretching her arms out across the table.

"Now!" he yelled, and it startled her.

She set the gun down, pushed back her chair, and walked away.

It took the general two weeks before he could find someone he could convince to shoot him, and this was only after he offered payment. The seventh expression meant nothing to the man who'd promised to do the job. What he was after, he said, were the three shrunken Harvang heads the general had kept as souvenirs of certain battles. They'd sell for a fortune on the black market. After the deal was struck, the general asked the man, "Did you see that face I had on a little while ago?"

"I think I know what you mean," said the man.

"How would you describe it?" asked the general.

The man laughed. "I don't know. That face? You looked like you might have just crapped your pants. Look, your famous expressions, the pride of an era, no one cares about that stuff anymore. Bring me the heads."

The next night, the general hid the illegal shrunken heads beneath an old overcoat and arrived at the appointed hour at an abandoned pier on the south side of town. The wind was high and the water lapped at the edges of the planks. The man soon appeared. The general removed the string of heads from beneath his coat and threw them at the man's feet.

"I've brought a ray gun for you to use," said the general, and reached for the weapon in his jacket pocket.

"I brought my own," said the man and drew out a magnum-class beam pistol. He took careful aim, and the general noticed that the long barrel of the gun was centered on his own throat and not his forehead.

In the instant before the man pulled the trigger, the general's strategy centers realized that the plot was to sever his head and harvest his intelligence node—"The Knot." He lunged, drill bits whirring. The man fired the weapon and the blast beam disintegrated three-quarters of the general's neck. The internal command had already been given, though, so with head flopping to the side, the robot general charged forward—one drill bit skewered the heart and the other plunged in at the left ear. The man screamed and dropped the gun, and then the general drilled until he himself dropped. When he hit the dock what was left of his neck snapped and his head came free of his body. It rolled across the planks, perched at the edge for a moment, and then a gust of wind pushed it into the sea.

The general's body was salvaged and dismantled, its mechanical wizardry deconstructed. From the electric information stored in the ganglia of the robotic wiring system it was discovered that the general's initial directive was "To Serve the People." As for his head, it should be operational for another thousand years, its pupils spinning, its lips rippling without a moment of peace in the cold darkness beneath the waves. There, "The Knot," no doubt out of a programmed impulse for self-preservation, is confabulating intricate dreams of victory.

The Stoker Memorandum

Lavie Tidhar

ABRAHAM STOKER'S JOURNAL

—From the archives of the Bureau of Secret Intelligence, Pall Mall, London, Classified Ultra, for Head of Bureau Eyes Only—

BUCHAREST—

I had finally arrived at this city, with darkness gathering, casting upon the city a most unfavourable appearance. Having checked into my hotel I drank a glass of strong Romanian wine, accompanied by bear steak, which I am told they bring from the mountains at great expense. I had not enquired as for the recipe.

I am sitting in my room, watching the dance of gas light over the city. Tomorrow I set off for the mountains, and as I write this I am filled with trepidation. I have decided to maintain this record of my mission. In the event anything were to happen to me, this journal may yet make its way, somehow, back to London.

Let me, therefore, record how I came to be at this barbarous and remote country, and the sorry torturous route by which I came to my current predicament.

My name is Abraham Stoker, called Abe by some, Bram by others. I am a theatrical manager, having worked for the great actor Henry Irving for many years as his personal assistant, and, on his behalf, as manager of the Lyceum Theatre in Covent Garden.

I am not a bad man, nor am I a traitor.

Nevertheless, it was in the summer of 18— that I became an unwitting assistant to a grand conspiracy against our lizardine masters, and one which I was helpless to prevent.

It had begun as a great triumph for my theatrical career. Due to a fight between the great librettist W. S. Gilbert and his long-time manager, Richard D'Oyly Carte, over—of all things—a carpet, I had managed to lure Gilbert and his collaborator, the composer Arthur Sullivan, to my own theatre from D'Oyly Carte's Savoy. We were to stage their latest work, titled *The Pirates of the Carib Sea*, a rousing tale of adventure and peril. The first part, and forgive me if I digress, describes our lizardine masters' awakening on Caliban's Island, their journey with that foul explorer Amerigo Vespucci back to the British isle, their overthrowing of our human rulers and their assumption of the throne—a historical tale set to song in the manner only G&S could possibly do it.

In the second part, we encounter the mythical pirate Wyvern, the one-eyed royal lizard who—if the stories in the *London Illustrated News* can be believed—had abandoned his responsibilities to his race, the royal Les Lezards, to assume the life of a blood-thirsty pirate operating in the Carib Sea, between Vespuccia and the lands of the Mexica and Aztecs, and preying on the very trade ships of his own Everlasting Empire, under her royal highness Queen Victoria, the lizard-queen.

Irving himself played—with great success, I might add!—the notorious pirate, assuming a lizard costume of some magnificence, while young Beerbohm Tree played his boatswain, Mr. Spoons, the bald, scarred, enormous human who is—so they say—Wyvern's right-handman.

It was at that time that a man came to see me in my office. He was a foreigner, and did not look wealthy or, indeed, distinguished.

"My name," he told me, "is Karl May."

"A German?" I said, and he nodded. "I represent certain…interests in Germany," he told me. "A very powerful man wishes to attend the opening night of your new show."

"Then I shall be glad to sell him a ticket," I said, regarding the man—clearly a conman or low-life criminal of some sort—with distaste. "You may make the arrangements at the box office. Good day to you, sir."

Yet this May, if that was even his real name, did not move. Instead, leaving me speechless, he closed and then locked the door to my office, from the inside, leaving me stranded in there with him. Before I could rise the man pulled out a weapon, an ornate handgun of enormous size, which he proceeded to wave threateningly.

"This man," he said, "is a very public man. Much attention is paid to his every move. Moreover, to compound our—" *our*, he said!—"problem, this man must meet another very public man, and the two cannot be seen to have ever met or discussed…whatever it is they need to discuss."

This talk of men meeting men in secret reminded me of my friend Oscar Wilde, whom I had known in my student days in Dublin and who had once been the suitor of my wife, Florence. "I do not see how I can help you," I said, stiffly—for it does not do to show fear before a foreigner, albeit one with a gun in his hand.

"Oh, but you can!" this Karl May said to me. "And moreover, you will be amply compensated for your efforts—" and with that, to my amazement, this seeming charlatan pulled out a small, yet heavy-looking bag, and threw it on my desk. I reached for it, drawing the string, and out poured a heap of gold coins, all bearing the portrait—rather than of our own dear lizard-queen—of the rather more foreboding one of the German Kaiser.

"Plenty more where that came from," said this fellow, with a smirk on his face.

I did not move to touch the money. "What would you have me do?" I said.

"The theatre," he said, "is like life. We look at the stage and are spell-bound by it, the scenery convinces us of its reality, the players move and speak their parts and, when it's done, we leave. And yet, what happens to *make* the stage, to move its players, is not done in the limelight. It is done behind the scenes."

"Yes?" I said, growing ever more irritated with the man's manner. "You wish to teach me my job, perhaps?"

"My dear fellow!" he said, with a laugh. "Far from it. I merely wished to illustrate a point—"

"Then get to it, for my time is short," I said, and at that his smile dropped and the gun pointed straight at my heart and he cocked it. "Your time," he said, in a soft, menacing voice, "could be made to be even shorter."

I must admit that, at that, my knees may have shaken a little. I am not a violent man, and am not used to the vile things desperate men are prepared to do. I therefore sat back down in my chair, and let him explain and, when he had finished, I have to admit I felt a sigh of relief escape me, for it did not seem at all such a dreadful proposition and they were willing to compensate me generously besides.

"You may as well know," Karl May said to me, "the name of the person I represent. It is Alfred Krupp."

"The *industrialist?*"

May nodded solemnly. "But what," I gasped, "could he be wanting in my theatre?"

For I have heard of Krupp, of course, the undisputed king of the armaments trade, the creator of the monstrous canon they called Krupp's Baby, which was said to be able to shoot its payload all the way beyond the atmosphere and into space...a recluse, a genius, a man with his own army, a man with no title and yet one which, it was rumoured, was virtually the ruler of all Germany...

A man who had not been seen for many a year, in public.

"Fool," Karl May said. "My lord Krupp has no interest in your pitiful theatre, nor in the singing and dancing of effeminate Englishmen."

"I am Irish, if you don't mind," I said. "There really is no need to be so *rude—*" and May laughed. "Rest your mind at ease, Irishman" he said. "My master wishes only to meet certain...interested parties. Behind, as it were, the scenes."

"Which parties?" I said. "For surely I would need to know in order to prepare—"

"All in good time!" Karl May said. "All in good time."

BUȘTENI—

This is a small mountain village near to my destination. I had taken the train this morning with no difficulty, yet was told the track terminated before my destination, which is the city of Brașov, nestled, so I am told, in a beautiful valley within the Carpathian Mountains.

This region is called Transylvania, and a wild and remote land it is indeed. The train journey lasted some hours, in relative comfort, the train filled with dour Romanian peasants, shifty-looking gypsies, Székelys and Magyars and all other manner of the strange people of this region. Also on board the train were chickens, with their legs tied together to prevent their escaping, and sacks of potatoes and other produce, and children, and a goat. Also on board the train were army officers of the Austro-Hungarian empire of which this was but a remote and rather dismal outpost, with nary a pastry or decent cup of coffee to be seen.

I had wondered at the transportation of such military personnel, and noticed them looking rather sharply in my direction. Nevertheless I was not disturbed and was in fact regarded with respect the couple of times we had occasion to cross each other in passing.

The train's passage was impressive to me, the mountains at first looming overhead, then—as the train rose up from the plains on which sat Bucharest—they rose on either side of the tracks, and it felt as though we were entering another world, of dark forests and unexplored lands, and I fancied I heard, if only in the distance, the howl of wolves, sending a delicious shiver down my spine.

But you did not ask me for a travel guide! Let me be brief. The train terminated, after some hours, at a station in the middle of a field. It was a most curious thing. I could see the tracks leading onwards—presumably to Braşov—but we could not go on. The train halted within these hastily erected buildings, lit by weak gas lamps planted in the dirt, and all—peasants and chickens and soldiers and gypsies and goat—disembarked, including this Irishman.

At this nameless station waited coaches and carts—the peasants and local people to the carts, the soldiers and more well-to-do visitors to the coaches. I stood there in some bewilderment, when I was taken aside by the military officer who seemed to be in charge of that platoon. "You are going—there?" he said, and motioned with his head towards the distance, where I assumed this Braşov lay.

"Yes," I said.

"To visit…him?"

I nodded at that, feeling a pang of apprehension at the thought.

The officer nodded as if that had settled matters, and shouted orders in the barbarous tongue of his people. Almost immediately a coach had been found for me, its passengers emptied out, and I was placed with all due reverence into the empty compartment. "You will go to Buşteni this night," the officer said, "it is too late now to go further." Again he spoke to the driver, who gave me a sour look but daren't refuse, and so we took off in a hurry, the horses running down a narrow mountain path that led upwards, and at last to a small village, or what passes for a town in these parts, which was indeed called Buşteni, or something like it, and had beautiful wooden houses, a church, and a small inn, where I had aligned and where I am currently sat, writing this to you, while dining on a rather acceptable *goulash*.

I do not wish to labour details of what took place following that scoundrel Karl May's visit to my office at the Lyceum. You know as well as I what had happened, you had suspected long before you had approached me, three months ago, in order to recruit me to this desperate mission.

The facts are as they stand. To an outside eye, nothing had happened but that *Herr* Krupp, on a rare visit to England, went, one night, to the theatre—and so did any number of other personages, including, if I remember rightly, yourself, Mr. Holmes.

The Queen herself was there, in the Royal Box, stately as ever, with her forked tongue hissing out every so often, to snap a fly out of the air. I remember the prince regent did not come but Victoria's favourite, that dashing Harry Flashman, the popular Hero of Jalalabad, was beside her. So were many foreign dignitaries and many of the city's leading figures, from our now-Prime-Minister Mrs. Beeton, my friend and former rival Oscar Wilde, the famed scientists Jekyll and Moreau (before the one's suspicious death and the other's exile to the South Seas), the Lord Byron automaton (always a gentleman), Rudolf Rassendyll of Zenda, and many, many others. Your brother, the consulting detective, was there, if I recall rightly, Mr. Holmes.

It was a packed night—sold out, in fact, and I had been kept off my feet, running hither and yon, trying to ensure our success, and all the while…

All the while, behind the scenes, things were afoot.

I was aware of movement, of strangers coming and going in silence, of that German villain Karl May (I had found out much later the man was not only a convicted criminal but worse, a dime novel hack) following me like a shadow, of a tense anticipation that had nothing to do with the play.

There are secret passageways inside every theatre, and the Lyceum is no exception. It has basements and sub-basements, a crypt (from when it was a church), narrow passageways, false doors, shifting scenery—it is a *theatre*, Mr. Holmes!

It was a game of boxes, Mr. Holmes. As I told you when you found me, three months ago, listening to me as if you already knew. How *Herr* Krupp appeared to be in the box when in fact it was a cut-out in the shadows; how he went through the false wall and into the passageway between the walls, and down, to the crypt, now our props room.

And the others.

For I had been unfortunate enough to see them.

BUŞTENI—

A letter had arrived for me in the morning. A dark baruch-landau had stopped outside the inn, a great hulking machine, steam-driven, the stoker standing behind while the driver sat in front, in between their respective positions a wide carriage for the transport of passengers or cargo.

The driver had disembarked—I watched him from my window—and what a curious being he was!

I had seen his like before, though seldom enough. Like the vehicle he was driving, he was huge, a mountain of a man, and a shiver of apprehension ran down my spine.

He would have been human, once upon a time.

"What *are* they?" I had asked Karl May. The play was going on above our heads, but I could not concentrate, I was filled with a terrible tension as we prepared for the summit—as May called it—down below, in the bowels of the theatre. The *they* I was referring to were beings of a similar size and disposition to the driver now sitting in the inn's dining room, awaiting my pleasure.

"Soldiers," Karl May told me. "Of the future."

"What had been done to them?"

"Have you heard of the Jekyll-Frankenstein serum?"

I confessed I had not.

"It is the culmination of many years of research," he told me, with a smirk. "We had stolen the formula from the French some time back. They have Viktor von Frankenstein working for them and he, in his turn, improved upon the work done by your Englishman, Dr. Jekyll. This—" and here his hand swept theatrically, enfolding the huge hulking beings that were guarding, like mountain trolls, the dark corridors—"is the result."

"Can they ever...go back?" I said, whispering. May shook his head. "And their lifespan is short," he said. "But they do make such excellent soldiers..."

It was then that *Herr* Krupp appeared, an old, fragile-looking man, yet with a steely determination in his eyes that I found frightening. "You did well," he said, curtly, and I was not sure if he was speaking to May or myself. He disappeared behind his monsters, and into the crypt.

"Who else are we expecting?" I said.

When, at that moment, the sound of motors sounded and a small, hunched figure came towards us in the darkness, half-human, half-machine…

BUŞTENI—

My landlady has been fussing over me ever since seeing the arrival of the carriage. "You must not go!" she whispered to me, fiercely, finding reason to come up to my room. "He is a devil, a monster!"

"You know of him?" I said.

"Who does not? They had closed the valley, Braşov had been emptied, they are doing unspeakable things there, in the shadow of the mountains." She shivered. "But *he* does not reside in Braşov."

"Where does he reside?" I said, infected by her fear.

"Bran Castle," she said, whispering. "Where once Vlad Tepeş made his home…"

"Vlad Tepeş?" I said. I was not familiar with the local history and the name was unfamiliar to me.

"Vlad the Third, prince of Wallachia," she said, impatiently. "Vlad Tepeş—how you say Tepeş in your English?"

"I don't know," I said, quite bewildered.

"Impaler," she said. "Prince Vlad of the order of the Dragon, whom they called Impaler."

I shook my head impatiently. Local history sounded colourful indeed, but irrelevant to my journey. "The man I am going to see is an Englishman," I said, trying to reassure her. "Englishmen do not impale."

"He is no man!" she said, and made a curious gesture with her fingers, which I took to be some Romanian superstition for the warding of evil. "He had ceased being human long ago."

At last I got rid of her, so I could return to my journal. Time is running out, and soon I shall be inside that baruch-landau, travelling towards my final destination.

Have mercy on my soul, Mycroft!

For I saw him, too, you see. I saw him come towards us, Karl May and me, in the subterranean depths of the Lyceum, that fateful night.

An old, old man, in a motorised chair on wheels, a steam engine at his back, and withered hands lying on the supports, controlling brass keys. His face was a ruined shell, his body that of a corpse, yet his eyes were bright, like moons, and they looked at me, and his mouth moved and he said, "Today, Mr. Stoker, we are making history. Your part in it will not be quickly forgotten."

I may have stumbled upon my words. He had not been seen in public for five years. His very presence at my theatre was an honour, and yet I was terrified. When the small get entangled in the games of the great, they may easily suffer.

"My Lord," I said. "It is an honour."

He nodded that withered head, just once, acknowledging this. Then he, too, disappeared towards the crypt.

Yes, you suspected, did you not, Mycroft? You suspected this summit, your people were there that night, in the audience, trying to sniff scent of what was happening. Yet you never did.

For they did not meet, just the two of them, My Herr Krupp and he, my summoner, the lord of the automatons.

Another was there.

A monster…

For I had gone down into the dark passages, I had gone to check all was secure, and I saw it. I saw the ancient sewer open up and something come crawling out of it, a monstrous being like a giant invertebrate, with feelers as long as a human arm, slithering towards that secret meeting…a vile, alien thing.

Which, three months ago, when we first met, you finally gave a name to.

The Bookman, you told me.

So that was that shadowy assassin.

A thing made by the lizardine race, long ago.

Those lizardine beings which came to us from Caliban's Island, in the Carib Sea, and yet were not of a terrestrial origin at all.

An ancient race, of scientifically advanced beings…crash-landed with their ship of space, thousands of years ago, millions perhaps, on that island.

And awakened by Vespucci, on his ill-fated journey of exploration…

And the Bookman, that shadowy assassin, one of their machines?

I do not know, Mycroft, but I remember the fear I felt when I saw that…
that *thing*, slither towards the crypt.

A summit indeed.

And now, I must leave.

THE BORGO PASS—

The driver says we are going through something called the Borgo Pass, though
it appears on no map of the area. I am the sole passenger of this baruch-landau,
the driver ahead, the stoker behind, and I in the middle, staring out over a
rugged terrain.

This is the letter I had received at the inn:

My friend—Welcome to the Carpathians. I am anxiously expecting
you. I trust that you slept well. My driver has instructions to carry you
in safety to my quarters and bring you to me. I trust that your journey
from London has been a happy one, and that you will enjoy your stay. I
look forward to seeing you.

Yours—Charles Babbage.

What awaits me beyond these mountains, is it to glory, or to death, that I ride?

CASTLE BRAN—

The baruch-landau, gathering speed, shot along the lone mountain road, and
in the distance a great valley opened up, and within…

But no, for we did not head directly there, to that strange shimmering city
in the distance, but elsewhere, down a slope that led into a beautiful valley, and
beyond it, growing gradually in my field of vision as we drew nearer—

On top of a cliff, overlooking this pleasant place—

A castle.

It loomed out of the peaceful surrounding, a stout old building, painted
white, so unlike our own castles. It had that Eastern influence, as though one
could sense Asia and the lands of the Turks being just around the corner, as it
were. Here Vlad Dracul had lived, that minor Wallachian prince the landlady
at the inn had told me about, who had fought the Turks—

He appears to have had a rather understated taste in architecture.

As we approached the castle I noticed things that had certainly not been there during those long gone days of Vlad the Impaler. Such as the armoured, steam-powered trucks moving along newly paved roads, or the two black airships rising like storm clouds over the castle, tethered to a nearby landing.

Storm clouds…

Far in the distance a storm *was* raging, and I could see the lightning strike, again and again, as if they were hitting at one particular spot, there beyond the shimmering mirage of the city I could see, which resembled no place I had ever seen before.

The baruch-landau stopped, at last, at the foothills of the cliff, and I disembarked—

To find a most curious individual there to greet me.

"You are Abraham Stoker?" he said.

His voice surprised me. It was high and somewhat reedy, yet came out of a mountainous exterior—a man completely bald, and extensively scarred, who towered over me, and smiled a smile in which no good could be deciphered.

"I am," I said.

"I am Spoons," he said. "You may call me Mr. Spoons."

I started at that. For, if you recall, Mycroft, that long ago production of *Pirates of the Carib Sea* did feature such a character, the rumoured boatswain of the notorious Captain Wyvern.

Could that possibly be the man himself?

I could see immediately that young Beerbohm Tree, playing him, did not do him justice. This man required no prosthesis or makeup to make him formidable.

But how had he come into my Lord Babbage's service?

"Come with me," he said.

Seldom does a man find all the answers to the questions in this world. I followed this Mr. Spoons—who carried, I could not help but notice, a Peacemaker in a holster on his hip, and a cutlass, of all things, on its opposite side—up the winding path that led to the castle above.

A bustle of activity welcomed us. Military personnel of the sort I had seen on the train—that is, of the Austro-Hungarian persuasion—mingled with black-clad men who had had a stylised B as their insignia.

B-men, I knew them to be.

The Babbage Company's private security force.

"Lord Babbage has instructed for suitable accommodation to be found for you in the castle," Mr. Spoons said. His tone suggested his idea of *suitable* would have been the stables. "He is anxious to meet with you."

"As I, him," I said, and yet unable to hide my nervousness. Mr. Spoons smiled grimly at that.

"I am told you are to be Lord Babbage's…biographer?" he said.

I nodded, equally grimly, at that, and we did not pursue conversation further. Mr. Spoons accompanied me to my new living quarters, an airy room at the very top of the castle, through narrow passageways and too many flights of stairs, and left me there. I could hear a military drill taking place outside, and saw one of the airships detach from its moorings and begin to journey away, towards that mysterious city I could see in the distance, in the shadow of the mountains.

I sat down on the bed as soon as the door had closed and clutched my head in my hands.

What had I let myself into?

Castle Bran—

Night settles over the castle and in the distance the lightning continues to strike at the same spot, a rising tower of metal, needle-like, out there in that city that had once been Braşov.

It is a strange sight, from high up here, looking at the valley, and at the vast machines slowly taking shape here in secret…

That first night was long ago. Lord Babbage had disappeared from public life, and of Krupp nothing more was heard. In eighty-eight Mrs. Beeton ascended to Prime Minister, beating Moriarty, and a new balance of power established itself, with the lizard-queen ceding some of her former power to a coalition of human, automaton and lizard: a true democracy, of sorts.

There had been rumours in the London papers, during that time, as to the mysterious demise of the Bookman, though none could vouch as to their veracity. In any case, my life continued as before, at the Lyceum, and I had all but forgotten that terrible, night-time summit deep below my beloved theatre, when there came a knock at the door.

"Enter," I said, preoccupied with paperwork on my desk, and heard him come in, and shut the door behind him. When I raised my head and looked, I stepped back, for there before me stood that same German con man and hack writer, the source of all my troubles—Karl May.

"You!" I said.

The fellow grinned at me, quite at ease. "Master Stoker," he said, doffing his hat to me. "It has been a while."

"Not long enough!" I said, with feeling, and with shaking hands reached to the second drawer for the bottle I kept there—for emergencies, you see.

May mistook my gesture. The old gun was back in his hand and he *tsked* at me disapprovingly, like a headmaster with an errand pupil.

God, how much I hated him at that moment!

"A drink?" I said, ignoring his weapon, and bringing out the bottle and two cups. At that his good humour returned, the gun disappeared, and he sat down. "By all means," he said. "Let us drink to old friends."

I poured; we drank. "What do you want, May?" I said.

"I?" he said. "I want nothing, for myself. It is Lord Babbage who has shown a renewed interest in you, my friend."

"Babbage?" I said.

"I will put it simply, Stoker," he said. "My Lord Babbage requires a… chronicler of the great work he is undertaking. And there are precious few who can be brought in. You, my friend, are already involved. And you had proved yourself reliable. It is, after all, why you are still alive."

"But why *me?"* I said, or wailed, and he smiled. "My Lord Babbage," he said, "has got it into his head that you are a man of a literary bent."

At that I gaped, for it was true, that I had dabbled in writing fictions, as most men do at one point or another, yet had taken no consideration of showing them to anyone but my wife.

"I thought so," Karl May said.

"But you're a writer," I said. "Why can't you—"

"My work lies elsewhere," he said, darkly.

I could not hold back a smirk, at that. "He does not value your fiction?" I said. At this he scowled even more. "You will make your way to Transylvania," he said. He took out an envelope and placed it on the desk. "Money, and train tickets," he said.

"And if I refuse?"

This made him smile again.

"Oh, I wish you would," he said, and a shiver went down my spine at the way he said it. I picked up the envelope without further protest, and he nodded, once, and left without further words.

Castle Bran—

I must escape this place, for I will never be allowed to depart alive, I now know.

Mycroft, you had come to me, two weeks after that meeting with Karl May. I remember you coming in, a portly man, shadows at your back. You came alone.

Without preamble you told me of your suspicions back at that opening night, and told me of the conspiracy you were trying to unravel. An unholy alliance between Krupp and Babbage and that alien Bookman. What were they planning? You kept saying. What are they after?

You had kept sporadic checks on me, and on the Lyceum. And your spotters had seen the return of Karl May.

Now you confronted me. You wanted to know where my allegiance lay.

Choose, you told me.

Choose, which master to serve.

For Queen and Country, you told me.

My name is Abraham Stoker, called Abe by some, Bram by others. I am a theatrical manager, having worked for the great actor Henry Irving for many years as his personal assistant, and, on his behalf, as manager of the Lyceum Theatre in Covent Garden.

I am not a bad man, nor am I a traitor.

Today I met my Lord Babbage.

Mr. Spoons came to escort me. I am a prisoner, if kept in comfort. Wordlessly he led me down the corridor, to a metal door. At the press of a button the door opened and we entered a lift, what the Vespuccians call an elevator. Down it went, and down, beyond the foundations of the castle, below the ground, into the castle's crypts. The metal doors opened, and I found myself in a dimly lit room, the air hot and humid, and orchids growing in profusion everywhere under the strange blue lights. Mr. Spoons motioned for me. I took a step forward, and another. A sound, as of bellows, working, a rhythmic mechanical sound of air being inhaled and exhaled. I took another step forward, already sweating from the high temperature and the humidity. A shape before me, in the shadows…one more step and I near cried out.

Before me sat a...a...picture an ancient mummy, a once-human body, a dried husk of one, yet with large, wet, living eyes set in that ruined face, that awful body, blinking—looking at me. Pipes led into the body, pipes running out of it like the hairs of Medusa, and an engine working beside, and mechanical bellows pumping air in and out, keeping that aged *thing* alive.

Horrified, I could only watch as those terrible eyes turned their attention on me, and that ruined, dried-out mouth moved, almost soundlessly, and an amplification of some sort took place, magnifying the dying whisper, and he said, "I am...Babbage, and I bid you welcome, Mr. Stoker, to my house."

"My Lord Babbage," I said, forcing out the words. The dry smell of him hung in the air, of old rotting skin, and machine oil, and I was sweating profusely. Those ruined lips moved. I think he tried to smile.

"We are...engaged," he said, "on a work of the greatest magnitude. You will...record it, for prosperity."

The sound of his breathing machine filled the air, in, out, I could see his chest rising and falling mechanically.

"Go," he said. "Your work...begins."

"My Lord—"

His lips moved again. Then his eyes closed. I felt Mr. Spoons' vice-like grip on my arm, pulling me away.

"Come," he said.

An airship is moored to the tower near my room. It is not used.

Have you ever seen the moon rising, full, over the valley of Braşov?

I must steal away from this place.

Mr. Spoons took me up in the elevator. We found ourselves at the base of the castle. That same baruch-landau was waiting, its driver a monstrosity of the type I had last seen, accompanying Krupp, at the Lyceum and that secret summit. A man injected with a J-F Serum.

A man who had become a monster.

We climbed into the carriage, and the driver cranked the steam engine and we were off, along the valley floor.

Spoons, smiling faintly, sat before me, watching me as I watched the road. At last I stuck my head out of the window, and the distant vista grew large and clear before me, and I gasped.

A city...

A city of metal spikes, a city of needles rising into the sky. A city burning with inhuman fire, with rising flames, a city under a full moon, as if each needle and spike were aimed at that heavenly body, wanting to do it harm.

"What...what is it?" I whispered.

Mr. Spoons said, "Rockets."

Night-time, the castle is surrounded by B-men, there is no escape on land, through these wild mountains, through the Borgo Pass, to Bucharest or the sea.

I have to make the attempt, must get word of Babbage's plan to Mycroft, to the Queen...

In a moment I shall open my window, and go out there, on the ledge, and...

I am deathly afraid.

In the air, somewhere above Transylvania—

Wounded. My blood drips on the page as I write. The airship moves silently above the Borgo Pass, to freedom. The engines drive it, fast and dark. For the first time I feel hope.

Rockets.

The valley had been filled with rockets.

They shot at me as I escaped. Beyond the window the wind howled, pushing at me, and I tottered, and nearly fell. A fall would mean death, it was a long way down. I held on to the mooring line and then, gathering myself, I pulled myself up, legs wrapped around the line, and with my hands pulled myself, step by torturous step, towards the airship.

A black sky above me, countless stars shining, the same distant stars Les Lezards may have come from...the same stars that were my Lord Babbage's destination.

He was mad.

But I had seen the valley, Mr. Spoons had taken me there, in the baruch-lan-dau, and I had seen: the city of Braşov, an old, beautiful place of stone, transformed now. Thin needle spires rose into the air and mechanical vehicles moved every-where, and in a converted palace of culture I saw Babbage engines beyond count, operating, and beyond the city the rockets stood, immense, metallic, strange...

"The stars," Mr. Spoons said, in his menacing, high-pitched voice. "Our destination."

"Why?" I said.

Slowly, he turned, looking at me.

"Because they're coming," he said, and said no more.

Somewhere above Europe—

I had bandaged my wounded shoulder. The airship moves almost without guidance, it is very fast, and the night is cold.

I look up at the stars. Could humanity really go there? It seems impossible, and dangerous.

And something else…

I had escaped too easily.

And now I wonder, Mycroft.

Have I truly gone there to record Babbage's story?

Or did he bring me there for another reason entirely?

Did he know you would approach me?

Was this just one more step in the great game we play, was I allowed to escape, in order to bring you this document?

They are coming, Mr. Spoons said.

Over the Channel—

Home, soon. I hope my signal is detected. Soon I shall reach my destination. I am afraid, yet filled with wild hope, too. Could this nightmare journey really be over?

Richmond Park, London—

Flares rise into the night, signalling the landing site. As I come down low the lights illuminate men down below, and as I watch I see a larger flare rise, and then—

My hand slips, the side of the airship is in flames—

Tilting—

The ground approaches fast, I—

—end of Stoker Memorandum. Retrieved successfully by Bureau operative Lucy Westenra. Classified Ultra, for Head of Bureau Eyes Only—

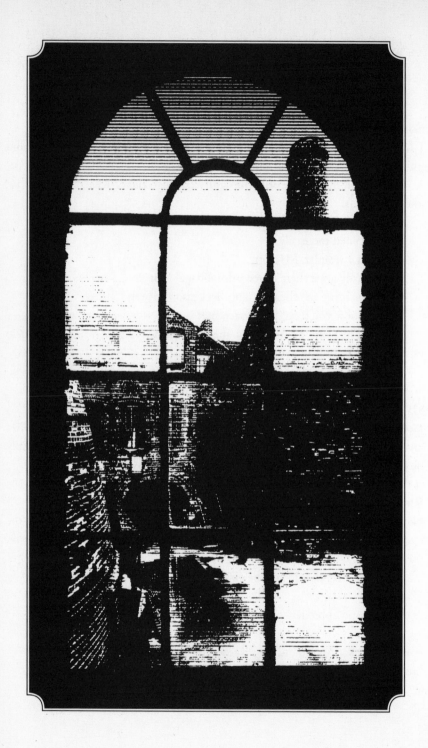

Smoke City

Christopher Barzak

ONE NIGHT, I woke to the sound of my mother's voice, as I did when I was a child. The words were familiar to my ear, they matched the voice that formed them, but it was not until I had opened my eyes to the dark of my room and my husband's snoring that I remembered the words were calling me away from my warm bed and the steady breathing of my children, both asleep in their own rooms across the hall. "Because I could not stop for death," my mother used to tell me, "he kindly stopped for me." They were Dickinson's words, of course, not my mother's, but she said them as if they were hers, and because of that, they were hers, and because of that, they are now mine, passed down with every other object my mother gave me before I left for what I hoped would be a better world. "Here, take this candy dish." Her hands pushing the red knobbed glass into my hands. "Here, take this sweater." Her hands folding it, a made thing, pulled together by her hands, so that I could lift it and lay it on the seat as my car pulled me away. Her hand lifted into the air above her cloud of white hair behind me. The smoke of that other city enveloping her, putting it behind me, trying to put it behind me, until I had the words in my mouth again, like a bit, and then the way opened up beneath me, a fissure through which I slipped, down through the bedsheets, no matter how I grasped at them, down through the mattress, down through the floorboards, down, down, down, through the mud and earth and gravel, leaving my snoring husband and my steadily breathing children above, in that better place, until I was floating, once more, along the swiftly flowing current of the Fourth River.

When I rose up, gasping for air, and blinked the water from my eyes, I saw the familiar cavern lit by lanterns that lined the walls, orange fires burning behind smoked glass. And, not far downstream, his shadow stood along the water's edge, a lantern held out over the slug and tow of the current, waiting, as he was always waiting for me, there, in that place beneath the three rivers, there in the Fourth River's tunnel that leads to Smoke City.

It was time again, I understood, to attend to my obligations.

History always exacts a price from those who have climbed out to live in the world above. There is never a way to fully outrun our beginnings. And here was mine, and he was mine here. I smiled, happy to see him again, the sharp bones of his face gold-leafed by the light of his lantern.

He put out his hand to fish me from the river, and pulled me up to stand beside him. "It is good to see you again, wife," he said, and I wrapped my arms around him.

"It is good to smell you again, husband," I said, my face pressed against his thick chest. They are large down here, the men of Smoke City. Their labor makes them into giants.

We walked along the Fourth River's edge, our hands linked between us, until we came to the mouth of the tunnel, where the city tipped into sight below, cupped as it is within the hands of a valley, strung together by the many bridges crossing the rivers that wind 'round its perimeter. The smoke obscured all but the dark mirrored glass of city towers, which gleamed by the light of the mill-fired skies down in the financial district, where the captains sit around long, polished tables throughout the hours and commit their business.

It did not take the fumes long to find me, the scent of the mills and the sweaty, grease-faced laborers, so that when my husband pulled me toward the carriage at the top of the Incline Passage, a moment passed in which my heart flickered like the flame climbing the wick of his lantern. I inhaled sharply, trying to catch my breath. Already what nostalgia for home I possessed had begun to evaporate as I began to remember, to piece together what I had worked so hard to obscure.

I hesitated at the door of the Incline carriage, looking back at the cavern opening, where the Fourth River spilled over the edge, down into the valley, but my husband placed two fingers on my chin and turned my face back up to his. "We must go now," he said, and I nodded at his eyes like chips of coal, his mustached upper lip, the sweat on his brow, as if he were working, even now, as in the mill, among the glowing rolls of steel.

The Incline rattled into gear, and soon we were creaking down the valley wall, rickety-click, the chains lowering us to the bottom, slowly, slowly. I watched out the window as the city grew close and the smoke began to thicken, holding a hand over my mouth and nose. An Incline car on the track opposite passed us, taking a man and a woman up to the Fourth River overlook. She, like me, peered out her window, a hand covering her mouth and nose as they ascended the tracks. We stared at each other, but it was she who first broke our gaze to look up at the opening to the cavern with great expectations, almost a panicked smile on her face, teeth gritted, willing herself upward. She was on her return journey, I could tell. I had worn that face myself. She had spent a long year here, and was glad to be leaving.

They are long here, the years in Smoke City, even though they are finished within the passing of a night.

At the bottom, my husband handed me down from the Incline car, then up again into our carriage, which was waiting by the curb, the horses nickering and snorting in the dark. Then off he sent us, jostling down the cobbled lane, with one flick of his wrist and a strong word.

Down many wide and narrow streets we rode, some mud, some brick, some stone, passing through the long rows of narrow workers' houses, all lined up and lean like soldiers, until we arrived at our own, in the Lost Neighborhood, down in Junction Hollow, where Eliza, the furnace, blocks the view of the river with her black bulk and her belching smoke. They are all female, always. They have unassuming names like Jeanette, Edith, Carrie. All night long, every night, they fill the sky with their fires.

Outside, on the front stoop of our narrow house, my children from the last time were waiting, arms folded over their skinny chests or hanging limply at their sides. When I stepped down from the carriage onto the street, they ran down the stairs, their arms thrown wide, the word "Mother!" spilling from their eager mouths.

They had grown since I'd last seen them. They had grown so much that none of them had retained the names I'd given them at birth. Shauna, the youngest, had become Anis. Alexander was Shoeshine. Paul, the oldest, said to simply call him Ayu. "Quite lovely," I said to Anis. "Very good then," I told Shoeshine. And to Ayu, I said nothing, only nodded, showing the respect due an imagination that had turned so particularly into itself during my absence. He had a glint in his eyes. He reminded me of myself a little, willing to cast off anything we'd been told.

When we went through the door, the scent of boiled cabbage and potatoes filled the front room. They had cooked dinner for me, and quite proudly Anis and Shoeshine took hold of either elbow and led me to the scratched and corner-worn table, where we sat and shared their offering, not saying anything when our eyes met one another's. It was not from shame, our silence, but from an understanding that to express too much joy at my homecoming would be absurd. We knew that soon they would have no names at all, and I would never again see them.

We sipped our potato soup and finely chewed our noodles and cabbage.

Later, after the children had gone to bed, my husband led me up the creaking stairs to our own room, where we made love, fitting into one another on the gritty, soot-stained sheets. Old friends, always. Afterward, his arms wrapped around my sweaty stomach, holding me to him from behind, he said, "I die a little more each time you are away."

I did not reply immediately, but stared out the grimy window at the rooftops across the street. A crow had perched on the sill of the window opposite, casting about for the glint of something, anything, in the dark streets below. It cawed at me, as if it had noticed me staring, and ruffled its feathers. Finally, without turning to my husband, I said, "We all die," and closed my eyes to the night.

The days in the city of my birth are differentiated from the nights by small degrees of shade and color. The streetlamps continue burning during the day, because the sun cannot reach beyond the smoke that moves through the valley like a storm that will never abate. So it always appears to be night, and you can only tell it is day by the sound of shift whistles and church bells ringing the hours, announcing when it is time to return to work or to kneel and pray.

No growing things grew in Smoke City, due to the lack of sunlight. On no stoops or windowsills did a fern or a flower add their shapes and colors to the square and rectangular stone backdrops of the workers' houses. Only fine dusty coatings of soot, in which children drew pictures with the tips of their fingers, and upon which adults would occasionally scrawl strange messages:

Do Not Believe Anything They Tell You.
Your Rewards Await You In Heaven.
It Is Better That Others Possess What I Need But Do Not Understand.

I walked my children down the road, past these cryptic depictions of stick men and women on the sides of houses and words whose meanings I could not fathom, until we came to the gates of the furnace Eliza, whose stacks sent thick plumes of smoke into the air. There, holding the hands of my two youngest, I knelt down in the street to meet their faces. "You must do what you are told," I instructed them, my heart squeezing even as I said the words. "You must work very hard, and never be of trouble to anyone, understand?"

The little ones, Anis and Shoeshine, nodded. They had all been prepared for this day over the short years of their lives. But Ayu, my oldest, narrowed his eyes to a squint and folded his arms over his chest, as if he understood more than I was saying. Those eyes were mine looking back at me, calling me a liar. "Do you understand, Ayu?" I asked him directly, to stop him from making that look. When he refused to answer, I asked, "Paul, do you understand me?" and he looked down at his feet, the head of a flower wilting.

I stood again, took up their small hands again, and lead them to Eliza's gates, the top of which was decorated with a flourish of coiled barbed wire. A small, square window in the door opened as we stood waiting, and a man's eye looked out at us. "Are they ready?" he said.

I nodded.

The window snapped shut, then the gate doors began to separate, widening as they opened. Inside, we could see many people working, sparks flying, carts of coal going back and forth, the rumble of the mill distorting the voices of the workers. The man who had opened the gate window came from around the corner to greet us. He was small, stocky, with oily skin and a round face. He smiled, but I could not manage to be anything but straight-faced and stoic. He held his hands out to the little ones, who went to him, giving him their hands as they'd been instructed, and my heart filled my mouth, suffocating me, so that I fell to my knees and buried my face in my hands.

"Stupid cow," the gateman said, and as soon as I took my hands away to look up, I saw Ayu running away, his feet kicking up dust behind him. "See what you've done?" *Do not look back,* I told Ayu with my mind, hoping he could somehow hear me. *Do not look back or you will be detained here forever.*

Then the gates shut with a metallic bang, and my small ones were gone from me, gone to Eliza.

The first month of my year in the city of my birth passed slowly, painfully, like the aftereffects of a night of drunkenness. For a while I had wondered if Ayu would return to the house at some point, to gather what few possessions he had made or acquired over his short lifetime, but he stayed away, smartly. My husband would have only taken him back to Eliza if he found him. That is the way, what is proper, and my husband here was nothing if not proper.

We made love every night, after he returned from the mill, his arms heavy around my waist, around my shoulders. But something had occurred on the day I'd given up the last ones: my womb had withered, and now refused to take our love and make something from its materials.

Still, we tried. Or I should say, my husband tried. Perhaps that was the reason for my body's reluctance. Whenever his breath fell against my neck, or his mouth on my breasts, I would look out the window and see Eliza's fires scouring the sky across the mountaintops, and what children we may have made, the idea of them, would burn to cinders.

"You do not love me anymore," my husband said one night, in my second month in the city; and though I wanted to, badly, I could not deny this.

I tried to explain. "It is not you, it is not me, it is this place," I told him. "Why don't you come with me, why don't we leave here together?"

"You forget so easily," my husband said, looking down into his mug of cold coffee.

"What?" I said. "What do I forget?"

"You have people there, in the place you would take me."

I looked down into my own mug and did not nod.

"It is what allows you to forget me, to forget our children, our life," said my husband.

"What is?" I asked, looking up again. Rarely did my husband tell me things about myself.

"Your bad memory," said my husband. "It is your blessing."

If my memory were truly as bad as my husband thought, I would not have been returned to the city of my birth. He was incorrect in his judgment. What he should have said was, *Your memory is too strong to accomplish what you desire,* for

I would not have been able to dismiss that. It is true, I wanted nothing more than to eradicate, to be born into a new world without the shackles of longing, and the guilt that embitters longing fulfilled.

But he had said his truth, flawed as it was, and because he had spoken this truth we could no longer look at each other without it hovering between us, a ghost of every child we had ever had together, every child I had taken, as a proper wife and mother, to the gates. They stared at me for him, and I would turn away to cook, clean, mend, to keep the walls of the house together.

Another month passed in this way, and then another. I washed my husband's clothes each day in a tub of scalding water. The skin on my hands began to redden, then to peel away. I began to avoid mirrors. My hair had gone lank and hung about my face like coils of old rope, no matter how I tried to arrange it. I could no longer see my own pupils, for there was no white left in the corners. My eyes had turned dark with coal dust and smoke.

One day a knock at the front door pulled me away from the dinner I was making for my husband's return from another sixteen-hour shift. When I opened the door, a man from the mill, a manager I vaguely recognized, was standing on my stoop. He held a hat against his protruding stomach, as if he had taken it off to recite a pledge or a piece of poetry. "Excuse me," he said, "for interrupting your day. But I come with sad news."

Before he could finish, I knew what he would say. Few reasons exist for a mill manager to visit a worker's wife.

"Your husband," he said, and I could not hear the rest of his words, only saw the images they carried within them: my husband, a slab of meat on the floor of the mill, burned by Eliza. My husband, a slab of meat on the floor of the mill, dragged away to be replaced by another body, another man, so that Eliza could continue her labors.

"You will need time to rest, of course," the manager said. "I'm sure it is quite a shock, but these things happen."

I nodded, dumbly, and stood there, waiting for something.

"We will be in touch, of course," said the manager as he stepped off my stoop back onto the cobbled street.

If I would have had any sense left in me, I would have done what Ayu had done, I would have run away as fast as possible, I would have done what I had done before, a long time ago, when I'd left the first time, with my mother's hand raised in the air above her cloud of white hair, waving behind me.

Instead, I sank down into my husband's chair in the front room and wept. For him, for our children, wept selfishly for myself. What would I do without him? I could feel him all around me, his big body having pressed its shape into the armchair, holding me in its embrace.

Within a week, a mass of suitors arranged themselves in a queue outside my door. They knocked. I answered. One was always waiting to speak to me, big and hulking like my husband had been, a little younger in some cases, a little older in others. Used up men and men in the process of being used. They wanted me to cook, clean, and make love to them. I turned them away, all of them. "No thank you," I said to each knock, glancing over their shoulders to see if the line of suitors had shortened. It stretched down the street and around the corner, no matter how many men I turned away.

There was a shortage of women, one of the suitors finally informed me, trying to make his case as a rational man, to explain himself as suitable for someone like me. There were many men in need of a good wife.

"I am not a good wife," I told him. "You must go to another house of mourning," I told him. "You must find a different wife."

The suitors disappeared then. One by one they began to walk away from the queue they had formed, and for a while my front stoop was empty. I went back to sitting in my husband's chair, grieving.

My memory was bad, he had told me, but he was wrong. My memory kept him walking the halls and the staircase, my memory refused to let go of him completely, as it had refused to let go each time I left. *I die a little more each time you are away,* he had said the first night of my return to the city. Now he was dead, I thought, there would be no more dying. Upon realizing this, I stood up from his chair.

Before I could take a step in any direction of my own choosing, though, a knock arrived at the front door, pulling me toward it. How quickly we resume routine, how quickly we do what is expected: a child cries out, we run to it; something falls in another room, we turn corners to see what has fallen; a knock lands upon a door, we answer.

Outside stood three men, all in dark suits with the gold chains of pocket watches drooping from their pockets. They wore top hats, and long waxed mustaches. They wore round spectacles in thin wire frames. I recognized them for what they were immediately: captains of industry. But what could they be doing here, I wondered, on the front stoop of a widow at a forgettable address in the Lost Neighborhood, down in Junction Hollow.

"Forgive us for intruding," they said. "We do not mean to startle you."

They introduced themselves, each one tipping his hat as he delivered his name: A. W., H. C., R. B. All captains' names are initials. It is their badge of honor.

"We understand," they said, "that you have recently lost your husband."

I nodded, slow and stupid.

"And we understand that you have turned away all the many suitors who have come requesting your hand in marriage," they continued.

I nodded again.

"We are here to inquire as to your plans, madam, for the future," they said, and took their pocket watches out to check the time, to see if the future had arrived yet. "Do you mean to marry again?" they asked. "Do you plan to provide us with more children?"

I shook my head this time, and opened my mouth to ask the purpose of their visit. But before I could form one word, they tapped at my chest with their white-gloved hands.

"Now, now," they said, slipping their watches back into their pockets. "No need for any of that."

Then they took hold of my arms and pushed me back into my house, closing the door behind them.

Within the passing of a night I became sick with their children; within a week, the front of my housedress began to tighten; and within a month, I gave birth: three in all. One by one, their children ripped away from me and grew to the size of the children I had walked to the gates of Eliza.

I did not need to feed them. They grew from the nourishment of my tears and rages. They knew how to walk and talk instinctively, and began to make bargains with one another, trading clothes and toys and whole tracts of land.

Soon their fathers returned to claim them. "Thank you very much," said the captains, as they presented each child with a pocket watch, a pair of white gloves, a top hat. Then they looked at me. "In return for your troubles, we have built you a library."

They swept their arms in wide arcs to the opposite side of the street. Where once a row of houses stood shoulder to shoulder, now a three-story library parked its bulk along the sidewalk. "Where are my neighbors?" I asked. "Where are my friends?"

"We have moved them to another part of the city," said the captains. "Do not worry. We are in the midst of building them their own library at this very moment. We do not take, you see, without giving back."

Then they clapped their hands and curled their index fingers over and over, motioning for their top-hatted, white-gloved children to follow, checking the time on their new pocket watches as they walked toward the financial district.

A dark rumor soon began to circulate throughout the back rooms in pubs and in the common rooms of the libraries of Smoke City. The captains' children were growing faster than their fathers could manage, it was said. The captains themselves, it was said, were having difficulties with their wives, who remained in their stone mansions on top of the mountains ringing the city, above the strata of smoke. One wife had committed suicide and another had snuck out of her mansion in the middle of the night, grew wings, and flew across the ocean to her home country, where her captain had found her many years ago sitting by a river, strumming a stringed instrument and singing a ballad of lost love. Those of us who lived below their homes above the point where the wind blew smoke away from the captains' houses had never seen these women, but we knew they were aching with beauty.

I could see it all now, what lay behind that terrible evening, and the plans the captains' children had been making as they'd left with their fathers, opening the backs of their pocket watches to examine the gears clicking inside, taking them out to hold up to the nonexistent light.

Indeed, the future spread out before me, a horizon appearing where the captains' sons were building machines out of the gears of their pocket watches, and more men lumbered away from the mills every day to sit on porches and frustrate their wives, who did not know how to take care of them while they were in their presence.

A future will always reveal itself, even in places like Smoke City.

But smoke nor soot nor the teeth of gears as they turned what arms once turned, as they ground time to chafe and splinters, could not provide the future I desired. I had seen something else—a long time ago, it seemed now, or a long time to come—and though it came with the price of unshakable memory, I began the journey that would return me to it.

Through the streets I trudged to the Incline platform, where I waited for my car, wearing nothing but my worn-out housedress, my old shoes covered in mud, and the stinking feces of horses. No one looked at me. I was not unnatural.

When the car arrived, I climbed in. And when the car began to lift, rickety-click, I breathed a small sigh. This time, though, as I turned to peer out the back window, my mother was not there, waving her hand in the air. Only the city. Only the city and its rooftops spread out behind me. This time, I was leaving without the cobwebs of the past clinging to me.

On the way up, a car went by in the opposite direction, carrying a woman with her man inside it. I stared at her for a moment, staring at me through her window, a frightened look on her face, before I broke our gaze to look up at the mouth of the Fourth River's cavern, and the water spilling from it.

When the car reached the top, I exited to wander through the lantern-lit cavern, the river beside me, until the walls were bare and no lanterns lit the way any longer, and the roar of the river was in my ears and the dark of the cave filled my eyes.

At some point, I felt the chill of rising water surround me. It trickled over my toes at first, then lifted me off my feet. I began to swim upward, pulling my arms through the current, kicking my legs furiously. Up and up and up I swam, until I opened my eyes to sunlight, blue skies that hurt to look at, yellow bridges, vast hills of green, and somewhere on the other side of this city my husband in this place would be waking up to find I had left him in the middle of the night again. He would wake the children next, the children I would never give over, and together they would walk to the place where I found myself surfacing. They have come across me here before. My husband would take my hand, say, "Early riser," and I would bring his hand to my lips to kiss it.

I gasped, taking the blue air into my lungs, the light into my eyes. The city, the city of my refuge, spread out before me, the rivers on either side of me spangled with light, a fountain spraying into the air, the towers of downtown gleaming. The smoke of that other city was gone now, the fires in that other sky were nowhere on this horizon. The smoke and the fires were in some other world, and I found that I could only weep now, selfishly grateful that it was no longer mine.

Goggles (c. 1910)

Caitlín R. Kiernan

I.

ELEVEN-YEAR OLD SAMUEL is sitting alone at the entrance to the Confluence Park bunkers, huddled against the hot, stinking wind, ruffling his hair even though they've all been forbidden to go alone to the entrance. It's long past midnight, and the dreams have been keeping him awake again. The ruins and the storm-wracked sky outside are less frightening than the dreams—all of them taken together as a whole, or any single one of the dreams. Better he sit and stare out through the gate's iron bars, fairly certain he can be back in his berth before Miss makes her early-morning rounds. He always feels bad whenever he breaks the rules, going against her orders, the dictates that keep them all alive, the children that she tends here in the sanctuary of the winding rat's maze of tunnels. He feels bad, too, that he's figured out a way to pick the padlock on the iron door that has to be opened in order to stare out the bars, and Samuel feels worst of all that he thinks often of picking that lock, too, and disobeying her first and most inviolable rule: never, ever leave the bunker alone. Still, regret and guilt are not enough to keep him in his upper berth, staring at the concrete ceiling pressing down less than a metre above his face.

Outside, the wind screams, and sickly chartreuse lightning flashes and jabs with its forked lightning fingers at the shattered, blackened ruins of the dead city of Cherry Creek, Colorado. Samuel shuts his eyes, and he tries to ignore the afterimages of the flashes swimming about behind his lids. He counts off the seconds on his fingers, counting aloud, though not daring to speak above a whisper—sixteen, seventeen, eighteen full seconds before the thunder reaches him, thunder so loud that it almost seems to rattle deep down in his bones. He divides eighteen by three, as Miss has taught them, and so he knows the strike was about six kilometres from the entrance to the tunnels.

Sam, that's much too close, she would say. *Now, you shut that door and get your butt back downstairs.*

He might be so bold as to reply that at least they didn't have to worry about the dogs and the rats during a squall. But that might be enough to earn him whatever punishment she was in the mood to mete out to someone who'd not only flagrantly broken the rules but then had the unmitigated gall to sass her.

The boy opens his eyes, blinking at the lightening ghosts swirling before them. He stares at his filthy hands a moment, vaguely remembering when he was much younger and his mother was always at him to scrub beneath his nails and behind his ears. When she saw to it he had clean clothes every day, and shoes with laces, shoes without soles worn so thin they may as well be paper. He stares at the ruins and half remembers the city that was, before the War, before men set the sky on fire and seared the world.

Miss tells them it's best not to let one's thoughts dwell on those days. "That time is never coming back," she says. "We have to learn to live in *this* age, if we're going to have any hope of survival."

But all they have—their clothing, beds, dishes, schoolbooks, the dwindling medicinals and foodstuffs—all of it is scavenged remnants of the time before. He knows that. They all know that, even if no one ever says it aloud.

There's another flash of the lightning that is not quite green and not quite yellow. But this time Samuel doesn't close his eyes or bother counting. It's obvious this one's nearer than the last strike. It's obvious it's high time that he shut the inner door, lock it, and slip back through the tunnels to the room where the boys all sleep. Miss always looks in on them about three, and she's ever quick to notice an empty bunk. That's another thing from the world before: her silver pocket watch that she's very, very careful to keep wound. She's said that it belonged to her father who died in the Battle of New Amsterdam in those earliest months of the War. Miss is, Samuel thinks, a woman of many contradictions. She admonishes them when they talk of their old lives, yet, in certain melancholy moods, she will regale them with tales of lost wonders and conveniences, of the sun and stars and of airships, and her kindly father, a physician who went away to tend wounded soldiers and subsequently died in New Amsterdam.

Walking back to his bed as quietly as he can walk, Samuel considers those among his companions who are convinced that Miss isn't sane. Jessamine says that, and the twins—Parthena and Hortence—and also Luther. Sometimes, when Miss has her back to them, they'll draw circles in the air about their ears and roll their eyes and snigger. But Samuel doesn't think she's insane. Just very lonely and sad and scared.

We keep her alive, he thinks. *Because she has all of us to tend to, she's still alive, against her recollections.* He knows of lots of folks who survived the bombardments, and then the burning of the skies and the storms that followed, and whom the feral dogs didn't catch up with, lots of those folks did themselves in, rather than face such a shattered world. Samuel thinks it was their inescapable memories of before that killed them.

He crawls back into bed, and lies on the cool sheets and stares at the ceiling until the dreams come again. In the dreams—which he thinks of as nightmares—there's bright sunshine, green fields, and his mother's blonde hair like spun gold. In his dreams, there's plenty of food and there's laughter, and no lightning whatsoever. There is never lightning, nor is there the oily rain that sizzles when it touches anything metal. He's never told Miss about his dreams. She wouldn't want to hear them, and she'd only frown and make him promise not to dare mention them to the others. Not that he ever has. Not that he ever will. Samuel figures they all have their own good-bad dreams to contend with.

2.

The storm lasts for two days and two nights. Miss reads to them from the Bible, and from *The Life and Strange Surprising Adventures of Robinson Crusoe,* and from Mark Twain. She feeds her filthy, rawboned children the last of the tinned beef and peaches, and Samuel has begun to resign himself to the possibility that this might be the occasion on which they starve before an expedition for more provisions can be mounted.

But the storm ends, and no one starves.

Early the morning after the last peals of thunder, after a meager breakfast—one sardine each and tea so weak that it's hardly more than cups of steaming water—Miss calls them all to the assembly room. They know it was not originally *intended* as an assembly room, but as an armory. The steel cabinets with their guns, grenades, and sabers still line the walls. Only the kegs of black powder and crates of dynamite have been removed. The children line up in two neat rows, boys in front, girls behind them, and she examines them each in their turn, inspecting gaunt faces and bodies, looking closely at their shoes and garments, before choosing the three whom she will send out of the bunker in search of food and other necessaries.

Once, there were older kids to whom this duty fell, but with every passing year there were fewer and fewer of them. Every year, fewer of them survived the necessary trips outside the bunker, and, finally, there were none of them left at all. Finally, none came back. Samuel suspects a brave (or cowardly) few might have actually run away, deciding to take their chances in the wastelands that lie out beyond Cherry Creek, rather than return. However, this is only a suspicion, and he's never spoken of it to anyone else.

The lighter sheets of rain that fall towards the end of the electrical storms are mostly only water, and after an hour or so it will have diluted most of the nitric acid. It'll take that long to hand out the slickers and vulcanized overshoes and gloves, the airtight goggles and respirators, and for Miss to check that every rusty clasp is secure and every fraying cord has been tied as tightly as possible. Samuel imagines, as he always does, that the others are all holding their breath as she makes her choices. There have been too many instances when someone didn't return, or when they returned dying or crippled, which is as good as dead, or worse, here in their bunker in the world after the War. Samuel also imagines he's one of the few who ever *hopes* that he'll be picked. He doesn't know for certain, but he strongly suspects this to be the case.

If volunteers were permitted, he would always volunteer.

"Patrick Henry," says Miss. Patrick Henry Olmstead takes one step forward and stares at the toes of his boots. His hair is either auburn or dirty blond, depending on the light, and his eyes are either hazel green or hazel brown, depending on the light. He's two years younger than Samuel. Or, at least he thinks he might be; a lot of the younger children don't know their ages. Patrick Henry has a keloid scar on his chin, and he's taller than one might expect from his nine years. He's shy, and speaks so softly that it's often necessary to ask him to please speak up and repeat himself.

"Molly," says Miss.

"Please no, Miss," Molly Peterson replies.

"You have good shoes, Molly. Your shoes are the best among the lot."

"I'll let someone else wear my shoes. I won't even ask for them back afterwards. Please choose another, Miss."

Molly is only eight, and her hair is black as coal tar. She's missing the pinkie finger from her left hand, from a run in with the dogs before they found her at the corner of East Bateman and Vulcan Avenue. Before an expedition brought her back to the bunker two years ago. The dogs got her sister, and she's only left the bunker once after her arrival. Molly has nightmares about the dogs, and sometimes she wakes screaming loudly enough that she startles them all from sleep, as her cries echo along the cavernous corridors. Her skin is very pale and freckled. She's small for her age. Samuel fancies if he were to ever court a girl, Molly would do just fine.

"You will go, Molly. Your name has been read, my choice has been made, and we will not have this argument. No one will go in your stead."

Molly only nods and chews at her lower lip.

"You will have eight hours," Miss tells them, just like always. "After eight hours...."

Samuel tunes out her grim and familiar proclamations. No one's ever come back after eight hours, and that's all that matters. The rest, Miss only says to be sure his two companions fully understand the gravity of their situation, and Samuel understands completely. This will be his fifth trip out in just the last year. He's good at scavenging, and Miss knows it. He enjoys entertaining the notion he's the best of them all.

"Eight hours," Miss says again.

"Eight hours, Ma'am," the chosen three repeat in perfect unison, and then she shepherds them away to the room where the outside gear is stored. She gives them each a burlap sack and a Colt revolver and a single .44-calibre bullet; the bunker's munitions cache is running too low to send them off with any more than that single round. She once whispered in his ear, "For yourself, or for one of the dogs. That has to be your decision." He has no idea whether or not she's ever said the same thing to any of the others. He doesn't actually *want* to know, because maybe it's a special acknowledgement of his bravery and approaching manhood, and if it's a jot of wisdom she imparts to one and all, Samuel would be more than a little disappointed.

3.

As almost always, Samuel is given the responsibility of carrying the map. It's a

15-minute topographic map of the Cherry Creek metropolitan area. It's folded and tucked into a watertight leather-and-PVC case, so he can see it, yet there's minimal danger of its getting wet. But Samuel knows exactly where he's going today, even through the dense fog, so he hardly needs the green and white topo sheet, with its black squares marking buildings and all its contour lines designating elevation. He and Patrick Henry and Molly are heading to what's left of the Gesellschaft zur Förderung der Luftschiffahrt's Arapahoe Station dirigible terminal. A few months back, he and two others were rummaging about in one of the airships that crashed when Cherry Creek was hit by the first wave of blowbacks from Tesla's teleforce mechanism. Deck B was still more or less intact, which meant the kitchen was also mostly intact, along with its storerooms. The two boys with him hadn't wanted to enter the crash, so Samuel had climbed alone through a ragged tear in the hull. He spent the better part of an hour picking his way through the crumpled remains of the gondola, always mindful of the hazards posed by rusted beams overhead and the rotting deck boards beneath his feet. But, at last, he found the storeroom, the shelves still weighted down with their wealth of cans and crates of bottles and jars, a surprising number of which hadn't shattered on impact, thanks to having been carefully packed in excelsior.

Samuel had retraced his steps, marking the path with debris placed *just so,* then cajoled his two fellows to follow him back inside. The three of them had returned with enough food to last several weeks, including fruit juice that had not yet spoiled. The discovery had earned Samuel one night of double rations.

"Are you certain we're not lost?" asks Patrick Henry, his already quiet voice muffled by the respirator covering the lower half of his face.

"I don't get lost," Samuel replied, then tossed half a brick against a lamppost. Someone had long ago shattered the globe crowning the post, or, more likely, a lightning storm had taken it out. "I've never gotten lost, not even once."

"Everyone gets lost sometime," says Molly. "Don't be such a braggart." She was so scared that she jumped at the thud of the brick hitting the lamppost.

"Then maybe I'm not everybody."

"Now, you're not even making sense," mutters Molly.

"Are you sure we're going west?" Patrick Henry asks.

Samuel stops and glares back at the younger boy. "Holy hell and horse shit, I wish Miss had let me come alone. Why are you asking me? *You're* the one with the Brunton."

No one—not even Samuel—is ever allowed to carry both the map *and* the Brunton compass. Just in case. Patrick Henry blushes, then digs the compass from the pocket of his overalls.

"Waste our time and take a reading if it'll make you feel better, but we ain't lost."

"Aren't," whispers Molly.

"But we *aren't* lost," Samuel sighs and rolls his eyes behind the smudgy lenses of his old blowtorch goggles

"It won't take long," says Patrick Henry, and so Samuel kicks at the dirt and Molly frets while he squints into the compass' mirror and studies the target, needle, and guide line, finding the azimuth pointing 270° from true north.

"Satisfied?" Samuel asks after a minute or two.

"Well, we're off by—"

"We're *not* lost," Samuel growls, then turns and stalks away, as though he means to leave the other two behind. He never would, but it works, and soon they're trotting along to catch up.

"It's not as though we can see the sun," Molly says, a little out of breath. "It's not as if we can see the mountains."

"I know the way to the station," Samuel tells her. "That's why Miss picked me, because I know the way."

"It pays to be sure."

"Fine, Molly. Now we're sure. Shut up and walk."

"You don't have to be such a bloody, self-righteous snit about it," she tells Samuel.

"Yes he does," sneers Patrick Henry, and Samuel laughs and agrees with him.

The going is slower than usual, mostly due to deep new washouts dividing many of the thoroughfares. Patrick Henry takes a bad tumble in the one bisecting Davies and Milton streets, where the dead city's namesake waterway has jumped its banks and carved a steep ravine. But he doesn't break or even sprain anything, only almost loses the revolver Miss has entrusted to him. Samuel and Molly pull him free of the mud and help him back up to street level, Samuel admonishing him for being such a clumsy fool every step of the way. Patrick Henry doesn't bother to say otherwise. The three sit together a few minutes with Molly, catching their breath and staring upstream at the wreckage that had once been Beeman's Mercantile before the building slid into the washout.

It's afternoon before they reach the airship, and Samuel has begun to worry about getting back before their eight hours are up, before Miss writes them off for dead. Besides, with the dogs on the prowl, he knows from experience that every passing minute decreases their chances of not meeting up with a pack of the mongrels.

"It's enormous," Molly says, gazing up at the crash, her voice tinged with awe. All three were too young to recall the days when the Count von Zeppelin's majestic airships plied the skies by the hundreds. And this was the first time that either Molly or Patrick Henry had actually seen a dirigible, other than a couple of pictures in one of Miss' books.

"It's like a skeleton," says Patrick Henry, and Samuel supposes it is, though the comparison has never before occurred to him. Once, almost a year ago, he'd crawled through the ruins of the late Professor Jeremiah Ogilvy's museum on Kipling Street. He'd seen bones there, or stones in the shape of bones, and Miss had explained to him afterwards that they were the remains of wicked sea monsters that lived before Noah's Flood and that were not permitted room on the Ark (he was polite and didn't ask her why sea creatures had drowned in the deluge). The petrified bones had much the same appearance of the crushed and half-melted steel framework sprawling before them.

Samuel points to the narrow vertical tear in what's left of the gondola. It's black as pitch beyond the tear. "The larder isn't too far in, but it's rough going. So, we'd best—"

"I'm not going in there," declares Patrick Henry, interrupting him.

"Hell's bells you ain't," says Samuel, whirling about to face the other boy.

"Aren't," Molly says so quietly they almost don't hear her. "You *aren't* going in there."

"You shut up, Molly, and yes he most certainly is. I don't care if he's a damned yellow-bellied coward. There ain't no *way* I can carry all the food we need out alone."

"I *won't* go in there, Samuel."

Samuel shoves Patrick Henry with enough force that the younger boy almost loses his balance as falls to the tarmac.

"You will, or I'll kick your sorry ass to Perdition and back again."

"Then you do that, Samuel. 'Cause I *won't* go in, no matter how hard you beat me, and that's all there is to it."

"You slimy, piss-poor whoreson," snarls Samuel between his teeth, and then he knocks Patrick Henry to the ground and gives him a sharp kick in the ribs.

There's a click, and Samuel turns his head to see Molly pointing her Colt at him. With both thumbs, she has drawn back the hammer and cocked the gun, and has her right index finger on the trigger. The barrel gleams faintly in the dingy light of the day. Her hands are trembling, and she's obviously having trouble holding the revolver level.

"You leave him alone, Samuel. Don't you dare kick him again. You step away from him, right this minute."

"Molly, you wouldn't dare," Samuel replies, narrowing his eyes, trying hard to seem as if he's not the least bit afraid, even though his heart's pounding in his chest. No one's ever held a gun on him before.

"Is this the day you want to find out if that's for true, Samuel?" she asks him, and her hands shake a little less.

Samuel turns away from her and stares down at Patrick Henry a moment. The boy's curled into a fetal position, and is cradling the place where the kick landed.

"Fine," says Samuel. "If you're lucky, maybe the dogs will find the both of you. That'd be better than if Miss hears about this, now wouldn't it."

"You just don't hit him no more."

"You just don't hit him *again*," Samuel says, and the act of correcting her makes him feel the smallest bit less scared of the gun. "You might be a slattern, but you don't have to sound like one, Molly Peterson."

Patrick Henry coughs and squeaks out a few unintelligible words from behind his respirator.

"May the dogs find you both," Samuel says, because there aren't many worse ways left to curse someone. He puts his back to the both of them and climbs into the dark gondola. It'll take time for his eyes to adjust, and he leans against a wall and listens to Molly consoling Patrick Henry. Samuel grips the butt of his own Colt, tucked into his waistband.

If I had another bullet, he thinks, but leaves it at that. Miss will take care of them, and oh, how he'll gloat when the coward and the turncoat bitch get what's coming to them. Unless, like he said, the dogs find them first. He thinks, *Molly knows all about the dogs firsthand,* then chuckles softly at his unintentional pun, and begins making his way cautiously, warily, through what's left of the passengers' observation deck.

4.

As has been said, Miss has told all her charges there's no point dwelling on what was, but has been forever lost.

"That time is never coming back," she said, on the occasion Samuel ever asked her about how things were before the War. "We have to learn to live in *this* age, if we're going to have any hope of survival."

"I only want to know *why* it happened," he persisted. "Didn't everyone have everything they wanted, everything they needed? What was there to fight over?"

She smiled a sad sort of smile and tousled his hair. "Some folks had everything they needed, and a lot more besides. You might look up at the dirigibles, or see the brass and silver clockworks, or the steam rails, or go to a great city and wonder at the shining towers. You could do that, Samuel, and imagine the world was good. You could listen to the endless promises of scientists, engineers, and politicians and believe we lived in a Golden Age that would last forever and a day, where all men were free from want. But those men and women were arrogant, and we all swallowed their hubris and made it our own. Ever wonder why folks who never went near a foundry or flew a thopter, people who never even got their hands dirty, used to wear goggles?"

"No," he told her, after trying very hard to figure out why they would have. Admittedly, it didn't make much sense.

"Because wearing goggles made us feel like we were more than onlookers, Samuel. It made us feel like we all had our shoulder to the wheel, that we'd all *earned* what we had. We wanted to believe there *was* finally enough for everyone, and everyone did, indeed, *have* everything they needed."

"But they didn't?"

"No, Samuel, they didn't. Not by half. We didn't talk about Africa, the East Indies, or the colonies elsewhere. They didn't talk about the working conditions in the mines and factories, or the Red Indian reservations, the people who suffered and died so that a few of us could live our lives of plenty. Most of all, though, they didn't talk about how *nothing* lasts forever—not coal, not wood, not oil or peat—and how one nation turns against another when it starts to run out of the resources it needs to power the engines of progress. They didn't tell us about the weapons the Czar and America and Britain, China and Prussia and lots of other countries were building. Our leaders and scholars and journalists didn't talk about these things, Samuel, and very few of the lucky people never bothered to ask why."

"So, we weren't good people?"

She stared at him silently for almost a full minute, and then she said, softly, "We were *people,* Samuel. And that's as good an answer as any I can offer you," she told him, then said they'd talked quite enough and sent him away to bed. He paused outside the room where the boys sleep and looked back. She was still sitting on the concrete bench, and had begun to weep quietly to herself.

5.

Lugging his bulging burlap bag loaded with cans and bottles back through the perilous gauntlet of Deck B, Samuel isn't thinking about the conversation with Miss. The sweat stings his eyes, and his head aches from having bumped it hard against a sagging I-beam. His back aches, too, and he's lost track of time in the darkness of the gondola. He isn't thinking about much at all except getting back before their eight hours have passed, and how many they might have left. He has room to worry about that, and he has energy to fume about Molly Peterson and Patrick Henry Olmstead, the dirty cowards shirking their duty and leaving him to do all the hard work. He takes satisfaction in knowing what Miss will do to them back at the bunker, how they'll go a day and a night without meals, how everyone will be forbidden to speak to them for a week. Miss doesn't tolerate deadbeats and cowards.

Samuel's footsteps and breath are so loud, and he's so lost in thought, that he's almost reached the tear in the hull before he hears the dogs. He eases the burlap bag to the floor and slowly draws the Colt from inside his jeans and his slicker. His hand is sweaty, and feels loose on the gun's stock. All at once, the snarling and barking and low, threatful growls are so loud that the dogs might as well be inside the dirigible with him. He knows better, knows it seems that way because he wasn't listening before. He was breaking another of Miss' rules: never, ever lower your guard. But he had. He'd become distracted, and here was the cost.

"Damn it all," he says, but the words are no more than the phantoms of words riding on a hushed breath. He knows well enough how sharp are the ears of the packs. He puts his back to the wall and edges towards the breach. Samuel knows he should retreat and seal one of the hatchways behind him, then pray the dogs go on about some other business before too long. But Molly and Patrick Henry are out there. He *left* them out there, and all his anger is dissolved by the fierce, hungry noises the dogs are making.

As cautiously as he can, Samuel peers through the tear, and sees that the dogs are wrestling over what's left of his dead companions. The pack is a terrible hodgepodge of timber wolves, coyotes, the descendants of dogs gone feral, and hybrids of all these beasts. In places, their fur has been burned away by the rain, and some are so scarred it's difficult to be sure they are any sort of canine at all. Two of the smaller dogs are wrestling over one of Molly's legs, and a gigantic wolf is worrying at a gaping hole in Patrick Henry's belly. Samuel wants to vomit, but he doesn't. He almost cocks his revolver, but, instead, he drags his eyes away from the sight of the massacre and quietly returns deeper into the bowels of the crashed airship.

I never heard a gunshot, he thinks, wiping at his eyes and pretending that he isn't crying. He's too old and too brave to cry, even at the horror outside the gondola. *I never heard even a single shot, much less two.*

But he knows the dogs are fast, and it's likely as not that neither Molly nor Patrick Henry had time to get a shot off before the animals were on them. Not that it would have made any difference, unless they'd used the guns on themselves. Which is what a clever, clever scavenger does, when a pack finds them. *For yourself, or for one of the dogs. That has to be your decision,* Miss had told him, as she always did. But he'd always understood she *meant* the former, and the second half of her instructions were only an acknowledgment of his choice in the matter.

With the hatch sealed, the corridor is completely black, and Samuel sits down on the cold steel floor. At least he can't hear the dogs any longer. And at least he won't starve, unless he can't find his way back to the storeroom and manage to fumble about in the dark kitchen until he finds a can opener. Not that he dares stay long enough to grow hungrier than he is already. Miss' silver pocket watch is ticking, and for the first time it occurs to Samuel to wonder why she allots the expeditions beyond the bunker only eight hours. Why not nine, or twelve, or fifteen?

Maybe she's not much saner than the men and women who started the War, he thinks, then pushes the thought away. It's easier to dupe himself and credit her with *some* reason or another for the time limit. *Like all those people who never got their hands dirty, but wore goggles,* he thinks, tugging his own pair from off his face. He does it with enough force that the rubber strap breaks. Samuel drops them to the floor, and they clatter noisily in the darkness. Then he sits in the lightless corridor, and he listens to the beat of his heart, and he waits.

For Jimmy Branagh, Myrtil Igaly, Loki Elliot, and for the New Babbage that was.

Peace in Our Time

Garth Nix

THE OLD MAN who had once been the Grand Technomancer, Most Mighty Mechanician, and Highest of the High Artificier Adepts was cutting his roses when he heard the unmistakable *ticktock-tocktock* of a clockwerk velocipede coming down the road. He started in surprise and then turned toward the noise, for the first time in years suddenly reminded that he was not wearing the four-foot-high toque of state, nor the cloak of perforated bronze control cards that had once hung from his shoulders, both of which had made almost anything but the smallest movement impossible.

He didn't miss these impressive clothes, but the old man concluded that because what he heard was definitely a clockwerk velocipede, however un-likely it seemed, and that a velocipede must have a rider, he should perhaps put something on to receive his visitor. Although he was not embarrassed himself, the juxtaposition of a naked man and the sharp pruning shears he held might prove to be a visual distraction, and thus a hindrance to easy communication.

Accordingly, he walked into his humble cottage, and after a moment's consideration, took the white cloth off his kitchen table and draped it around himself, folding it so the pomegranate stain from his breakfast was tucked away under one arm.

When he went back out, the former Grand Technomancer left the shears by the front door. He expected to be back cutting roses quite soon, after he got rid of his unexpected visitor.

The surprise guest was parking her velocipede by the gate to the lower paddock. The Grand Technomancer winced and frowned; the vehicle emitted a piercing shriek that drowned out its underlying clockwerk ticktocking. She had evidently engaged the parking retardation muffler to the mainspring before unlocking the gears, a common mistake made by those unfamiliar with the mechanism and yet another most unwelcome noise to his quiet valley.

After correcting her error, the girl—or more properly a young woman, the old man supposed—climbed down from the control howdah above the single fat drive wheel of the velocipede. She was not wearing any identifiable robes of guild or lodge, and in fact her one-piece garment was made of some kind of scaly blue hide, both the cut and fabric strange to his eyes.

Perhaps even more curiously, the old man's extraordinarily acute hearing could not detect any faint clicking from sandgrain clockwerk, the last and most impressive advance of his colleagues, which had allowed modern technology to actually be implanted in the body, to enhance various aspects of physique and movement. Nor did she have one of the once-popular steam skeletons, as he could see neither the telltale puffs of steam from a radium boiler at back of her head nor the bolt heads of augmented joints poking through at elbow, neck, and knee.

This complete absence of clockwerk enhancement in the young woman surprised the old man, though in truth he was surprised to have any visitor at all.

"Hello!" called out the young woman as she approached the door.

The old man wet his lips in preparation for speech, and, with considerable effort, managed to utter a soft greeting in return. As he did so, he was struck by the thought that he had not spoken aloud for more than ten years.

The woman came up to the door, intent on him, watching for any sign of sudden movement. The man was familiar with that gaze. He had been surrounded by bodyguards for many years, and though their eyes had been looking outward, he saw the same kind of focus in this woman.

It was strange to see that focus in so young a woman, he thought. She couldn't be more than sixteen or seventeen, but there was a calm and somewhat chilling competence in her eyes. Again, he was puzzled by her odd blue garment and lack of insignia. Her short-cropped hair, shaved at the sides, was not a style he could recall ever being fashionable. There were also three short lines tattooed on each side of her neck, the suggestion of ceremonial gills, perhaps, and this did spark some faint remembrance, but he couldn't pin the memory down. A submarine harvesting guild, perhaps—

"You are Ahfred Progressor III, formerly Grand Technomancer, Most Mighty Mechanician, and Highest of the High Artificier Adepts?" asked the woman quite conversationally. She had stopped a few feet away. Her hands were open by her sides, but there was something about that stance that suggested that this was a temporary state and that those same hands usually held weapons and shortly would again.

The old man couldn't see any obvious knives or anything similar but that didn't mean anything. The woman's blue coverall had curious lumps along the forearms and thighs, which could be weapon pockets, though he could see no fasteners. And once again, he could not hear the sound of moving metal, not even the faintest slither of a blade in a sheath.

"Yes," he said scratchily and very slowly. "Ahfred...yes, that is my name. I was Grand Technomancer. Retired, of course."

There was little point in denying his identity. Though he had weight, his face was still much the same as it had been when it had adorned the obverse side of millions of coins, hundreds of thousands of machine-painted official portraits, and at least scores of statues, some of them bronze automata that also replicated his voice.

"Good," said the woman. "Do you live here alone?"

"Yes," replied Ahfred. He had begun to get alarmed. "Who...who are you?"

"We'll get to that," said the young woman easily. "Let's go inside. You first."

Ahfred nodded shakily and went inside. He thought of the shears as he passed the door. Not much of a weapon, but they were sharp and pointed.... He half turned, thinking to pick them up, but the woman had already done so.

"For the roses?" she asked.

Ahfred nodded again. He had been trying to forget things for so long that it was hard to remember anything useful that might help him now.

"Sit down," she instructed. "Not in that chair. That one."

Ahfred changed direction. Some old memories were coming back. Harmless recollections that did not threaten his peace of mind. He remembered that it didn't matter what armchair he took; they all hid the same controls and equipment. The house had been well prepared against assassins and other troubles long ago, but he had not restarted or checked any of the mechanisms after…well, when he had moved in. Ahfred did not choose to recall what had happened and preferred in his own head to consider this place his retirement home, to which he had moved as if in normal circumstances.

Even presuming that the advanced mechanisms no longer functioned, he now had some of the basic weapons at hand, the knives in the sides, the static dart throwers in the arms. The woman need merely stand in the right place.…

She didn't. She stayed in the doorway, and now she did have a weapon in her hand. Or so Ahfred presumed, though again it was not anything he was familiar with. It looked like a ceramic egg and was quite a startling shade of blue. But there was a hole in the end, and it was pointed at him.

"You are to remain completely still, your mouth excepted," said the young woman. "If you move, you will be restrained, at the expense of some quite extraordinary pain. Do you understand?"

"Yes," said Ahfred. There had always been the risk of assassination when he was in office, but he had not thought about it since his retirement. If this woman was an assassin, he was very much puzzled by her origins and motivation. After all, he no longer had any power or influence. He was just a simple gardener, living a simple life in an exceedingly remote and private valley.

"You have confirmed that you are Ahfred Progressor III, the last head of state of the Technocratic Arch-Government," said the woman. "I believe among your many other titles you were also Key-Holder and Elevated Arbiter of the Ultimate Arsenal?"

"Yes," said Ahfred. *What did she mean by "last head of state,"* he wondered. He wet his lips again and added, "Who are you that asks?"

"My name is Ruane," said the woman.

"That does not signify anything to me," said Ahfred, who heard the name as "Rain."

He could feel one of the control studs under his fingers, and if his memory served him correctly, it was for one of the very basic escape sequences. Unlike most of the weapons, it was not clockwerk powered, so it was more likely to have remained operational. Even the chance of its working lent him confidence.

"Indeed, I must ask by what right or authority you invade my home and force my acquiescence to this interrogation. It is most—"

In the middle of his speech, Ahfred reached for a concealed knife on one side of the chair and the escape stud on the right-hand arm,

Something shot out of the egg and splatted on Ahfred's forehead, very like the unwelcome deposit of a bird. He had an instant to crinkle his brow in surprise and puzzlement before an intense wave of agony ran through the bones of his skull and jaw and—most torturously for him—through his sensitive, sensitive ears.

Ahfred screamed. His body tensed in terrible pain. He could not grip the knife, but his fingers mashed the control stud on the chair. It rocked backward suddenly, but the panel that was supposed to open behind him slid only halfway before getting stuck. Ahfred was thrown against it rather than projected down the escape slide. He bounced off, rolled across the floor, and came to rest near the door.

As the pain ebbed, he looked up at Ruane, who had kept her place by the door.

"That was the least of the stings I could have given you," said Ruane "It is only a temporary effect, without any lasting consequence. I have done so to establish that I will ask the questions and that you will answer, without further attempts to derail the proceedings. You may sit in the other chair."

Ahfred slowly got to his feet, his hands on his ears, and walked to the other chair. He sat down carefully and lowered his hands, wincing at the faint ringing sound of the escape panel's four springs, which were still trying to expand to their full length.

"I will continue," said Ruane. "Tell me, apart from you, who had access to the Ultimate Arsenal?"

"There were three keys," said Ahfred. "Two of the three were needed to access the arsenal. I held one. Mosiah Balance V, Mistress of the Controls, had the second. The third was under the control of Kobediah Oscillation X, Distributor of Harm."

"What was in the arsenal?"

Ahfred shifted a little before he remembered and made himself be still.

"There were many things—"

Ruane pointed the weapon.

"All the weapons of the ages," gabbled Ahfred. "Every invention of multiple destruction, clockwerk and otherwise, that had hitherto been devised."

"Had any of these weapons ever been used?"

"Yes. Many of the older ones were deployed in the War of Accretion. Others had been tested, though not actually used, there being no conflict to use them in."

"The War of Accretion was in fact the last such action before the formation of the Arch-Government, twenty-seven years ago," said Ruane. "After that, there was no Rival Nation, no separate political entities to go to war with."

"Yes."

"Was the absence of military conflict something you missed? I believe you served in the desert—in the Mechodromedary Cavalry—during the war, rising from ensign to colonel."

"I did not miss it," replied Ahfred, suppressing a shudder as the memory, so long forgotten, returned. The mechodromedaries had joints that clicked, and the ammunition for their shoulder-mounted multiguns came in bronze links that clattered as they fired, even though their magnetic propulsion was silent. Then there had been explosions, and screaming, and endless shouts. He had been forced to always wear deep earplugs and a sound-deadening spongiform helmet.

"Did Distributor Kebediah miss military conflict? She, too, served in the Accretion War, did she not?"

"Kebediah was a war hero," said Ahfred. "In the Steam Assault Infantry. But I do not believe she missed the war. No."

"Mistress Mosiah, then, was the one who wished to begin some sort of war?"

Ahfred shook his head, then stopped suddenly and gaped fearfully at his interrogator.

"You are permitted to shake your head in negation or nod in the affirmative," said Ruane. "I take it you do not believe Mistress Mosiah was the instigator of the new war?"

"Mosiah was not warlike," said Ahfred. A hint of a smile appeared at the corner of his mouth, quickly banished. "Quite the reverse. Bui I don't understand. May I...may I be permitted to ask a question?"

"Ask."

"To what war do you refer?"

"The war that approximately ten years ago culminated in the deployment of a weapon that killed nearly everyone on Earth and has destroyed all but fragments of the Technocratic civilization. Did it start with some kind of revolt from within?"

Ahfred hesitated a moment too long. Ruane pointed the egg weapon but did not fire. The threat was enough.

"I don't think there was a revolt," said Ahfred. Small beads of sweat were forming in the corners of his eyes and starting to trickle down beside his nose. "It's difficult to remember—I am old, you know…quite old…I don't recall a war, no—"

"But a weapon of multiple destruction *was* used?"

Ahfred stared at her. The sweat was in his eyes now, and he twitched and blinked to try to clear it.

"A weapon was used?" repeated Ruane. She raised the egg.

"Yes," said Ahfred. "I suppose…yes—"

"What was that weapon?"

"Academician Stertour, its inventor, had a most complicated name for it… but we called it the Stopper," said Ahfred very slowly. He was being forced to approach both a memory and a part of his mind that he did not want to recall or even acknowledge might still exist.

"What was the nature and purpose of the Stopper?" asked Ruane.

Ahfred's lower lip trembled, and his hands began to shake.

"The Stopper…the Stopper…was a development of Stertour's sandgrain technology," he said. He could no longer look Ruane in the eyes but instead stared at the floor.

"Continue."

"Stertour came to realize that clockwerk sandgrain artifices could be made to be inimical to other artifices, that it would only be a matter of time before someone…an anarchist or radical…designed and constructed sandgrain warriors that would act against beneficial clockwerk, particularly the clockwerk in augmented humanity…."

Ahfred stopped. Instead of the pale floorboards, he saw writhing bodies, contorted in agony, and smoke billowing from burning cities.

"Go on."

"I cannot," whispered Ahfred. He felt his carefully constructed persona falling apart around himself, all the noises of the greater world coming back to thrust against his ears, as they sought to surge against his brain. His protective circle of silence, the quiet of the roses, all were gone.

"You must," ordered Ruane. "Tell me about the Stopper."

Ahfred looked up at her.

"I don't want…I don't want to remember," he whispered.

"Tell me," ordered Ruane. She raised the egg, and Ahfred remembered the pain in his ears.

"The Stopper was a sandgrain artifice that would hunt and destroy other sandgrain artifices," he said. He did not talk to Ruane, but rather to his own shaking hands. "But it was not wound tightly and would only tick on for minutes, so it could be deployed locally against inimical sandgrain artifices without danger of its...spreading."

"But clearly the Stopper did spread, across the world," said Ruane "How did that happen?"

Ahfred sniffed. A clear fluid ran from one nostril and over his lip,

"There were delivery mechanisms," he whispered. "Older weapons. Clockwerk aerial torpedoes, carded to fly over all significant cities and towns, depositing the Stopper like a fall of dust."

"But why were these torpedoes launched?" asked Ruane. "That is—"

"What?" sniffled Ahfred.

"One of the things that has puzzled us," said Ruane quietly. "Continue."

"What was the question?" asked Ahfred. He couldn't remember what they had been talking about, and there was work to be done in the garden. "My roses, and there is weeding—"

"Why were the aerial torpedoes launched, and who ordered this action?" asked Ruane.

"What?" whispered Ahfred.

Ruane looked at the old man, at his vacant eyes and drooping mouth, and changed her question.

"Two keys were used to open the Ultimate Arsenal," said Ruane. "Whose keys?"

"Oh, I took Mosiah's key while she slept," said Ahfred. "And I had a rapture cylinder of her voice, to play to the lock. It was much easier than I had thought."

"What did you do then?" asked Ruane, as easily as asking for a glass of water from a friend.

Ahfred wiped his nose. He had forgotten the stricture to be still.

"It took all night, but I did it," he said proudly. "I took the sample of the Stopper to the fabrication engine and redesigned it myself. I'm sure Stertour would have been amazed. Rewound, each artifice would last for months, not hours, and I gave it better cilia, so that it might travel so much more easily!"

Ahfred smiled at the thought of his technical triumph, utterly divorcing this pleasure from any other, more troubling, memories.

"From there, the engine made the necessary ammunition to arm the torpedoes. One thousand sixteen silver ellipsoids, containing millions of lovely sandgrain artifices, all of them sliding along the tubes, into the torpedoes, so quietly.... Then it took but a moment to turn the keys...one...two...three... and off they went into the sky—"

"Three keys?" asked Ruane.

"Yes, yes," said Ahfred testily. "Two keys to open the arsenal, three keys to use the weapons, as it has always been."

"So Distributor Kebediah was present?"

Ahfred looked out the doorway, past Ruane. There were many tasks in the garden, all of them requiring long hours of quiet, contemplative work. It would be best if he finished with this visitor quickly, so he could get back to work.

"Not at first," he said. "I had arranged for her to come. A state secret, I said, we must meet in the arsenal, and she came as we had arranged. Old comrades, old friends, she suspected nothing. I had a capture cylinder of her voice, too. I was completely prepared. I just needed her key."

"How did you get it?"

"The Stopper!" cackled Ahfred. He clapped his hands on his knees twice in great satisfaction. "Steam skeleton, sandgrain enhancement, she had it all. I had put the Stopper on her chair...."

Ahfred's face fell, and he folded his hands in his lap.

"It was horribly loud," he whispered. "The sound of the artifices fighting inside her, like animals, clawing and chewing, and her screaming, the boiler when the safety valve blew...it was unbearable, save that I had my helmet...."

He looked around and added, "Where is my helmet? It is loud here, now, all this talking, and your breath, it is like a bellows, all a-huffing and a-puffing—"

Ruane's face had set, hard and cold. When she spoke, her words came out with slow deliberation.

"How was it you were not affected by the Stopper?"

"Me?" asked Ahfred. "Everyone knows I have no clockwerk enhancement. Oh, no, I couldn't stand it, all that ticking inside me, that constant *tick...tick... tick....* It was bad enough around me, oh, yes, much too awful to have it inside."

"Why did you fire the torpedoes?" asked Ruane.

"Tell me who you are and I'll tell you," said Ahfred. "Then you may leave my presence, madam, and I shall return to my work...and my quiet."

"I am an investigator of what you termed the Rival Nation," said Ruane.

"But there is no Rival Nation," said Ahfred. "I remember that. We destroyed you all in the War of Accretion!"

"All here on Earth," said Ruane. The lines on her neck, that Ahfred had thought tattoos, opened to reveal a delicate layering of blue flukes, which shivered in contact with the air before the slits closed again. "You killed my grandparents, my great-uncles and great-aunts, and all my terrestrial kin. But not our future. Not my parents, not those of us in the far beyond, in the living ships. Long we prepared, myself since birth, readying ourselves to come back, to fight, to regain our ancestral lands and seas, to pit the creations of our minds against your clockwerk. But we found not an enemy, but a puzzle, the ruins of a once-great, if misguided, civilization. And in seeking the answer to that puzzle, we have at last found you. *I* have found you."

"Bah!" said Ahfred. His voice grew softer as he went on. "I have no time for puzzles. I shall call my guards, assassin, and you will be...you will be...."

"Why did you fire the torpedoes?" asked Ruane. "Why did you use the Stopper? Why did you destroy your world?"

"The Stopper," said Ahfred. He shook his head, small sideways shakes, hardly moving his neck. "I had to do it. Nothing else would work, and it just kept getting worse and worse, every day—"

"What got worse?"

Ahfred stopped shaking his head and stood bolt upright, eyes staring, his back rigid, hands clapped to his ears. Froth spewed from between his clenched teeth and cascaded from his chin in pink bubbles, stained with blood from his bitten tongue.

"The noise!" he screamed. "The noise! A world of clockwerk, everybody and everything ticking, ticking, ticking, ticking—"

Suddenly the old man's eyes rolled back. His hands fell, but he remained upright for a moment, as if suspended by hidden wires, then fell forward and stretched out headlong on the floor. A gush of bright blood came from his ears before slowing to a trickle.

It was quiet after the Grand Technomancer fell. Ruane could hear her own breathing and the swift pumping of her hearts.

It was a welcome sound, but not enough, not now. She went outside and took a message swift from her pocket, licking the bird to wake it before she sent it aloft. It would bring her companions soon.

In the meantime, she began to whistle an old, old song.

White Fungus

Bruce Sterling

As I was explaining to you last time, I named the boy "Vitruvius." I was younger then, and maybe a little too proud of my architecture degree. It was one of the last, full, cum-laude degrees from a major European university.

After I graduated, the Education Bubble burst. Universities were noble institutions nine hundred years old, but their business model had failed. Their value chain had been delinked. Their unique value proposition was declined by the consumer. Globalization had routed around the Academy.

Maybe you can remember how people used to talk back then. We were impotent in our long emergency, but we were wonderfully glib.

So Petra and I, and baby Vitruvius—"Rufus" for daily use—went home to the Eurocore. The world was in turmoil, but I was young, I was strong, I had training. It was time to make a go of my architectural career.

I wanted to build in the place where I grew up. Our home was not Brussels, or Lille, or Luxembourg, or any of the formal venues in the Eurocore that were legal, historical cities. My home was that nameless locale that my professors called "White Fungus."

White Fungus was the edge-city. Semiregulated, semiprosperous, automobilized expanses of commercial European real estate. Mostly white brick, hence the name. White Fungus had paved the region, while city planners were bored, or distracted, or bought off.

We were natives of White Fungus. After eight years in school, I understood architecture, but White Fungus was what I knew.

There were six huge, civilization-crushing reasons why White Fungus could not survive. First, the energy problems. Second, the weather crisis. Third, the demographics. The elderly people in charge of our law and finance were hiding in gated enclaves. They still had the votes, they held the official positions, but they pottered around in their shabby-genteel misery, terrified by the weird turn the world had taken. They lived in a computer game where they pretended to have incomes, pretended to obey laws, and pretended to lobby nonexistent world governments. We were their children. So we pretended to read their e-mails.

The world financial crisis was world-smashing factor number four. I'd like to explain that financial crisis. Nobody can do that. Let's just say that a nineteenth-century method of mapping value no longer fit the networked reality of the 2020s. Money had tried to cover too much of existence. Money was overstretched, like an abacus that fails to do advanced math. The euro was long gone. Tiny national currencies made no more economic sense than local newspapers.

I tried to explain some of this to Petra, including crisis number five, which was our huge public health crisis, and also world crisis number six, which, frankly, I've forgotten now. Number six was a major issue at the time.

I explained that the lives that our parents had led had no further relevance for us. We were a modern European couple with a child, yet we were beyond help. No "man on horseback" was going to save us. No authority had coherent answers for our woes. I had every piece of music recorded in the past two hundred years inside a backup the size of a match-head. But computers were not sources of wealth for us. Moore's Law had smeared computers around the planet, with silicon cheaper than glass. The poorest people in the world had cell phones: cell phones were the emblems of poverty. So we were badly off. We were worse off than former Communists in 1989 missing their Nomenklatura. We didn't even have the *ability to begin to define* what had gone wrong with our existence.

We would have to architect some other order. Another way of life.

This was not what Petra perceived as our marriage bargain. We were two children of privilege with arty instincts. Our worst problem should have been picking the storage units for last year's couture. We also had a baby, a bold act Petra now regretted.

Our young family's safety and security was supposed to be my responsibility. There were better places in the world than White Fungus; why not flee there, why not rush over and emigrate? Petra could see those cities just by clicking on her screen. London, New York, Barcelona, these ancient cities still existed, they hadn't vaporized. They were, however, visibly panicking as the seas rose at their docks, washing in boats full of the rootless and hopeless.

Petra had a screen; I had a screen; everybody in the world had those screens. Any city that looked like a lifeboat would surely be besieged by émigrés. I knew that. We were safer in White Fungus, where we belonged. There we were humble, nameless, and steeped in massive urban failure, which was our heritage.

The truth was that I was born a regional architect. I wanted to build where I lived, in the locale that had shaped me. The ruins of the unsustainable were the one frontier fully open to the people of my generation. Our great challenge was not the six great bogies that we feared so much. It was our own bewilderment, our learned helplessness.

As things worsened by fits and starts, Petra tossed in her recurring nightmares. She was sure that the lights would go out all over Europe. We would freeze and starve in the dark. We were doomed to a survivalist dystopia, with leather-clad science-fiction savages picking meat off each other's thighbones. I could not convince Petra that there were no savages in our world. In the 2040s, everybody from the Abidjan slums to the Afghan highlands was on the Internet. The planet was saturated, networked from the bottom up like the mycelial threads of white wood rot. So we could access anything, and yet we could solve nothing.

Unfortunately, my brilliant theoretical framing could not assuage her primal fears. Our marriage failed as fully and glumly as our other institutions. Petra left me and the boy. She fled to the south of France. There she became the girlfriend of a French cop. This gendarme couldn't protect her, any more than I could, but his jackboots and body armor made him resemble security.

Rufus and I moved in with my father. That seemed to work for a small while—then my father left us, too. He left us to engage in European politics, which he considered his duty. Sooner or later, my father assured me, our turmoil would return to a coherent European order, with a tax base, a social safety net, designer parking meters, and regulation low-flow green flush toilets. In stark reality, Europe was swiftly becoming a giant half-mafia flea market where even Denmark behaved like Sicily.

In Brussels, the full repertoire of our golden civilization was still sitting there, on paper. All the codes, the civil rights, the human rights, the election rituals, the solidarity, the transparency, the huge regulation. Yet Brussels itself, as a badly overloaded urban entity, was visibly imploding. The surreal emanations from Brussels sailed right over the heads of the population without encountering the least resistance from the fabric of reality.

Despair is a luxury for a single father. I was rich in self-pity, but one fine day, I forgot about that. I had lost so much that the fabric of my new existence had a lively, parametric texture: it was like sand dunes, like foam. Rufus was beginning to walk, to talk. Rufus was never my burden: Rufus was my client. He was my strength.

My goal was to map the structure for his needs.

Food, of course. Young children are very keen on the idea of food. Where to get food? Like most European politicians, my father imagined that European cities were frail, artificial constructions, cordially supported by European yeoman farmers—the sturdy peasantry who pocketed the EU tax grants. This perception was untrue. Except for a few small-town hucksters clowning it up for the food-heritage industry, there were no European peasants. The reality was massive agro-business technicians organized in state-supported conglomerates. They enjoyed regulatory lock-in and vertical monopolies through big-box urban grocery chains.

That system no longer functioned. These apparatchiks were all broke. The rural zones of Europe were, if anything, worse off than the cities, which at least had some inventive options.

Logically, industrial farmers should move into places like White Fungus and industrially farm the lawns. Derelict buildings should be gutted and transformed into hydroponic racks. White Fungus was, in fact, an old agricultural region: it was ancient farmland with tarmac on top of it. So: rip up the parking lots. Plant them.

Naturally, no one in White Fungus wanted this logical solution. Farming was harsh, dull, boring, patient work, and no one was going to pay the locals to farm. So, by the standards of the past, our survival was impossible.

The solution was making the defeat of our hunger look like fun. People gardened in five-minute intervals, by meshing webcams with handsets. A tomato vine ready to pick sent someone an SMS. Game-playing gardeners cashed in their points at local market stalls and restaurants. This scheme was an "architecture of participation." Because the local restaurants were devoid of health and employee regulations, they were easy to start and maintain. Everything was visible on the Net. We used ingenious rating systems.

People keenly resented me for this intervention. My coldly logical scheme was about as popular as Minimalism. I did it anyway. I designed the vertical racks for the outsides of old buildings, I designed the irrigation systems, and I also planted the webcams to deter the hordes of eager fruit thieves. I performed this labor in my "free time," because the need to eat is not a "business model." However, my child was eating fresh produce. All the children were eating. Once other parents grasped this reality, I received some help.

No mere fuel crisis could stop movement on the roads of Europe. The Romany came into their own in these surreal conditions; suddenly, these stateless, agnostic hucksters became the genuine Europeans. The gypsies still looked scary, they were still chiseling us, and they still couldn't be bothered to obey the law. But demographically, there were hordes of them. They roamed the continent in booze-fueled bus caravans, which spat out gaudy mobile marketplaces. The Romany bartered anything that wasn't nailed down. They were saving our lives.

At this point in our epic, Lillian appeared. Yes, Lillian. I must finally talk about her now, although Lillian is an issue I've been avoiding for years. Lillian never seemed like a major issue, even when I tried to make her into one. Still, she was what she was.

Lillian was the first true citizen of the new White Fungus. Lillian was native to White Fungus in the way that Cubism was native to Montparnasse.

Certain people have an ability to personify a place, to become an instantiation of it. There are Cockneys more native to London than a chimney-pot, and Milanese more Milanese than a glassed arcade. Lillian had that quality. She was the White Fungus in its mushroom flesh.

White Fungus never lacked for vagrants, interlopers, and derelicts. We even had a mafia and some amateur terrorists. After all, Europe was suffering six major forms of turmoil. That meant that troubled, evil people shared our daily lives. These wretches were not primitive or ignorant people; they were net-savvy and urban, just like us. So every one of these marauders had some beautiful rhetorical justification. They were "entrepreneurs." They were "community organizers," or "security forces," or even "rescue personnel." The worst of the lot were religious zealots eager to abolish all things "secular." The second-worst were Marxists "critically resisting" something long dead.

Lillian never went in for that behavior. Lillian was a backpacker, a silent drifter. Lillian was "undocumented." She was on the run from something, from someone—her creditors back in the former USA, presumably. Being American, Lillian was from a society that could no longer afford itself. Europe had blown six fuses, but the troubles in the United States of America were as dense as Sanskrit; the Americans had all our troubles, plus several lost wars.

When I pressed the matter—I was impolite that way—Lillian told me that she had grown up in a trailer. Her parents had "home-educated" her, inside some Beatnik tin contraption, randomly rambling the American continent. Lillian had never owned a home, she had not so much as a postal code. Criminals had stolen her identity. When I looked her up on the Net, there were thirteen Lillian J. Andertons, every one of them in debt and most of them on parole. It seems entirely possible that Lillian had somehow restolen her own identity—deliberately vanishing into bureaucratic ineptitude.

When Lillian appeared among us, with her agenda cinched round her waist like a secret money-belt, a new vernacular architecture was already gripping White Fungus.

The region had been designed for cars, of course. Built for portly car-driving suburbanites, people eager to plunge into individual home ownership, into its unsustainability, its eventual chaos.

White Fungus was a developers' mélange of mass-produced skeuomorphic "styles," realized in lath, plaster, wire, glulam, and white brick. Those structures, dependent on climate control, were rapidly peeling and rotting. The structures that survived had permanently opened doors and windows, and had vomited open their contents. Their occupants, deprived of delivery trucks and package services, were hustling permanent garage sales, living from barter. Abandoned buildings were torched by bored teens or ripped apart to tack, bolt, and staple onto the living properties.

This denser, digital-feudal housing was easier to patrol, defend, and heat. Almost everyone was growing marijuana, in the touching illusion that this fast-growing weed had some value. This was the new vernacular look of White Fungus: this tottering Frankenstein make-do patchwork, this open-air Lagos-style junk space.

Lillian looked like that. That was her milieu. An indifferent female vagrant with a backpack, a billed hat, thick rubber boots, multipocketed work jeans and, to top it all, a man's high-visibility jacket in tarnished silver and aviation orange. Never any lipstick, scissored-off hair. Never anxious, never in a hurry. She had no more origin or destination than a stray cat. Asking for nothing, demanding nothing. Commonly she was munching something from a small canvas bag and reading a used paperback book. Lillian had mushroomed among us when no one was looking.

In times of turmoil, people love to talk about their troubles. I still talk about those times, as you can see. That was years ago, and life has become quite different now, but those were my formative times, my heroic times. That's the consolation of a general catastrophe: that misery loves its company so dearly.

Lillian did not want to talk about her troubles, or about anyone's. Lillian wanted to act. Demands for conversation bored her: they sent her out the door, into the street. There she merged into the fabric of the urban. She became unfathomably busy.

Lillian was on a mission: a one-woman rescue of junk space. "Guerrilla urbanist" might describe Lillian, except that I'm flattering myself. In truth, I was the guerrilla urbanist in White Fungus. I like to think my efforts drew her there.

I was very busy, like she was. Once my boy was fed, the boy had to be schooled. White Fungus had a school of course, but it had no budget and its teachers had fled. It sat dark, paralyzed and useless at the end of a long commute.

We had no money for new construction. This meant that the children had to build their own school. Their parents were not particularly public spirited, but they were driven mad by their children's incessant presence underfoot. So these parents commandeered, they squatted, a dead retail box store. We built the new school inside this vast, echoing space.

The school was made of cardboard: a ramifying set of parametric cardboard igloos. An insulated playground. Because there was no educational bureaucracy left, there was no more reason to build a school like a barracks. Let the children wreck their school, paint it, pierce it, kick holes in it; after all, it was cardboard.

My son's school, a playground set of ramifying continua without doors or right angles, was generated out of package-strapping, Velcro, and glue. The structure was a blatant fire hazard, in brutal opposition to a hundred building codes, and it had to be rebuilt every five weeks. This did not matter. The "curriculum" had nothing to do with previous school systems, either.

The school was no monument; as I said, the costs were mostly borne by sweat equity, and that mostly from sweaty little children. Still, it was the first new building in White Fungus that looked like us—like the *new* us, like something novel we ourselves had created, that wasn't a rip-off or a hand-me-down of the old ways. We were poor people with computers, so we had to set our computers to work on the poorest and humblest materials. On recycled paper. On fiberboard. On bundled straw. On recycled plastic, on cellulose glue, on mud, on foam.

On the abject. Machine processing always looked best when applied to the abject. Because the simplicity of the materials made one see the brilliance of the process. And what we could see, we could inhabit.

Because Rufus never wanted to "come home" from his wondrous new playground, I moved in with him. As a resident intellectual, the locals were keen to have me to teach school. I of course had no salary and no pedagogical clue. So I taught the rubrics of assemblage, the complexity of dynamic systems, and the primacy of experience in the philosophy of Charles Sanders Peirce. Those Peirce studies interested the children most. Indeterminate phenomenology was the one issue they couldn't master through Wikipedia in five minutes.

Lillian had no visible interest in children. The school brought Lillian out of hiding because of her silent passion for abandoned buildings. I remember that she owned a thin, shiny hammock made of heat-reflective fabric, some American astronaut toy. The hammock came with anchors. She would dig her rubber boot heels in, climb the junction between two walls—and reach the overhead corners, which are the deadest spaces in architecture. There she would fix her mirror-colored hammock, climb inside it, and vanish.

Whenever Lillian was gone, she was commonly four meters above people's heads, invisibly sleeping. Sometimes I'd see the glow of a solar-battery booklight up there, as she silently paged through the works of Buckminster Fuller.

There was a legendary period in Fuller's life, when Fuller dropped out of society, said nothing for two years, and invented his own conceptual vocabulary. In retrospect, I'm quite sure Lillian had experienced something similar. Fuller, for instance, realized that mankind lives on a globe and not a Euclidean plane. Fuller therefore used to refer to the direction "down" as "in," and "up" as "out." Fuller theorized that walking "instairs" and "outstairs" might help us pilot SpaceShip Earth. In the long run, we got neither Utopia nor Oblivion; we got what we have.

Lillian took some similar approach, but she never spoke about it. Her practice had to do with junk spaces. Useful work could be done in junk spaces, but never within the parameters of reason. Junk space was everywhere in White

Fungus. Traffic islands. Empty elevator shafts. Gaps within walls, gaps between administrative zones and private properties. Debris-strewn alleys. Rafter space. Emergency stairs for demolished buildings. Nameless spaces, unseen, unserviced, and unlit. No economic, social, or political activity ever transpired there. They were just—junked spaces, the voids, the absences in the urban fabric. This is where Lillian existed. This was her homeland.

She was always busy. Living in spaces no organized system could see, she took actions no organized system would take. For instance: if cars become rare or nonexistent, then bicycle lanes should appear. Of course, this rarely happens. Someone has to study the streets with care, find the paint, and perform the work. The administration taxed with such labor no longer exists. Worse, no shame-faced official wants to admit that the cars are truly gone, that a glorious past has collapsed through sucking its own exhaust, and that the present is abject.

Physically, it is quite simple to repaint a street for a horde of bicycles. One small, determined adult could do this useful task in two or three nights. If they asked no permission from anyone. If they demanded no money for doing it. If they carried out that act with cool subterfuge and with crisp graphic precision, so that it looked "official." If they calmly risked any possible arrest and punishment for this illicit act. And if they told no one, ever, about the work they did, or why, or how.

This was what Lillian was doing. At first, I simply couldn't believe it. Of course I noticed her interventions, though most untrained eyes never saw them. I saw the work and I was, I confess, thunderstruck by its tremendous romantic mystery.

Here was this uncanny female creature, diligently operating outside any comprehensible reward system. Lillian was not a public servant, an activist, a political campaigner, a nun devoted to religious service; she wasn't working for money, or ethics, or fame, or to help the community. She wasn't even an artist, least of all a prankster, or a "subversive" of anything in particular. When she dropped sunflower seeds in a dead tree pit, when she replaced and rerouted useless traffic signs, tore out the dead surveillance cameras—she was just… being herself.

Those mushroom spores. Surely that was the strangest part of it. A mushroom pops out overnight, but the mushroom itself is a fruiting body. The network of the mushroom, those tangled mycelial threads, are titanic, silent, invisible things, some of the oldest living beings on Earth. Seeding flowers is one thing—your grandmother might do that, it's warm, it's cuddly, it's "green"—but seeding mushroom spores? Or spreading soil bacteria? To "befriend" the bacteria: who would ever see that? Who on Earth would ever know that you were the friend of microbes?

Well, I would know. Myself. Of course I would learn that, in the way that a man's obsession with a woman makes it necessary for him to know. There's nothing commoner than a lonely man, with his "chivalrous concern," stalking a woman—whether she returns his feelings or not.

They say—well, some sociobiologists say—that every creative work of the male species is a form of courting behavior. I could never make Lillian come to visit me, but, infallibly, I could get her to visit a project.

The projects started small, with the children, who were also small. The new architectural order scarcely looked like order, because it was growing in a different ontological space: not "utilitas, firmitas, and venustas," but massing, structure, and texture. My personal breakthrough came when I began practicing "digital architecture" without any "computers." I was adapting and upgrading the materialist methods of Gaudi and Frei Otto. I don't want to go into that subject in depth, because there are so many learned treatises written about it now. At the time, we were not learning it, we were living it. Learning becomes so tiresome.

Let me simply summarize it as what it was: white fungus. A zeitgeist growing in the shelter of decay. First, it silently ate out the dead substance. When that work was done, it burst up through the topsoil. Then it was everywhere.

Our architecture did not "work." We ourselves were no longer "working," as that enterprise was formerly understood. We were living, and living rather well, once we found the nerve to proclaim that. To manifest our life in our own space and time.

"If we can crack the design of the models necessary to accomplish this, it will propagate virally across the entire world." I didn't say that, but I did hear it.

The Internet—we used to call it a "commons." Yet it was nothing like any earlier commons: in a true commons, people relate directly to one another, convivially, commensally. Whereas when they train themselves, alone, silently, on a screen, manifesting ideas and tools created and stored by others, they do not have to be social beings. They can owe the rest of the human race no bond of allegiance. They can be what Lillian was: truly, radically alone. A frontier wanderer with no map for her territories. Hard, isolated, stoic, and a builder.

Bruce Sterling

She was the worst lover I ever had: worse than you could imagine. To be in her arms was to encounter a woman who had read about the subject and was practicing sexual activity. It was like banging into someone on a sidewalk. Other aspects of our intercourse held more promise, because there were urban practices a single individual could never do within a reasonable time. Exploring, patching, and clearing sewers. Turning swimming pools into aquaculture sumps. Installing park benches and bicycle parks. Erecting observation towers on street corners, steel aeries made of welded rebar where Lillian liked to sit and read, alone.

Lillian was no engineer, she had no fondness for electrical power or moving mechanical parts, but there were urban interventions that required such skills. There, at least, I could be of some service to her.

Inevitably, I could feel her growing distant, or rather, distant from me. "You don't need a woman," she said at last, "you need a nest." That was not a reproach, because, yes, in White Fungus we did need nests. Lonely women were never in short supply.

Lillian appeared at my construction sites less frequently, then not at all. Then her friends.... I wouldn't call them "friends," but they were clearly associates of hers, people who had intuited her aims and who mimicked her activities. Women, mostly. A cocktail party or a knitting bee had more social cohesion than these women. They had no logo, no budget, and no ideology. They were mercilessly focused, like the Rubble Women of postwar Berlin. They were dusty women with shovels and barrows, and with no urge to discuss the matter. They did things to and for the city, in broad daylight. We learned not to fuss about that.

These women were looking after Lillian, it seemed, in the way that they might take in a stray cat. With no thought of reward, no means and no ends. Just to do it, because stray cats are from the street. So Lillian was gone, as she was always gone. Several months passed.

When she at length reappeared, I never saw her. She left me with a basket and a note. "My work here is done," said the note. My second son was inside that basket. Not much need for talk about the subject: he was my futurity, just like my first one.

NONFICTION

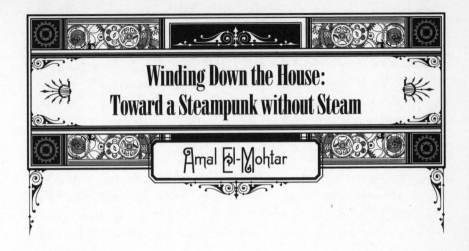

Winding Down the House: Toward a Steampunk without Steam

Amal El-Mohtar

I WANT TO destroy steampunk.

I want to tear it apart and melt it down and recast it. I want to take your bustles and your fob watches and your monocles and grind them to a fine powder, dust some mahogany furniture with it and ask you, *is this steampunk?* And if you say yes, I want to burn the furniture.

Understand, I want to do this out of love. I love what I see at steampunk's core: a desire for the beautiful, for technological wonder, for a wedding of the rational and the marvelous. I see in it a desire for nonspecialized science, for the *mélange* of occultism and scientific rigor, for a time when they were not mutually exclusive categories. But sadly I think we've become so saturated with the outward signs of an aesthetic that we're no longer able to recognize the complex tensions and dynamics that produced it: we're happy to let the clockwork, the brass, the steam stand in for them synecdochically, but have gotten to a point where we've forgotten that they are symbols, not ends in themselves.

Now, I am a huge fan of the long nineteenth century. I am a scholar of the long eighteenth century, which, depending on whom you ask, begins in the seventeenth and overlaps with the nineteenth, because centuries stopped being a hundred years long in the twentieth—which is, of course, still happening, and began in 1914. But the nineteenth century holds a special place in my Lit Major heart. When, about ten years ago, I began to see the locus of the fantasy I read shifting from feudal to Victorian, swapping torches for gas lamps, swords for sword canes, I was delighted. I was excited. There was squee.

I could write about this, I thought. *I could write about how steampunk is our Victorian Medievalism—how our present obsession with bustles and steam engines mirrors Victorian obsessions with Gothic cathedrals and courtly love. I could write about nostalgia, about the aesthetics of historical distance, and geek out!*

And I could. I have, to patient friends. But I'm not going to here, because I think we're past the point of observing what constitutes a steampunk aesthetic, and should be thinking instead of deconstructing its appeal with a view to exploding the subgenre into a million tiny pieces. We should be taking it apart, unwinding it, finding what makes it tick—and not necessarily putting it back together in quite the same way. In fact, maybe we shouldn't put it back together at all.

A case in point: I was recently asked to contribute a story to *Steam-Powered: Lesbian Steampunk Stories*, an anthology that does what it says on the tin. I wrote a story in what, to my mind, would be a steampunky Damascus: a Damascus that was part of a vibrant trading nation in its own right, that would not be colonized by European powers, where women displayed their trades by the patterns of braids and knots in their hair, and where some women were pioneering the art of crafting dream-provoking devices through new gem-cutting techniques.

Once I'd written it, though, I found myself uncertain whether it was steampunk. It didn't look like anything called steampunk that I'd seen. Sure, there were goggles involved in gem-crafting, and sure, copper was a necessary component of the dream-device—but where was the steam? My editor asked the same question, and suggested my problem could be fixed by a liberal application of steamworks to the setting. Who could naysay me if my story had all the trappings of the subgenre?

Syria, you may be aware, is a fairly arid country. There are better things to do with water than make steam.

So to add that detail would have meant acknowledging that steampunk can only occur in Victorian England—that it is bound to a time and a place, without which it must be something else. It would have meant my Damascus would be London with Arabic names tacked on, and that Syria could not participate in the exciting atmosphere of mystifying science that characterized Britain in the same period without developing precisely the same technology. It would mean that the cadence of my characters' speech would need to change.

I changed other things. I gave my protagonist an awareness of world politics. I raised the stakes of the technology she was developing. I tried to make my readers see that the steampunk with which they were familiar was happening somewhere within the bounds of this world, but that I would not be showing it to them, because something more interesting was happening *here*, in Damascus, to a girl who could craft dreams to request but rarely dreamed herself. And my editor liked it, and approved it, and I felt vindicated in answering the question of whether it was steampunk with, *well, why not?*

I submit that the insistence on Victoriana in steampunk is akin to insisting on castles and European dragons in fantasy: limiting, and rather missing the point. It confuses cause and consequence, because it is fantasy that shapes the dragon, not the dragon that shapes the fantasy. I want the cogs and copper to be acknowledged as products, not producers, of steampunk, and to unpack all the possibilities within it.

I want retrofuturism that plays with our assumptions and subverts our expectations, that shows us what was happening in India and Africa while Tesla was coiling wires, and I want it to be called steampunk. I want to see Ibn Battuta offered passage across the Red Sea in a solar-powered flying machine of fourteenth-century invention, and for it to be called steampunk. I want us to think outside the clockwork box, the nineteenth-century box, the Victorian box, the Imperial box. I want to read steampunk where the Occident is figured as the mysterious, slightly primitive space of plot-ridden possibility.

I want steampunk divorced from the necessity of steam.

Eighteen Months Later

This essay originally appeared as a blog post for Tor.com on October 29, 2010. It received dozens of comments, most of which were in excited agreement, but many of which were critical of my stated goal to expand our ideas about what could constitute "steampunk." When the story in question ("To Follow the Waves," which also appears in this volume) was broadcast on *PodCastle* a few months later as part of a special steampunk episode, many listeners chimed in on the forums to say they had enjoyed it—but they didn't think it was steampunk. When I occasionally asked why not, or pointed them toward the essay, they would respond with protests similar to those voiced by Tor.com's readers: that I couldn't just take an established term and personalize it for my purposes. Words have meanings, and I have no business seeking to change them.

I would also sometimes get asked why I was so invested in steampunk, anyway? Why not call what I was doing "gempunk," leave steampunk to its steam in an amorphous Victorian setting while I pursued other things?

The answer is simple: steampunk was popular. Steampunk—at least from 2007 to 2010, in my view—was a very commercially visible, very vibrant site in which these discussions could take place. When grounded in the context of the British Empire of the nineteenth century, steampunk collapsed within itself multiple intersections of marginalization—race, gender, class, disability—which absolutely cried out for new treatment, for examination, for subversion. I wanted my response to those issues in fiction to be called steampunk, to be visible beneath its bronze-handled umbrella; the more reluctant people were to call it so, the more important it became for me. I was trying to participate in a high-profile conversation, and any response that said, "This isn't steampunk" told me I wasn't welcome within it.

I wonder if, now, that's one of the reasons I haven't seen much new literary treatment of steampunk in the last two years—that too many people were reluctant to have that conversation. I remember feeling that, at least where the Internet and convention circuit were concerned, the tide was turning even in late 2010, when writers who had been enthusiastic about steampunk in the year or two before seemed to tire of it and of the conversations people like me wanted to have about it, on Tor.com and elsewhere. *Go write your own things,* seemed the prevailing current, *and stop criticizing what's already there.*

But the latter is absolutely crucial to the former: how can we write new, vibrant things without first examining and then rejecting that which is outworn and problematic? And how can we write our own things, informed by our critiques, when they won't get read as steampunk specifically because they are informed by our critiques?

Revolutions, by definition, come from within. Unless we're willing to take a good hard look at the spirit of steampunk and adapt it to our needs, we'll continue to be bound by its letters, its cogs, its gears isolated from any productive purpose. I feel like steampunk is, at the moment, an antikytheraean mechanism trapped in amber, only able to generate static electricity by means of that which displays it in pleasing sepia tones.

I look forward to seeing it break out.

Steampunk Shapes Our Future

Margaret Killjoy

IF YOU COULD live in any era, when would it be?

If you ask a steampunk, the answer might surprise you. Sure, a lot of us are as aware of the politics of the 1880s as the 1980s, and it's clearly the case that we promote anachronism as a lifestyle. But steampunk is, all told, firmly rooted in the present. Steampunk speaks at least as much to our aspirations for the future as it does to our reverence—and critique—of the past. Retro-futurism is still, at its core, futurism.

It's no coincidence, I would argue, that the genre of steampunk took two decades to grow into a subculture and really take off. Because it's only now that we, as a society, have learned how far back we have to go to start having some hope for our future. Steampunk offers a level-headed (and top-hatted) critique of modernity that is neither blinded by the myth of linear progress nor lost in the romanticization of the pretechnological era.

In the 1980s when steampunk was just fiction, we didn't yet know how completely consumerism and industrialized society had failed us. Most environmental problems were seen as localized or surmountable—people were worried about acid rain, hazardous waste disposal, and the threat of nuclear meltdown. These were and still are all valid concerns, but they pale when held up against the apocalyptic vision that climate change threatens to be today. What's more, most critiques leveled at consumerism two decades ago were on the grounds of homogeny—consumer culture is boring, it limits variety. Mainstream environmentalism was often reduced to "recycle" or even "cut up your six-pack plastic before you throw it out." And although plastic litter is a wildlife-endangering reality, it still simply can't compete with the mass extinction that threatens to strike if we don't mend our ways.

We've always had oil crises, as well. This isn't the first time oil has become scarce. But things are a scale of magnitude more serious now. As late as the 1840s, streets were lit with whale oil, a clearly limited resource. Then we moved to coal (and its derivative kerosene) and now petroleum. Oil production and availability has cycled historically. But it's only in the last decade or so that the realization that oil is a finite resource has become widespread and that indeed our oil production might have already peaked. More recently still, climate-change scientists are finally starting to agree with environmentalists that perhaps fossil fuels are best left in the ground, that carbon is best suited sequestered within the Earth and not out in the atmosphere.

But steampunk isn't doom and gloom. It lacks the hopelessness and nihilism of cyberpunk, its predecessor. Why? Because at the time it was first being written, cyberpunk wasn't retro-futurism, it was simple futurism. It was a more realistic approach than that taken by science fiction historically—now that it is the twenty-first century, we've got almost no spaceships but we sure have plenty of giant corporations, mercenary armies, and subliminal advertisements. But cyberpunk, while it played and continues to play its part in the imagining of the present and future, is locked into a version of the world that takes the scientific progress of the twentieth century for granted. Because of that, cyberpunk is perfect for societal critique but it isn't in a place to offer us much in the way of hope.

Retro-futurism, however, is. Steampunk lets us trace a path back through history to find places of departure that might be more interesting with which to craft a future. Steampunk denies historical determinism—the idea that what has happened is what must have happened, the idea that history progresses linearly and that what is new is more worthy than what is old. To a steampunk, an airplane is not *better* than a zeppelin or even a hot-air balloon—it is simply a different thing. Steampunks don't take the primacy of the internal combustion engine as a foregone conclusion. Steampunks think outside the box because they focus on the age when the box had not yet been built.

Steampunks love technology, it's true. And it is humanity's obsession with technology that has gotten us into this mess in the first place. But what we celebrate in our machinery is entirely different than what the industrialists celebrate in technology. We have no love for economic efficiency. We romanticize an era, perhaps a fictitious one, when individuals and teams built machines with love and attention to detail, sacrificing neither expense nor ornamentation to fill the world with wonders. The assembly line was the wrong direction for us to take, if you ask me—the scale and speed of reproduction are not more important than process. Money is not more important than the mental and physical health of the crafters and workers.

I'm not arguing for a steampunk world. I don't think we need to revel in the steam engine or make everyone become a tinkerer. I sincerely doubt we need to wear eye protection all the time. Colors other than brown are excusable. I don't have a strong opinion one way or the other on anthropomorphic robots, either. But what I *am* suggesting is that steampunks are in a brilliant place to apply their anachronistic skills to the creation of some kind of future worth living in. It's not a steampunk future I'm looking for, as much as suggesting that steampunk-inspired philosophy might be useful for imagining what ought to come.

There's a chance that the airship can become the perfect green form of air travel. A jet is faster, yes. Airplanes are better suited to military use and they're better suited for a fast-paced economy. But I don't see that applicability to war or global capitalism ought to be the determining factors of what technology we promote. An airship, once filled with hydrogen or helium, might never need to be refilled when redesigned with a modern understanding of gas—that its density and therefore lifting power can be changed through heating and cooling. An airship uses a lot less fuel than a jet as well and, because it won't fall from the sky if it stops moving forward, it can make use of alternative sources of energy, such as solar, wind, or biomass. Airships might be safer, too. The most famous airship crash in history, the *Hindenburg,* left only 35 of its 97 riders dead. I'll take those odds over a plane crash any day.

Steampunk culture is also fiercely Do It Yourself and Do It Ourselves. Not only do we celebrate the artisan—a practically revolutionary idea in an age of consumerism—but we expect our artisans to share their skills widely and freely. As science-fiction author Bruce Sterling puts it in "The User's Guide to Steampunk," "If you meet a steampunk craftsman and he or she doesn't want to tell you how he or she creates her stuff, that's a poseur who should be avoided."

But it's here too that steampunks are not simply looking back blindly and promoting values of the nineteenth century. Before the industrial revolution, artisan-craft was an important part of the economy. But it is in the modern world that more people have access to the means of production and tools with which to create a larger variety of things than they have at any other point in our industrialized society. Maker culture, which overlaps profoundly with steampunk, exists to teach people how to craft. Now you can be a dressmaker and a blacksmith both. A computer programmer and an author. You can record an album in your living room and share it with the world before going back to your leatherwork. What steampunks are doing, though, is challenging modernity to really start taking this culture seriously. What would it mean if we slowly gutted and replaced the whole of industrial civilization? Eating local food, working with horizontally created communications infrastructure, traveling a heterogeneous world of wonder? I'm for it.

The twin horrors of contemporary life are ecological crisis and the control of society by economic elites. A steampunk is poised to confront both these problems by scavenging the junkyards of history to find the parts needed to construct something new, something better, something more interesting. And that process of crafting something new is maybe the most interesting thing of all. To quote the situationists of May 1968 France, "In a society that has abolished every kind of adventure the only adventure that remains is to abolish the society."

If I could live at any time in history, I would live right now. Not the 1960s, not the 1880s. I would be living in 2012. The world is changing, for better or for worse, and we get to be part of that. Together, we get to shape history.

From Airships of Imagination
to Feet on the Ground

Jaymee Goh

WE LIVE IN a post-modern era, where everything can be mixed-and-matched; identities can be bought for a price, whether through clothing, or the educational marketplace. People, too, can be mixed-and-matched, traded on the job market, left on the shelf. We work in accordance to deadlines, assignments, quotas, trying to reach productivity levels at ever-increasing rates, just to feed and clothe and shelter ourselves. It is a cruel mix of the Protestant work ethic, bootstrap mythology, and consumerist individualism.

No wonder the clunky, hand-made, strikingly mismatched look and feel of the steampunk aesthetic is such a draw. Steampunk has grown into a large-scale fashion trend, a cosplaying escapist funfair that has no canon to draw upon except in one's own imagination. There is comfort in a creative outlet that doesn't demand accuracy but encourages research into minute detail, that allows us to indulge both in instant gratification through consumerism and the satisfaction of learning a skill to bring a project to fruition. These things are not mutually exclusive; it is simply reflective of the complex, variegated nature of being human.

Thus, despite the outward appearances of steampunk as a fashion trend, it has a potential to be more, much more, and the dress-up and role-playing are simply scratches on the surface of steampunk's potential. By rethinking our relationship to technology, we can reclaim and center marginalized identities, create stronger communities and learn accountability for the actions of our ancestors and ourselves. And we can use steampunk to do all this, if we ask the right questions.

RETHINKING TECHNOLOGY

In steampunk, the most prominent feature is the imaginary technology. At a steampunk event, you'll see any of the following: goggles, glasses with several lenses, prosthetic limbs, canes with ornate wires and tubes and pipes and whatnot, backpack tanks that could be a jet engine or respirator, and guns. Very, very big guns.

The German philosopher Heidegger explored the relationship between humanity and nature extensively in his later writing. In a post on technofantasy and military technology, I paraphrased Steve Garlick's summary of Heidegger's thesis as follows: "in Europe before the 18th century, we largely saw our relationship to nature as one where we adapted to nature, because nature is its own entity, which we're a part of. There came a shift in how we viewed nature: rather than seeing it as it is, something to adapt to, we started seeing it as a resource, and considering ways to make it adapt to us. This was right before the Industrial Revolution. So modern technology, or rather, what we think of as technology, is a reflection of a philosophy in which we see nature as something to be conquered, something to be overcome, something to use. In other words, technology is a manifestation of our relationship to nature."

Today's technology, such as iPhones and computers, have somewhat magical workings for a very short lifespan, or, if you wanted to fix it up, requires specialized knowledge that isn't easily available. One is hard-pressed to see where they begin and end, and are sometimes hailed as space-age, transcendent of crude nature.

The technologies we dream of in steampunk, however, are not like that. The Catastrophone Orchestra and Arts Collective wrote, in *Steampunk Magazine #1*: "steampunk machines are real, breathing, coughing, struggling and rumbling parts of the world. They are not the airy intellectual fairies of algorithmic mathematics but the hulking manifestations of muscle and mind, the progeny of sweat, blood, tears and delusions. The technology of steampunk is natural; it moves, lives, ages and even dies." We can touch these things: we can make them, we can break them down, we can retool them, we can change them, as organically as life changes itself. The body can change itself; the steampunk machine can be modified. At death, the body will transform, into broken down little minerals and dirt; the steampunk machine can be taken apart, its components finding new use in other machines.

It's probably why prop makers like to design their work to look old; it implies a lifespan, and a history. It implies that eventually this thing will fall apart and stop working and will need to be retooled and changed. But moving beyond props, this is a philosophy that acknowledges that even a thing made of steel comes to an end of its purpose. It asks us to consider what technology means to us.

This in turn leads to us asking, what kind of relationship do we want with nature? What do we expect from the sleek cases that intimidate us from exploring their innards, versus the machine that invites us to take it apart and put it back together again? What does life look like when we have a relationship with technology that's not based on consumption? In this day and age of copyrighted technology, where brands create products with parts that aren't interchangeable, it is easy to lose touch with the inner workings of our everyday objects. The film project "Hacking Hope" from Dutch art group Studio Needs Must explores how household machines have become systems that generate more waste because of our consumer culture of convenience. "Hacking Hope" offers us an understanding of these systems that allow us to live more efficiently. What is the point of getting a machine only to replace it when a small part breaks down?

Obviously, these are not specifically steampunk questions. The DIY ethos so prevalent in steampunk is easy to enact because the steampunk aesthetic draws inspiration from any pre-postmodern era where machines were still easily taken apart. (It is also why any far-future steampunk usually still has the appearance of rudimentary technology, "as seen by Victorians" as it were.) These are living skills that people learned as part of growing up, before generations of schools rendered these skills specialized and, in many cases, lower-class. Steampunk DIY, then, evokes a longing within us for technology that we are not beholden to, crying in tragic despair when the motherboard crashes because we forgot to backup our hard drive. It calls into question our consumer relationship, pondering another that has us engaging more with the technologies of our lives.

This is a sentiment that has been around long before steampunk. In her "Musing about Native Steampunk," Monique Poirier considers Native American attitudes towards technology: "NDN technologies have historically tended to be green and sustainable—not because NDN folks are *magically spiritually attached to Mother Earth* but because NDN cultures tend to value foresight and cycles, considering generational consequences of technological adoption and understanding of systems over flat utilization of resources." Is there a way we can relate to nature instead of forcing it to change to suit our desires, so that we can adapt to get the most out of it? Keep in mind that such little projects of using rudimentary technology to better lives is already happening all over the world, in more official capacities: Adlens Ltd. produces and distributes a "universal" eyewear frame with fluid-filled lenses that can be adjusted on the spot. Non-profit organizations are dedicated to getting these kinds of glasses out to areas where optometrists and corrective lenses are expensive. The Amish, famous for being Luddites, often have their own version of technology that enables them to remain "off-grid" as it were, "in the world but not of it"; their embrace of modern technology is slow, to prevent technology from getting the better of them. In the Philippines, the NGO Isang Litrong Liwanag uses the very basic principles of prisms distributing light to create lightbulbs from discarded water bottles. In many neighbourhoods across North America, community gardens bring locals together, helping fill not just physical needs, but psychic ones.

It's a common adage that sometimes the answer to complex problems lies in simple solutions. Similarly, our complex industrialized lives could use some simple hands-on technology. If you took stock of your possessions, what could you fix yourself? What would you have to keep buying? Unfortunately, we are beset by the pressure to consume as much as possible to get our money's worth—what can we produce ourselves instead?

Addressing Ability and Accessibility

The use of the DIY ethos so encouraged in steampunk has applications beyond costuming and props, beyond replicating little Victorian machines and refurbishing vintage gadgets. Steampunk believes in constant improvement; few Makers ever stop fiddling with their work.

Yet the concept of the perfect human body has always dogged us, becoming even more entrenched during the era of scientific progress. Many Western cultures are fixated on this, and aberrations from this ideal are medical conditions that must be treated and "fixed." Going back to our relationship with nature made manifest in our technology, so, too, has our relationship to human bodies changed, and now ruled, by the technology that a culture of consumerist convenience produces. Things must be made easily and cheaply; everything should be standardized; anything that does not fit this standard must be customized at greater cost.

This affects a wide range of people, as there is no such thing as a standard human being, with a standard body, and a standard mental capacity. Yet we live with expectations of bodily averages: you can't be too fat, or too thin. You should be able to walk, or be mobile to some extent, according to the average person's capacity. The reality that many people do not, and cannot, is so disregarded, that laws, such as the American with Disabilities Act (ADA) must be created before it is even a consideration. Even then, loopholes are constantly sought after, just to cut costs.

In steampunk, prosthetic limbs, mechanical appendages, and assorted gadgets already exist as assistive devices, making up for some part of human weakness. Although it's easily read in pulp fiction as a common desire to be stronger, it also offers an alternative way of thinking about the human body—namely, that what is a physical disability is simply only an obstacle because too often, people with no physical problems don't do anything to help people who do have any variety of physical conditions.

Steampunk favours visible technology, and people with physical disabilities can lay claim to that, to raise their own visibility, and assert their right to participate in public spaces without obstacle. Such technology reveals the flaws of an able-bodied society that strives so hard for bodily averages, people with disabilities are ignored at best, killed at worst, simply because mainstream society doesn't want to "accommodate" people with disabilities. Disabled steampunks are already involved across various physical spectrums: witness the accessorized wheelchairs and scooters, the canes and crutches. Any steampunk revolution must be wheelchair-accessible.

In steampunk, con-goers are already mindful of the amount of space taken up by costumes and props; we must extend this mindfulness towards people who require physical space in daily life, not just in costume. If you have a physical disability, how do you want your assistive devices shaped and made? How can we create them so these can be easily repaired? If steampunk DIY places the power of creation and modification in the hands of people, not corporations, then it should also empower those of us who use assistive devices in meaningful ways.

This extends to how we think of other bodies that don't conform to what we consider to be "average" and thus "human." If we lay aside any claims to bodily norms, how does our thinking towards transgender, transsexual, or intersex people change? We must let go of the harmful ideals of what humans should look like, in favour of a society that enables people to just be themselves.

And what of non-evident disabilities, such as mental illness and autism? If we let go of a bodily ideal, how does our perception of what is "neurotypical" or mental health change? Steampunk is a valuable creative outlet for people with mental health issues. However, the mad scientist trope, combining both pathological behaviour and physical disability in a dangerous conflation, remains a popular trope. How do these tropes change with a shift in attitudes towards disability?

Visibility and Representations

Such considerations remind us that treating everyone equally is not treating everyone *the same*. It is thus worthwhile exploring how non-normative bodies are represented in steampunk media, especially media that draws heavily from history. This also applies to racialized peoples, living with histories that are either co-opted, rewritten or erased.

Due to the focus on steam technology (as evidenced by its name), steampunk tends to center around the era that most utilized and developed steam: the nineteenth century, which just so happened to be the height of European conquest and colonialism. As many assume historical distance from the events that set the world on its current course, they feel free to re-imagine the era as a more positive time: of change (capitalism!) and discovery (Darwin!), when visible progress was achieved (the Industrial Revolution!). Because of cultural imperialism, it is difficult to divorce British/Western European supremacy from historical narratives. However, with the rising prominence of antiracist activism, it is not impossible to dream of alternatives. In fact, there are very few reasons why we should not address stereotypes created and perpetuated in the past while refraining from creating new, equally destructive ones.

Unfortunately, too often it is assumed that people who do not have an Anglo cultural/historical background would find no appeal in steampunk. Many people of colour performing non-white steampunk are still told that steampunk must remain rooted in Victoriana, or subscribe to racist stereotypes of the period, to be recognizable. This is untrue and unfair, as it implies that narratives that do not have the same standards of success as the dominant one are not worth as much, and thus not worth owning. Marilyn French wrote in the preface of the first book in her four-volume *From Eve to Dawn*, "I wrote this history because I needed a story to make sense of what I knew of the past and what I saw in the present." Similarly, those of marginalized histories can explore these histories to make sense of the past that led to our present. Doing this can connect us to our heritage and root us in an identity larger than ourselves, if that is what we want.

But where to begin as a non-white person participating in a discourse that either spends too little time fitting in non-white peoples, or tokenizes them? There are many steps to take as people of colour, among them reclamation of the histories that are so rarely spoken of in mainstream media. N. K. Jemisin's story in this anthology, "The Effluent Engine," is a clear example of this, exploring white supremacy and various mechanisms of racism between black people of different shades. It uses steampunk to break away from the narrative of Haiti's dependence on the States and Europe for support.

Paolo Chikiamco's "On Wooden Wings," also in this anthology, infuses steampunk with Filipino history and a story of race relations specific to the region, centering Filipino actors in a genre that often sidelines them. Chikiamco had been working on the reclamation of Filipino heritage before writing "On Wooden Wings," editing *Alternative Alamat*, an anthology that places a modern SFF spin on Filipino myths and legends. Or, further from literature into the realm of the material, we have Massoud Hassani's Mine Kafon, a large ball of sticks shaped like a dandelion head designed to be blown by the wind onto minefields, detonating mines. While not specifically steampunk, Massoud Hassani's project draws directly on his personal history in Afghanistan, and his invention draws direct attention to the effects of U.S. military imperialism in the region and its continued echoes in the present.

There are questions people of colour must ask of themselves as well: do I participate in the auto-exoticism? Am I perpetuating a racial stereotype in my dress, media, and performance? Do I dress to stand out, and how? Or do I dress to blend in, somewhat, while still participating in an extraordinary aesthetic? It is only when people of colour participate fully and honestly in steampunk without holding ourselves back from the common fear of discrimination that we can truly celebrate inclusivity and multiculturalism in steampunk.

However, "multicultural steampunk" has become a new social cachet in many white steampunk circles; it is often code for non-white (or non-Victorian) steampunk imagined through a white gaze. It is also very aesthetic-based, and more to do with play than with engagement. The knowledge gained is rarely connected to the humanity of the people whose culture is being re-imagined, but rather is turned into a commodity item that can be mixed-and-matched at will, while the people whose culture is being explored remain sidelined.

Steampunks must recognize the politics of terms such as "multiculturalism" and "cultural exchange" versus "cultural appropriation," because the power to aestheticize a cultural product that is representative of a culture is not an artistic license, but is granted by a long history of imperialism and cultural domination. It has enormous implications for non-white peoples, who remain "stigmatised, exotified, and patronised, if not subjected to physical violence, for practicing their culture, [while] white people selectively taking on aspects of these cultures often gain a great deal of fame and praise" (Fire Fly, 2012). Individual intention stops mattering in the face of these global trends, but in many conversations between white people and people of colour, this is often where we reach a stand-still, as white people scramble to defend themselves from accusations of racism on a personal level.

This is why multicultural steampunk must move from mere aesthetic into active policies that center non-white steampunks and steampunks of colour, and provide ample opportunity and encouragement to reclaim, retell, re-present their own histories in narratives that will run counter to a world that would rather do violence to them than let them speak. We must move beyond racism as individual acts towards people of colour, and mark how whole societal trends bend towards favouring white people, and people privileged by whiteness must figure out how to confront their complicity without becoming paralysed with guilt. Since cultural appropriation is more than non-white people getting mad that you're using the wrong buttons, what becomes the next step towards acknowledging the act without resorting to self-defensiveness and the insistence of innocence and goodness?

So many histories are ignored to uphold racist systems; every person of colour inherits at least one such history. And these histories are told as if they are separate and irrelevant, rather than interwoven into the larger narrative. Or suppressed so they do not threaten the status quo. We must be able to reconnect with our own histories if we are to be able to truly connect between peoples for solidarity purposes. Where better to do this, than in the spectacle of steampunk? We can claim our place there, and our right to write the next chapter of our stories for ourselves.

CONNECTING ACROSS HISTORY

Steampunk is fascinating for many reasons, among them a curiosity about and love for history. Steampunks find themselves connecting between generations as younger participants outfit themselves with fashions that older people recognize. Depending on your personal history, this can be an occasion of joyous reconnection, or an awkward moment of unfamiliarity and distance. While steampunk is certainly an outlet to create whole worlds from scratch, steampunk is also a communal aesthetic.

We live in a world where corporations and various institutions demand that people pick themselves, their families and their lives up from one end of the country to the other. We are encouraged to be rugged individuals, moving out of our parents' place to form our own nuclear family households. We are encouraged to be prettier, stronger, healthier, and more efficient by buying and consuming various products, as individuals.

Steampunk has already provided people with excuses to get out and meet— witness the conventions and groups that keep popping up all over the Americas, from Sociedad Steampunk Argentina to the Toronto Steampunk Society. Steampunk groups now dot Europe. Whole families get involved. Younger people have access to the knowledge of the past held by the elder generation, and children get to see multigenerational friendships in action.

This calls for us to think about what we produce, and how these products affect our relationships with other people. If we know how to connect intergenerationally between living people, and how to connect with people long faded into history, then we have the tools to connect with future generations. If we can understand how the past has affected us today, then the next logical step is to understand how our actions will affect future generations.

Steampunk differs from other reenactment groups: it is not married to historical accuracy. It is driven by a modern sensibility that has the affluence to wield and understand technology, using technology to comprehend the intergenerational reverberations of actions taken today and in the past. If steampunk can teach us something, perhaps it is to revise our relationship to history. Many of us all over the world have access to information about the past that is assumed to be long-dead. However, the Victorian era is not long-dead; it set in motion an age of colonialism and imperialism that still reverberates today. This is not a history to "get over" as if it existed in a bubble separate from ourselves; it is part of the process that has shaped our modern lives.

ESCAPISM AND ACCOUNTABILITY

Steampunk is fun. In between connecting with many types of people, researching different fields of knowledge, seeing tangible projects come to life, dressing up and reading, there is a whole world of imagination.

However, too often, we decontextualize the knowledge we come across, not out of malice, but out of a self-centered desire for entertainment. We filch and stereotype, we create rules for our world of imagination, and in due process we exclude or re-create problematic representations that continue marginalizing people. Then we cover it up with the excuse of "it's just fiction" or "it's not real," allowing colonial performance to pass under "satire."

Everything that we do in any imagined world is informed by what is in our world. Thus, as much as we would like to celebrate other cultures or ways of being in our play, by insisting on the falseness of our worlds, we often put real problems of institutional prejudice at arm's length and refuse to acknowledge the damage done to living people. We justify it under the spirit of seeking knowledge, and ignore the colonial power dynamics that allow for this kind of intellectual query. We hide behind enlightenment, claiming that anyone who doesn't see beyond the problematic facade just isn't "getting the joke."

This is not limited to steampunk. It is simply more visible because of the subject matters that steampunk deals with: real and lived histories. Even claiming only the aesthetic for separate worlds draws clear lines back to our world. Perhaps steampunk is so compelling because it is an imaginative aesthetic that refuses to give up the real. The best steampunk draws fine lines between the real and the imagined, and uses the familiar to create the extraordinary.

The desire to stay true to the real is sometimes the dig. In conversations about multicultural steampunk regarding cultural appropriation, there are two axioms: "do your research" and "say sorry." They are arguably applicable to most anything to do with marginalized groups, except few have recognized crip-drag as an actual problem. We often assume that doing research and saying sorry are good steps to avoiding flagrant displays of bigotry, that it is enough. But saying "sorry" means someone got hurt in the first place and has to accept the apology.

This is the problem with the axioms: it is not enough, and does nothing to address the underlying systems that allow these prejudices to continue unchecked. For all our love of history, we have yet to connect how our systems of institutionalized bigotry are present in the abuses that living people go through, normalized by the very histories that we play with in steampunk. Some of us must suffer microaggressive blunders that cut deep reminders of our marginalized bodies and must hold our tongues to keep the peace. Others play anticolonials, seeking to right the wrong of long-dead imperialists, but this instils a false sense of comfort that "we" know "better" while ignoring the continued imperialism of today.

We must not be afraid to hold ourselves and our peers accountable for any acts that we recognize as continuing the horrifically normalized legacy of the past. We must have the intellectual courage to confront the idea that we, too, participate in the perpetuation of systemic bigotry today and address it not just while we perform steampunk, but in all aspects of our lives. If we are to steampunk our lives, we must do it beyond play and ornamentation, and translate our skills of making the material into reshaping the immaterial.

STEAMPUNK: REVOLUTION

Steampunk is a very visual and materially oriented subculture. A sentiment I often hear is, "How would you steampunk that?" "That" being anything: how do you steampunk Chinese culture? How do you steampunk your clothes? How do you steampunk your food? (Jury's still out on the last one.) Where do you buy this, how did you modify that, where did the materials to build such-and-such come from…? These are all questions that are common in steampunk spaces. It is easy to imagine, not so easy to enact.

But what does all this have to do with revolution? Historically, revolutions are a replacement of one kind of hierarchy for another kind of hierarchy. So long as any group places a premium on power and hoards resources, there can be no meaningful replacement of hierarchies. Revolutions often happen in too short a time, on too shallow a scale, for everyone to truly benefit from any change in management.

Steampunks have loud ambitions of taking over the world, but our methods of doing so are to toddle around with mostly munitions props and spout the same rhetoric that diminishes the presence of the marginalized from the picture. The strength of steampunk communities do not come from these posturings.

They do not even come from the prettiness of the people. That's all show. The fact that steampunks often exchange money buying each other's products is often a show of support for the community. That's all business.

Steampunks often share time, know-how and resources with each other. This is a community aspect that many comfortable people take for granted as we turn to monetary exchange value to determine our investment in people. It is, however, very much a survival mechanism for various marginalized communities. Without each other, we quickly sink. Isolated in the mainstream, we are marked for death. Sharing to create beauty is an exercise for the privileged, but it is also an action that can be extended above and beyond.

There is value in practical hands-on skills and the benefits of sharing work-space, of being around other people to build and cultivate friendships and community. There is a muted necessity of human contact to acknowledge and take note of one's existence. Some of the arguably most popular people and active groups in steampunk demonstrate this: every fan of Jake von Slatt's Steampunk Workshop site bows to his skills and know-how, but Jake von Slatt remains just a man who decided to share everything he's doing with random people on the Internet. Airship Archon of Columbus, Ohio, is a group that comes together every once in a while to have a "Build Day," which goes beyond a meet-and-greet to bring people together with any current projects to share and get help with. The most radical part of this work, then, is not gaining all this knowledge and spreading it around. Rather, it is the work of gathering the sum of all this knowledge, and remembering it to the many who have been asked, told, even commanded, to forget it all.

There is a reason why the world order of capitalist consumerism constructs systems defined by monetary value, encourages hyper-individualism, consistently distracts us with new must-have technology, rewards bigotry, and punishes critique: beware the peoples who have learned to understand each other, work with one another, share what little they have, and build their own worlds. Beware the peoples who can see beyond props, fashion, performance and rhetoric, and know how to use them all. Beware the peoples keenly aware of how to identify history's repeated cycles. We are not just in our airy-fairy airships of imagination, but in the plumbing and machinery of the world, the urban forests and suburban sprawls.

Some descend, some rise, and beware the peoples who do this together.

CITATIONS AND ACKNOWLEDGEMENTS:

The Catastrophone Orchestra and Arts Collective. "What Then, Is Steampunk? Colonizing the Past so we can Dream the Future." *Steampunk Magazine #1*. March 3, 2007.

Chikiamco, Paolo. "On Wooden Wings." *Philippine Speculative Fiction 6*. Eds. Nikki Alfar and Kate Osias. Kestrel DDM, 2011. *Alternative Alamat*. Ed. Paolo Chikiamco. Rocket Kapre, 2011.

Fire Fly. "What is cultural appropriation." The Long Way Home. 26 February 2012. ARDHRA.WORDPRESS.COM/2012/02/26/WHAT-IS-CULTURAL-APPROPRIATION

French, Marilyn. *From Eve to Dawn: A History of Women in the World*. Feminist Press at CUNY, 2002.

FWD/Forward: Feminists with Disabilities for a way forward. DISABLEDFEMINISTS.COM

Garlick, Steve. "What Is a Man? Heterosexuality and the Technology of Masculinity." *Men and Masculinities* 6:2 (October 2003): 156–172.

Hassani, Massoud. "Mine Kafon." MINEKAFON.BLOGSPOT.CA

Isang Litrong Liwanag (1 Liter of Light.) ISANGLITRONGLIWANAG.ORG

Jemisin, N. K. "The Effluent Engine." *Steam-Powered: Lesbian Steampunk Stories*. Ed. JoSelle Vanderhooft. Torquere Press, 2011. 3–37.

Kurji, Zuleikha. "Adaptive Eyewear: Glimpsing the Obvious." *Science 2.0.* 15 October 2009. WWW.SCIENCE20.COM/AVOCADO039S _ NUMBER/BLOG/ ADAPTIVE _ EYEWEAR _ GLIMPSING _ OBVIOUS _ I

Pho, Diana and Jaymee Goh. "Steampunk: Stylish Subversion and Colonial Chic." *Fashion Talks: Undressing the Power of Style*. Eds. Shira Tarrant and Marjorie Jolles. SUNY Press, September 2012.

Poirier, Monique. "Musing about Native Steampunk." Moniquilliloquies. 19 December 2011. MONIQUILL.TUMBLR.COM/POST/14393053317/MUSING-ABOUT-NATIVE-STEAMPUNK

Studio Needs Must. "Hacking Hope: Consequences of Design." Netherlands, 2011. STUDIONEEDSMUST.COM/INTRO/INDEX.HTML

The Technium. "Amish Hackers." 10 February 2009. WWW.KK.ORG/THETECHNIUM/ARCHIVES/2009/02/AMISH _ HACKERS _ A.PHP

The (R)Evolution of Steampunk

Austin Sirkin

EVERYTHING CHANGES, AND Steampunk is no exception.

Looking in from the outside, it's easy to spot all the trappings that would lead someone to believe that Steampunk is a movement that is made up of people who want to live in the past. After all, Steampunk is full of women in restrictive corsets, men wearing impractical outfits, and outdated technology. None of that has anything to do with the present, right?

In reality, the idea that Steampunks live in the past couldn't be more wrong. The Steampunk movement not only embraces change, but at its heart, the movement embodies change.

When I first became aware of Steampunk as more than just a few novels and films, the year was 2006 and people were just beginning to wear Steampunk costumes. Like so many others, I was immediately taken by the intricacy and beauty of the clothing and props. They were unlike anything I'd ever seen in the costuming world, full of brass and leather and gadgets and gizmos.

Before Steampunk came along, the sort of costuming done at fan conventions like DragonCon or San Diego Comic-Con was movie-replica stuff. The idea was to create a costume that closely matched a character, such as Captain Jack Sparrow or Superman, in order to emulate and embody that character. It's an extremely rigorous, time-consuming activity, and the people who are seriously involved in it are very skilled craftspeople. The problem, though, is that there is no real creativity in it; the designs are already done!

Many of the very first people who jumped to make impressive Steampunk outfits were already members of the costuming community, but had gotten tired of the lack of creativity involved in emulating premade designs. For example, Danny Ashby of Outland Armour, whose work inspired many early Steampunks, got his start making costumes like Spawn or Boba Fett, and Thomas Willeford of Brute Force Leather used to dress up as Thor or Wolverine before his Steampunk work awed millions. In many ways, those first costumers were pioneers. Most of them had never read a Steampunk book in their lives, and were instead drawing on old Scientific Romances from the Victorian era (or often the films based on them) and using a liberal dash of their own imaginations. It was at this time that the airship pirate became a cliché; it was the go-to Steampunk costume and no one really had much of a chance to think of any others.

Steampunk was very misunderstood at that point, not only by the outside, but by the very people who were doing it. After all, those first pioneers in Steampunk costuming weren't considering the social or political ramifications of what they were doing; most of them just wanted to make cool costumes!

However, as the pictures of these costumers began to spread across the Internet, an amazing thing happened: People responded. It was as if a lightbulb (or carbon-filament lamp, if you prefer) suddenly turned on as people began to realize that they, too, could partake in this hobby. No longer would they have to look like any specific actor or character, and as an added bonus, they could even express themselves creatively. The Internet practically exploded with posts and pictures about this new thing, Steampunk.

Many of the people who became involved in Steampunk at that time weren't aware that Steampunk (in other artistic forms) had been around for many years. I frequently cite the television show *The Wild, Wild West* (1965) as the first example of the Steampunk genre, but there were many similar films around that time, including *The Great Race* and *Chitty Chitty Bang Bang*, that also embodied a Steampunk aesthetic. Of course, it wasn't until 1987 that author K. W. Jeter coined the term "Steampunk," but again, most early Steampunks had no idea of that.

As the movement gained more and more popularity, an interesting phenomenon arose: People began arguing about Steampunk on the Internet. What exactly was Steampunk, and what did it mean? It had become popular so quickly that there had been no time to develop an ideology or philosophy, so the movement was suddenly swamped with many people who loved Steampunk yet had no idea what it was or what it was about.

The first theories focused mainly on the Victorian aspect of Steampunk, because that was the most easily-identifiable visual aspect. Clearly, Steampunks love the Victorian era. After all, it was a time of exploration and adventure, when the world was larger and so were the machines. The industrial revolution was changing the world, and mainstream society was convinced that the future held great things. For lack of an alternative theory, many people found themselves agreeing with the simplicity and allure of that explanation.

However, that simply wasn't a broad enough explanation to encompass all of Steampunk and that became clear as the costumes started to move further and further away from historical accuracy. For example, women wearing skimpy outfits made exclusively of strategically-placed belts were hardly something that would have been seen during the Victorian era (at least in public!), and yet there was still something inherently Steampunk about them. How could you capture the essence of Steampunk without wearing a Victorian outfit if Steampunk was primarily about the Victorian era? The answer, of course, was that you couldn't.

It didn't help that the very idea of romanticizing the Victorian era was problematic, because the real Victorian era was a rather harsh place. Not only was it physically very dirty, it was also a time of unapologetic oppression, subjugation, child labor, and colonialism. Many of those things still go on, and it pained early Steampunks to think that they may have in some way been unintentionally endorsing them.

While some of us struggled to come to terms with our own movement, it went right on moving without us. The airship-pirate cliché could only last for so long, and as more and more people got involved with costuming, the very creativity that drew them to Steampunk also drew them on to forge new territory for themselves. Soon we had Steampunk miners, doctors, scientists, soldiers, and every other occupation that could be expressed visually, along with some that couldn't. But it didn't stop there; it spread out even further and began to encompass other forms of media by "Steampunking" them. We had Steampunk *Star Wars*, *Doctor Who*, *Star Trek*, *Ghostbusters*, and many, many more. People were combining their favorite fandoms with Steampunk and turning what used to be simple emulation into unique creations.

It was around this time that it became apparent that Steampunk, as a movement, wasn't really about the past at all, but about the present. The example I started with was of the costumers who wanted more creativity in their work, but there are many different reasons why people come to Steampunk; trying to shoehorn everyone into the same box just isn't feasible or productive or even desirable. Some people come to Steampunk because modern commercial design is extremely minimalist, and they crave more aesthetic variety. Some come because they want to make things with their hands and Steampunk gives them that opportunity. Steampunk resonates with people because of a shared anxiety about technology, and easily understandable machines help people come to terms with their lack of control over our nigh-incomprehensible modern machines.

These are just a small sampling of reasons why people come to Steampunk, and those reasons also include reactions to mass production, planned obsolescence, lack of etiquette, devaluation of education, increased casualization, and many more, but no single one of them describes everyone. Additionally, you may have noticed that although all these issues are unique, none of them have anything to do with the past; they're all things that society is dealing with right here and now in the present. As that realization slowly spread throughout the community, it rocked the Steampunk movement. Everyone breathed a collective sigh of relief that their cool costumes weren't unintentionally glorifying atrocities, but then they realized that if Steampunk is about the present, wouldn't that mean that they had a responsibility to make the present a better place?

Soon Steampunks began trying to do exactly that, and it became commonplace to do everything from raising money for charity to pushing for greater acceptance of all races and genders both inside and outside the movement. Miriam Rosenberg Rocek, who is also known as Steampunk Emma Goldman, performs at political rallies, petitioning for women's rights, among other things, and Noam Berg, a musician known as Painless Parker, writes and plays songs that are against class-based discrimination. Once a few brave and vocal individuals started spreading these messages, the waves rippled outward in an ever-increasing radius, drawing more and more people who were already socially active into the movement. Now nearly every Steampunk convention in America holds fund-raisers for the charities that they support, such as Atlanta's AnachroCon with Reading Is Fundamental, or New Jersey's Steampunk World's Fair with the Leukemia and Lymphoma Society. Some conventions even host discussions about how to use Steampunk to enact social change. It's clear that a pattern had emerged that showed Steampunk changing from a simple aesthetic toward a primarily liberal, socially progressive movement that's working to create a better world.

This may seem like it was a fairly straightforward and logical progression, but as is always the case with change, it doesn't happen everywhere simultaneously. This story starts with the costumers because costuming is where the genre or aesthetic of Steampunk transitioned into a full-fledged movement. Of course people around the world had been making Steampunk art, sculptures, and novels for years by the time the costumers really got involved with the scene, but those early artists and writers had mostly languished in obscurity until Steampunk made the leap into costuming. The very nature of costuming as a participatory activity was what most helped it take off, because people could see themselves in those outfits.

The books, comics, and movies that are considered Steampunk are an entirely different phenomenon than the costuming, and part of what makes them different is exactly what makes most Steampunks so socially conscious. Books and movies tell a complete story—context already included—but costumes have no inherent context other than the real world in which they are worn. In book or movie form, that context is what provides the relief from reality that many call escapism. Due to a lack of a Steampunk "canon" for people to emulate, everyone who participates in Steampunk costuming has to create his or her own personal context. With no shared space of interaction, all of us have to participate in the real world rather than in a fantasy world of our own imagining. That's why Steampunk is expression rather than escape, and once people are participating in the real world, it's only a short step to addressing real-world issues.

Steampunk is more than just a bunch of people running around in strange clothes; it's a part of the extensive dialogue between this generation and its accompanying mainstream culture. It represents all the problems in modern societies not just in America but around the world, and it's a way of acting out and telling everyone in a very visual way that we want more than what we've been given. We're the disillusioned and the dissatisfied, and Steampunk is our revolution.

Acknowledgments

Ann VanderMeer

I'd like to thank the following editors, writers, and creators who shared their work with me, inspired me, and/or pointed me in the right direction: Margaret Killjoy, Jess Nevins, Selena Chambers, Rosemary Lim, Maisarah Bte Abu Samah, JoSelle Vanderhooft, Scott Andrews, Zachary Ricks, Bart Leib, Phillip E. Carroll, Kelly Link, Gavin Grant, James Carrott, Byrd MacDonald, Diana Pho, Emma Goldman, Sean Wallace, Stephen Segal, Paula Guran, Liz Gorinsky and John Coulthart. In addition, many thanks to Tessa Kum, Dominik Parisien, and Alan Swirsky for continuing on as editorial assistants on various projects. And of course to my husband, Jeff VanderMeer, who inspires me in so many ways each and every day.

Contributor Biographies

Christopher Barzak grew up in rural Ohio, went to university in a decaying postindustrial city in Ohio, and has lived in a Southern California beach town, the capital of Michigan, and in the suburbs of Tokyo, Japan. His stories have appeared in a many venues, including *Nerve*, *The Year's Best Fantasy and Horror*, *Interfictions*, *Asimov's*, and *Lady Churchill's Rosebud Wristlet*. His first novel, *One for Sorrow*, won the Crawford Award. His second book, *The Love We Share Without Knowing* was a finalist for the Nebula Award for Best Novel and the James Tiptree Jr. Award. He is the coeditor of *Interfictions 2* and has done Japanese-English translation on *Kant: For Eternal Peace*, a peace theory book published in Japan for Japanese teens. Forthcoming in August 2012, his story collection *Birds and Birthdays* will be published by Aqueduct Press. Currently he lives in Youngstown, Ohio, where he teaches fiction writing in the Northeast Ohio MFA program at Youngstown State University.

Paolo Chikiamco runs Rocket Kapre (WWW.ROCKETKAPRE.COM), an imprint and blog dedicated to publishing, facilitating, and promoting works of the fantastic (in prose and comics) by Filipino authors. Once an associate at a top Philippine law firm, he came to realize that although fact is often stranger than fiction, it's not quite as creatively fulfilling. He is the editor of *Usok* and *Alternative Alamat*, and his fiction has been published in such venues as *Scheherazade's Façade*, *Philippine Genre Stories*, and the *Philippine*

Speculative Fiction series. He is also the writer of *High Society*, the first in a series of steampunk comics set in the same world as "On Wooden Wings."

Amal El-Mohtar is an Ottawa-born Lebanese-Canadian, currently pursuing a Ph.D. in the UK. She is a Nebula Award nominee and a two-time winner of the Rhysling Award for Best Short Poem as well as the author of *The Honey Month*, a collection of poetry and prose written to the taste of twenty-eight different kinds of honey. Her fiction and poems have appeared in multiple venues online and in print, including *Strange Horizons*, *Apex*, *The Thackery T. Lambshead Cabinet of Curiosities*, *Welcome to Bordertown*, *Stone Telling*, and *Mythic Delirium*. She also edits *Goblin Fruit*, an online quarterly dedicated to fantastical poetry. You can find her online at AMALELMOHTAR.COM.

Jeffrey Ford is the author of the novels *The Physiognomy*, *Memoranda*, *The Beyond*, *The Portrait of Mrs. Charbuque*, *The Girl in the Glass*, *The Cosmology of the Wider World*, and *The Shadow Year*. His story collections are *The Fantasy Writer's Assistant*, *The Empire of Ice Cream*, and *The Drowned Life*. Ford's fiction has been widely translated around the world and is the recipient of the Edgar Allan Poe, Shirley Jackson, Nebula, and World Fantasy awards, and the Grand Prix de l'Imaginaire. His latest collection, *Crackpot Palace*, will be published in August 2012 by Morrow/Harper Collins.

Jaymee Goh is the steampunk postcolonialist of Silver Goggles (SILVER-GOGGLES.BLOGSPOT.COM). Her work engages with historicity, identity, cultural appropriation, imperialism, and neocolonialism in steampunk. She graduated from McMaster University with an M.A. in Cultural Studies and Critical Theory, having written a thesis on the application of postcolonial theory to steampunk. She has written on racialized steampunk for the *WisCon Chronicles* (Aqueduct Press, 2011 and 2012), and contributed to Tor.com, Racialicious.com, the Apex Book Company Blog, Beyond Victoriana.com, and *Steampunk II: Reloaded* (Tachyon Publications, 2010). Her fiction has been published in *Expanded Horizons*, *Crossed Genres*, and *Steam-Powered 2: More Lesbian Steampunk Stories*.

Lev Grossman is the author of four novels, including the *New York Times* bestsellers *The Magicians* and *The Magician King*; NPR called *The Magician*

King "triumphant." He is the book critic for *TIME* magazine, and his journalism has appeared in the *Times*, the *Believer*, the *Wall Street Journal*, *Salon*, *Wired*, and the *Village Voice*. He also makes frequent appearances on NPR. In 2011 Grossman won the John W. Campbell Award for Best New Writer from the World Science Fiction Society. His alignment is chaotic good.

Samantha Henderson lives in Covina, California, by way of England, South Africa, Illinois, and Oregon. Her short fiction and poetry have been published in *Realms of Fantasy*, *Strange Horizons*, *Goblin Fruit*, and *Weird Tales*; the anthologies *Running with the Pack* and *Fantasy*; and reprinted in *The Year's Best Fantasy and Science Fiction*, *Steampunk II: Steampunk Reloaded*, and the *Mammoth Book of Steampunk*. She is the co-winner of the 2010 Rhysling Award for speculative poetry and is the author of the Forgotten Realms novel *Dawnbringer*.

Leow Hui Min Annabeth is a Southeast Asian student with an interest in postcoloniality and feminism. She currently holds a diploma in maths and science, which is admittedly rather odd for a literature-loving girl who never got the hang of integral calculus, but the more you know.... Her essays have been published in *Transformative Works and Cultures*, *Bitch*, and *POSKOD. SG*, and her fiction has appeared in *Quarterly Literary Review Singapore* and *Crossed Genres*, among other places. Things she does not like include cultural imperialism, crushed dreams, and tea with non-non-dairy creamer.

N. K. Jemisin is a Brooklyn author whose short fiction and novels have been nominated for the Hugo and the Nebula, shortlisted for the Crawford and the Tiptree, and have won the Locus Award for Best First Novel. Her speculative works range from fantasy to science fiction to the undefinable; her themes include the intersections of race and gender, resistance to oppression, and the coolness of Stuff Blowing Up. She is a member of the Altered Fluid writing group and a graduate of the Viable Paradise writing workshop. Her latest novel, *The Killing Moon*, will be published in May 2012 from Orbit Books. Her website is NKJEMISIN.COM.

Morgan Johnson has been pretending to be a giant squid on the Internet for twelve years. He is a cofounder of *Poor Mojo's Almanac(k)* with David Erik

Nelson and Fritz Swanson and blogs at NEWSWIRE.POORMOJO.ORG. He lives in Oakland, California.

Caitlín R. Kiernan is the author of several novels, including *Low Red Moon*, *Daughter of Hounds*, and *The Red Tree*, which was nominated for the Shirley Jackson and World Fantasy awards. Most recently, her seventh novel, *The Drowning Girl: A Memoir*, was published by Penguin. Since 2000, her shorter tales of the weird, fantastic, and macabre have been collected in several volumes, including *Tales of Pain and Wonder*; *From Weird and Distant Shores*; *To Charles Fort, With Love*; *Alabaster*; *A Is for Alien*; *The Ammonite Violin & Others*; and *Confessions of a Five-Chambered Heart*. In 2011, Subterranean Press released a retrospective of her early writing, *Two Worlds and In Between: The Best of Caitlín R. Kiernan (Volume One)*. She lives in Providence, Rhode Island, with her partner, Kathryn.

Malissa Kent grew up listening to her father's stories about heart surgeries (he was a nurse in the heart center at a nearby hospital). And though she carried a pacemaker in her purse as a teenager (just because), this is her first story about hearts. When she's not injecting Steampunk or Fantastic elements into French history, she's planning her next trip to France, where she lived for three years. She studied Creative Writing and French at Knox College and earned her M.F.A. in Creative Writing at Stonecoast. She lives in Seattle and is currently putting the finishing touches on her epic Fantasy novel. This is her first publication.

Margaret Killjoy is a nomadic author, editor, anarchist, and activist. He is the founder and current editor of *SteamPunk Magazine* as well as the author of *A Steampunk's Guide to the Apocalypse*, the Choose-Your-Own-Adventure book *What Lies Beneath the Clock Tower*, and *Mythmakers & Lawbreakers: Anarchist Writers on Fiction*. He publishes with the zine-publishing group Strangers in a Tangled Wilderness as well as the collectively run genre-fiction publisher Combustion Books. He speaks and writes about the social significance of fiction and the rich political history of Steampunk as a genre and an emerging culture.

Andrew Knighton lives and occasionally writes in Stockport, England, where the gray skies provide a good motive to stay inside at the word processor. When not working in his standard-issue office job, he battles the slugs threatening to overrun his garden and the monsters lurking in the woods. He's had more than thirty stories published in such places as *Murky Depths*, *Redstone SF*, and *Steampunk II: Steampunk Reloaded*. He occasionally scrawls down thoughts about his latest stories at ANDREWKNIGHTON.WORDPRESS.COM. "Urban Drift" was inspired by nineteenth-century Chicago, where the buildings really did move, and a review of a comic, because Andrew will take inspiration anywhere he can.

Nick Mamatas is the author of several novels, including *Sensation* and *Bullet-time*, and of more than eighty short stories. His work has appeared in periodicals including *Asimov's Science Fiction*, Tor.com, *Weird Tales*, *New Haven Review*, and *subTERRAIN* and in such anthologies as *The Mammoth Book of Steampunk*, *Long Island Noir*, and *Lovecraft Unbound*. His reportage and essays on radical politics and literature have appeared in *Clamor*, *Village Voice*, *In These Times*, *The New Humanist*, *H+*, and the anthologies *You Are Being Lied To* and *Everything You Know Is Wrong*. His editorial work and fiction have been nominated for the Hugo, World Fantasy, Bram Stoker, International Horror Guild, and Shirley Jackson awards and for the Kurd Lasswitz Prize.

David Erik Nelson is a freelance writer and author of the geeky DIY book *Snip, Burn, Solder, Shred*. His steampunky fiction has appeared in *Shimmer*, *Asimov's*, and *Steampunk II: Steampunk Reloaded*. Kindle and other digital editions of his celebrated steampunk novella "Tucker Teaches the Clockies to Copulate" are now available online. Find him at DAVIDERIKNELSON.COM or on Twitter as SquiDaveo.

Garth Nix is a bestselling Australian writer best known for his young adult fantasy novels. His books include the award-winning novels *Sabriel*, *Lirael*, *Abhorsen*, *Shades Children*, and *Lord Sunday*. He has also written for RPGs and magazines and journals. His latest book is *A Confusion of Princes*, a YA space opera.

Ben Peek is the critically acclaimed and controversial author of *Twenty-Six Lies/One Truth*, *Black Sheep*, and half the author of *Above/Below*. His collection *Dead Americans* will be published in early 2013. Currently, he lives in Sydney with a living American, a cat, and books that he and his partner organize based on the year the author was born. He keeps a low-fi blog at BENPEEK. LIVEJOURNAL.COM.

Cherie Priest is the author of a dozen novels, including the steampunk pulp adventures *Ganymede, Dreadnought, Clementine,* and *Boneshaker. Boneshaker* was nominated for the Hugo Award and the Nebula Award; it was a PNBA Award winner and winner of the Locus Award for Best Science Fiction Novel. Cherie also wrote *Bloodshot* and *Hellbent* from Bantam Spectra; *Fathom* and the Eden Moore series from Tor; and three novellas published by Subterranean Press. In addition to all the above, her first foray into George R. R. Martin's superhero universe, *Fort Freak* (for which she wrote the interstitial mystery), debuted in the summer of 2011. Cherie's short stories and nonfiction articles have appeared in such fine publications as *Weird Tales, Publishers Weekly,* and numerous anthologies.

Margaret Ronald is the author of *Spiral Hunt, Wild Hunt,* and *Soul Hunt* as well as a number of short stories. Most of her steampunk work is available at *Beneath Ceaseless Skies.* Originally from rural Indiana, she now lives outside Boston.

Christopher Rowe has published a couple of dozen stories and been a finalist for the Hugo, Nebula, World Fantasy, and Theodore Sturgeon awards. His work has been frequently reprinted, translated into a half-dozen languages around the world, and praised by the *New York Times Book Review.* His story "Another Word for Map Is Faith" made the long list in the *Best American Short Stories 2007* volume, and his early fiction was collected in a chapbook, *Bittersweet Creek and Other Stories,* by Small Beer Press. A Forgotten Realms novel, *Sandstorm,* was published in 2011 by Wizards of the Coast, and he is hard at work on a new novel, *Sarah Across America,* about maps and megafauna. He is currently pursuing an M.F.A. in Creative Writing at the Bluegrass Writers Studio of Eastern Kentucky University and lives in a hundred-year-old house in Lexington, Kentucky, with his wife, Gwenda Bond, and several pets.

Vandana Singh teaches physics at a state university near Boston and writes in her nonexistent spare time. She was born and raised in the city of Dilli (aka Delhi, India), where medieval ruins lie strewn among modern-day edifices. Her work has been published in numerous magazines and anthologies and has frequently been reprinted in Year's Best publications. She is a winner of the Carl Brandon Parallax Award. Her most recent publication is a story for *Lightspeed* magazine.

Austin Sirkin has traveled to the present from the future, and in that future he participated in a movement called "iPunk," wherein people would scrape off the intricate detailing on their technological devices to make everything look sleek and smooth. Upon arriving in the past, Austin was dismayed to discover that his iPunk made him fit in and that he was no longer "cool," so he reluctantly became a Steampunk. This has given him a unique perspective on Steampunk and life in general.

Bruce Sterling is the bestselling author of novels including *Heavy Weather*, *Involution Ocean*, *The Artificial Kid*, *Schismatrix*, *The Zenith Angle*, and *The Caryatids*; the short-story collections *Gothic High-Tech* and *Globalhead*; and the nonfiction titles *The Hacker Crackdown* and *Shaping Things*. He coauthored, with William Gibson, the critically acclaimed novel *The Difference Engine*. Sterling also edited *Mirrorshades*, the definitive cyberpunk anthology, and he is considered one of the founders of the cyberpunk movement.

Fritz Swanson's work has appeared in such places as *McSweeney's*, the *Christian Science Monitor*, *Esopus*, and the *Mid-American Review*. He lives in Manchester, Michigan, with his wife, Sara, and their children, Abigail and Oscar. Visit him at WWW.MANCHESTER-PRESS.COM.

Karin Tidbeck lives in Malmö, Sweden, and writes speculative fiction in Swedish and English. She occasionally teaches creative writing and works for the local writers' center. Her short fiction has been published in *Weird Tales*, *Shimmer Magazine*, and *Unstuck Annual*, as well as the *Odd?* anthology from Cheeky Frawg Books. She made her book debut in 2010 with the Swedish story collection *Vem är Arvid Pekon?* The dystopian novel *Amatka* will follow in September 2012. Her first English short story collection, *Jagannath*, is due out in October 2012. Her website can be found at KARINTIDBECK.COM.

Lavie Tidhar is the author of the BSFA Award–nominated *Osama*, which has been compared to Philip K. Dick's seminal work *The Man in the High Castle* by the *Guardian* and the *Financial Times*. He is also the author of the Bookman Histories novels, comprising *The Bookman*, *Camera Obscura*, and *The Great Game*, and of many other novellas and short stories.

Catherynne M. Valente is the *New York Times* bestselling author of more than a dozen works of fiction and poetry, including *Palimpsest*, the Orphan's Tales series, *Deathless*, and the crowd-funded phenomenon *The Girl Who Circumnavigated Fairyland in a Ship of Her Own Making*. She is the winner of the Andre Norton, Tiptree, Mythopoeic Award, Rhysling, and Million Writers Award. She has been nominated for the Hugo, Locus, and Spectrum awards and the Pushcart Prize, and she was a finalist for the World Fantasy Award in 2007 and 2009. She lives on an island off the coast of Maine with her partner, two dogs, and enormous cat.

Genevieve Valentine's fiction has appeared or is forthcoming in *Clarkesworld*, *Strange Horizons*, *Journal of Mythic Arts*, *Fantasy Magazine*, *Lightspeed*, and *Apex*, and in the anthologies *Federations*, *The Living Dead 2*, *The Way of the Wizard*, *Running with the Pack*, *Teeth*, and more. Her nonfiction has appeared in Tor.com, *Weird Tales*, and *Fantasy Magazine*, and she is the coauthor of *Geek Wisdom* (out from Quirk Books). Her first novel, *Mechanique: A Tale of the Circus Tresaulti*, won the 2012 Crawford Award and was nominated for the Nebula Award.

Jeff VanderMeer is a two-time winner of the World Fantasy Award and has had stories published by Tor.com, *Clarkesworld*, *Conjunctions*, *Black Clock*, and several Year's Best anthologies. Recent books include the Nebula finalist novel *Finch* (2009) and the short-story collection *The Third Bear* (2010). His *The Steampunk Bible* was featured on the *CBS Morning Show* and was a finalist for the Hugo Award for best related book. He also recently coedited the mega-anthology *The Weird* compendium. A cofounder of Shared Worlds, a teen SF/F writing camp, VanderMeer has been a guest speaker at the Library of Congress and MIT, among others. He writes book reviews for the *Los Angeles Times*, the *New York Times Book Review*, and the *Washington Post*. VanderMeer's latest novel, just completed, is *Annihilation*.

Carrie Vaughn is the bestselling author of a series of novels about a werewolf named Kitty. *Kitty Steals the Show*, the tenth installment, is due out in summer

2012. She has also written for young adults (*Voices of Dragons, Steel*) and two stand-alone fantasy novels, *Discord's Apple* and *After the Golden Age*. Her short fiction has appeared in many magazines and anthologies, and she's a graduate of the Odyssey Fantasy Writing Workshop. She lives in Colorado with a fluffy attack dog. Learn more at WWW.CARRIEVAUGHN.COM.

JY Yang is a scientist-turned-writer-turned-journalist who gets the odd SF/F short story published every now and then. She likes chicken rice and furry hats. She blogs at MISSHALLELUJAH.NET and lives in Singapore, in the company of the occasional Pomeranian and an overactive imagination.

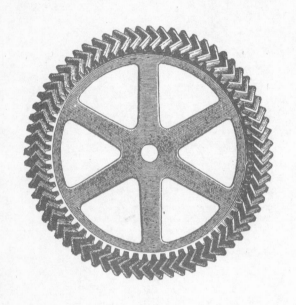